Praise for *The Grift*

**Named a *New York Times Book Review* Notable Book
of 2008**

A SCIBA Bestseller

"[A] novel of slow-burn spookiness . . . Ginsberg shows a remarkable capacity to inhabit the minds and motives of others. . . . *The Grift* is a gift with no strings attached . . . a satisfyingly voyeuristic vision of a mysterious stranger's supernaturally charged fortunes." —*New York Times*

"Ginsberg smoothly sketches captivatingly flawed characters."
—*Entertainment Weekly*

"An interesting read from the psychic side of the crystal ball, with sleazy characters and some good twists. A-." —*Rocky Mountain News*

"A complicated puzzle, a murder mystery that keeps readers guessing . . . a great read." —*Las Vegas Review-Journal*

"A rollicking novel, full of lies and uncontrollable fictions."
—*Los Angeles Times*

"Pleasantly chilling, end-of-summer read." —*Daily News*

"[A] clever thriller . . . Ginsberg has a way with offbeat characters."
—*New York Times Book Review*

"Compelling second novel . . . *The Grift* isn't so much a mystery as a story about a woman forced to take a hard look at herself and find the courage to change." —*Boston Globe*

"Mixes mystery and romance with enough silliness to keep it from getting too serious." —*Chicago Sun-Times*

"Smart observations of life on the con." —*San Diego Union-Tribune*

"An entertaining whodunit and an invigorating tale." —*Publishers Weekly*

"Memoirist and novelist Ginsberg mixes supernatural and film noir elements in this mystery about a woman whose living as a psychic falls apart when her psychic powers become too real." —*Kirkus Reviews*

"The story flows along, and readers looking for a different twist on the psychological novel will enjoy the trip." —*Library Journal*

"*The Grift* is a gift—a fresh voice and story, with a winning heroine. Another triumph for Debra Ginsberg, who clearly has many gifts of her own." —Laura Lippman, *New York Times* bestselling author of *Life Sentences*

"Debra Ginsberg has done it again in this compulsively readable, suspenseful, and very this-worldly tale of a psychic and her desperate clientele." —Janet Fitch, *New York Times* bestselling author of *Paint it Black* and *White Oleander*

Praise for *Blind Submission*

"A hilarious insider's look. . . . Makes for a clever mystery as Ginsberg adroitly amps up the suspense." —*New York Times Book Review*

Prada genre—and enough mystery to keep a reader turning pages late into the night." —*Boulder Daily Camera*

"This debut novel's sharp writing and intriguing mystery elements turn what could be the same old story into something fresh and new. . . . The suspenseful 'who-wrote-it' sets the novel apart from other so-called 'assistant lit'. . . . Ginsberg clearly knows the ins-and-outs of the publishing world, and *Blind Submission* offers an engaging look." —*BookPage*

"A page-turner." —*People* Style Watch

"A gleefully caustic tale that is not so much a whodunit as a who-wrote-it. . . . An affectionate skewering of the ludicrous side of the book business and a claws-out send-up of the perversities of power, Ginsberg's blithe blend of mystery, romance, and satire is smart, classy, and fun." —*Booklist* (starred review)

"The book-within-a-book hook adds a clever twist to this tale of entry-level angst." —*Library Journal*

"Memoirist Ginsberg gracefully transitions into fiction with a fresh twist on the aggrieved publishing assistant. . . . The plot is twisty enough to keep readers guessing to the end." —*Publishers Weekly*

"Welcome, Debra Ginsberg! *Blind Submission* is a debut novel that kept me turning the pages. Wicked fun and suspense from a talented new writer with an original, clever voice."
—Lisa Scottoline, author of *Look Again*

"*Blind Submission* is a wonderful read from start to finish. Ginsberg's writing is clever and seductive as she spins this tale of psychological peril and illumination." —T. Jefferson Parker, author of *The Renegades*

Also by Debra Ginsberg

Blind Submission

NONFICTION

About My Sisters
Raising Blaze
Waiting: The True Confessions of a Waitress

The G[r]ift

A NOVEL

Debra Ginsberg

THREE RIVERS PRESS • NEW YORK

Published in the United States by Three Rivers Press, an imprint of the
Crown Publishing Group, a division of Random House, Inc., New York.
www.crownpublishing.com

Three Rivers Press and the Tugboat design are registered trademarks of
Random House, Inc.

Originally published in hardcover in the United States by Shaye Areheart Books,
an imprint of the Crown Publishing Group, a division of Random House, Inc.,
New York, in 2008.

Library of Congress Cataloging-in-Publication Data
Ginsberg, Debra, 1962–
The grift : a novel / by Debra Ginsberg.
1. Swindlers and swindling—Fiction.   2. Psychics—Fiction.
3. California—Fiction.   1. Title.
PS3607.I4585G75 2008
813'.6—dc22   2008000947

ISBN 978-0-307-38273-3

Printed in the United States of America

Design by Lynne Amft

10 9 8 7 6 5 4 3 2 1

First Paperback Edition

For my family

grift – *n. a group of methods used for obtaining money falsely through the use of swindles, frauds, etc.*

gift – *n. a special ability or capacity*

Prologue

September 1976

Madame Z had been sitting in her spot on the boardwalk for hours and the only forms of life she'd seen were a few listless seabirds. It was too hot and bright for casual strollers and too late in the season for vacationers. And for Madame Z, it was both too hot under the crushing blue sky and too late in a long life to wait much longer. It seemed unlikely that she would tell any fortunes today. Nor did she think she'd be back tomorrow or perhaps ever again. But this was not something that caused her anxiety. For some time now Madame Z had sensed her own end drawing near and she'd made her peace with it.

She watched as a seagull pecked at a shell a few feet in front of her, lost interest and flapped away. Madame Z looked up to follow its flight and saw a woman and a little girl walking toward her through the hot shimmering air.

So, she thought, *one last fortune to be told.*

As they approached her small table, Madame Z could see that the woman and child were mother and daughter and that their roles were working in reverse. The woman was unkempt, twitchy and petulant while the girl was quiet, serious and unnaturally self-contained. As they got closer, Madame Z could see that they were both dark-haired and green-eyed, and she could feel waves of unhappiness emanating from both of them.

"How much?" the woman asked.

"Twenty dollars for your future," Madame Z answered.

"That's a lot," the woman said. "Too much."

"It's your future."

The woman scratched the side of her face and scowled at the fortune-teller. "I want the *ten-dollar* future. I was told you could give me that."

Madame Z pursed her lips and tried to contain her disgust. She could smell it now, that chemical odor mixed with stale sweat. She'd been approached by desperate, misinformed drug seekers before, but this was the first time she'd seen a child in tow.

"You are mistaken," the fortune-teller said. "I don't have what you are looking for."

The woman pulled a few grimy bills from the front pocket of her dirty jeans. "Listen, I only have fifteen and I have to feed the kid, okay? Give me a break. I can do ten." She cast a backward glance at her daughter, who was standing very still, eyes wide and expressionless, hands folded in front of her. "Ten," she repeated, a note of panic edging her voice. "Okay?"

"You are not understanding," Madame Z said. "I do not have the thing you want. I read the future. That is all." The woman eyed her with suspicion and then faltered, comprehending at last, her arms falling to her sides in a gesture of defeat.

"Well, that's just great, isn't it?" the woman said, pulling a crumpled cigarette pack and matches from her back pocket. "Now what am I supposed to do?" She walked back a few steps, sat down on the ground and lit a cigarette. "What the hell am I supposed to do now?" she repeated to herself.

After watching her mother smoke in silence for a few moments, the little girl approached Madame Z and dropped four shiny quarters on the faded green felt of the fortune-teller's table.

"I want to know my future," the girl said.

Madame Z wanted to tell the girl to keep her coins. It didn't take second sight to know what was in store for this child. A quick glance at the mother, still smoking and softly cursing to herself, was all that was needed. But the girl's eyes, the same sparkling green as the sea, forbade pity or sympathy, and Madame Z found herself sliding the quarters into her pocket and gesturing for the girl to sit down in the folding chair next to her.

"What's your name?" the fortune-teller asked. The girl continued to give her a steady, unwavering gaze and held her hands out, palms up, toward Madame Z, the gesture quick and easy as if she'd done it many times before. "Here," the girl said instead, "tell me my future."

Madame Z took the small soft hands in her own and peered down as if she were deep in concentration, wondering what this solemn child would most like to hear. Perhaps that she'd get a favorite toy or some new clothes or . . . Madame Z's eyes were old and playing tricks on her. The lines of fate cut deep slashes through each of the girl's hands, slicing through the head and heart lines. And there was something else she had never seen before. She checked one palm and then the other. There was no life line on either hand.

Madame Z dropped the girl's hands and reached for her deck of tarot cards. "Let's do this," she said. "You choose a card and I will—"

"I know this game," the girl interrupted. "I choose the man with the eight over his head."

"The eight?" Madame Z positioned the deck in front of the girl. "What do you mean?"

"This one," the girl said, plucking the top card from the deck and turning it over to reveal the Magician holding a wand aloft. Above his head was the symbol of eternity, a sideways figure eight.

"That's very good," the fortune-teller said, sliding the card to the bottom of the deck. "Why don't you pick another?"

The girl picked the next top card and turned it over. Impossibly, the Magician stared back at her again.

Madame Z repeated her movements, again replacing the card at the bottom of the deck and again instructing the girl to draw another. And again the girl turned over the Magician from the top of the deck.

"This game is boring," the girl said. "I want a different card. I want you to tell me my future."

Trembling, Madame Z looked up from the cards and into the girl's face, but it was no longer the girl that she saw in front of her. Her own reflection stared back at her as clearly as if she were looking into a mirror. She saw her own face crease with pain and her hand reach up to her heart. She saw the shadow creep into her eyes and block out the light of life. There, in the girl's face, Madame Z watched herself die.

"Hey. *Hey!* What do you think you're doing?"

Madame Z blinked, her eyes watering. The woman was standing next to her now, too close, shouting. Her daughter, once again just a child with wide green eyes, had moved away from the table and stood near her mother. "What are you telling her, huh? What do you think you're doing?" The woman grabbed the girl's arm and yanked her close. The girl's expression never changed—still that same self-possessed, impassive stare.

"She . . ." Madame Z had to catch the breath that was coming short and labored. She pointed to the girl. "She has the gift."

The woman raised her eyebrows, a momentary curiosity flashing across her face.

"What does she mean, Mama?" Madame Z noticed for the first time how deep the girl's voice was.

"Nothing," the woman snapped. "It doesn't mean anything. This crazy freak doesn't know what she's talking about. Do you hear me, freak? There's something wrong with you," she said, starting to turn around. "Let's get out of here. I've wasted enough time." She walked away fast, dragging the girl in the direction from which they had come.

"She has the *gift!*" Madame Z called out after them. They kept walking, out into the sunlit distance. The girl turned once, staring hard as if to imprint the image behind her. Madame Z watched as they became smaller and smaller in her field of vision. She watched through the pains that had started shooting through her chest and kept watching until the light became too bright and burned her vision to black.

Part I

The Grift

August 2005

Chapter 1

Marina Marks had been sweating for weeks. Constant, skin-crawling perspiration ran in tiny rivers across her body. Sweat started at the base of her skull and ran down her neck and back, traveling the length of her zodiac tattoo, sliding over the ram's head symbol for Aries between her shoulder blades and finishing with the swimming fish symbol for Pisces at the very base of her spine. In front, the moisture condensed on her chest, disappeared in droplets between her breasts and pooled in the marsh between her legs. It didn't matter how many showers she took in a day or how long she stood under the water. By noon, she was wrung out and flattened.

They said the body was better equipped to deal with the dry bake of a desert than with the wet heat of a swamp. Meteorologists pointed to this fact when they talked about the heat index. It might be only eighty-five degrees outside, but when the air scorched wet and heavy it *felt* as if it were over a hundred. Babies, the elderly and the infirm were all at risk in this kind of heat, they said. Weak bodies might just give up and give out; even the healthy ones would struggle with discomfort. And they were right, Marina thought. She was one of the strong ones, but this relentless steam-box humidity was killing her.

This morning had been the worst yet in a season that had already offered more than its share of bad days. She'd slept hard but badly, as if she were being slowly suffocated. At dawn, she'd startled into full consciousness, hot and gritty and thinking about her mother, a clear indicator of just how uncomfortable a night she'd spent. Marina never thought about her mother voluntarily, and when visions of that woman—always the horrible way she'd looked the last time Marina had seen her—managed to press their way to the surface from deep in her subconscious, Marina knew that she was stressed and uneasy.

Marina lifted her heavy hair away from her neck and angled herself toward the standing fan next to her table, even though it helped very little and served mostly to just move the heat around. Three weeks earlier, her air conditioner had groaned as if it were in pain, spat ice for the length of an afternoon and then died. Living without an air conditioner in South Florida at the height of summer was ridiculous, even crazy, but Marina hadn't fixed hers or replaced it. Either option would have required much more money than she was willing to spend for a couple months' worth of relief. She had calculated that two months—three at the very outside—was all the time she needed to clear out and get herself set up in California, and there was no room in her budget for any expenses that weren't strictly necessary. But it wasn't just the money, because Marina could have found that if she'd really wanted to. Fixing the air conditioner would have made it too easy to stay longer, might even have implied a kind of permanence. The constant sticky discomfort was an ongoing reminder and incentive to leave as soon as possible.

Marina bent closer to the warm stream of air. What small relief the breeze provided was canceled out by the thought that she'd have to turn off the fan and move it before Mrs. Golden arrived, which would be within the next fifteen minutes. Appearances counted for so much more than people ever imagined. Marina could not have a plastic fan on display in her house, where it would clash badly with her crystals, tarot cards and delicate silk scarves. Nor could she be seen as a person who suffered the effects of heat, humidity or any other physical indignity. She needed to be perceived as above and beyond the pains and ills of the flesh. This was the package her clients were buying and the likely reason why nobody had yet complained about how hot it was in her house. She could have played it straight—just your average work-at-home woman dressed in casual cottons who also happened to be a psychic—but Marina knew how well most minds responded to subliminal advertising. Looking the part without going over the top into some kind of caricature was one of her key selling points. This was why Marina wore darker makeup on her green eyes than she would have liked ("Witches' Brew" eye shadow and "Voodoo" eyeliner, no less), dressed in a collection of flowing skirts and gauzy blouses vaguely reminiscent of Stevie Nicks in her "Gypsy" heyday and had dyed her hair "Midnight Black" for so long that she couldn't remember its natural color. Marina would have cut that long, thick, *hot* hair short long ago had it not been such an important element of her image.

But for this godforsaken place, Marina thought, none of it would matter. Florida, especially this piece of it, felt to her like hell on earth. It was no wonder the word *muggy* was used to describe weather that seemed to attack you every time you exposed yourself to it. No wonder, too, that the elderly, the ill and the spiritually lame all converged in this hot, soupy trough—misery coming to misery. She should have known better, or at least earlier, that she'd never find happiness here.

When she'd arrived in Florida, the end of her slow drift down the eastern seaboard, Marina hadn't intended to stay long. She traveled light, but even so it took weeks before she unpacked all her clothes and longer still before she started adding new items to the small house she was renting. Gradually, almost in spite of herself, Marina bought a lamp to go here or a chair to go there, until her place finally looked more like a home than a temporary box she'd moved into. She started earning money quickly as almost all of her early clients became regulars, and before she knew it she was settled in, making appointments for the months ahead, her feet firmly planted on the Florida ground. But the further entrenched she became, the more Marina wanted to leave. And it wasn't just the weather or the general malaise of the place that was pushing her out. Underlying those things—and the real reason Marina had decided to head as far west as possible—were the *others,* those who were making it almost impossible for her to get on with her business.

Slowly, and not very subtly, Marina was being squeezed. She had landed in a community where Gypsies, *santeros* and *voodooiennes* existed in a delicate and wary balance. Marina was an outsider, and she played by her own rules. It wasn't her way, for example, to go for a big score with a client and then never see that client again. Hers was a slow build of confidence and a fostering of need. Many of her clients treated her with the same deference to authority that they showed their doctors. Marina had always believed that it took more skill to develop trust than inspire fear. It paid better in the long run, too, and was much less likely to end with angry clients feeling as though they'd been shafted. That she held herself to her own set of standards wasn't really the problem, though; it was her refusal to ally herself with or pay her respects to any particular group. She didn't try to make nice, and it wasn't long before she discovered that she wasn't welcome.

She noticed little things at first: a few cold stares, the barely perceptible clicking of tongues. But then the friendly neighborhood cop stopped by one day, just wanting to make sure she was "okay," telling her that there'd been "some trouble" in the area, that she should keep her eyes open just in case. Oh, and if she were doing any kind of business out of her house, she should make sure that her licenses and permits were in order; she wouldn't want to be on the wrong side of the law in case she ever needed help of any kind . . .

After that, she started hearing whispers everywhere, started seeing eyes in the bushes. She didn't like to admit it, but she'd allowed herself to become spooked. How she hated Florida. She couldn't wait to get out of this backward swamp with its ignorance and heavy superstitions. Two more months and she'd be breathing in the light California air and making some real money without having to contend with sacrificed chickens and pin-holed dolls. Californians loved the weird and the illusory as much if not more than anyone, but they never seemed to take anything too seriously, least of all themselves. But that wasn't the only reason she had chosen southern California as her destination. She'd lived there once, though so long ago it seemed like a recollection from another life. She was only a little girl and it had been a very short stay, too short for Marina to attend school or to remember now which beach city it had been. But Marina recalled it as a bright moment in an otherwise hard and miserable childhood. That shining memory beckoned her now like a lighthouse glow across the darkness.

Marina flicked off the fan and pushed it into a storage closet behind a bead-covered doorway. Sweat formed instantly, trickling down her ribs. The crawling sensation made her shiver, and she closed her eyes. There was a quick flash of light behind her lids and she flinched, blinking them open. Marina stared at nothing for a moment, wondering if the heat was short-circuiting her brain. She closed her eyes again and focused. The flash came again, but this time Marina could see its form—a fork of lightning illuminating rain—and then she remembered. This storm behind her eyes was an echo of a dream she'd had . . . was it last night? She'd woken up so abruptly, strangled in the damp, tangled sheets, her mother in her mind. Maybe there had been thunder outside—a real storm. But no, the day was cloudless, no sign of rain. Marina prickled with irritation at herself, not wanting to recall her dreams, good, bad or otherwise. The heat was now driving her mad as well as making her uncomfortable. A knock on the door reminded her that she needed to pull herself together. Mrs. Golden, usually punctual to the minute, had inexplicably chosen this day to come early. *If only it were just five degrees cooler,* Marina thought as she made her way to the door.

She pulled her front door open to the wet air outside and the smell of rot hit her like a wave. There was an empty rectangle of light in her doorway. Mrs. Golden was nowhere in sight. It took only a second for Marina to look down and see the dead snake, stuffed with foul dark matter, coiled on her front step. Even as she was slamming the door shut, adrenaline shooting through her veins, Marina knew she had to open it again and get rid of the thing. Sweat sprang from every pore in her body as she moved fast to the closet to pull out a broom and a rolled-up grass mat. No time to make this neat. Perspiration pooled under her eyes like still tears. Marina opened the door again, breath held and eyes averted, and hit the thing hard with the broom, sweeping it off the step and into a clump of half-dead birds-of-paradise. One more swipe at the grimy black smear it left behind and then Marina threw the broom after it. She didn't have time to look for a hose or a bucket now. She unrolled the mat and tossed it on the step. She could still smell the thing, but at least she couldn't see it.

Marina went back inside and scrubbed her hands until her palms were red and throbbing. She wiped the slick sweat from her neck and pulled her thin shirt away from where it had become glued to her back. She laughed; a hard crazy sound that had nothing to do with amusement. So now they'd decided to leave their voodoo trash at her doorstep. Curses, spells and hexes—Marina believed in none of them. But she did believe in the power of bad intentions. The snake was a particularly crude warning, and Marina suspected there wouldn't be many more. She couldn't afford to wait two more months. She had to find a way to get out now.

There was another knock at the door. Mrs. Golden had arrived exactly on time. Marina pictured her client standing on the grass mat and knew she needed to answer the door before the old woman smelled what was hiding in the flowers. *But if I make her wait,* Marina thought, *she'll be frantic and desperate by the time I let her in.* Frantic and desperate were good for business, and that was exactly what Marina needed right now. She had to think, calculate, speed up her mental process. She glanced at her table, where she'd laid out the cards for Mrs. Golden, and a decision began forming in her mind.

This would be Mrs. Golden's last reading, and it would be very expensive. Mrs. Golden knocked again. "Hello? Are you there? Hello?" Her voice was high and urgent. *Yes,* Marina thought, *Mrs. Golden was ready.*

The old woman was always on the edge anyway and hardly even needed a push. Her worries had been escalating over the last few readings. Concerns over the state of her own health had turned into irrational fears that her dead husbands—she'd outlived two of them—were unable to rest in peace. She'd developed a morbid curiosity about the nature of her own death: when and how it would happen. Mrs. Golden's need for bad news had been increasing with every appointment, and she'd been scheduling her sessions closer and closer together. *Tell me something bad, Marina. Tell me something terrible.* Her eyes begged for it, searched for it every time she came for a reading. Today, her search would be over. It wasn't Marina's business to understand why Mrs. Golden or any of her clients had such a powerful need for calamity. But it *was* her business to give it to them.

Marina smoothed the folds of her skirt and wiped the beads of moisture from her lip. She willed herself into stillness for a few seconds, controlling her breath and allowing her professional mask to drop and settle over her. She could feel her face relax, her back straighten and her eyelids fall. When finally she made her way over to the door, Marina had, by sheer force of will, transformed herself from a frazzled, ordinary woman in her thirties to an ethereal, ageless psychic.

Appearances counted for a great deal indeed.

"Hello, Mrs. Golden."

"Marina . . . I was worried that you . . . you . . ."

Marina fixed her eyes on Mrs. Golden with the careful, studied gaze she'd perfected over years of training. Mrs. Golden's usually well-maintained auburn hair was showing white roots, and her cheekbones were sharp against the glare of the afternoon sun. Her fingernails, digging into the tired beige leather of her handbag, were uncharacteristically unpolished and uneven in length. The coral lipstick she had hastily applied was dry and feathery, long past its prime. She was wearing polyester taupe slacks and a matching blouse. The outfit was outdated and too warm for the weather. Nor did it go with the shoes, child-size clear jelly sandals available for $1.99 at any drugstore. She was letting herself go, Marina thought, and it wasn't for lack of money. Marina knew the old woman had plenty of cash on hand and much more in the bank. So either dementia was setting in or Mrs. Golden was just sick of keeping up the facade. Marina could certainly relate to that.

"Not to worry, Mrs. Golden. Please come in." Marina's voice was low and even, but friendly and familiar.

The old woman stepped inside and blinked in the dimness of Marina's small shuttered house. "I thought you . . . when you didn't answer—"

"Don't be silly," Marina interrupted. "You know I'll always be here for you."

Mrs. Golden smiled, showing the perfect white teeth available only to those who could afford them, and loosened her grip on her handbag. "Yes, dear, of course you will."

Marina offered the smallest of smiles in return and gestured toward her table. Today, she would be the daughter Mrs. Golden had never had—one of many roles she was able to adopt. She was sometimes the best friend, sometimes the mistress, the child or the parent. The medium became the message—and it was all the same to Marina as long as they paid in cash.

Chapter 2

"Let's get started, shall we?" Marina said.

Her table was covered with a dark blue silk square, bare but for the stack of tarot cards in the center. Mrs. Golden eased herself into a low wingback chair on one side of the table while Marina slid into her own slightly higher chair across from her. Marina dipped her head, narrowed her eyes to slits and breathed deeply. This was the part where she contacted her spirit guides, marshaled her psychic energy and opened her aura. At least, this is what the clients believed she was doing. In reality, Marina used these moments to organize her observations, detect the client's mood and plan the reading accordingly.

Marina had been making her living as a psychic for so long that this little act of hers was pitch-perfect. So immersed had she become in her own psychic persona that she was sure she could have passed a lie detector test. The deep irony of it was that Marina did not—now or ever—believe that psychic ability existed at all. She did believe in intuition and that everyone possessed it in equal amounts but that most people couldn't or wouldn't tap into it. But what Marina considered intuition had nothing to do with the unexplainable "woo woo" visions of the future that everyone so desired. Intuition, for Marina, was all about observation and appropriate response. It was as simple as being able to pick up on what the people in front of you were thinking or feeling based on what you knew about them. And people gave away so much about themselves in their words, gestures, clothing and faces—*especially* those people who came to a psychic for readings. Half the time, Marina was convinced that her clients knew this was exactly what they were doing. This was the best part of the reading, really, for both her and the client. The client telegraphed what he or she wanted to hear and Marina picked up the message.

Mrs. Golden was perhaps one of Marina's easiest clients in this regard. Although Marina never got emotionally attached to her clients, she did appreciate the old lady's generosity, and not just the financial end of it. For Marina, Mrs. Golden's willingness to both lead and be led counted for just as much. As they both waited now, Marina strategizing and Mrs. Golden anticipating, it occurred to Marina that she was sorry to leave this woman behind and that she might even miss her a little. But there was no time for sentimentality. Marina had a job to do and needed to get on with it. She raised her head abruptly and stared straight ahead, focused on some unseen point.

"Please touch the cards," she instructed. Mrs. Golden placed her blue-veined hands on top of the stack and Marina covered them with her own. Mrs. Golden's hands were cold, even in this heat, and Marina could feel them trembling. After a moment, Marina lifted her hands and gestured for Mrs. Golden to do the same.

"I have had a dream," Marina said, "and I am very disturbed by it." Again the strange lightning flash crossed Marina's eyes, followed by the fading image of her mother and a sharp spike of discomfort. There were probably better ways to handle Mrs. Golden than summoning a nonexistent dream, and normally Marina would have taken another approach. But today, maximum impact was necessary, and now that she'd plunged in there was no turning back.

"A dream about me?" Mrs. Golden asked. There was a note of hope in her voice. *Tell me something bad. Please tell me something awful.*

Marina watched as the woman raised her right hand to her neck and unconsciously began to rub the ring that dangled from the end of a long chain. Marina knew this ring well, having long ago extracted the details of its provenance from her client. The multicarat trillion-cut ruby set in a simple gold band had been a gift from Mrs. Golden's only son. It was extremely valuable, Mrs. Golden had told Marina, because "rubies are rarer and worth much more than diamonds, you know." She didn't trust a safe-deposit box to hold this one-of-a-kind piece and never left her house without it. In addition, it was "a good luck thing," and Mrs. Golden made no secret of being intensely superstitious. The ring had been given to her with love and it would be bad karma to put that kind of love away in a dark place where nobody could see it. So she wore it on a chain because, she'd told Marina with pride, it was "too heavy" for her finger.

Mrs. Golden's eyes searched Marina's face for an answer while her thumb rubbed, back and forth, against the ring. The son *was* her greatest love, Marina knew, and with the greatest love came the greatest fear. *This is what she wants,* Marina thought. *And I can give it to her one last time.*

"The dream was about your son," Marina said.

Mrs. Golden's reaction was instantaneous. Her hand formed a fist around the ring, her eyes widened and her mouth dropped open. "What about my son?"

"He is in danger," Marina said without hesitation, "but he doesn't know it."

"But I spoke with him the other day. He's fine. He told me—"

"I know," Marina said. "The problem is that he *thinks* everything is fine. But my dream was clear." She sighed heavily as if struggling under a great weight. "It is very unusual for me to have these kinds of dreams," she said. "My visions are usually in the conscious moment. It has to be this way or I would never rest. I would be tormented day and night with the cries and wishes of the dead and living alike. I don't *want* to dream. But the dreams come when they must. We've never discussed my dreams before, have we?"

Mrs. Golden shook her head. "No," she said, "we never have."

"This is why I know we *have* to pay attention to this one. I saw your son. I saw the danger surrounding him. Dark, evil forces around him."

"Evil forces . . ." Mrs. Golden seemed momentarily stunned. And then, as if something peculiar had just occurred to her, she drew back, eyebrows raised, furrows deepening on her forehead. "You saw my son?" she asked. "What does he look like?"

Marina's face was set in its professional mask and gave no indication of her surprise. Clearly, Mrs. Golden's tatty outfit and grown-out roots had nothing to do with dementia. Mentally she was still all there. Marina smiled inwardly. Good for the old girl, making her work a little harder. Marina liked to earn her money. Nothing of real value was free. She looked into her client's eyes now, for the first time since the session had started. They were a deep brown; no hint of lighter color. Dark, Marina thought. Dark meant dominant.

"He has . . . your eyes," Marina said. The words found their mark. Mrs. Golden bowed her head and clasped her hands.

"What danger is he in?" she whispered. "You have to tell me."

Marina straightened in her chair. "I need to be sure," she said. "Let's look at the cards. They may tell me something different or give me more information than the dream."

"Yes," Mrs. Golden said. "Yes, please."

"Would you like to choose the cards today?" Marina asked, but she already knew what the answer would be.

"No, no." Mrs. Golden shook her head hard and drew back from the table. "You choose them."

Marina breathed in and held her hands over the cards for half a minute. Then she cut them three times and fanned them out in the center of the table. She selected a card and placed it facedown in front of Mrs. Golden. The next card Marina chose went to the left. The final card went to the right. This three-card spread was less exotic than the more complicated Celtic Cross or pyramid spreads, but it packed more of an immediate punch, which was exactly what Marina was going for. She gathered the remaining cards and made a neat stack of them on the edge of the table.

"The first card represents the Issue," Marina said, turning over the center card, the Knight of Cups. She gave Mrs. Golden a few moments to absorb the image of the armor-clad knight on horseback. "This is your son," Marina said. "He is kind, dedicated. Cups signify water. Your son is a water sign—a Cancer, born in July." Mrs. Golden's sharp intake of breath, along with another reflexive hand movement to the ruby—July's birthstone—gave Marina license to continue. She turned over the second card and Mrs. Golden gasped. The card showed three swords piercing a heart, with a violent rainstorm in the background. "This is the Situation," Marina said. "Your son is involved with . . . evil people. He has business dealings with people who want to harm him. There are people, one person in particular, whom he trusts. That person is plotting against him with the help of two others." Marina watched as Mrs. Golden processed the information, wondering, no doubt, who her son trusted and why anyone would be plotting against him. Marina sat patiently, waiting for Mrs. Golden to imagine and conjure suspects in her mind. At last, she gestured to the final card. "This card represents the Outcome," she said, and turned it over.

The Death card stared up at them.

"No," Mrs. Golden said, her voice hushed.

"This is very serious," Marina said, after allowing the image of black skeleton Death atop his white horse to sear itself into Mrs. Golden's brain. For a moment, Marina wondered if she might have gone too far. The Death card was so recognizable that it was almost a cliché, yet it never failed to make an impression. The irony of it was that in traditional interpretation of the tarot, the Death card didn't signify physical death at all, but a profound spiritual change. But Mrs. Golden did not know that. Nor, Marina suspected, would she want to.

"He's going to die?" Mrs. Golden whispered finally. "Are you saying he's going to die?"

"I'm not saying anything," Marina answered. "But the cards—and my dream—are saying plenty. I am just the vessel through which the spirit guides speak." She paused, almost able to hear the turmoil raging in

Mrs. Golden's head. On the table, the Knight of Cups stared at Death as if waiting for an answer.

"The person . . . ," Mrs. Golden began. "The one who wants to hurt him. Is she . . . is it a woman?"

Marina placed her hand on top of the Knight of Cups and closed her eyes, calculating. There was fear in Mrs. Golden's voice, but also a faint thread of territorial jealousy. It was ever so with mothers and their sons, Marina thought. "I see . . ." Marina paused and furrowed her brow. "I see someone very . . . beautiful. An image of beauty—that is what I am receiving. Beautiful . . . but deceptive. Yes, I believe it is a woman." Marina opened her eyes and stared at Mrs. Golden, gauging her expression. "A woman who uses her beauty to mask inner ugliness."

"Yes." Mrs. Golden sighed. "Yes, that's her. I told him about her. He laughed at me, told me I was meddling . . ."

Marina leaned forward and looked directly into Mrs. Golden's eyes. "A mother's intuition is the most powerful of all," she said. "You were right to suspect. I am just so glad you're here before it's too late."

The two women sat in unsettled silence, the space between them thick and weighted with the mingled scents of sandalwood incense and Mrs. Golden's rose perfume.

"What can I do?" Mrs. Golden asked finally. "Can you help me?"

"I believe I can," Marina said. "And I believe that is why I had the dream. But it is not easy to reverse a destiny. It will take some time and . . . certain resources."

"What kind of resources? Please tell me. I'll do anything."

Marina shifted in her chair, aware once more of the heat, of the moist motionless air in the room. She could feel her scalp prickling with fresh perspiration and the damp in the small of her back. Mrs. Golden's hand had gone once more to the ring around her neck. Marina caught the deep red gleam of the ruby as it shifted between the woman's worn fingers. Once more, unbidden and unwanted, the vision of her mother skirted the corner of Marina's mind. Although she'd never had the means or the inclination, had Marina ever given her mother a gift like that, it would have disappeared instantly, transformed into the only thing that had real worth to her. Nothing that couldn't be smoked, swallowed or injected had any resonant meaning for her mother. In this way her mother was a true alchemist, with the ability to turn anything beautiful into ugliness and waste. Tiny slivers of resentment stabbed at Marina now and old wounds, long scarred over, began to ache. She felt a hot wave of anger pulsing through her throat. The hellish heat, the dead snake, the unrelenting tension and even the sight of this superstitious old woman were starting to swirl into a potent brew, and Marina could feel herself losing the control she'd worked so hard to maintain.

Mrs. Golden was staring at her, waiting for her response. *"I'll do anything,"* she had said, and Marina knew it was true. Everyone did whatever they needed to survive. She took a deep quiet breath. It was time to pull herself together. It was time to close the deal.

"There is a way," Marina said. "There is always a way."

December 2005

Chapter 3

The girl was beautiful, naked and covered with an array of brightly colored fresh sushi. She lay perfectly still on a banquet table in the middle of the huge living room without so much as a tremor of her lip or a twitch of her pale waxlike fingers to indicate she was made out of living flesh. From her own spot in the corner of the room, Marina had a clear view of the girl and the guests as they milled around the red silk-draped platform, using black lacquered chopsticks to remove packets of wrapped fish from their human platter. Marina could hear nervous giggles and noticed how the women hesitated, cautious about eating off a naked female body. The men were less tentative, choosing delicately wrapped salmon eggs from the leaves on the girl's breasts. Some guests were less than graceful—or already drunk on sake and Japanese beer—and dropped their yellowfin tuna rolls on the floor or inadvertently poked their chopsticks into the girl's thighs as they reached for the eel between her legs. Throughout all of it, the girl never moved or smiled or gave any indication that she inhabited her own skin. Marina wondered how much the girl was getting paid for her services and if that price was comparable to what Marina was getting paid to be the party's psychic.

Was it worth more to have people eat off your nude body or to provide a glimpse into the unknowable future? Marina couldn't decide. Both were titillating in their own ways. Both played on the very human need to explore what was off-limits and mysterious. Marina thought her own services required more skill than those of the girl, but she wouldn't have traded places with her, either. And it had to be somewhat difficult to find jobs doing this sort of thing. You couldn't exactly print up a stack of business cards, as Marina had, and hand them out. That was the kind of talent people had to find by knowing where to look. Naked Sushi Girl was probably getting paid very well, Marina decided. After all, this party was being held in one of the wealthiest enclaves in a county that was already full of millionaires. It was exactly the place for such a pretentious and expensive shindig.

In a way, serving naked sushi *and* providing a psychic seemed a bit like overkill, an ostentatious display of theme party one-upmanship. But ostentation itself seemed to be the theme of this event. Marina was sitting under an actual tent, which was designed to look as if it had come out of a Depression-era carnival. There was straw at her feet, a round table covered with velvet and an extremely tacky crystal ball that Marina had surreptitiously stashed behind her brocaded chair. The living room of this mansion was so large that the tent fit comfortably, even looked as if it might belong there. At least nobody had asked her to wear gold hoop earrings and a head scarf to complete the tableau. Marina had been hired by a party planner and had barely spoken with the hostess, the lavishly named Madeline Royal. It was a holiday party, the planner had explained, but sushi and psychics had nothing to do with Christmas or even the New Year. It didn't seem to matter, though. Clearly Madeline Royal had plenty of ready cash with which to impress her guests. Rich people were easily bored. It was why they had these kinds of parties in the first place.

Marina had never liked parties and had never opted to host one of her own. They were predictably unpredictable. Someone would have a fight; someone would throw up, pass out or break something. Parties always brought trouble of some kind; that was the predictable part. What form the trouble would take was the surprise.

Marina might have felt differently if she'd had any positive experiences to draw from, but as a child she'd had precious few parties of her own to celebrate birthdays or other childhood passages. When her mother would emerge from her stupors or benders for long enough to remember she had a kid and try to organize such events, they ended up being wildly inappropriate affairs filled with adults and drugs and missing key elements like cake or other children. So Marina had never associated parties with fun, a critical disconnect that persisted even when she was long past the age of Pin the Tail on the Donkey. Many of the parties Marina had experienced were, in fact, tinged with darkness.

It was at a party—a completely different scene than the one going on around her now—when her mother first realized that Marina could be useful. Marina's memories of that night were thick with the dirty haze of smoke that had blanketed the scene. She was seven or eight, dressed up in thrift-store red velvet and big gold earrings. Her ears hurt from the piercings, done by her mother's boyfriend, Rafe, a wiry tattoo artist covered in ink. They hadn't left the posts in long enough and hadn't sterilized them, either, and Marina's ears throbbed with the infection. Her mother put her at the kitchen table, surrounded by overflowing ashtrays and a bottle of Jack, and slapped a worn deck of tarot cards in front of her. There were traces of white lines on the brown Formica table. The room was full of ugly strangers, men and women alike.

"Go ahead," her mother had said to the group at large. "Test her out. This kid can tell the future, I'm not joking. Go on—let her read your cards, your hand, whatever."

Marina knew to be quiet and give her mother what she wanted. In this case, it wasn't difficult. When they came up to her, glassy-eyed with bent smiles, all she had to do was look at them. Even at that age, Marina knew how to read body language. Not that she considered this any kind of great feat. How difficult was it to see sadness in a pair of eyes that were red from crying, or to recognize fear in trembling fingers and tightly crossed arms? Marina just had to pay attention to what she was seeing and then feed it back with words. And these early fortune seekers were generally so wasted that they didn't know any better anyway. A little girl in a red velvet dress twiddling the Judgment card in her hand was a cosmic experience for them. Marina didn't like being the center of attention (bad things happened when adults started looking at you too closely), but she liked the feeling of power those early sessions gave her. She couldn't understand why adults were stupid enough to be awestruck over something that even a child could do, but for a while, it gave her a feeling of safety.

Soon after that, Marina's mother started to make them pay. Her young daughter became a profitable side business for them, reading tarot cards or palms and eventually astrology. Marina had always understood her mother's desire to extract a quick buck from wherever she could find it, but what she would never know was whether her mother actually believed in the product she was selling. Sometimes, in the midst of a reading, Marina would sense a sort of controlled nervousness from her mother that didn't have anything to do with her usual drug-induced jitteriness, as if she'd discovered her daughter playing with live ammunition. At some point, Marina realized that her mother was worried that the fraud would be discovered and that she'd lose her new source of income. It made Marina panicky to think what would happen if she became useless to her mother and so she was spurred to do better, to act even more like the psychic prodigy she wasn't. This was also why she hadn't complained—not voiced even a murmur of dissent—when her mother had instructed Rafe to give her daughter that tattoo.

Marina had lain facedown, naked, on a filthy couch while Rafe made a permanent painting of the twelve signs of the zodiac between her shoulders and the top of her buttocks. It was astonishing if you thought about it; her back was so small that there was barely enough room to contain all the symbols. But Rafe (the closest thing she'd ever had to a father figure— her own father had been killed in a motorcycle accident when she was too young to remember) had somehow managed it, working off a sheet showing the various symbols with their crosses, lines and circles. It had taken so long and it had hurt so much. Even now, she could feel the pain of the needle piercing her back.

Marina squeezed her hands into tight fists until the pain of her digging fingernails pushed aside the memory of Rafe's needle. She couldn't allow herself to drift, to remember things that would only serve to make this night longer and her work harder. She looked out into the living room again, forcing the thoughts out of her mind.

The cluster of people thickened around the platform and Marina lost sight of the girl. She leaned back in her chair and idly shuffled her tarot cards. She checked her watch. She was scheduled to start at 8 P.M., in exactly ten minutes. Money or not (and she *was* getting paid well for this effort), Marina hoped this was the last party she'd have to work. There was something cheap and tawdry about being a psychic for hire at a party, and everybody knew it. Psychics at the top of their game didn't need parties or 900 numbers to generate cash and clients. But Marina was still new to California, and although she'd made the most of the last few months, she still needed a wider base of steady clients with deep pockets. For now, there was no better place than this house to find them.

As a way of passing the time, Marina tried to calculate the net worth of the revelers, but it was beyond her powers of estimation. There were dozens of people wandering around, yet the house was so massive it didn't even appear crowded. It was hard to believe that there were only two people living here, Madeline and her husband. While keeping her instructions brief and the small talk to a minimum, the party planner had let slip that the house had been built—almost literally—on a foundation of gold and gems. The husband was the founder and CEO of Royal Rings, a huge West Coast engagement ring franchise that, with the help of the Internet, was moving eastward at a brisk pace.

Marina's hand wandered unbidden up to her chest as she thought about Royal Rings, her fingers touching the chain on which her own ring hung and then moving down to the ring itself, feeling the sharp edges of the gold and the deep red gem inside it. It had been four months since she'd first put it on and she hadn't taken it off since. She felt a slight twinge of guilt—not for having it or wearing it, because she'd actually been implored, almost forced, to take it—because she knew she'd made herself very hard to find. Returning the ring, which she had every intention of doing *someday,* would therefore happen on her own timetable. That was the part she hadn't exactly made clear to anybody when she'd left Florida.

"Hey there. I'm a little early. Thought I'd beat the crowd. You mind?"

Marina smiled at the tall, dark-haired man creeping into her tent. He was wearing a hundred-dollar T-shirt, jeans that probably cost twice that and a black designer sport jacket. All three items flattered his well-but not excessively muscled form in the way that only the most expensive clothes can. His tan, just a shade or two darker than the permanent glow of most southern Californians, was rich and flawless. His features, Marina thought, were fairly close to perfect as well. She noted this as an art lover might admire a particularly lovely painting without any desire to possess it. Marina felt no personal attraction to this man, who was in any case gay—something else Marina had observed immediately and filed accordingly.

"Come in," she said. "I don't see any reason why we shouldn't get started."

"I'm Cooper," he said, and he took a seat opposite her at the small table. Marina saw his eyes move to her chest, which perplexed her for only a second until she realized that he was staring at her ring. Swiftly, she tucked it back inside her shirt and reached out to shake his offered hand. It was large, with strong fingers and a moist palm, and she could feel his nervousness in their brief touch.

"Marina," she said. In her peripheral vision she noticed another man, slight, with thinning blond hair, hovering near the entrance to the tent and trying to appear as if he wasn't looking in. Cooper glanced at him quickly

and turned back to Marina. They knew each other, but neither acknowl-
edged it. Sometimes, Marina mused, her work was almost too easy.

"Some party, huh?" Cooper asked. There was too much lightness in
his tone. He was covering something, Marina thought.

"It does seem pretty elaborate," she agreed.

"This whole thing with the naked sushi," Cooper said, gesturing in
the general direction of the buffet, "is so trendy right now. People think
it's some kind of ancient Japanese ritual, that they're being all authentic,
but it isn't. It's called *nyotaimori*—means like, naked woman on a plate
or something. It's what the Yakuza—you know, Japanese organized
crime?—what they do for fun. It's prostitution, basically. Sort of. Also,
it's kind of disgusting, even if she *is* totally clean and hairless. Can't imagine how she got every strand of hair out—must be some kind of magic
hot wax she's got going." Cooper drew a long breath and Marina smiled
pleasantly at him. "I'm sorry," he said. "I tend to talk really fast when I
get nervous."

"Why are you nervous?" Marina asked.

"Because you're psychic," Cooper said. "I'm assuming you can see all
my secrets."

"And I can see that you've nothing to be nervous about," she said
warmly. "Only people with evil in their hearts have reason to be nervous."

"So I'm one of the good guys?" Cooper laughed. "You can tell that,
huh? There are probably people who would disagree with that, you
know."

"Really?" she asked him. "Do you believe that?"

"Maybe not."

"You see? No need to worry," Marina said. "Do you have a specific
question or would you like me to read the cards?"

Cooper looked at the tarot cards on the table and sighed. "Actually,
the cards scare me a little," he said. "Can we do something else?"

"All right," Marina said. "Why don't you give me your hands? Just
relax; it's okay."

Cooper made a show of wiping his palms on his expensive jeans before taking a long theatrical breath and laying his hands on the table. Marina clasped them in hers and closed her eyes. She felt a sudden pang of sympathy for the man sitting opposite her, but she tamped it down. He didn't seem to be in any worse shape than the vast majority of the moneyed and overly privileged people who had time to attend a party like this. *Shake it off,* she told herself, *and move on.*

"Congratulations," she said, opening her eyes after a few moments.

The corner of Cooper's mouth turned up in a little half-smile. "Really?" he asked. "Congratulations on what?"

"You're in love," Marina said, allowing him a small smile of her own. Cooper raised one dark eyebrow skeptically. "Not so sure that's a reason to congratulate me," he said.

"Maybe not in other circumstances," Marina said. "You've been in love before. But this time it's the real thing for you. When that happens— when the heart opens so widely—it's always a cause for celebration."

"Well, I suppose you have a point there," Cooper admitted. "But the course of true love—"

"Never does run smooth," Marina finished for him. "And so it is now. The man you love . . ." She trailed off, waiting for the assent in Cooper's eyes. It wasn't long in coming.

"Is it that obvious?" he asked her. There was resignation but also a bit of defiance in his voice.

"No," Marina said, and gave him a moment to process this. "But my job is to see what *isn't* obvious."

"Of course it is," Cooper said. "So? The man I love is what?"

"He's not free," Marina said. "He's tied to another person or . . . another ideal. Still, he's attached to you. But there is something he's hiding. He is in a trap of his own making."

"Yes," Cooper said. Then, his voice calmer, "That's exactly right." He stole another glance through the tent's entrance, where Marina could see the blond man shifting around with a plate of sushi he wasn't eating. "He thinks . . ." Cooper seemed to catch himself and trailed off. Marina was familiar with this as well. People either opened up completely when they sat down at her table or they forced themselves to clam up and make her prove her psychic worth. But the skeptics always wound up being the biggest believers.

"He thinks *you* are the one with the problem," Marina finished for him. "That's how out of touch he is with himself."

Cooper's face softened, moisture forming in the corners of his eyes. "I've told him that," he said. "I've said those very words. It's like you pulled them out of my head." He paused. "You know, he *asked* me to come here with him. Madeline and Andrew aren't even my friends. Well, I guess technically they are now, but anyway, the point is he asked me to come here with him and now he won't even talk to me. He's acting as if he doesn't even know me."

"Yes," Marina said. "This man will be your biggest challenge. There is a struggle ahead for you and him both."

"But what can . . . what should I do?" Cooper asked.

Before Marina could answer, a young woman holding a glass of plum wine entered the tent. "Oh, sorry," the woman said, although she clearly wasn't. "I didn't know anyone was in here. We're lining up out there." She gestured to the tent entrance with the hand holding the wine, splashing some of it on the straw. "Oops. Okay, sorry—again. I'll just go wait." She half stumbled back out, and Marina could see a queue was indeed forming. Marina heard laughter and the clinking of glasses.

"Well, I guess we're done," Cooper said with a sigh.

"It's difficult to get too far in such a short time," Marina said, smiling. "That's the problem with these kinds of . . . meetings."

"Do you think you can help me?" Cooper stood up and fixed Marina with a look that beseeched and denied her at the same time.

"I think I can help you help yourself," Marina said, handing him one of her business cards. "You don't need to be rescued."

Cooper's smile reached all the way to his eyes as he tucked Marina's card into his jacket pocket. "Well, I guess we'll see about that," he said. "It was good to meet you."

Marina nodded as he turned and made his way back into the throng. The three hours she'd been paid for began now, and she steeled herself for the onslaught.

Chapter 4

"He's a Scorpio," the girl was saying, "and you know how they are—so secretive and all. So I think this would be a great birthday present for him. I want to shake him up a little. Well, I want *you* to shake him up. What do you think?"

What Marina thought was something she couldn't say, namely, that the girl seemed terrifically out of place at this party, and that with the Scorpio in question, she was likely in way over her head. Marina's head was buzzing. The two hours so far felt very much like ten, a mad kaleidoscope of hopes, dreams and fears shoved into every minute. The thick flow of people into her tent showed no sign of letting up and her throat was parched. She couldn't wait to pack up and leave. One more hour. She turned her attention back to the girl—Kelly, Katie . . . no, *Cassie,* her name was Cassie—who was waiting for an answer.

"Well, I'm biased," Marina said, "but I think a reading is a terrific and unusual gift to give someone. I'm sure he'll appreciate it."

"You know what?" Cassie said. "I think he will." She bent down to retrieve her oversize purse from the straw-covered floor and started rummaging through it. "What do you take? Like, Visa or, um, a check? Or I might have . . ." Cassie brought out a few crumpled bills and placed them on the table.

"Cash is always great." Marina smiled. "I do take that."

"I'm so glad I came to this party!" Cassie exclaimed as she searched her purse for more money. "I wasn't going to because I thought it would be, you know, some kind of weird boring thing. When Madeline invited me—she's a client of mine, I do her hair. I'm a stylist, by the way. I should give you *my* card, too, in case you ever need . . . oh, good, I *knew* there was another twenty in here. Anyway, I'm really glad I decided to drive all the way out here tonight, because I met you. It's a sign!"

Marina kept smiling and nodding until Cassie had emptied enough cash from her voluminous purse to cover the reading she was buying for her Scorpio. Then, as soothingly as she could, Marina placed her hand on top of Cassie's and said, "I look forward to meeting him. He's very fortunate to have someone as thoughtful as you in his life."

"Yes," Cassie said. "He is, isn't he?" She nodded slowly, hypnotizing herself into believing it. "It's never easy being in love, is it? I mean, maybe I'm just an incurable romantic, but I've always believed that the power of love can conquer everything. Well, it should, anyway."

Marina bristled. Being in love would be a damn sight easier for this girl if the object of that emotion wasn't a married man who was clearly using her for "love" in its most physical, base sense. Not that Cassie had told her in so many words that her Scorpio was committed to another woman, but she hadn't needed to. The information was as visible as if it had been branded on her face. How to answer her? Marina disliked being made into an advice columnist. "I suppose you're right about that," she said. "If it were easy, there would be much less unhappiness in the world." It was a banal, vanilla-flavored statement, but it was what Cassie wanted to hear.

"Are you . . . You must be in love with someone," Cassie stated. "I can tell you know exactly what I mean."

Marina felt irritation crawling across her skin and struggled to keep it at bay. She wanted badly to tell Cassie that she not only wasn't *in love* with anyone now, she'd never been in that kind of love: the heavy turbulent undertow that drove one to extremes of action and emotion. Every working day brought Marina these tales of love lost, out of reach or gone bad. Even the happy ones were constantly on edge. *Does he love me as much as I love him? Is he going to leave me? Will we be together forever? Is he the one?* For most people, it wasn't even about love, it was about not wanting to be alone. But Marina was not afraid to be alone. Not that her personal life was any of Cassie's—or anyone's—business.

"I do know what you mean," she told Cassie, straining to keep her voice sincere. "The heart is its own mistress."

"That's beautiful," Cassie whispered and stood up. "Thank you. Thank you so much."

Marina had barely enough time to deposit Cassie's payment into her own purse before another fortune seeker strode in, grabbed the chair and planted himself at the table. This one was close to fifty, Marina gauged, if he wasn't already there, and was trying unsuccessfully to look younger or at least hipper than he was. There were the hair plugs, for one thing, and the glaringly white Nikes, for another. This wasn't a man who spent much time in his sneakers. Nor did he seem comfortable in the professionally faded jeans and silk crewneck he was wearing. He held a drink in one hand and the other reached up to adjust a tie that wasn't there. This was a man who lived in expensive suits, if his casual clothes were any indication—a man who made a great deal of money and wanted everyone to know it. He leaned back in his chair, stretched out his legs and polished off the last of his drink with a single swallow. He regarded Marina with an air of ownership and played with the thick elaborate gold band on his ring finger as if it were a small toy.

"Everything okay in here?" he finally asked. Marina could smell the alcohol on his breath.

"Oh, yes," Marina answered, touching her tarot cards. "Would you like a reading?"

"Nah," he said. He pointed to the cards. "Never touch the stuff. I just wanted to check in. People"—he gestured toward the living room—"are very happy with you—so I had to see for myself."

"Are you sure I can't interest you in a reading, then?" Marina asked, hating the flirtatious tone she'd adopted but knowing it was necessary just the same. "Since I've come so highly recommended."

"Right," he said, and shook the ice in his glass. "I don't need a reading, sweetheart. This is my house. I'm the schmuck paying for this shindig."

So this was the man who'd made his fortune selling expensive tokens of love, Marina thought. How appropriately ironic that he seemed so loveless and angry himself. "Well," she began, and looked directly into his slightly bloodshot brown eyes. "It's a lovely shindig. And you have a beautiful home."

"Thanks. Can't take credit for the party, though. This was all my wife's idea. I'm just paying. That's what I do." He shook his ice again and Marina knew that it would probably take several more drinks to slake the kind of thirst he had going. The word *resentful* presented itself and lodged in her brain. It was as if everything and everybody in this big beautiful house annoyed and chafed at him, including Marina, whom he now looked at with growing disdain.

"I'm Andrew, by the way." He extended his hand and Marina took it in hers. She wasn't surprised that he had a crushing grip.

"I'm very pleased to meet you, Andrew."

"Yeah, pleased to meet you, too." Andrew stood but did not turn to leave. "You're psychic, huh?"

"Yes, I am."

"Psychic like you can see into the future and all that? How about dead people? You talk to dead people, too?"

"I see what I am allowed to see," Marina answered. "Some call it having second sight. Some call it being psychic."

"So I suppose you can 'see' that I think this whole thing is a bunch of bullshit, right?"

Marina hesitated, unsure of whether to suggest again that he sit down for a reading, though she knew she couldn't tell him what an angry person he was, his pent-up fury pulsing so close to the surface it was almost visible. In any case, Andrew didn't give her a chance to speak.

"Doesn't really matter what I think, though, does it?" he said. "As long as people are getting their money's worth. *My* money's worth." He took a last swallow from his thick etched glass. "I have to hand it to Maddie. I wouldn't have been able to think up this crap in a million years." He growled out a laugh. "A psychic at a party. Whatever." He marched out of the tent calling out, "Next!"

At exactly 11 P.M., Marina threw her tarot cards into her purse and returned the fake crystal ball to the table. There were still people milling around the tent, but the partygoers had become progressively drunker as the night wore on and most of them were slow and swaying now, giving in to alcoholic entropy. It was easy enough for Marina to brush by the thinning crowd and head into the center of the house. It was slightly more challenging to find someone who could tell her where to find a bathroom. The likeliest candidate would have been Madeline, but the party's hostess, who had not paid a visit to Marina's tent, was nowhere in sight. Her husband, Andrew, whom Marina spied across the room, would have been her second-best bet, but he was deep in conversation with Cooper's blond man. It looked to Marina like they were whispering, their conversation vaguely furtive, although with Coldplay blaring over some unseen sound system there was hardly any need to worry about being overheard. Cooper himself was absent and Marina wondered if he'd had enough of his date's cold shoulder and gone home.

Marina finally found the room she was looking for, but it was more like a chamber than a bathroom, complete with dressing table, stage lights and marble flooring. The toilet itself was behind another door, which Marina found to be locked. Marina waited for a minute, then two, then five. Just as she was debating whether to find another bathroom, the door to the toilet opened and Naked Sushi Girl emerged, now dressed in a pink miniskirt, a micro T-shirt and strappy heels, her long black hair straight and flowing down her back. She was disconcertingly beautiful, Marina thought; her face, to which she was now applying lipstick and mascara, was just as pale and expressionless as it had been when she was nude and covered with raw fish.

"Can I help you?" the girl asked. Marina realized she'd been staring.

"Some party, huh?"

The girl shrugged. "Whatever."

"Is it difficult?" Marina asked.

"Is what difficult?" The girl had a slight lisp, which made her sound as if she had a foreign accent.

"It must be hard to lie that still when people are poking you with chopsticks."

"You want to know how I can stand to have people eating off me. You think it's some kind of sex thing, don't you?"

"Not at all."

"You're the psychic, right?"

"Yes."

"So you know, then."

"Know what?"

"It's a job, just like yours. You sat in a tent. I lay on a table. I just happened to be naked."

"I didn't mean—"

"Let me ask *you* a question: Are you a whore?"

Marina shook her head. "No, obviously I'm not."

"Yeah, well . . . neither am I."

The girl adjusted her skirt, pulled her tiny top down to cover her navel, turned away from Marina and exited, slamming the door behind her. It was only after a couple of stunned moments that Marina noticed the girl had left her lipstick behind. Marina picked it up and held it, feeling the small weight of it in her palm, and then she dropped it into her purse. She wasn't often surprised by people, but Naked Sushi Girl had done just that. It wasn't her hostility or her unusual profession that had Marina perplexed; it was that the girl hadn't seemed the least interested in getting a reading or even a quick bit of psychic insight for free. What kind of person, Marina wondered, had no need to know what was in store for her?

February 2006

Chapter 5

In southern California rain fell with a great deal of flash and excitement. The wind tore at wet palm fronds, flinging them into driveways; gutters poured out miniature waterfalls. Exit ramps flooded and cars inevitably spun into guardrails. It was rarely catastrophic, but in Encinitas, located on the northern coastal edge of San Diego County, rain refused to be ignored. Here, rain was not a weather condition, it was a cinematic performance.

It was the rain, or rather the sound of it beating against the studio windows, that kept Madeline from fully relaxing into *savasana* after a particularly challenging hour of yoga. This was usually the best part of the session, when her muscles unwound and her breath came easy and slow. But the hammering rain had been bothering her since the minute they'd started. Usually she could think about nothing but getting through each asana as the instructor, Lydia, put them through their paces, but today Madeline had been completely distracted by the noise. She lay still now, eyes closed, wrists and ankles loose, but her brain refused to stop twitching. Rain was supposed to be soothing, but to Madeline it sounded like a spray of bullets hitting the glass.

Maybe it wasn't the rain, Madeline thought as she tried to keep her fingers from squeezing the sides of her yoga mat. Maybe it was the hormones that were making her teeth grind and her synapses crackle. She was on the fourth cycle of her Clomid prescription and the only thing growing inside her was nausea, bloating and excruciating tenderness in the tissue surrounding her C-cup breast implants. If nothing happened in the next two months, it would be time to start talking about in vitro, a process that Madeline was not eager to experience. But Andrew was unlikely to give up his quest for progeny. He was fifty years old and had suddenly decided that time was running out. Well, not that suddenly. He'd been talking about having a baby for a while. In truth, Madeline had to admit that Andrew had been on this quest since they'd married six years ago. No, even before. *"Sure,"* Madeline had agreed, *"of course I want kids. Sure, sooner rather than later. But not just yet. Let's enjoy this time for ourselves. Let's redecorate the house, take an extended honeymoon . . . We'll never be able to see Europe with a baby in tow."*

Now Madeline wasn't sure why she'd resisted at all. She'd known all along how important children were to Andrew. Madeline was positive that if she was unwilling or unable to avail herself as an incubator, Andrew would find someone who wasn't. And he wouldn't have to look far. It was pretty clear to everyone that Andrew was *loaded*. As the head of Royal Rings, a wildly successful chain of jewelry stores that specialized in "the unusual, the spectacular and the best" engagement and wedding rings, Andrew had been voted San Diego's "most eligible bachelor" by *America's Finest City* magazine before Madeline had taken him off the market. He was so wealthy that his lawyers had insisted she sign a prenuptial agreement. Having a baby was not only an insurance policy but an extremely small sacrifice to make for her future security. Women routinely did far worse for much less.

God, that was a terrible thought. It wasn't as if having a baby was such an awful thing. It was just that Andrew had been so *desperate* about it lately. Madeline clenched her left hand into a fist, feeling the small, reliable bite of her beautiful and very expensive Royal engagement ring and wedding band. Damn it, she was trying everything she could to conceive:

a low-fat, high-protein diet, organic foods, no caffeine, yoga twice a week
and Pilates almost as often. She'd even asked her stylist, Cassie, to stop
highlighting her hair with the standard bleach lest it affect her fertility.
Madeline had also given up alcohol, surprisingly the most difficult thing
to do. She hadn't thought of herself as much of a drinker before, but she
missed that nightly glass or two or three of good red wine.

And then there was the sex. For months, she and Andrew had been
copulating daily. Andrew had gotten himself a refillable prescription for
Viagra and was drinking wheatgrass and vitamin E smoothies every day.
Madeline couldn't remember the last time she'd gone more than twenty-
four hours without Andrew banging away at her. Madeline had always enjoyed sex with Andrew before all of this—he was a considerate lover and
he knew what made a woman feel good. Occasionally, he was even in-
spired, which made Madeline want to please him in ways that most wives
avoided like the plague. But then she'd always wanted to please Andrew
sexually. She wasn't blind enough to ignore the fact that Andrew had married down with her, and that her own best assets were a beautiful face and
a great body. And she had no money of her own.

When she met Andrew, she was just getting by, running a small business making gift baskets out of her tiny apartment. He had been enjoying
his success for years already and knew exactly what he wanted out of life:
a wife, children and a big house in Rancho Santa Fe, a neighborhood so
exclusive that the houses had no mailboxes. Madeline had wanted that,
too, which was why she was not only willing but happy to please Andrew,
in bed and out of it. It was also why she didn't complain that what they
were doing now had no feeling in it and nothing to do with lovemaking.
They were trying to make a baby. *She* was trying—hard.

No, it wasn't she who wasn't cooperating, it was her body, and she
couldn't be held accountable for what her body decided to do or not do.
Unless . . . Madeline sighed and opened her eyes. Unless the reason she
couldn't get pregnant didn't have anything to do with her body but with
something much less easily defined. Maybe, deep down, she had some

kind of mental block about having a baby. Madeline supposed she could spend more of Andrew's money on a psychiatrist to discover if she had any buried memories, motivations or issues that were keeping her from getting pregnant, but she didn't trust psychiatrists. One of Andrew's friends, Max, was a shrink and he was absolutely nuts. How else to describe a *therapist* who was gay but pretended otherwise? Not that he'd ever come out and said that, but come on, it was so obvious. When she'd first met him, Madeline thought that maybe Max kept up the heterosexual pretense because of Andrew's homophobia (it was subtle but it was there), but it soon became clear that the guy actually thought he was straight. It didn't exactly inspire confidence in the profession.

For Madeline, the likelier possibility was that there was some problem with the combination of her body and Andrew's that was preventing them from *ever* having a baby of their own. Madeline felt a clutch of panic twist her insides. What if that *was* the problem? How long would it take for Andrew to run out of patience? He'd made it very clear that he was in no way interested in adoption. No Chinese, Russian or Guatemalan babies for Andrew. No babies that hadn't sprung directly from his own loins. So there was really only one option. But what if that option was unavailable?

What she really needed, Madeline thought, was to get some kind of glance into the future so at least she could be prepared for what was coming. This Madeline *did* trust in—she'd been seeing an astrologer/psychic in La Jolla regularly until a few months ago when the woman decided to *retire*, of all things. How did you retire if you were a psychic? Wasn't that against some kind of code? Not that her ex-psychic was that great to begin with. Madeline's panic turned to anger. Her psychic had actually sucked when you got right down to it, even at a hundred dollars a session.

Madeline's mind shifted to the psychic whom her event coordinator had booked for their holiday party back in December. What was the woman's name? Marina. That was it. Madeline hadn't had a chance to speak to her, let alone get a reading, because there was so much going on that night. Between getting that whole sushi thing set up, making sure everyone was getting enough but not too much to drink and Andrew's foul mood, Madeline had spent the whole night in a state of dithering anxiety. But people were raving about the psychic, she remembered. They'd *loved* her.

"Namaste." Lydia had to raise her voice considerably against the sound of the rain, robbing her ending cue of its intended peacefulness.

"Namaste," Madeline mumbled along with the other would-be yogis, and she was off her mat and putting on her sweatshirt before the rest of them could even roll over and sit up. This was one of the best yoga classes in a city that had them by the gross, but today Madeline couldn't wait to leave. Besides, she was now on a mission; she wanted to find this Marina and make an appointment as soon as possible. Maybe even today.

"Damn it." Madeline stood at the door, staring out at what had become a full-on winter storm. In this part of the world, *winter* was a term used mostly to delineate holidays rather than temperature changes, and was only somewhat helpful in predicting periods of precipitation. This was why Madeline had decided to park her car several blocks away in Moonlight Beach. The clouds had looked heavy and she'd thought it *might* rain, but with the selfish optimism of most southern Californians, she'd figured it wouldn't rain on *her*. It was this very type of thinking that kept the locals from buying, selling or using umbrellas.

"Really coming down out there, isn't it?"

Madeline turned to the voice and saw Lydia smiling behind her. "I was so stupid," Madeline said. "I should have parked closer, but I wanted to get in a walk before yoga. There's no way I'm running through this now. I'll drown before I get to my car."

"I actually biked down here this morning," Lydia said. "I'm going to wait it out at Darling's across the street. I could use a hot drink, anyway. Do you want to join me?"

"I don't know," Madeline said, staring out at the wet streets. "I should probably . . ." Probably what? There was nothing Madeline *had* to do: no cooking, no cleaning and certainly no child to take care of. Her one goal for the day was to track down a psychic. Sudden tears formed behind her eyes and she struggled to contain them. This was her third rapid change of emotion in the space of fifteen minutes and she felt like she was going crazy. These hormones were going to kill her.

"Are you okay, Madeline? You seemed a little distracted today." Lydia's broad face radiated concern. Madeline decided to take a chance.

"I'm going through kind of a rough patch right now," she said. "Wish I had a little direction or guidance or something."

"Don't we all?" Lydia said. "Seems like it's getting harder and harder to maintain equilibrium these days, doesn't it?"

"Yes, it does," Madeline said, feeling fresh tears push at the backs of her eyes. She wiped at them quickly and drew in a deep breath.

Lydia tipped her head slightly to one side and gave Madeline a penetrating look. "Come on, Madeline, have a cup of coffee with me. We can talk. I won't keep you forever, I promise. How long can it rain, right?"

Madeline smiled. She could feel her muscles loosening and her jaw relax. Parking so far away hadn't been such a stupid move after all. She needed more friends; better friends, *real* friends. Maybe Lydia would be that kind of friend. "Okay," she said. "I'm game."

"Great," Lydia said. "It's before lunch, so with any luck we'll get a table by the window."

"Luck," Madeline repeated. She had a feeling hers was about to change.

Chapter 6

I
t was a bit of blind luck that Eddie happened to look up from his *San Diego Union-Tribune* at the exact moment two women made their dash across Highway 101. Had he given the right-wing Republican bullshit on the editorial page three more seconds of his time, he would have missed a glorious vision: two wet, bouncing, beautiful sets of tits coming straight at him.

Eddie stared out through the rain-bleared window of Darling's and revised his opinion slightly as the women crossed and ran, laughing and soaked, into the restaurant. Only one of the two pairs of braless breasts was truly outstanding—firm, round, probably fake—but he wasn't complaining. Wet T-shirts in a coffee shop on a Tuesday morning were a rare treat indeed.

Eddie watched with pleasure as the two women begged the hostess for a table next to the window. The one on the right had a plain face—Eddie had finally allowed his gaze to travel up that high—but came with a nice, well-toned body. The one on the left, though, long-legged, tan, with damp and tousled blond hair, was *prime*. She looked extremely well maintained, Eddie thought, and that probably meant there was a man—and money—at home. As if to prove him right, the blonde raised her left hand to push the hair out of her eyes and flashed a giant rock on her ring finger. Had to be three, maybe four carats at least, Eddie reckoned, although he'd never been close enough to a diamond that size to judge. His own wife wore a plain gold band, same as the one he wore, with the date of their wedding inscribed on the inside. It had been Eddie's experience that the bigger the diamond, the bigger the bitch who wore it and the bigger the asshole who had given it to her. It had also been Eddie's experience that women tended to writhe and flail their arms when they came and those goddamn rings scratched like hell.

Eddie noticed that the two women and the tiny black-haired hostess were staring at him staring at them, and he busted out his trademark grin. He had been doubly blessed with dimples and good teeth and he never failed to use them to his best advantage. The hostess came over to his table, clutching a couple of plastic-covered menus to her flat chest.

"Hey," she said, "how're you doing?"

"Just fine," Eddie answered. "Soon as I get my breakfast I'll be even better."

"Oh, you haven't eaten yet?"

Eddie saw that the two women were still standing at the door, straining to hear their conversation. "No, I have not," he told the hostess. "What's the problem?" He glanced again in the direction of the ladies at the door.

"Oh, no, I just . . . We were wondering if you'd mind . . . those people"—and here she gestured at the door—"are dying for a window table, and since you're only one person sitting at a table for four, we were wondering if you'd mind moving to the bar?"

Eddie considered the situation and weighed his options. "I'd rather not move to the bar," he told the hostess, watching her little face fold into a scowl. "Got a bad back—don't do too well on a stool, if you know what I mean. But I'd be happy to have the ladies join me here." He turned his smile up to full wattage and shouted across the restaurant, "Ladies— plenty of room over here for two more!"

"Whatever," the hostess said, making her way back to the door, where she relayed Eddie's message. He wasn't particularly surprised when he wasn't taken up on his offer. Plain Face looked like she'd probably have gone for it, but Diamond Ring was just pissed. "Thanks anyway," Diamond Ring called as the hostess led them to two cramped stools at the bar. The flat tone of her voice was the very definition of insincerity. Hell with her, then.

Eddie shrugged, turned back around to face the window and picked up his newspaper. Goddamn it, women were such a pain in the ass. But he loved them—all of them. Women were Eddie's drug of choice, and like any addiction they caused great pleasure, made him do stupid things and left him with great regret. It was because of a woman that he was even sitting here right now, allowing himself to be snubbed by the likes of Diamond Ring.

Although Eddie managed a large hardware and home repair shop one exit up the freeway in Leucadia, he never spent any time in this glossy, New Age, tofu-eating part of San Diego, preferring to keep himself removed from the foolish, faddish trends that went along with this side of the social spectrum. He lived down south and inland in El Cajon with his wife, Tina, and their two teenage boys. Tina worked down there, too, as a secretary at his boys' high school. It was a perfect arrangement: she kept an eye on them, they had her close by and nobody worried themselves about him. That kind of privacy was worth every minute of his daily commute, which kept Eddie's two worlds separate, although at seventy miles round-trip, the goddamn gas prices were killing him. Normally, he'd be taking this rare weekday off to do some work around his own house. He'd been installing those kitchen cabinets for what seemed like years already, his wife on him all the time about them, but he'd told Cassie—no, he'd promised her—he'd do this other thing today.

The waitress interrupted Eddie's musings by delivering his breakfast: scrambled eggs, bacon and cheesy potatoes. None of these items was available to him at home. Eddie's wife had taken him off red meat and anything else worth eating after his last cholesterol test had come back close to three hundred. She wouldn't let him drink, either. Eddie felt a stab of guilt about cheating with this heavy breakfast. It was, oddly, a less comfortable guilt than the one he felt when he cheated on her with Cassie.

But Cassie . . . There was no way to resist her even if he'd tried. Little red-lipped face shaped like a heart to match that heart-shaped pleasure palace between her legs. Cassie would go for it—and enjoy it—anywhere, at any time. Damn, she was hot. And so willing. Eddie never could figure out why.

He'd decided long ago that it was pointless to try to pretend he wasn't married or to lead a girl to believe there might be some kind of future beyond some good conversation and some excellent fucking. All modesty aside, he knew he was great in the sack—women never faked it with Eddie. He also had a sense of humor—wasn't afraid to laugh at himself, either—and they liked that. But if you couldn't laugh at yourself after where he'd been (although he *never* talked about his time in prison with anyone, not even his wife), then you were on a slow road to hell for sure.

But even knowing that he'd never leave his wife, knowing that he *loved* his wife—because Eddie didn't dish out that crap about his wife not understanding him or not having sex with him or whatever—even with all of that they were still willing to get what they could and to ride it out as long as possible. This was the thing that just confused the hell out of him. Great in bed could only get you so far, right? There was never time for cuddling and movies and weekends. Snatch and run. Why did so many of them go for that?

But they did. And he had to be careful, because sometimes they acted like it was all okay, like they wanted it this way themselves, but then they got too involved. Take Cassie, for example. She was so good at always turning the conversation back to him, asking him questions about what kinds of books he'd read when he was a kid, what kinds of movies he liked to watch, what kinds of music he liked to listen to now and how was it different from the music he listened to when he was younger. She wanted to know about his tattoos, how old was he when he got them and what was he thinking about at the time. Eddie was well practiced in keeping off the topic of that time in his life and found that a strong, pained silence usually shut off more questions. That was another thing about women—they got turned on by dark secrets as long as they didn't know what those secrets were. But that was Cassie's business. She cut hair and had to talk to people about themselves all day long—that was how he'd met her in the first place.

Almost a year ago already, he'd needed a haircut and his usual guy was on vacation, so he'd stopped into the little place in the strip mall where Cassie worked, and she'd had a chair available. Right away he knew they'd end up naked together sooner or later. She smelled so good, like fresh-cut flowers, and he could see the yes in her eyes as she leaned over him, brushing her plump little tits against his shoulders, trailing her fingers down the back of his neck.

He tipped her ten dollars on a twenty-dollar haircut and told her, "You're gorgeous and I'm very attracted to you."

"Thank you," she said, "and I feel the same about you."

"Shall we do something about it?"

She touched his wedding ring with her fingertip. "Isn't *that* going to be a problem?"

"Not for me," he said. After that it was only a matter of the details.

Thinking about her now, Eddie was almost drooling. He thought about Cassie often—more than he wanted to—and sometimes lately she was in his dreams and he woke up hard. He'd gotten too tangled up with Cassie, he knew it, and soon he'd have to find a way to cool the whole thing off. She was sweet—so sweet—but she wasn't stupid. She was starting to want more than he could give her. He knew the signs. She was starting to cry—quietly but wetly—after they had sex now, and a few weeks ago she'd told him that she loved him. No, she'd told him that she had *fallen in love* with him. More often now she was starting her sentences with "I wish" or "If only" and ending them with "Never mind; it's okay."

Cassie knew the rules, but it was only a matter of time before her desire reached that critical mass peculiar to women. If she got to that point, it would result in one of two outcomes. She'd either tell him that she was sorry, but it was too hard to keep giving herself emotionally to a man who was unavailable and they'd have to end it, or she'd go *Fatal Attraction* on him and start looking for bunnies to boil.

It was because he feared turning Cassie toward the latter scenario that Eddie had agreed to go to this psychic whatever-her-name-was. Cassie had given him the reading as a birthday present months ago, explaining that she couldn't give him an *object* of any kind that might be discovered by his wife. The reading could give him some insight into his past, Cassie had said, and maybe some into his future. It would mean *a lot* to her if he didn't make any noises about how ridiculous these kinds of things were and would just open his mind and *go*. Even though he suspected Cassie was hoping the psychic would tell him to dump his wife and take up with her (maybe she'd even planned this out in advance), Eddie promised he'd go. Well, he owed her that much. And even though she was a reasonable girl, you could never really tell. There weren't too many things in the world that frightened Eddie, but the unpredictability of a woman's mood was one of them.

Eddie checked his watch as he gulped down the rest of his coffee. Still had an hour before he was supposed to be at this thing and the address was practically around the corner, but he didn't want to sit in Darling's anymore. The place was starting to fill up in spite of the pouring rain and the atmosphere was getting steamy and loud. Thinking about his situation with Cassie was starting to give him a headache and the cheesy potatoes were giving him heartburn. He caught the waitress's eye and gestured for his check.

Too bad it was raining so hard. This would be a perfect time to go sit on the beach, maybe have a smoke (although Eddie was supposed to have given that up as well). He lived so close to it, but Eddie rarely saw the ocean. Two, maybe three blocks from where he sat now, the waves were breaking against the hard, wet sand. There were probably surfers out there, too. There wasn't any kind of weather that kept those guys out of the water.

That's what he'd do, Eddie decided. He'd get in the truck, park at the beach and watch the waves and surfers. Maybe even take a quick nap. He had time and the ocean was beautiful in the rain.

Chapter 7

Cooper washed down his dry cranberry scone with the end of his double soy latte and shoved his napkin into the empty paper cup. Not much of a lunch, but he was preparing a big, intricate dinner for Max tonight and he didn't want to load up ahead of time. He cooked much better on an empty stomach, anyway. He should be at the Harvest Ranch Market right now, in fact, buying salmon and blueberries, not sitting in his car in front of the giant green glass–and–marble building where Max had his psychiatric practice. This building also housed a group of plastic surgeons and a fertility clinic. It was a bizarre combination of specialties, Cooper thought, but he supposed it made some sense. They were all very costly, and elective, medical services. Where else should you go than some of the most expensive real estate in the country with a drop-dead gorgeous view of the Pacific Ocean? And it *was* beautiful—even in the rain. Made you want to get liposuction or go crazy just so you could watch the waves from the waiting room.

It was still catting and dogging out there, Cooper observed. Even if he made a run for it, he'd get soaking wet. Of course, he shouldn't actually go in at all. He was probably out of his mind to see Max at his office. It was one of Max's cardinal rules—*Don't show up at the office*. As if Cooper would go ballistic, scream or do something so incredibly *gay* that Max would somehow be found guilty (read: queer) by association. As if Max's patients didn't do the same every damn day of the week. *They* were the crazy ones, not him. *He* was normal. Actually, it was *Max* who was off his head. It was 2006, for crying out loud. Gay was so *out in the open* (for lack of better words) that it was almost passé. Hello, *Brokeback Mountain?*

Yet here he was, tiptoeing around like a frightened mistress whose married lover had threatened to end the affair if it ever went public. Ridiculous and humiliating is what it was. Cooper didn't know why he put up with it.

Yes, he did.

He was unfortunately and insanely in love with Max—an insanely smart man who unfortunately couldn't admit he was gay. Well, that wasn't quite right, either. Max admitted that he had sex with men (it was kind of difficult to deny when he was lying naked next to Cooper, who was undeniably a man), but he thought of it as a phase. Max, a *psychiatrist,* an *M.D.,* actually thought—had convinced himself—that he was a closet *heterosexual.* He'd even told Cooper that he planned to get married—to a *woman.* That was a "someday" scenario, of course, and one that Cooper had gotten a good laugh out of. But lately Cooper was getting the feeling—a lover's intuition—that Max was getting ready to *really* start dating a woman, and Cooper needed to make his presence felt in some way. Needed Max to realize how much he meant to Cooper. How much Cooper meant to him. So maybe this visit was some kind of shock therapy. They'd talked ad nauseam about boundaries (boundaries were Max's business), and maybe this was Cooper's way of crossing a boundary to get on the right side. Or something like that.

Cooper popped a Xanax into his mouth to take the edge off his nerves and followed it with a piece of Arctic Chill gum to get rid of his coffee breath. He was probably hitting the Xanax a little too hard lately, but what the hell. It was either that or X or coke, and Max didn't approve of any drugs he couldn't prescribe. So for now it was Xanax and Shiraz.

Fuck, Cooper thought suddenly, he used to have fun before he hooked up with this fucked-up closet case.

Well, never mind.

Cooper checked his reflection in the rearview mirror, grimacing to see if there were any wayward cranberry bits stuck in his recently whitened teeth (done with lasers, not those stupid strips). They looked good and so did the rest of him, Cooper decided. Max was crazy, but he had good taste. Cooper was who women referred to when they said all the hot guys were gay. He worked at it, sure. You didn't have a perfect year-round tan without a little help (even if this was southern California), and you couldn't maintain a crisply defined six-pack without hitting the gym. But, and this was important, Cooper had very good genes. If the thick mops on both sides of his family were any indication, he wasn't going to lose a single hair on his head anytime soon. And while you could nip and tuck almost anything, you couldn't buy good bone structure, and Cooper's basic architecture was pure F. L. Wright. So the question was definitely not why Max was attracted to him, but why he was attracted to Max.

Max was Cooper's opposite in almost every way. He was about five seven, short for a guy, and skinny, with thinning strawberry blond hair. Max didn't give a crap about working out beyond an after-dinner walk, and he had to wear a hat in the sun to keep from burning. Not exactly an imposing figure. But they had exactly the same color eyes: hazel with hints of green and gold. It was strange but also really compelling to look into Max's face and see himself reflected there.

The eyes they shared had also made a good conversation starter—Cooper's opening gambit on the night they met, at a fund-raiser for a children's hospital that Cooper's father supported as one of his many philanthropic projects. Cooper was there because he earned his very generous keep by organizing his father's events, and Max was there as a thousand-dollar-a-plate donor. Cooper needed very little small talk to understand which team Max batted for, and so early on, before his second martini even, he came out with it.

"You seem to be wearing my eyes," he told Max, "so you must know what I'm seeing right now."

It was kind of lame, but Max laughed, getting it right away. That was the thing about Max—he got Cooper. If only he could get himself as well. That party had been—what—almost a year ago now. They'd broken up twice during that time (well, not really, since they were never officially "seeing" each other), and Cooper had been so miserable that he'd come running back the minute Max called him, both times with no apology or explanation, just "Are you busy right now? Because I can call back if you're busy." Although it was never explicitly stated, the reason for both breakups was Max's insistence that he didn't see a future for their relationship because eventually he was going to live—and be happy—straight.

"I want to have children, Cooper," he'd said.

"I don't know if you've noticed, but gay men can have children in this century," Cooper had answered.

"You know that's not what I mean," Max had said, and that had been the end of that conversation. It would have been easier, Cooper thought, if Max had been a bitch about it—or about anything. But that was another thing about Max; he was kind, he really cared about people and he was very generous. Not just with money, because Cooper had plenty of his own, but in other, less flashy ways. Already a year and only a year.

Cooper was smart enough to know that his relationship with Max probably fell into some kind of classic definition of dysfunction. The more Max pushed Cooper away, the more Cooper wanted to be with him. And then as soon as Cooper got used to the idea that he couldn't be with Max, Max would reel him back in. Self-help manuals would tell Cooper he deserved better, that Max was using him or was too confused to give Cooper what Cooper needed. And it had occurred to Cooper that possibly he was living in his own denial. But deep down Cooper really believed that the two of them were meant to be together. Why, he couldn't say, but love wasn't meant to have clear explanations. You couldn't help who you fell in love with. And this was something Max still didn't understand.

For a moment Cooper was torn. It wasn't too late to change his mind and leave. Max would never be the wiser and they would just have a nice dinner later tonight, maybe a movie. . . . No, he was going in. Cooper gathered the elegant glass vase in which he'd arranged five fat sunflowers as a sort of for-your-office-which-I've-never-seen ruse, locked the car door behind him and ran to the clinic entrance with one arm shielding his head from the rain.

The lobby was so plush that it looked like a hotel foyer. Impressive, Cooper thought. No surprise Max got two bills for each fifty-minute session. He could only imagine what the good doctors in the plastic surgery clinic got for a boob job. At the end of the lovely lobby was a large steel-and-glass reception desk shaped like a half moon. At the center of this desk was a woman shaped, Cooper thought unkindly, like a *full* moon. It was kind of weird that a group so obviously concerned with appearances would hire such a large woman to helm the front desk. He'd have to ask Max what was up with that, Cooper decided as he approached.

"Hi—um—" Cooper couldn't find a name tag on her. "I'm here for Dr. Raymond."

She looked up and regarded Cooper with cool, dark eyes. "Do you have an appointment?" she asked. She'd actually be really pretty if she weren't quite so heavy, Cooper thought. She had smooth olive skin and lovely hair—a rich chestnut color that he could tell was totally natural— that fell like a curling waterfall down her back. Fifty pounds, he thought. If she could lose fifty pounds she'd be a knockout. He had a sudden irrational fear that this was the woman Max had set his sights on.

"Sir? Do you have an appointment with Dr. Raymond?"

"Sorry, no. No, I don't. Can you just buzz him for me?"

"What's your name please, sir?"

"Cooper." He had started to sweat. The lobby was too hot. It wasn't like this was the goddamn North Pole. Why did they keep it subtropical in here?

The receptionist gave him a manufactured smile as she dialed Max's extension. "Still raining out there?" she asked.

"Um, yeah, it's raining. Yes."

"Dr. Raymond? Hi, there's a Mr. Cooper down here? He doesn't have an appointment. Yes. No. Yes. Okay. You, too, Dr. Raymond. You're welcome." She hung up her phone and smiled at Cooper again. "Dr. Raymond asked me to tell you that he's sorry but he won't be able to meet with you today. He had an emergency session this morning and has to work through lunch. But if you want, I can schedule an appointment for you." Two of the multiple lines on her phone started ringing and she held up a finger in the "please wait" gesture as she answered them. Cooper could feel his heart pounding and his ears burning.

Yes, he'd been a fool to come here. He had nobody to blame but himself.

Before the woman could get off her calls, he placed the sunflowers on top of her desk, mouthed the words "These are for you" and stalked out of the lobby.

His cell phone started ringing before he could even get into the car.

"What the *fuck,* Max?" Cooper slid into the driver's seat and quickly swallowed another Xanax.

"Cooper, what are you doing? I've told you—"

The asshole never raised his voice. It was amazing—no matter what was going on, he always sounded like a shrink. "Told me *what?* I wanted to see you. You're not with a patient. You had me tossed out like some . . . some . . ."

"Cooper . . ."

"No, forget it Max, just fucking forget it!" And then, to his horror, Cooper started to cry.

"Cooper, are you crying? Listen to me, okay? It's not—"

"I can't talk to you right now. Fuck you and fuck dinner." Cooper punched the "end" button on his phone and tossed it onto the passenger seat. He put his head on the steering wheel and allowed himself to wail like a stuck pig for two full minutes. How he *hated* this feeling—this part of it. If only he could walk out of this relationship like he had with every other man he'd ever been involved with.

It was going to take more than love to turn Max around. He was a shrink, for God's sake—he *treated* people like himself. And Cooper needed something more powerful than Xanax, because he was starting to turn into a basket case. He pulled a couple of tissues from the glove compartment and blew his nose loudly. Fuck it, he was calling Marina. Max *loathed* when he did that—said Cooper was being ripped off and might as well light a fire with his money. Said it would be better if he *did* burn his money, because psychics were dangerous: they gave you false hope, told you what you wanted to hear and lied through their teeth. This was, probably, the only topic on which Max came close to losing his cool—it was almost funny in a way.

Cooper had gotten a good vibe from Marina as soon as he'd met her at that ridiculous holiday party. The rest of the evening had been a total disaster—Max avoiding him like the plague, even though they'd shown up together—but it had been worth it for those few minutes with Marina. She'd called right away that he was gay—okay, not much work guessing that, even though generally he flew under most people's gaydar—but what was interesting was that she also told him that he was in love with someone who wasn't free. Hit the nail on the head right there, she did.

Cooper had called her to make an appointment a few weeks later, when he and Max were on one of their mini breakups. She was really good—knew all about Max and came out with it before Cooper even had a chance to settle into his chair. Their session was short—Marina said she always kept the first visit that way so that she didn't absorb too much of her new client's energy—but she'd told him that he and Max would get back together and that she saw a rough road ahead unless Cooper was willing to do some "spirit work." Just as she'd said, they'd gotten back together, and when he told Max about her he got all that hell. So out of some weird respect for Max and his *opinions,* he hadn't called Marina again. But fuck him.

Cooper punched the numbers into his cell phone and listened to it ring. He looked out of his window. It had finally stopped raining and the clouds were starting to break. A shaft of sunlight slipped through one of these and shone through Cooper's windshield. After several rings, just when he was starting to tear up again, she picked up.

"Hi, Marina," he said. "It's Cooper. Can you help me?"

November 2006

Chapter 8

Marina woke up to the dry howl of a mad wind. The Santa Ana wind, known simply in some circles as *el diablo* or "the devil," had arrived on schedule and with a sly wink in time for Halloween. Twenty-four hours later, it was still swirling around caved-in pumpkins and blowing remnants of bathroom tissue and black crepe toward the ocean. Marina heard her windows rattle and her first thought was that she was going to have a busy day. Her second thought was that it was a good thing, because it was her birthday. Turning thirty-five meant that she had only two years left to reach her goal, which was to have enough money to stop working and do whatever she wanted. She wouldn't call it *retirement,* a sad word that conjured images of golf clubs and guided tours. What she was after was the opposite of retirement—a new life. Today, at least, the weather would help.

There were reasons why Marina welcomed this wind that so many hated. When it raced down the mountains and out to the coast, the Santa Anas grew hot and arid, sparking wildfires and setting nerves on edge. People complained of dry skin, flat hair, nosebleeds and headaches. But it also swept away haze and fog, leaving the landscape so bright that the colors seemed supersaturated and the air sparkled with particles of desert dust blown west. Marina relished that clarity and the way she felt when the wind moved through her body, so dry it made her shiver.

The main reason Marina liked the Santa Ana season was that it brought in business. There were better and worse times of year for psychics, and people usually moved wavelike with them. The holidays, for example, were busy, whereas late spring and early summer were slow. Days that were warm and sunny were generally quiet, and when it rained there was always a rush. But nothing brought in wanderers desperate for psychic counsel like the Santa Ana winds.

Marina had slept well, in spite of or maybe because of the wind, and it took more effort than usual to pull herself from her large down-covered bed. Frugal in most other ways, Marina splurged on anything related to the luxury of sleep. Both her four-poster pine bed frame and her mattress were top of the line and covered with thick, rich linens. Filmy white mosquito netting flowed over the frame, making the whole effort look and feel like an island devoted to slumber. If she had been explaining the elaborate bed to a client, Marina would have pointed to the influence of Neptune and Pisces in her birth chart. Pisces, at the very end of the zodiac, was weary and loved the escape of sleep. But Marina knew that her own sleep shrine had more to do with the avoidance of dreams.

Marina knew that she dreamed—everybody did—because biology demanded it, but she also knew that her mind was powerful enough to choose not to remember these dreams. Lately this had not been as easy as she would have liked. Weird flashes of light and ominous images had begun creeping into her unconscious, and she'd been plagued by an insistent feeling of dread. In her dreams she was running, and sometimes she woke up with a start, the smell of smoke thick in her nostrils, only to find there was nothing in the house to account for the odor. Worse than this, though, Marina's mother had lately made a few walk-on appearances in her dreams—always Marina's personal signal of subconscious unrest, like the achy feeling one got before the flu took hold. But there was nothing to be gained by trying to interpret dreams, Marina told herself. As far as she was concerned, they were nothing more than random electrical impulses. Of course, she'd never admit as much to her clients. Portentous dreams were powerful tools in the psychic's arsenal.

Rubbing the last traces of sleep from her eyes, Marina laid out her clothes for the day and took a quick hot shower. She'd cut her hair short after leaving Florida and had finally stopped coloring it, too. It had grown out to the color of strong tea, a darker brown than she remembered it's being, and now curled around her shoulders. There was also no longer any need for the heavy theatrical makeup she'd once worn, but Marina continued to use the black liner and deep shadow on her green eyes. California was as forgiving as Florida had been demanding, but Marina still wanted some camouflage.

All in all, Marina was pleased with the progress she'd made since she'd left that swamp. It had taken some time to set herself up, of course, and more time to stop looking over her shoulder, but her own fear had finally given way to something resembling confidence. And this was ironic, because what one really needed to make it in her business was access to fear. Not one's *own* fear, mind you, but fear in general. If she allowed herself to become frightened as she had in Florida, she was ineffective, almost paralyzed. It wasn't difficult to find fear. Wherever there were people, there was fear. And fear was what motivated people to come to Marina. Everyone was afraid of something—afraid of being alone; afraid of not having enough money, love or recognition; afraid of the unknown, the unusual, failure, pain and death. Death was the big one, the underlying fear of so many smaller ones. Fear was Marina's stock in trade, and there was no shortage of it to go around.

Of course, there was the argument that people consulted psychics because of desire, because they wanted love or money or fame. But Marina knew that desire merely masked fear. People wanted to know what the stars predicted, what the cards foretold and what their futures held, because they wanted to make sure that their futures *existed.* In many ways it didn't matter what the future held as long as there was a future to look into. That at any moment it would all stop, that there would be a vast maw of blank, unknowable eternity to contend with, was what frightened people most of all. Marina had always understood this—had always known that the color of the human heart was very dark.

Fear existed in abundance here, twenty miles north of "America's Finest City," as it did everywhere else. But what made this place special and what made Marina's job so much easier was that this population was not only fearful but so *willing*. People here had an unlimited appetite for the cosmic, supernatural and extrasensory with very little of the usual skepticism. She hadn't quite figured out if this willingness came from innocence or an openness of spirit or was just geographically based stupidity. Perhaps, Marina thought, it came from an underlying sense of optimism. Perhaps hope made up the fabric of belief in the first place.

At any rate, it was working for her. She'd been able to set up shop in Encinitas with little problem other than competition from the three other psychics in town. The only things Marina had to do were to be better and to be more expensive. Better was easy. Since she didn't believe in "real" psychic ability, Marina had no doubt that her competition was made up of charlatans with varying degrees of talent in the art of deception. There were likely several who practiced *self*-deception as well—a big problem for many psychics. Once you started buying into your own line of bullshit you were finished. This had never been an issue for Marina. Since she was a child she'd known that people would pay well to hear things about themselves that they could figure out if they just looked into the mirror. There was a big difference between a talent and a gift, and Marina never confused the former, which she did have, with the latter, which didn't exist. She also knew that when she was on her game there was nobody who could beat her. Not that anyone seemed particularly willing to try.

As far as what she charged, Marina had learned this: people didn't want to skimp on their psychic services. Paying more meant you were getting quality. You wouldn't buy your future off a sale rack, would you?

Marina's decision to charge more, to take in as much as she could, had resulted in a small but growing nest egg. It wasn't enough to make her feel totally secure (she didn't know how much money it would take to accomplish *that*), but it certainly took the edge off. Marina was determined to never again feel the sense of desperation that had tortured her those last few months in Florida, not least because she despised what it brought out in her. It was a point of pride for her that despite plenty of opportunity, she never drained her wells dry. She took what she could get from her clients, sure, and sometimes more than they should have given her considering how much they had, but there was always a line she drew and would never cross. Except she had crossed it, in Florida, when that back-against-the-wall insecurity had made her weak and greedy.

It took no effort for Marina to summon the memory of the sweltering, nightmarish day when she'd looked into her tarot cards and predicted disaster for Mrs. Golden's son. She could still see the interplay of fear and excitement on the old woman's face as she'd turned the cards. It was almost as if Mrs. Golden wanted the worst possible news, as if she was goading Marina on. "I'll do anything," she'd said, almost an invitation.

Marina bit her lip, ashamed even now at what had happened next. No need to get so worked up, she'd told Mrs. Golden. There was always a way of warding off evil, but she'd need money—quite a bit more than usual—for certain candles and crystals that could only be obtained in certain places. Marina had never before stooped to that level. Candles and crystals were the oldest Gypsy fraud tricks in the book—low-class all the way—and she hated herself for resorting to it even as she pushed forward. But Mrs. Golden was completely unfazed. Oh, yes, the candles, she knew all about those, she'd told Marina. Another psychic she saw—well, actually a couple, but please don't be jealous, dear, you're far and away the best—had told her to buy those candles before. She knew they were expensive, but what did it matter, this was her son they were talking about.

And Mrs. Golden had come prepared, as if she'd known in advance that this was going to be a costly reading. Her tatty purse contained a stack of hundred-dollar bills, which she took out and placed next to the tarot cards. "How much do you need?" she'd asked, and after that it was only a matter of Marina's calculating the difference she needed to get herself to California. But as forthcoming as she'd been with her cash, Mrs.

Golden still surprised Marina with what she offered up at the end of their session.

Marina held it in her hand now, the brilliant ruby ring dangling from its golden chain. Mrs. Golden had taken it off and pressed it into Marina's hand so firmly that the sharp edges of the stone dug into her palm.

"Please," she'd said, "I want you to wear this. You can keep him safe if you wear it. Until the danger is past him."

Marina had studied Mrs. Golden's face carefully then, her first instinct telling her it was some kind of trap. It wasn't possible for this woman to entrust her with such a valuable and sentimental piece.

"It's not necessary," Marina told her. "I don't need—"

"Please, Marina, please. I know it will work. Wear it next to your heart. It will help you protect him." Marina started to protest one more time, but Mrs. Golden interrupted again before the words could fall from her mouth. "When he's safe, you can give it back to me," she said. A flicker of indecision passed over her face. "Or the next time we see each other. All right?"

That would have been the moment, Marina thought now, to make a final protest—to tell Mrs. Golden that she couldn't take the ring because there wasn't going to be a next time. But the old woman continued to fix Marina with a look that was both searing and pleading. And then Marina saw herself slipping the chain around her own neck and heard herself promising the woman that she would keep the ring close to her body, away from the eyes of all others, until the moment she returned it.

She'd at least made good on that promise, Marina thought, staring at the ring's sparkle before replacing it in the soft place between her breasts, the spot it had occupied since that August day. It felt heavier than usual today and Marina had to adjust it several times to keep it from poking into her flesh. It had been six months before she tried to contact Mrs. Golden. Marina had never intended to keep the ring, but there was always a reason why it wasn't yet time to return it. She didn't want anyone from her old life to know where she was, she'd rationalized at first. And then it was that she'd wanted to wait until Mrs. Golden—who was probably upset about her sudden absence—had time to settle down. And when she did make the call at last, the phone number was no longer in service. Marina had tried, although not very hard, to track down Mrs. Golden once or twice after that and had came up empty each time. Now, more than a year since she'd last seen the woman, Marina had arrived at a sort of peace with the idea that she'd made an attempt to return the ring and that by keeping it she was honoring Mrs. Golden's wishes. What Marina was less easy with was that she'd come to view the ring as a sort of lucky charm, the kind that would stop working as soon as she let it go. For someone who believed in neither luck nor charms, this bit of superstition was like a small but troublesome pebble trapped in a tight shoe.

Marina patted the ring in its place and shrugged off her doubts. It was her birthday, after all, not a time to be morbid. Instead of grinding beans in her own kitchen, she decided to treat herself to a large cup of coffee and drink it down on Swami's Beach, where she could watch the surfers negotiate the waves. The beach was situated in the corner angle between Marina's small house in the scrubby hills of Cardiff-by-the-Sea and her storefront office off the Coast Highway in Encinitas. There were any number of coffeehouses between those two points, but Marina favored Rosa's, a tiny shacklike stop that served strong coffee, fresh-squeezed citrus juices and a limited selection of baked goods. There was no special language one had to learn to order (the coffee came in two sizes, small and large) or chatter to engage in while one stood in line. Rosa herself, often the only person working the counter, didn't talk to her customers beyond what was absolutely necessary to fill their orders. All of which suited Marina perfectly.

Outside, the air was electrified and warm. Marina could feel the static crackle in the atmosphere even before the inevitable sparks flew from her keys and car door to her fingers. She parked in a lot next to the beach and walked the short distance to Rosa's stall. As she stood in front of Rosa contemplating whether to have an apple fritter or a pumpkin empanada, the dry wind pressed her skirt to her legs, then lifted it from underneath like a hand.

"I'll have a large coffee and one of those," Marina said, pointing to the empanadas.

Rosa nodded without offering a smile and prepared the order in silence. Marina noticed that a few strands of Rosa's usually neat ponytail had come loose and were falling across her eyes, which looked strained and dark-circled. Normally placid and efficient, Rosa slipped pouring Marina's coffee, spilling some on her hand and provoking a couple of whispered oaths. The wind, Marina thought. In one way or another it affected everyone.

Once on the beach, sandals in her hand and sand rough under her bare feet, Marina was relieved to find that despite Rosa's sour mood, her coffee was as good as ever. The empanada, too, surprisingly light and spiced with cinnamon and nutmeg, had been a good choice. A couple of curious gulls circled Marina, squawking their desire to share, but she ignored their pleas. It was likely that she'd be working through until dinner and wouldn't get a chance to eat anything substantial in the meantime, so she was going to consume every last bite. Marina enjoyed a good meal as much as the average person, but had never been passionate about food. Plus, staying slim was as important to her success as any learned skill.

Marina looked out at the ocean, awed by its churning array of colors. Green and gray mixed with patches of deep blue and the swirling red of seaweed. The waves were high and she wondered at how few surfboards she saw dipping in and out of the foam. Usually there was nothing that kept those dedicated surfers out of the water: not vicious undertows, storms or even the threat of dumped sludge and waste. But there were only a couple of wet-suited figures far out in the waves now. Marina's eyes wandered to the water's edge, where a barefoot couple strolled across the wet sand. They were physically mismatched; she was tall and thin and he was several inches shorter and thick around the waist, but they were laughing and holding hands and Marina could tell that they were comfortable with each other. They walked together in rhythm, each knowing the pace of the other's steps. There was an ease in their together-ness that suggested perfect complicity, and for the first time in a long while Marina felt a pang of loneliness.

Making a living as a psychic was similar to be being a masseuse when it came to dating. Potential partners were intrigued at first, maybe even dismissive, but pretty soon they started to want her "services" for free. Nor did she want to get into a discussion about her line of work with people she didn't know. And it wasn't as if she had a social network through which to meet men. She was closer to some clients than others and those connections were what passed as friendships these days. But it was an incontrovertible rule that she *never* become romantically involved with a client.

Besides all of this, though, Marina was smart enough to know that her early experience with sex and men—much of which could easily be considered child abuse—hadn't given her the best foundation on which to build a decent relationship. The word *damaged* flitted through Marina's head, as it had many times before. It was a fact of her business that she let precious few people get close to her, but that alone couldn't explain why she had always been unable to open herself up to a man. There was too much risk. The few times she'd come close, Marina had felt raw and ex-posed to the point of pain, as if her skin had been peeled from her body.

Still, she wasn't exactly a nun; there had been men in her life and in her bed, although none who had stayed for too long. But it had been a long time since Marina had felt even the most casual of caresses. She reached into her shirt to make sure the ring was secure in its position. It had been so long, in fact, that the only man who had gotten close enough to catch a glimpse of that precious gem was her gay client, Cooper, who had boundary issues and thought, before she'd set him straight, that it was okay to touch her hair, clothing and jewelry in the interest of assessing fashion. Of course, Marina mentally revised, she hadn't exactly set him *straight,* but she had gotten him to stop touching her.

The couple continued on their way and out of her field of vision. She wondered what was next for them today. A leisurely breakfast, perhaps at one of the many quaint little beach cafés? Or maybe they'd go home, to the house that they shared. She'd make him an omelet with chanterelle mushrooms and goat cheese. Maybe he'd make it for her. Or maybe they'd skip food altogether and go straight to bed, their bodies comfortable and knowing with their deep, quiet passion.

Marina swallowed the last of her coffee, tasting the sea salt that had blown onto her cup. A bitter taste had crept into her mouth and into her mood. It was too windy to be outside, she thought. Best to leave the beach now before that rush of air turned into a storm inside her head.

Chapter 9

Marina stood up, brushed the sand from the folds of her skirt and started mentally planning out her day. She'd get to her office early and, given the Santa Ana winds, might even get a walk-in before her first appointment. Although she preferred a set schedule, she had to keep time open for walk-ins. Every regular, after all, had once been a new client. And despite the fact that she had accumulated a nice, steady set of returning clients, most of Marina's regulars did not refer her to their friends or acquaintances. They didn't want to share her and probably felt that the more clients she had, the less time she'd be able to devote to them, as if there wouldn't be enough to go around when it came to their time at the table.

Marina preferred working in her office and tried to avoid making house calls. Sometimes, though, it was inevitable. She had one later today, in fact.

Right around rush hour, she'd be heading into the well-tended labyrinth of Rancho Santa Fe to see Madeline, who'd been ordered to bed rest by her obstetrician. Women like Madeline were Marina's bread and butter—rich, dissatisfied and looking for meaning anywhere but inside themselves. A couple of months after Marina had been hired to work at Madeline's house in December (the last party, thankfully, that Marina had worked), Madeline came to see Marina in a panic about not being able to get pregnant. Marina had run her standard game, which was to collect information over the course of the first couple of visits and judge how much a client was willing to invest to get the answers and outcomes they were looking for. Madeline, as transparent as a sheet of plastic wrap, had made it very easy.

There was a baby in Madeline's near future, Marina told her (the Empress card showed this in Madeline's first tarot spread), but there were also impediments that had to be cleared before conception could take place. Her aura, for one thing, was muddy and thick. This was creating a barrier that the baby's pure spirit could not cross. Another problem was the presence within Madeline that refused to yield the space needed to grow and nurture a new life. That presence was Madeline's younger self, Marina explained, her "inner child." That child had been neglected in some way and had refused to grow up with Madeline. Now that spirit was crying out against being forgotten again to make way for another being—crying out so loud, in fact, that Marina had heard the wail as soon as Madeline walked in.

Madeline's eyes got wider with each one of these pronouncements and she nodded along as if to say *Yes, yes, that is exactly right.* Her only question after absorbing it all was what Marina could do to help. Cost was no object.

Marina burned red and white candles and sage and directed her client to drink a blend of potent herbs imbued with special properties (in reality a combination of raspberry leaf and green tea) that would help her fertility. She gave Madeline small samples of these items and instructed her to perform the same rituals at home.

Marina's thinking was that as soon as Madeline felt that responsibility had been lifted from her—that some outside force was taking care of her situation—she would relax enough to get pregnant. It happened this way with women often enough. They tried and tried to no avail, but as soon as they gave up and decided to adopt or travel the world instead, they conceived. If this didn't end up happening, Marina had a backup plan: She would tell Madeline that the forces working against her were too strong, and that different spirit work was needed. If it came down to it, Marina would even tell Madeline that she'd been cursed for wrongdoing in a previous life and that she would have to work off the karmic debt.

Fortunately, Marina hadn't had to resort to her alternate plans. Although Marina had warned that the process might take up to a year, Madeline conceived five months later. Marina, not Madeline's husband or physician, was the first to hear the good news. Madeline flew into her office waving a positive pregnancy test stick and weeping tears of joy, completely convinced that the baby was entirely Marina's doing. That was the moment that Marina became the most important person in Madeline's life and was put on a very generous retainer—an unexpected but happy development.

At almost three months Madeline had started spotting and she'd been housebound ever since. Now, terrified of losing the baby, she needed Marina more than ever. This new wrinkle worried Marina a little. She had to weigh both possible outcomes and prepare for each one. If Madeline managed to get through her pregnancy without miscarrying, Marina would take the credit. If not, Madeline would need to be convinced that it was her own fault. Either way, Marina would have to remain necessary. Madeline was her most reliable and profitable client.

So she would travel to Madeline's big house in Rancho Santa Fe with its imported Italian marble, Chinese roof tiles and Danish furniture. She would take her tarot cards, her sage, her candles and her tea. She would set it all up in the large room that had been made into a nursery while Madeline reclined next to her on an oversize velvet couch. And then Madeline would talk and talk, spilling out the most intimate details of her life: her wishes, her fears, her secrets. Yes, Madeline was easy. It was the husband, Andrew, Marina wasn't so sure of. She hoped he wouldn't be home this evening, but his absence was unlikely; he'd been hovering over Madeline like an anxious cloud almost every time Marina had come to the house.

"My wife *loves* you," he'd told her on one visit, echoing the same sense of disbelief he had first offered at the party so many months before.

Andrew had gone through some physical changes since that night. His skin had become bluish gray around the jawline and there were shadows under his angry-looking eyes. There was always a bristling hostility about him; it was so strong that Marina sometimes thought she could hear him growl. The way he spoke to her, in fact, was very much as if he were a big guard dog just looking for an excuse to attack. "I hope you know what you're doing," he'd said on her last visit as she headed up the stairs to see Madeline. He'd added a little laugh at the end as if he was just joking, but Marina could hear the threat. Madeline had mentioned many times how important this baby was to her husband.

"He's worked so hard his whole life," Madeline had told Marina. "He made Royal Rings all on his own. And he wants to pass it on. You know, keep it in the family."

But Marina wasn't convinced that Andrew's anger and frustration could be explained as simply as that. She sensed a much deeper dissatisfaction—or maybe disappointment—inside of him that no amount of money or possessions could fix. And men like Andrew, who shoved his own emotions so far down that he completely lost touch with them, always looked to blame others for their own predicaments. It was worse when they had money, because money gave them power and power turned them into bullies. Marina didn't believe that a child would make him happy.

Irritation prickled at the edges of Marina's thoughts. These people had no idea how petty and meaningless their problems were in the greater scheme of things. It was a good thing; if they ever woke up and realized the insignificance of their own little troubles, Marina would be out of a job.

Marina's office was wedged between a nail salon and a tiny thrift shop, a space that was open and public but not overly so. She'd fashioned a waiting area in the front of the office, outfitted with shelves, used books and a couple of comfortable chairs. There was a smaller, private space partitioned off behind this area that Marina used for her readings, as well as a tiny bathroom and a back exit door that Marina never used. The office was tasteful and inviting, but it wasn't immediately obvious what kinds of services were provided there. Unlike other psychics, Marina didn't choose to hang neon signs or symbols in her window. A brass nameplate advertising "Intuitive Counseling" hung on her office door, and that was enough to attract the right kind of clientele. People here knew exactly what that meant. After Florida, she'd decided never again to work out of her house, and she found that her current clientele liked going to an office—it gave the whole process an air of legitimacy.

The wind was still blasting as Marina stuck her office key into the lock, and she could smell smoke. The bone-dry brush around the marine base just north at Camp Pendleton was probably already on fire, she thought. It seemed to burn regularly. Across the street, a waitress struggled to keep her long hair in place as she served coffee to a man sitting alone at one of the café's outdoor tables. The man must not be from around here, Marina thought, amused. The locals hated any kind of atmospheric interference with their meals; as soon as there was a hint of rain or a puff of wind they headed inside for shelter. And heaven forbid the temperature should fall below the mid-seventies. Outdoor heat lamps had to be lighted immediately. Marina noticed that the man seemed much more relaxed and unperturbed than his harried waitress. He smiled at the sulky girl, handed her his menu and then, as if he could feel her watching him, turned his eyes toward Marina. Surprised and embarrassed to be caught staring, Marina looked down at her keys and moved quickly to unlock her door.

"Some weather for Election Day. Guess we'll be getting some interesting results. But you probably know what those are already, don't you?"

Marina startled at the voice close behind her and whipped her head around, almost convinced that the man from the café had materialized at her back. But no, the voice belonged to Ed "call-me-Eddie" Perkins, who had come in for a reading back in February and had been making a periodic nuisance of himself ever since.

"I don't make political predictions, so you should go vote anyway," Marina said, unruffled by his swagger and sarcasm.

"Aw, come on, I didn't mean it that way," he said. "How are you, Marina?"

"Doing fine, Ed. What can I do for you?"

"You can call me Eddie to start." He grinned wide, making sure to maximize the effect of the prominent dimples on each cheek, and ran his hand through his longish salt-and-pepper hair.

"Eddie, fine. What else can I do for you?"

"Can we go inside first and then I'll let you know?"

Marina knew Eddie's type so well. He was the kind of guy she'd cut her psychic teeth on when she was a kid and men like him had trailed in and out of her mother's bedroom. Marina's mother would go off on a nod, too out of it to service them, so they'd start checking out her daughter like a piece of meat. Her razor-sharp powers of observation and her natural talent with her mother's worn-out set of tarot cards saved Marina from molestation on more than one occasion, because while these men were too morally impaired to see the wrong in having sex with a girl her age, they were too scared to attempt the same thing with a freaky little witch. At least, most of them felt that way. But Marina was now expert at avoiding those memories.

Marina sensed that Eddie was not a child molester, but thought his womanizing was the most insidious kind of abuse. She could see it all—his compulsion to use them and then move on to the next—the minute he walked into her office, mud and rain falling from his work boots, to get the reading that one of his many girlfriends had bought for him. Marina had gone easy, giving him what he'd find inside any fortune cookie and throwing in a bit of astrology (too technical and boring for most guys like him). She could tell he didn't have much extra cash and probably wouldn't be back for another reading. Plus he was obviously more interested in her body than in anything she had to say. So she didn't bother mentioning anything about what she'd learned by looking at his prison tattoos and the jagged scar above his collarbone.

But Eddie had come back. He bought his own reading a couple of months later and spent the whole time (mostly a repeat of the first) attempting to x-ray her blouse with his eyes. He told her that she was the most beautiful and unusual woman he'd ever met and that he hadn't been able to stop thinking about her since he'd met her. Marina couldn't imagine the kind of helpless innocence one would have to have to fall for a line like this, but she supposed there were still women out there who did. She'd set him straight right then—told him that she wasn't looking for a date and that unless he was serious about their sessions, he wouldn't be able to get any benefit out of them. He'd apologized and left, but the following month he was back again—not for a reading, but to drop off a half dozen red roses. A month later, he returned with a single white one, long-stemmed and elaborately wrapped. And this was how it had gone.

It had been a while since his last offering, and Marina had thought he'd found another new girlfriend or gotten tired of the game. But, naturally, Eddie was the kind of man who lived for this kind of challenge.

"Eddie," she said when they were both inside her office and out of the wind, "I've told you that I would never become involved with a client romantically. And that's not even considering the fact that you're married."

"I need a reading, Marina. A real one—I mean, a big one. No, I mean, I have a problem and I need you to . . . look into it for me."

Marina stared into his face, searching his eyes for his real motivation, and couldn't find it. "Do you want to do this now? Because I have—"

"No. I'll make an appointment. But if you have time this week, I'd appreciate it."

"Okay," Marina said, "but this is an appointment, Eddie. Don't bring flowers."

"Just money, right?"

Marina allowed him a smile and pulled her calendar from her desk drawer. *Fine,* she thought. Eddie wasn't a bottomless well, but he had some money, and as long as he was going to keep coming around, she might as well take it.

"What about Friday?" she asked him. "I have a cancellation at four. After that, it looks like I'm booked solid for a couple of weeks."

Eddie smiled. "I'll take it," he said.

Chapter 10

Marina's day had been even busier than she'd expected. Whether this was solely because of the weather or also because it was Election Day, giving people more than the usual need to know what the future held, she couldn't tell. After Eddie left, the hours had passed in a blur of beseeching faces seeking answers to all of life's major questions.

Kiki, a receptionist for a medical group, wanted to know when she would meet her soul mate on the Internet dating service she'd just joined. In her tarot cards, Marina had conveniently spotted a doctor—perhaps even someone where she worked—who would soon be making contact. Kiki blushed, excited. Well, in fact there *was* someone at work she'd had her eye on, she told Marina. Who would have thought?

Stephanie, a new client referred by a regular, wondered whether she should change careers from technical writing to nursing. Marina noted the strong healing energy in Stephanie's aura, but the cards showed that Stephanie would have to put that energy into caring for a sick relative. Then there was Jill, a young woman who had seen Marina's sign when she'd gone into the thrift store next door and had decided on an impulse to come in for a reading. Jill, who adopted the I'm-not-going-to-tell-you-anything-about-myself-because-you're-the-psychic-and-should-know attitude common to some first-timers, proved to be a major drain on Marina's own energy and flagging blood sugar. She sat there, pale and pouting, and refused to either agree or disagree with anything Marina was saying. Working much harder than she wanted to, Marina looked for the tiniest giveaways—or *tells*, as poker players called them—to clue her in to what Jill had really come in for. Nobody came to see a psychic if she was perfectly content. And nobody was ever perfectly content. So Marina observed the way Jill's eyes blinked hard at the sight of the Lovers card, the anxious way she twisted the still-shiny wedding band on her finger and the unconscious motion of her hand to adjust the collar of her shirt so that it covered a faint red mark on her neck.

"I'm seeing a third person," Marina said finally, "standing between you and your husband."

Jill hadn't mentioned that she was married nor had she asked about relationships, but Marina's words hit squarely on the mark. For the first time, Jill dropped her guard and gasped. From there, the session was easier, if still exhausting. By the time she ushered Jill to the door, Marina's stomach was growling in protest.

There was a small natural foods market a few blocks from Marina's office where one could find organic fruit, bagel sandwiches or vegan sushi next to bottles of vitamin-enriched water and shade-grown coffee to go. It was the perfect place for an overpriced snack if not for stocking up on household staples, and she calculated she could walk there and back before she met with Cooper, her last client before she had to head to Madeline's house.

Marina had returned to her office, finishing the banana she'd begun on the walk back, when she realized that the man she'd seen in the café across the street was still there. He was sitting at a different table, so he must have moved at some point during the day, but he was still outside, still alone and still nursing a cup of coffee. He'd picked up a newspaper and was staring at it in the way people do when they're pretending to read. Marina leaned against the doorjamb and tried to recall if she'd noticed him there at any other time during the day when she'd been letting clients in and out, but she couldn't remember registering his image between the morning and now. Marina peered across the street at the man, suddenly convinced he was watching her. Prickly cold anxiety began forming at the base of her spine and her stomach turned in a sick flip. The rational part of her brain insisted that he had nothing to do with her. But Marina's irrational self, the part of herself she tried her best to suppress, didn't need any proof—it *knew*. Was it even the same man, Marina questioned herself, or was she imagining the whole thing? But no, while there might have been two big men in faded blue jeans drinking coffee in Encinitas that day, there weren't two big men in faded blue jeans, a red lumberjack-looking shirt and worn tan work boots drinking coffee in the same café. And there was something about the way he held his head and shoulders, squared off and tilted forward, that made her sure it was the same man. She stood there, her hand on the jamb, unable to move or avert her eyes for several seconds. It was Cooper, who'd arrived early for his appointment and was gliding toward her on a wave of expensive cologne, who finally broke the spell.

"Marina, my love, you look more fetching than usual," Cooper said as he approached. "Were you waiting for me? That's very sweet." Although she knew them all very well at this point, Cooper was the only one of Marina's regulars who spoke to her with this kind of familiarity. Marina, who tacitly demanded a certain emotional distance from her clients, didn't mind Cooper's lack of formality as long as it didn't involve an invasion of her personal space. She felt something resembling affection for Cooper, although she wasn't sure why. Perhaps it had to do with the fact that he didn't seem to care whether or not she cared about him. Unlike most of her other clients, Cooper had no need for her approval. There was something about this that made him less pathetic in his quest for approval—and love—from a person who was never going to give it to him.

"Marina? What are you looking at?"

"Sorry, Cooper. I just want to see . . ."

"See what? Something good?" Cooper craned his neck to get a glimpse of whatever it was she was looking at.

"There's a man . . ."

"Well, that's never a bad thing, is it?"

"He's been sitting there at the café all day. I saw him when I got here early this morning. He's still there."

"And that's a problem because?"

"Not a problem," Marina said. "Just kind of odd."

Cooper squinted in the direction of the café. "That burly guy over there? Looks all right," he said. "From what I can see, anyway. He seems *tall*. Look at those long legs of his. And what's with that shirt? Very Paul Bunyan."

"Yes," Marina said, smiling in spite of herself, "I was just thinking that."

"Soooo . . . ?" Cooper said. "We're going to watch him now?"

"No," Marina said. "I'm sorry. Let's get to your reading."

Cooper knew his way around her office and headed immediately to her table in the back. He relaxed into the chair opposite Marina, who lit a candle scented with orange and sandalwood and set it between them. Cooper liked candles, incense and any other psychic accessories that were available. If she'd had one, Marina was sure he'd have enjoyed gazing into a crystal ball as well. He'd have believed in her without the trappings, Marina knew, but she still provided them for him. It was important that the client was comfortable. If that meant bells and whistles, fine. Most of Marina's clients here didn't seem to care one way or the other. This was so different from Florida, where her mostly elderly clients were attached to outdated images of what a psychic should look like.

Marina chased the unpleasant memories of Florida out of her head and turned her full attention to Cooper, who was leaning back in his chair, lips pursed as if to hold in words that were trying to burst out of his mouth. Still tired from her encounter with Jill and uneasy about the man in the café, she decided to let Cooper speak for as long as he wanted to.

"How have you been, Cooper? I'm sensing a lot of heightened energy around you right now. I think you have something you need to tell me?"

Cooper inhaled a huge breath and placed his hands, palms down and fingers splayed, on top of the table. His flair for the dramatic was sometimes subdued, Marina thought, but always somewhere in evidence—the result, she'd told him before, of having so many planets in the sign of Leo.

"I think Max is getting ready to ask me to move in with him," Cooper said after a pause. "I know, this is *big*." He looked at her for confirmation and continued. "I thought at first I was imagining it, like it was more of my wishful thinking, you know? So I've been playing it really cool, waiting for the other shoe to drop or something." He paused, but Marina didn't interrupt him. "We haven't had a fight for a really long time—not even about the little things like what movie to watch. He's been really . . . I don't know, *calm* or something. It's like he's accepted me, or *us*. Like he's accepted us. We haven't been talking about the future or anything, kind of taking it day by day, I guess, but he just seems more comfortable with having me around." Cooper stopped talking and cleared his throat. One corner of his mouth turned up in a little almost-smile. "Remember when I gave him that rosebush?"

Marina smiled noncommittally, not knowing if the rosebush was something she'd forgotten or if Cooper hadn't even mentioned it to her but just assumed in his benignly self-absorbed way that she would know.

"It was this gorgeous rosebush I got for his garden and he killed it. All right, maybe not *killed* it, but it died on his watch. He didn't do it on purpose. It was just . . . he just couldn't get it together, I guess. He said it got some kind of worm, whatever. So the other day, I brought over this beautiful pot I found at the Seaside Bazaar . . . I was going to keep it at my place, but I thought it would look great in his house—he's got this hallway that it's perfect for. And it doesn't require any *maintenance*. Anyway, I brought it over and he loved it. He said I 'beautified' his surroundings—that I had such great taste . . ." Cooper looked down at his hands and then up at Marina, his eyes begging for response, affirmation, anything.

"And?" Marina said gently. "And then what?"

"He said he liked seeing me in his house." Cooper smiled, as if re-membering something sweet. "We actually had our first holiday together the other night. I know, it's only Halloween—not like Christmas or any-thing like that—but it was really nice. Max really loves Halloween be-cause of the kids. You should see what he goes through to get the best, most nutritionally sound, politically correct candy. It's so funny. I told him that they don't care—you know, they probably prefer the really dis-gusting stuff—but it's like a *thing* with him." Cooper grew silent and shifted his eyes downward. "I need you to tell me, Marina. I need you to tell me whether I'm on the right track here. I can feel a change in him. I'm almost sure that he's going to ask me to move in, but I don't want to say anything until . . . until I'm positive. You have to tell me."

Marina was ready, having sifted through her own options while Cooper spoke. She knew details of Cooper's doomed relationship that he wasn't even aware of: information he'd given her just by his mannerisms and the clouds passing across his eyes. It was unlikely that Max had had a sudden change of heart where Cooper was concerned and much more probable that Max's recent attitude had to do with guilt. Meanwhile, Cooper played out his part as Charlie Brown to Max's Lucy. Max would lead Cooper on, make him feel it was safe to kick that football again, but soon Cooper would find himself flat on his back once more. It was a classic situation and Marina sus-pected that even Cooper knew it. But Cooper hadn't come to her for this kind of psychiatric deconstruction. What he wanted was psychic insight and that was what she was going to give him.

"Give me your hands, Cooper," she said, and he willingly offered them. Marina closed her eyes and felt the cool touch of his fingertips, the quick beat of his pulse against the skin of her hands.

"Marina, I—"

"Be still," Marina said softly. "The message is coming in."

Chapter 11

The sun had dropped behind the ocean when Marina finished with Cooper. The wind had picked up again, rushing through palms and eucalyptus and swirling dry leaves in circular patterns on the street. There were no slow sunsets at this time of year. Night came fast and fell hard.

"Kind of gloomy out, isn't it?" Cooper said, surveying the landscape as he donned an unnecessary scarf.

"Maybe," Marina said. "But it isn't too cold." She peered across the street at the café, but it had closed and its patio was empty. The man, whoever he was, had finally gone. She let out a breath that she hadn't realized she was holding.

"Looking for your mystery guy?" Cooper asked. "Want me to do a sweep of the area and make sure you're safe?"

Marina couldn't tell if Cooper was serious or trying to be funny, and she suspected that he didn't know himself. Now that their session was over, she sensed Cooper sliding into petulance. It was like this with her neediest clients; they liked her, even believed in her, but there was a part of them that resented her for not being entirely devoted to them. It was a particular kind of selfishness or possessiveness that was both self-protective and childish. This wasn't rational behavior, of course, and

Cooper likely knew it. But knowing about a behavior and changing it were two different things.

"Thanks for the offer," Marina told him, making sure to give him a broad warm smile to go with her words, "but I'm fine. It was nothing."

"Well," Cooper said, "*you're* the psychic."

"Exactly."

"I'm off, then," Cooper said. "Have we made our next appointment?"

"I have you down, Cooper. You know I do."

"But I might need you before then."

"Coop—"

"Okay, okay. Have a lovely evening, Marina."

"You too, Cooper. Remember—"

"I know," Cooper interrupted again, raising his hand. "I'll be good. I promise."

"It's not about being *good*," Marina said.

"I know that, too," Cooper answered. "As you know." He laughed and then was out the door. Despite the candles and incense, Cooper's spicy cologne overpowered the room and lingered in the air after he'd left.

Marina set about closing her office. She was filled with uncharacteristic trepidation and wished that she didn't have to negotiate the traffic to Madeline's house—or conversation with Andrew once she got there. This was one of the rare moments when she would have preferred to work as a hairstylist or a receptionist—something that had a finite end to each day; a profession where loose emotional ends weren't part of the job description. And it was her birthday. If she was a hairstylist she'd be eating cake and drinking with friends. *Stop it,* she thought. No use feeling sorry for herself; she had a job to do and a goal to meet. A few more hours and her day would be over.

The sky was fully dark now. Marina locked her office door and, unable to shake her feeling of uneasiness, gripped her keys in her fist with the sharp edges protruding through her fingers, all the better to gouge the eyes of an attacker if need be. Her car was close, just a few yards away in the parking lot. She was so caught up in getting there, visualizing how she would let go of her keys, unlock her door, climb in and drive away, that she missed what she was so carefully avoiding: a man-size shape emerging from the shadows and fast approaching her.

"Excuse me—miss? Hello? Excuse me, could I—"

He was almost on top of her, the polite tone of his words completely at odds with the speed he was using to catch up with her, and Marina couldn't help herself—she let out a frightened cry and flung her arm out wide. Her pursuer, who she could now see was the man from the café, leaned back to avoid connecting with her sloppy roundhouse. He smiled at her sheepishly. Even in the dim light of the street, Marina could see that he was embarrassed.

"Hey, I'm sorry. I didn't mean to startle you."

"What do you want?" Marina said, her voice rough from adrenaline.

"I meant to come to your office, but I was late. I saw you leaving just now and I didn't want to miss you. I'm sorry; I really didn't mean to scare you. I just wanted to make sure I spoke to you before you left."

Marina's throat was still constricted from fear and she forced herself to take a deep breath before she answered him. He *was* tall, as Cooper had noted, but now that he was so close, Marina could see that he was also broad and solid. He was a big man, someone who could overpower her in a second, but she didn't detect any menace in him. His demeanor was friendly, even conciliatory, and it just didn't jibe with the fact that he'd snuck up on her in the dark after hanging around and watching her all day in the café.

"Listen, I saw you sitting over there today," Marina said, gesturing across the street, "so I know you had plenty of time to talk to me before. There's no reason you suddenly had to talk to me *now.*"

"You got me," he said. "But I have an explanation . . . if you'll let me give it to you." He smiled again. Marina took notice of his tan face in the reflected storefront lights, its weathered lines and crow's-feet at the corners of his dark eyes, the sharp angles and smooth planes of nose, cheek and jaw. His teeth were straight and very white. His hair was thick and wavy, but she couldn't gauge the exact color, which was somewhere between blond and brown. She wanted a better look in real light. She wanted to see the details she was missing.

"I have to go," Marina said. "I have an appointment."

"Please," he said. "This will only take a minute."

"That's good," Marina said, "because a minute is all I have."

"Then I'll get right to it," he said. "You're Marina, right? Marina Marks?"

Marina could feel her legs stiffening with tension again, the fight-or-flight response kicking into overdrive. Her intellect told her not to trust him, but her gut warned against trusting her intellect. It was the most confusing mix of signals she'd ever received from her internal radar.

"My name is Marina, yes," she said.

"I'm Gideon," he said, extending his hand.

"Gideon who?" she asked.

"I'm sorry," he said again. "Gideon Black."

Marina finally released her grip on her keys and transferred them to her left hand in order to shake the one Gideon held out. It was large, like the rest of him, and it engulfed hers. His fingers were strong and his palm was warm. No, not warm—hot. Too hot, Marina thought, like electricity. As the thought formed in her mind, a shock shot up Marina's arm to her shoulder, causing her to pull her hand from his grip and give out a little yelp of pain. Her fingers were tingling and her arm ached.

Gideon looked down at his hand in confusion. "Did I hurt you?" he asked.

"I—it's so dry and the wind . . . I think I just got a shock from you," Marina said, rubbing her arm. "It happens this time of year. You didn't feel it?"

"No," he said, "but I have pretty thick skin." Again, Marina wished for the clarity of daylight. She couldn't read his expression in the dark. "It's nice to meet you, Marina, and I want to apologize again for creeping up on you like that. The thing is, you were recommended to me by someone

I trust, but I've never done this before—you know, gone to see a psychic—and I just didn't know how to go about it." He sounded like a criminal confessing after he'd been caught in the act, Marina thought. *Honestly, officer, I didn't know she was a prostitute. And I've never seen those drugs before in my life.*

"I don't know what you mean," she said.

"I just feel a little . . . silly. It's true, I spent a lot of time drinking coffee today, trying to decide whether or not to come over here. I'm the kind of person who tries to solve problems in a more conventional way. Maybe it's a man thing."

"What do you want?" Marina asked again.

"What I want . . ." Gideon paused and seemed to try to collect himself. "I've lost something very important to me. What I want is for you to help me find it. Like I said, you come highly recommended."

"Who recommended me?" Marina asked.

"I couldn't tell you her name, but she raved about you."

"You don't know her name?"

"Is her name important?"

"I just . . . I don't usually locate lost items. That isn't what I do."

"Is it something you *can* do?"

Marina didn't know why she was hesitating or why she was giving him such a hard time. She understood full well that men sought out her services far less often than women for precisely the reasons he was giving. Generally, unless they were hitting on her, as in Eddie's case, or they were gay, as in Cooper's, men tended to be wary of her. It was something she'd become used to long ago. Ironically, once her male clients saw what she could do, they became more ardent believers than the women. But money was genderless and Marina didn't care who it came from. Besides, what he was asking for seemed simple enough. He'd come at her in an odd way, but she was used to that as well.

"You'll need to make an appointment," Marina said. "And my book is in my office."

"And you're already late," Gideon said. "I understand. I guess I should

come back tomorrow? I know a place where I can get a cup of coffee."
He laughed. "Look, I know I must seem kind of weird. I'm not from
around here, in case that's not obvious by now. I guess I'm still getting
acclimated."

Marina teetered between two options, uncertain about both. She could
tell him to come back tomorrow or lead him back to her office, where she
could turn on the lights and get a closer look at him. The urge to see him
clearly was becoming stronger, almost turning into a need. She couldn't
remember the last time she had received such a blank first impression
from a stranger. It was as if who he was—and what he wanted—were obscured by the white noise of static. She would risk being late to Madeline's
house if she stopped now, but traffic was always a valid excuse and she'd
come to learn that punctuality had a very broad definition in southern
California. There was also something unsettling about having to wait for
him to show up again tomorrow.

"You're here now," Marina said finally. "We might as well set up an
appointment."

"Are you sure?" he asked. "I don't want to make you late for whatever
it is you have to do."

"Like I said, you're here now," she repeated, turning back toward her
office. "Let me see if I have any openings tomorrow." Gideon hesitated for
a moment, as if waiting to see if she'd change her mind, and then followed
her inside.

December 2006

Chapter 12

After all the pills, potions, incantations and doctor's visits, the one thing Madeline had not expected about pregnancy was that she would hate it so much. Maybe *hate* wasn't the right word exactly. *Resent* or *loathe* was more accurate. And maybe neither would have been applicable if she hadn't found herself so confined. She was imprisoned by her body—no, held hostage by the *baby* who had taken over her body—if you could even call it a baby at this point. Yes, she'd sighed with misty delight over the first grainy ultrasound pictures, but her initial delight at becoming pregnant had more to do with a feeling of triumph than of maternal instinct. And, of course, Andrew was beyond thrilled. In all the time she'd known him, in all their most intimate moments together, she'd never seen him so moved. He was so happy that he didn't even stay pissed when he found out he wasn't the first person to hear the news.

When Madeline told him about running over to Marina's with the pregnancy test stick, a wave of anger washed over his face, though he held it in check. Madeline had tried to make it a funny story, emphasizing how silly she must have looked bouncing around with a pee-soaked stick. It wasn't a dig at him, but when it fell flat she understood her mistake. He was jealous of Marina, she realized, and didn't like to think that his wife gave a psychic more credit for the baby than him. He was actually rude when Marina came over, and Madeline got the sense that had she not been in such a "delicate condition," he'd stop paying Marina's hefty fees. It was understandable, she supposed, but really, who had been more supportive during the whole nightmare? Madeline had caught herself then and prattled on about baby names, dates and the months to come. Andrew held her hand like a teenage boy on a first date. It was one of the happiest moments in their marriage, Madeline thought, which made the way she was feeling now even more depressing.

Very soon after that initial rush of joy she was ordered to bed and Andrew started drifting away from her. He was more distant now than he'd ever been before and seemed constantly irritated by her, always preoccupied by something that seemed to be chewing away at him from the inside out. It was as if she'd created this high-risk pregnancy on purpose. What made it even worse was that he was so *solicitous* toward her. He brought her juice and fruit salad on a tray. He made sure she had plenty to read. There were so many magazines in their bedroom that it looked like a doctor's office, and half the Borders bestseller rack was on their bedside table. He hired extra maid service and a personal chef. There was nothing—*nothing*—Madeline had to do for herself.

What bothered her about all this attention was that Andrew didn't seem to be giving it to *her*. All of his energy was for the baby. She was just the vessel carrying it. It wasn't her imagination that Andrew hadn't so much as touched her since she'd announced she was pregnant. At first she'd had outrageous morning sickness, but after that, it was just a series of excuses: he was done taking the Viagra; he wasn't as young as he used to be; he'd read somewhere that a man only had a certain number of orgasms allotted in his lifetime and he didn't want to speed the end of his. She'd asked him right away if he was having an affair, but the sad thing was that she didn't even need to hear his denial to know he wasn't. After she started spotting, he didn't even need to make excuses. Of course, they couldn't have sex *now;* it would almost certainly hurt the baby.

"Be reasonable, Maddie," he'd told her. "We tried so hard for this and it's something we want so badly. Why would we risk it all for a little quick fun? There will be so much time later."

"There are still things we can do," Madeline had whined then. "It's not all about straight missionary, you know. I can—"

"But I'm fine," Andrew had insisted.

"What man doesn't want a blow job from his *wife?*" Madeline had demanded. "What's wrong with you?"

"Are you listening to yourself?" he asked, disgusted, and that was the last time they'd so much as mentioned sex.

If she was being honest with herself, Madeline admitted that lovemaking didn't hold much appeal for her at the moment, either. But that wasn't the point. She wanted *Andrew* to want it, and the fact that he didn't was starting to make her feel ugly and frightened—as if she only had worth as a host body. Which was exactly what she felt like.

It was bad enough that she couldn't do yoga or Pilates anymore, but she couldn't even *drive.* She couldn't go for a walk on the beach. She was barely allowed to walk to the bathroom. She could feel the fat starting to spread across her hips and backside, even though everyone told her she was being ridiculous, she looked great and you were supposed to gain weight when you were pregnant. At least Cassie was willing to come to the house to cut her hair so she didn't look like a total wreck. And it wasn't as if she was in prison . . .

Except Madeline felt as if she *was* in prison and that what was waiting for her at the end of this sentence was as scary as what was happening during it. The first time the baby had kicked, she'd not felt the overwhelming joy and wonder you were supposed to feel when such a thing happened. It just felt weird, like there was some alien inside her, feeding itself off her life force. Madeline worried that after the baby was born she'd resent it even more than she did now. What if she had postpartum depression and couldn't care for the baby or wanted to drown it in a bathtub? Then what? Bad enough she had *pre*partum depression and couldn't take anything for it. Madeline craved a glass—a bottle—of wine. She felt as if she could chew glass. She felt as if she was going crazy.

But Marina understood. She was the only one.

Madeline picked up the phone as she had done so many times before and dialed Marina's number. Ringing, ringing and no answer. Damn voice mail again. *"Please leave your number and the time you called . . ."*

"Marina, it's Madeline. I've left a bunch of messages already, don't know if you got them. You must be super busy. Listen, I really need to talk. I need you to come over here. I know you said we don't need to see each other until next month, but I *need* to *see* you, Marina, okay? Please call me as soon as possible."

Madeline clicked off, her anger rising. She paid that woman a lot of money; the least she could do was answer her damn phone once in a while. Maybe that wasn't entirely fair. At their last session, Marina had told her that she needed to work on healing the inner child of her psyche so that her actual baby would have a welcoming place to grow. If they saw each other too often, Marina had said, they risked diluting the effect of the message and the guidance of the spirits. They needed at least two months' separation. Most of her clients visited her only once or twice a year (which Madeline suspected was bullshit but had no way of proving), and they had already gone way over the usual limit. Madeline agreed at the time. But it was easy to agree with Marina.

Madeline was partly worried that Marina was putting distance between them because of Andrew. She didn't understand his hostility toward Marina. She was sure Marina picked up on it even if Andrew hadn't said something to her, which she suspected he had. Really, he should thank her. It was only after she started seeing Marina that she got pregnant, after all. But that was only one fear. The other, darker fear was that Marina, like Andrew, was just getting sick of her. Marina had seemed so distracted the last time they'd seen each other. She'd shown up late, for one thing, which she never did, and hadn't even apologized. Then the whole time she was there, she went on about why she shouldn't be there. A horrible thought occurred to Madeline now: What if Marina was trying to slowly get rid of her? She had started seeing Marina because she couldn't get pregnant and now she was and what else needed to be known, aside from whether or not she'd miscarry or whether it was a boy or a girl? Pretty soon Madeline would be out of the woods and the baby would be able to survive outside the womb. Was that what Marina was waiting for?

Madeline dialed the numbers again but hung up before the sound of the voice mail beep. She had been in this room for so long, staring at the same patch of wall and the same corner of window showing the same triangle of darkening sky. Andrew wouldn't be home for hours. She could be there and back and he'd never know. She felt fine. She felt good. There was no cramping, no spotting, no sign that anything was wrong. As if to reassure her, the baby gave a small kick to her bladder. What would it really hurt? A visit to Marina's office could only make her feel better, in fact, help get her out of this funk. Marina would for sure be at her office; she worked all the time. Andrew wouldn't even have to know.

Madeline tested herself at every step of the way. She pulled on her yoga pants and a sweatshirt and then sat down on the couch. All fine. She brushed her teeth, put her hair in a ponytail and slowly descended the stairs. Still good. And she was good leaving the house, entering the garage and climbing into her Mercedes. She felt great all the way through Rancho Santa Fe and onto the Coast Highway. It wasn't until she passed the railroad tracks in Cardiff that she began to feel cramping, dull but insistent. She wondered if she should turn around and head to her doctor's office, but she gave it another mile and the cramps eased off.

There was no space in front of Marina's office, so Madeline had to double back and park in front of the Seaside Market a few blocks away. She was starting to think this was a bad idea. It had been so long since she'd been out in real air that she was feeling light-headed even in the car. But after a few deep yogic breaths Madeline felt fine again and renewed her resolve. Besides, once she got to Marina's everything would be fine; she could feel it. Madeline walked slowly, unaccustomed to her lopsided weight. The baby felt heavy. A few yards from Marina's office, a sharp pain in her midsection took her breath away for a moment before it subsided. And then she saw something that surprised her so much that she forgot the pain entirely. Marina was coming out of her office with a man behind her. He was a big, blond guy who looked like he worked outdoors, construction or something. Good-looking, too. They were talking and smiling, and then he reached over to her, gently moved some hair away from her face and leaned down to kiss her on the mouth. So it was a *guy,* Madeline thought. Marina was ditching her clients and her responsibilities for some beefcake? Madeline didn't know whether to be outraged or relieved. But Marina looked over before Madeline had a chance to decide, a look of recognition and then horror spreading quickly across her face.

"Madeline!" she called. "What are you doing here? Oh God, Madeline, what's going on?"

Madeline was completely confused by the look of fear on Marina's face. That man standing next to her looked freaked out as well and Madeline couldn't understand why they were both staring at her like that. She looked down, following the direction of their eyes. And that was when Madeline saw all the blood.

Chapter 13

It was the middle of the lunch rush and the overworked staff at Darling's wasn't keeping up. Eddie sat at a corner table not reading the newspaper in front of him and waiting for his long-overdue burger. He was hungry and had to be back at work in less than half an hour. If it took much longer he wouldn't even have time to wolf down his overpriced meat patty. Goddamn story of his life was what it was.

"Hey, 'scuse me," Eddie called to a waitress who he knew was not his server. The girl didn't bother answering as she brushed by him with two coffees in one hand and a plate of chicken salad in the other. Her attitude pissed him off, so he reached out and grabbed the edge of her apron and gave it a gentle tug. She stopped short then, jerking the coffees so that a little spilled over both edges and splashed on his table. "Hey, hon, can you tell me where my lunch has got to? I'm kinda on a timetable here." He followed this with a smile, flashing his dimples as usual, but now the waitress was pissed.

"Sir, could you not grab me, please? I'll get your waitress for you if you can wait a minute."

"That's kinda the problem. I *have* been waiting a minute. I've been waiting many, many minutes."

"I'll get your waitress," she said, scowling, and Eddie knew she wouldn't. Skinny little bitch; who the hell did she think she was? Goddamn women and their bullshit. He was just so sick of it. He didn't know why he came here anyway; the food wasn't that great and the service sucked. He'd be better off at the goddamn Burger King drive-through. Eddie folded his arms and leaned back in the hard wooden chair that was already starting to hurt his back. No sense getting angry; it wasn't going to solve anything. And nobody had forced him to eat at Darling's, where only people who didn't have to work could afford to wait this long for a meal. He came here because this was where he had sat the day he'd met Marina for the first time and so now it had become a habit. Eddie was nothing if not a creature of habit. And those habits were what had gotten him into the ridiculous fucked-up situation that he was in now.

Eddie ran his hand through his hair and sighed in frustration. He didn't know how things had gotten this out of control. It was sheer bad luck—again, the story of his life. He wasn't a bad guy. He'd made some errors in judgment, that's all. Like what happened to him when he was a kid. His life hadn't even started at eighteen years old and there he was, busted for selling weed to a cop. It was entrapment, really, but who had the money for a lawyer? His parents certainly hadn't given a shit. Two years in the federal pen for that. They made an example of him even though he was super small-time and he hadn't hurt anybody. He was just a kid, for crying out loud.

It could have gone way south after that. He could have gotten into more trouble, could have let that unspeakably bad experience ruin his whole life, but he hadn't. He worked hard, raised two kids, was good to his wife for the most part. He was a good boss, too. His employees liked him and a few of the younger guys even came to him for advice about their personal lives. Which was why Eddie couldn't help feeling that he had done nothing to bring on this mess his life was in now. He felt like he was in the middle of a giant knot and every time he moved he just made it tighter. What made it worse was that it was such a clichéd situation, the stuff of any low-rent soap opera.

First, there was Cassie. Eddie wasn't yet willing to admit that his *entire* involvement with her had been a mistake, just the last part, which was bad enough. He'd seen the writing on the wall a long time ago and he *had* done the right thing then. They'd had that huge argument after he went to see Marina. As he'd known she would, Cassie had expected Marina to tell him to ditch his wife and take up with her. It was a ridiculous notion on Cassie's part, but he realized now that hope and despair were two sides of the same coin, and no matter which side it landed on when it flipped, either one could make you believe in the impossible. So when Eddie told her that all he'd gotten from her psychic was a warning that his poor diet was leading to a muddy aura and that his planets or whatever showed a tendency to weak circulation, Cassie got annoyed first, then she turned on the waterworks. This irritated Eddie more than anything. He hated when women started in with the tears. Tears meant desperation, and desperation was definitely not sexy.

"Listen," he'd told her, "I think you put way too much stock in that psychic. It was a very nice gift and I appreciate it, Cassie, I really do. But you have to know this stuff is all bullshit, right?" He'd thought he sounded very reasonable, very believable. Of course, he'd left out the part about being so immediately and totally turned on by Marina that he could barely concentrate on what she was saying at all.

Cassie kept pushing his buttons, crying the whole time, and that had been pretty much it for Eddie. They were finally at the finish line. So, as difficult as it was, Eddie cut it off right there. He gave her the standard speech about how she was a wonderful person who deserved so much better than what she was getting from him. She was young and beautiful, with her whole life in front of her, and it had never been just about the sex. And as much as it hurt him to say it . . .

She took it well; much better, in fact, than he'd have thought. It was as if she'd known it was coming. They'd made love then, because good-bye sex was the hottest, sweetest there was, and then it really was good-bye. And that should have been it.

Eddie's waitress, who looked about ready to explode (she'd obviously been tipped off by the other one), appeared in front of him and slammed down his burger without so much as a good word. Eddie could tell that the plate had been sitting under the heat lamps for too long. The meat looked dry and overdone and the fries were limp and greasy. But Eddie didn't care. He wasn't even hungry anymore. Thinking about what had happened after he'd left Cassie that day and how it had been possibly the most colossal mistake of his life had made his appetite vanish.

He'd left well enough alone for months. He'd even finished the damn kitchen cabinets and had taken a vacation with the family over the summer, which he'd been promising his wife for years—an entire week in Las Vegas. Yes, it was ungodly hot in the desert in the middle of summer, but the rates were good and you didn't ever have to leave the comfort of the hotel pool if you didn't want to. The kids had a good time and his wife got her spa days. Eddie felt like a good husband. But then, as another year was closing in on him, he found himself wandering into Cassie's salon. Had it even taken a full twenty-four hours for them to wind up in bed again? Eddie didn't think so. It was just one time. Just once. They'd both been so clear about that.

Eddie cursed his own stupidity. The only reason he'd gone in there was because he was unbelievably frustrated over Marina. Yes, Marina, the psychic in whom he didn't believe, had become the object of every fantasy his mind could create. She was a cool customer, Marina was, and rebuffed him like no woman ever had. Mind you, she didn't mind taking his money. Turned out he paid handsomely for the pleasure of her company. Could have gotten the most expensive hooker in Vegas for what he'd paid her. And, of course, Marina's coldness had only made him hotter for her. He thought—he thought he might even be in love with her. That was what had driven him to Cassie. Call it ego, a need to have a woman want him in the way he wanted Marina. Call it sexual frustration. Call it what it was—plain crazy. Because his reward for that little indiscretion was a gigantic pile of shit.

Cassie was pregnant. At least, she claimed she was. It was the oldest fucking trick in the book. And now he had to deal with her because if he didn't, it was as good as telling her to call his wife to have a nice chat. Eddie wasn't sure he even believed Cassie was pregnant and, if she was, that it was even his baby. Not that he was going to wait and find out. He knew how this was going to play out. The threat of pregnancy and her being unsure of what she was going to do was enough to keep Eddie on the line, and Cassie knew it. He'd have to hang in long enough for her to abort or tell him that it was a false alarm, and then he'd have to get out all over again. Nobody to blame but himself for this.

The kicker, though, and why Eddie now found his hands forming fists in front of his uneaten burger, was that none of this had helped him stop thinking about Marina. If anything, he thought about her more. Even at the height of their affair he hadn't devoted this much mental energy to Cassie. It was—he hated to even think it—bordering on obsession. He had to figure out a way of getting close to her, because he knew it wasn't going to stop until he did. He'd tried to rationalize it, to tell himself that he only wanted her because she didn't want him, or that it was just because she was so exotic and sexy. But he was certain there was something about Marina—something deep below her surface—that *knew* him better than he knew himself. It wasn't anything to do with psychic voodoo, since Eddie didn't believe for a second that Marina was the real thing where that was concerned. She made a good living telling people fairy tales, and that was fine. What drew Eddie to Marina had nothing to do with that. It was something he couldn't name and didn't even want to understand.

He needed some reason to see her again outside of her office. If he could just get her in the open—on his own turf . . . It wouldn't be easy, and Eddie had himself all twisted up trying to think of how to do it. He'd already been warned off once, back at the beginning of November. He'd come in for a reading and they'd both run the usual line of bullshit with each other. At the end of the session she'd told him that it was enough, that she only saw her clients once or twice a year at most, and those were the serious ones. She didn't believe that Eddie was coming to her for psychic counsel. Lay off, she'd told him. Save your money.

But he hadn't. And the next time he'd come around there was some big macho bouncer type hanging out outside her office. Eddie didn't like the look of the guy *at all.* The thought crossed his mind that the guy was laying it to Marina and that made Eddie furious. How many times had she told him that she never dated her clients? And he had to be a client, because why else would he be sitting there like he was waiting for a reading? Eddie got as far as the door that time.

"How you doing?" he'd asked the guy.

"Good," the guy said. "How are you doing?"

"Good," Eddie said. "Is she in?" He gestured toward Marina's door with his thumb.

"Not yet," the guy said. "I'm waiting for her. I'm a little early. Do you have an appointment?"

"Yeah. Or no, not really. She knows me, though." Eddie was irritated that he had to explain himself to this asshole. But before he could say anything else, Marina appeared, all business.

"Gideon, hi," she said to the bouncer guy, and then to Eddie, "We're not going to do this again, are we, Ed?"

Eddie didn't want to remember the rest of the embarrassing details. Like how the guy had asked if there was a problem and how Eddie had told him to mind his own business and how that interchange seemed to really annoy Marina, who had then asked the guy—*Gideon*—to give them a moment, and when he did, told Eddie that she thought she'd made it pretty clear that he didn't need to be there.

The next time he came by, he didn't even get out of his truck—just parked it across the street and sat there. He was formulating an opening line when he saw a woman go into Marina's office, which meant there was nothing to do but watch the traffic and plot his next move. You got to see all kinds of people in this part of town: the wealthy, the day laborers, and the down-and-outers. He'd never really noticed just how wide a range there was. There was one guy, for example, in a shiny silver midlife-crisis Porsche who kept driving around the block looking for a place to park. The third or fourth time the car cruised by, Eddie started to feel suspicious and paranoid. It was pretty clear that the guy wasn't looking for a parking spot, because there were plenty of spaces. No, he was *watching*. Eddie strained to get a look at the driver when the car slowed in front of Marina's office, but he couldn't get a clear enough angle to see details. On the next loop he would take down the license plate number, Eddie decided, but he never got the chance. A tap on the passenger-side window made him jump, and when he looked over, he saw that it was Gideon coming up out of nowhere. So she had a bodyguard, Eddie thought. Ridiculous. He drove off before the guy could get into it with him. Decades after being released from prison, Eddie still had that knee-jerk fear of being busted, even if what he was doing was perfectly legal.

Now here he was, sitting at Darling's, a place that, if he was really being honest, he hated, trying to think of a way to get to her. It had to be some sort of grand gesture, something to make her come around. He felt irritated and maybe even a little hurt that Marina had that guy hanging around, doing whatever he was doing. It felt almost as if she was cheating on him, as crazy as even Eddie knew that sounded. He had to do something to get back into her good graces, even though he sort of resented her for making him . . . *beg* seemed like the only word for it. But first he was going to have to pay a visit to Cassie, the huge albatross now hanging around his neck. Eddie didn't have to look at his watch to know that in addition to everything else, he was also going to be late getting back to work. He flagged down his waitress with a big sweep of his arm. The hell with being polite.

"What can I do for you?" she asked, throwing the same attitude right back at him.

Eddie pointed to his cold, untouched food. "I'm going to need that to go," he said. "And I'd really appreciate it if you could do it now."

Chapter 14

Ring, ring, ring. Ring. Voice mail. Goddaaaaammmmmnnnniiitttt.
Cooper pushed "end" on his cell phone and then "1," "7," and "send." He had the bitch on speed dial. So fucking stupid. Who had a psychic on speed dial? Well, in fact a lot of fucking people did. Hello, the Psychic Hotline?

Not the same.

Ringing, then more voice mail. Fuck her. Seriously. Cooper picked up his house phone and hit "1" and "7." It took a while for him to realize that nothing was happening because there was no speed dial on this phone and he had to punch in the actual phone number. It took even longer to coordinate between his cell phone and cordless because, like everyone else in the world, he had electronic-device-induced ADD, which meant he couldn't remember phone numbers anymore, only the prompts attached to them. Finally, he got it all together only to listen again to the ringing followed by her voice-mail message. He'd almost believed that dialing from his house phone, which had a blocked caller ID, was going to fool her into picking up. His reflexes were pretty slow, so it was a second or two after the tone that he managed to leave a message. He kept his voice low and hissy, disguised. "You there, bitch? We need to . . . have . . . a little . . . *talk*." He hung up quickly. Had he really just prank called her?

Cooper giggled and slid farther down in his leather butterfly chair so that his head lolled off the side. It was getting too heavy to hold up any longer. Don't drink and dial. How many times had he heard that or said it himself? Well, it didn't matter, because he wasn't fucking drinking. Although . . . Cooper grasped at the prescription bottles that had fallen into the thick shag pile of his carpet. He was in his retro room, which was designed to look like some kind of mad Brady Bunch acid trip. Fun for parties. Fun for this. It was good, he decided. The combination of Xanax and Vicodin was just right. Really hit the spot. Took the edge off. Floated his boat. Got him through the night. Chapped his hide. No, wait, that last one was wrong. Hide, hide, hide. The word bounced around in Cooper's head and he laughed again. It was funny—Max thought he could hide.

"Thinggen," Cooper said out loud. Well, *that* didn't sound right. He'd meant to say *Think again.* Whatever. Nobody around to hear him anyway. But the point was . . . the point . . . He couldn't hide, that was the point. Oh, Max. Whywhywhywhy?

This wasn't anything like their other breakups. This time it had the flavor of a real ending. Cooper felt an ache somewhere in the vicinity of his chest. He'd have to take another one of these pills. They were supposed to stop *pain,* after all. If he could just pick up that bottle off the floor.

He wondered what she looked like. A dozen different possibilities came to mind. Blond, skinny, fat, brunette, short, tall, thick, leggy, masculine . . . Yeah, masculine, that would probably suit Max fine. Cooper tried to picture a tall, masculine woman and came up with an internal picture of himself—which would have been funny if it weren't so ridiculous and sad. No, of course she wouldn't look like that. Max would want a woman—a *woman!*—who was very feminine, the furthest possible thing from Cooper he could find. Not that he would admit that to Cooper or even tell him who it was. It could be anyone. Cooper's cell phone slipped from his hand and fell into the plush pile of the carpet. He stared down at the small screen, which displayed Marina's number, cued up and ready to send. Could even be Marina, Cooper thought. Now *that* was funny. And then not so funny.

All at once, Cooper felt his mood shift and slide into anger—toward Marina. Those little sessions of theirs might as well have taken place on any clichéd psychiatrist's couch. She knew the score as well as—no, better than—anyone. Come to think of it, it wasn't such a bizarre idea to think that Max was somehow involved with Marina. All that false *concern* Max had for him. He was probably in touch with Marina—probably shared some of that deep concern with her. No, that wasn't so far off at all. And then they'd both dumped him. Max for some woman and Marina for—well, who knew what for? He hadn't been able to get hold of her for a while now. Ever since . . . Wasn't the last time he'd spoken to her the very day that Max had tossed him out on his sorry ass? Cooper's sense of time was a bit fuzzy, like the rest of him, but it seemed right. The two events were linked in his mind in any case. And now she wouldn't answer her phone. He was *pissed off.* If you couldn't count on your damn *psychic* for a little support, who *could* you rely on? He pushed "redial" on his house phone. When had those rings gotten so looooong? Finally, the beep.

"Biiiiittchhhh," he growled into the phone and clicked off. What the hell was wrong with him? But, no, fuck her for abandoning him.

He should just get up and go over there was what he should do. Unfortunately, movement of any kind seemed totally out of the realm of possibility at that moment. Even his arm, reaching for the phone or the pill bottle, whatever he could get hold of first, seemed way too heavy to move. And it was at the wrong angle, too. Cooper realized he was looking up at the ceiling instead of down at the carpet. When had he gotten out of his chair? It was better here on the floor, no question, but also more difficult to move. Maybe he didn't need another pill after all. On the other hand, maybe he did. He was still awake and thoughts were shimmying around in his brain. He wanted to sleep without dreaming or be conscious without having to think. Or maybe what he wanted was just to get her on the phone. Sooner or later she had to answer, and he was going to keep trying until she did. As soon as he could reach the phone, which now looked like it was lying a mile away from him, buried deep in the carpet. He needed a minute. Just one minute to rest his eyes and then he'd try again.

January 2007

Chapter 15

*N*ighttime. *The sky is pinholed by stars that offer no light. There is no moon, no bright patches anywhere. She is on the Coast Highway, walking. There are no cars and the air is still, heavy with the sweet scent of roses. He is walking several yards ahead, hands in his pockets, looking down at the road. She is following, but her feet are bare and there are sharp little rocks pressing into the flesh of her heels, and she can't keep up. She needs to move faster. She needs to warn him. He turns, heading away from the ocean, and quickens his pace. She tries to run, but her feet stick to the road. The smell of roses becomes stronger, along with something new—the smell of smoke. She calls to him, but no sound comes from her throat. He stops walking. Why is he stopping? She has to tell him now before it is too late. Suddenly, she is right there, right behind him. They are in a parking lot. She knows this place, but it is too dark to make out the details. She is gagging from the smell of roses and now she realizes why. Her mouth is stuffed full of soft petals and she cannot speak. He starts to turn around. There is a flash of light and everything explodes. Then there is only darkness.*

*M*arina woke from her dream with a feeling of déjà vu. It was a repeating coda, always the same and always the last one she had before opening her eyes to consciousness. Every morning for the last two months, she'd woken up trying to speak through the roses in her mouth, trying to get the man to turn around. She never saw his face, but she knew that the man was Gideon. The first time she'd had the dream was the November night she'd met him, and she'd had it every night since. But even though there was so much anxiety within the dream itself, Marina never woke up feeling frightened by it. If anything she awoke, as she did now, with a feeling of inevitability, as if the end of the dream and whatever it meant were predestined.

Closing her eyes and burying her head deeper in her warm down pillow, Marina let her thoughts linger on Gideon. Their romance, which to this point had been an updated version of a Victorian love story, was about to take a turn into wilder territory. For weeks, they'd been exploring their physical attraction to each other, getting closer but never naked, nor fully horizontal. Marina knew that was going to change tonight, and she was as excited as any bodice-ripper heroine. He'd implied that something special was planned for their date later, although he wouldn't elaborate beyond that. The whole evening was meant to be a surprise, but Marina suspected they would go to Lucky, the Chinese restaurant where they'd had their first date, if *date* could be considered an appropriate term. Like her dream, that moment had a feeling of inevitability about it. Marina summoned the memory again, examining it for details she might have missed and for clues as to what was in store.

He'd come to see her because he'd lost something and he wanted her to help him find it. At least, that's what he'd told her. Marina had assumed at first that it was some kind of object that had gone missing, but soon after it occurred to her that he could have been talking about a person or even a feeling. At any rate, he didn't tell her what it was and she didn't get a chance to ask. After he'd flagged her down in the parking lot, she'd taken him inside her office and made an appointment for the following day. She'd thought about scheduling him later in the week, even later in the month, so that he wouldn't think she was completely available (and therefore subpar), but there was something different about Gideon from the beginning, and she didn't bother with the usual pretense. It was only the first of her own rules she would break.

The second happened as soon as the following morning, when she spent half an hour in front of the mirror, checking her clothing and makeup and searching for lipstick. Wanting to look pretty for a client was a mistake and a bad place to go. Marina hadn't worn lipstick for so long that the only tube she could find was the pink glittery lip color she'd pocketed on the long-ago night of Madeline's party. Marina didn't know why she'd kept it all this time, nor did she understand why she was using it now, when she could just as easily pick up something fresh, cheap and unused at the Rite Aid down the street. Marina could still see the angry pout on Naked Sushi Girl's face as she applied the girl's color to her own lips.

Marina had told Gideon to come by at midmorning, but when she arrived at her office at nine o'clock he was already waiting for her.

"You must think I'm a little crazy," he told her. "Here all day yesterday and now I show up early. But I have a good excuse."

"Not necessary," she told him and smiled to soften the clipped sound of her words. Her painted lips felt heavy and sticky and had he not been standing in front of her she would have wiped them clean. He looked less imposing in broad daylight, although still big and solid. He was wearing a dark gray T-shirt and faded jeans. *Clean and casual,* Marina thought. Appropriate for the occasion, unlike her made-up face and color-coordinated outfit.

"Why don't we get started?" Marina asked him and led him to her table. The office still smelled vaguely of Cooper's cologne and the sandalwood candles she'd burned the day before, and Marina wondered if Gideon was bothered by the lingering scents. Finally, she had a chance to study him as he sat down and made himself comfortable in the chair opposite her.

She figured him to be about her age, or maybe a few years older. He wore his dark blond hair a little longer than was fashionable, but it was thick and full and men past their twenties with that much hair tended to advertise their good fortune even if, like Gideon, they had some scattered white showing through. He smiled often, emphasizing the well-worn laugh lines in his face, but his eyes remained serious and guarded. There was something there she couldn't see and he wasn't showing her, even though dark eyes were usually the easiest for her to read. There was no wedding ring on his finger and no telltale white band of skin showing where one might have been recently removed.

His body language confused her. He leaned back in his chair, showing he was at ease, but kept his arms loosely folded in front of him, closing himself off. He was waiting for something, Marina thought, but it wasn't a reading. And then she realized what was different about him. He was studying *her* in the same assessing way she was studying him. Marina was used to being visually searched and evaluated, both personally and professionally. But this man wasn't studying her in a sexual way, nor was he gauging her psychic abilities. There was something else he was after entirely, and it set her off balance.

"Is there anything you need before we get started?" Marina asked him. "Would you like water or . . ."

"Or?" Gideon sounded amused, although there was still no yielding in his eyes. He seemed in no hurry for his reading, yet there was a sense of urgency about him.

"I don't know," Marina answered. "I just want to make sure you're comfortable."

"Sure," he said. "I'm fine."

"Well, then, I think we should start with your question; the reason you're here."

Gideon formed a steeple with the fingers of his hands and looked down at them for a moment before lifting his head and staring right into her eyes. "I've lost something," he said. "I think you can help me find it."

For the first time, Marina saw something she recognized in his eyes: a hint of doubt. She waited, but that was all he was willing to offer for the moment.

"Okay," she said. He was going to be difficult, offering no details, and she was going to have to go begging for clues. She could have moved it along right there—could have come out and asked him what it was he had lost and why he was being so elliptical about describing it, but Marina had a stubborn streak. Even in the face of this oddly unreadable and increasingly attractive man, she was determined to earn her fee through skill. She'd never been one to avoid a challenge.

"Have you seen these before?" she asked, holding up her deck of tarot cards. "Most people are familiar with a couple of the images, but I sense that this is a very new experience for you, isn't it?"

"Mm-hmm, yes, you could say that." He never broke eye contact with her, not even when she fanned the cards out on the table. Usually, Marina's clients would look down and their eyes would gravitate to the card that most closely represented what they were thinking about. But Gideon didn't shift his eyes to the table, and it was just as well, because Marina's fingers stuck to the Magician and when she lifted her hand, the card came up with it. She had to pull it free and then it stuck to her thumb. Flustered, she shook her hand to get it free and watched it fall to the table. Gideon's eyes never left her face.

"This isn't what I expected," he said.

Still ruffled from her sloppy performance, Marina smiled and tried to wipe her hands on her skirt without being noticed. "What isn't?" she asked. "The cards? Because I—"

"No, not the cards. *You.*" He tipped his head slightly to the side as if another angle would give him a better view.

"Well, what were you expecting?" she asked him.

He paused. "That's a fair question," he said. "I'm just not sure how to answer it. I suppose I thought you'd be older, for a start. And then, I guess I just assumed that this"—he gestured to the room—"wouldn't be so ordinary."

"Did you think I'd have a crystal ball and some chicken bones lying around?" she asked. "Maybe you were expecting some kind of *lair?*" She smiled so he wouldn't think she was angry, but she could feel her face flushing with heat. A brief, unpleasant memory of Florida flashed before her: the dead snake and the sweltering humidity.

"Maybe I did," he said. "Like I told you, I've never done this before. I suppose I have some preconceived notions about what you . . . your . . . about what you do."

Marina felt another uncomfortable wave. "Are you a cop?" she asked.

"Would it matter if I was?"

Marina bit her lip and tasted the sweet chemical flavor of another woman's lipstick on her mouth. She gathered the tarot cards and once again they refused to cooperate, falling out of the stack and sticking to her fingers as if her hands were covered in honey. "What is it you want?" she asked, trying unsuccessfully to separate the Lovers from Judgment. "You didn't come here for a reading, did you?"

"I'm sorry," Gideon said. "I've upset you. I didn't mean to do that." He reached across the table and touched one of her hands with his. Marina felt the same heated charge as when he'd shook her hand the night before, but this time it was accompanied by a wavering in the air and then what seemed to be a dimming of the light in the room. Had it not been broad daylight, Marina would have sworn they were in the middle of a brownout. There was no rational accounting for the feeling—unless the man himself was giving off sparks like some sort of electric eel. Gideon felt her tremble and removed his hand as quickly as he'd put it out.

"I really did come here for a reading," he said. "And I'm not trying to make fun of you."

Marina's hand tingled where he'd touched it. She found herself wishing that Gideon did have an ulterior motive, because she didn't know if she could give him a reading that would pass muster. She'd never been so badly betrayed by her own powers of observation. It wasn't even as if he was trying to hide something; she could always tell what people were trying not to give away. It felt instead as if he were holding up a reflective barrier so that all she could see was how badly she was stumbling. It had been stupid to ask him if he was a cop, and she didn't know what had possessed her to say it. She wasn't doing anything illegal, but something in his manner implied that she was. Now that he'd claimed he did want a reading, she didn't know how to proceed. She was going to have to busk it, throw out a little song and dance and buy some time.

"You're not from around here, are you?" she asked him. He'd already told her that in the parking lot, of course, but she didn't think he'd remember.

Gideon smiled, seemed pleased that she'd gone down that road, although Marina couldn't understand why. "No, I'm not," he said. "I haven't been here long at all. Is it that obvious?"

Marina remembered the lumberjack shirt, how he didn't blend in at all in these surroundings. "Where are you from?" she said, knowing that as a psychic she shouldn't have to ask. But Gideon didn't seem to be bothered by this. Instead, he hesitated to give her an answer. For the first time, his eyes left hers for a moment, darting up and to the left.

"I'm from Texas," he said, and Marina knew he was lying, the first tiny bit of information she'd been sure of since she'd met him.

"Big place, Texas," she said. "Lots of room to lose something."

"Sure is," he said. Then the two of them sat in silence for much longer than was comfortable. Gideon stared at her, his steady gaze holding just the shadow of a question and little else that she could define.

"Listen," he said, finally breaking the thick wall of tension between them, "I think we got started on the wrong foot here and it's my fault. Maybe I'm not ready for this." Marina waited for him to go on—clearly, he had more to say—but he held his tongue and looked down into her table as if the mysteries of the universe could be found in its faux wood grain.

"So . . . you *don't* want a reading?" It came out sounding much harsher than she'd intended it to. She didn't want him to leave, Marina realized, and that threw her completely off kilter.

"I do." He looked up from the table and directly into her eyes. "Or, I did." He faltered, unable to decide on a course of action. Marina couldn't tell what the options were, but his equivocation couldn't have been clearer if he'd had a cartoon angel on one shoulder and a devil on the other. "I'm sorry," he said finally. "I guess I don't want a reading. At least not right now."

He reached over again and put his hand on hers once more. Whether this was to punctuate his apology or just a reflex, Marina couldn't tell, but she didn't have a chance to figure it out, because she was suddenly startled by a movement behind him. She looked up and for a split second was sure she saw a woman walking into the small bathroom at the back of the office. Marina jumped up out of her seat, knocking into the table. Alarmed, Gideon stood up.

"What is it?"

"I— Just a minute—" Marina couldn't explain it. She walked the short distance to the bathroom and opened the door. There was nobody inside, of course. Nor was the exit door open or unlocked.

"Is something wrong?" Gideon was now standing close beside her, an expression of concern on his face.

"Kind of silly," Marina said. "I thought I heard something back here." She hadn't consciously substituted *heard* for *saw,* but she knew why she'd done it. Hearing things that weren't there was always more explainable than seeing things that didn't exist.

"Someone knocking at the door?" he asked.

"No," she said. "Nobody comes in this way. It was nothing."

"Are you sure?"

"Yes, absolutely." Marina turned and walked back to her table with Gideon following. The two of them stood there for a moment in an awkward silence. There was no reading to resume and therefore nothing else to say. Marina's professional exterior had slipped and she struggled to pull it back.

"Listen," Gideon said. "Can we . . . I'd really like to talk to you, Marina. Would it be . . . ?" He was going to ask her out, Marina thought, and she was both surprised that he was taking this sudden turn and disturbed that she wanted him to. "Would it be totally out of line to ask you if we could talk somewhere else? I think I've been rude and I'd like to make that up to you. What I mean is, I'm wondering if you'd join me for lunch—or dinner. Or drinks. I don't know, something involving food and beverages. What do you think?"

Marina allowed herself only the slightest hesitation. "I think that would be all right," she said.

"Well, that's great," he said, and his whole body seemed to relax into a smile. "How do you feel about Chinese food?"

And that was how they had ended up at Lucky, which was tiny and tacky-looking, but known for the high quality and authenticity of its food. At the end of the meal, Gideon had offered her the choice of two fortune cookies on a small square tray. Marina had taken hers and held onto it while Gideon opened his and broke the sweet hard crust neatly in half. His cookie was empty, and he laughed at what that could mean— out to dinner with a psychic and no fortune in your cookie. Then Marina opened hers and pulled out two small strips of paper, a double fortune.

"Looks like you're in luck," she told him. "I have enough for both of us."

And maybe it was luck that he'd lost, Marina thought, because after that moment, neither of them mentioned what he'd come looking for again.

Marina sat up in bed and stared at the outlines of her bedroom. What would their fortunes offer tonight? she wondered. The air was cold on her sleep-warmed body, but she was too lethargic to even pull the blankets up over her exposed arms and chest. It took a long time for her to get moving in the morning these days, and she knew the reason lay in several half-opened blister packs on her bedside table. For the last month, Marina had been sampling a variety of sleeping pills in an effort to turn off the nightly film festival that now made up her dreams. It wasn't just the one repeating dream any longer; her unconscious was now teeming with wild, colorful panoramas. The dreams made her edgy not because they were frightening but because she had no control over them. Marina hated feeling out of control about anything. But the pills did nothing to stop the dreams, no matter how many or what kind she swallowed each night. What they did do, magnificently, was make her groggy and slow from morning until afternoon. She felt more alert when she was sleeping, Marina realized as she slid out from under the warmth of her covers and shivered.

Gathering the pill packets in her hand, Marina decided that it was time to stop. She wouldn't throw them away—you never knew when you might need them for *real* insomnia—but she couldn't afford to spend her days in a state of wooziness anymore. Marina walked unsteadily into her bathroom and stuffed the packets into her medicine cabinet. Her eyes felt as if they were full of sand and her legs were stiff and heavy. And it was cold. The weather was all anyone could talk about lately. The temperature had dipped below freezing in southern California and the oranges were dying in the groves despite the burning peach-pit fires set to keep them warm. Marina felt the chill. It was going to take a very long, very hot shower and at least two cups of strong coffee to wake her body up enough to keep pace with her mind. There was more on her schedule today than Gideon, even if all her mooning and dreaming indicated otherwise.

For one thing, she needed to do something about the crank calls and hang-ups she'd been receiving for the past few weeks. She'd ignored them at first—the "bitch" messages left on her voice mail and the heavy breathing followed by dial tones—chalking them up to kids playing games or stray perverts who'd gotten bored with Internet porn. But they hadn't stopped, and it was starting to make her anxious. The most obvious solution would be to change her phone number, but she hadn't yet figured out how to do that without calling every one of her clients to let them know—something that would arouse suspicion at best and turn people away at worst. It just wouldn't look good. She'd call the phone company, Marina decided, and see what they could recommend.

More important than the phone, however, Marina's clients needed tending to—especially those regulars who had been more demanding than usual lately. They were like children, Marina thought. As soon as Mommy diverted her attention even a little, they started clamoring, *Look at me, look at me.*

Madeline was the only one whom Marina felt even remotely responsible for, even though she couldn't be blamed for doing anything wrong—the woman had clearly caused her own miscarriage. Marina grimaced, remembering the scene outside her office a few weeks earlier.

"I should call my doctor," Madeline had said. "I'm sure it's nothing." She was covered in blood from the waist down, Marina remembered, and her face was so pale. She was obviously going into shock. Still, in all the commotion of getting her inside and calling for an ambulance, Marina saw how venomously Madeline seemed to be staring at Gideon, who had arrived just a few minutes before she had. Where, in all the horror of losing the baby she had tried so hard to conceive and carry, had Madeline found the presence of mind to even notice that Gideon was there? It was just a moment—just a flash across Madeline's exhausted face—but it had chilled Marina.

It was a good thing Gideon *had* been there, actually. While Marina spoke soothingly to Madeline, holding her hand and looking deeply into her eyes to give her a focus point, Gideon called the ambulance. He was so quiet and efficient about it that Marina didn't even hear him make the call. The ambulance was just *there* suddenly and then Madeline was gone. Gideon had something to do with that, too. He managed to take control, get her out of there quickly, before anyone could stop to look and start asking questions. Marina supposed she owed Gideon for that, although it wasn't exactly a sense of obligation that drew her to him.

Marina had been expecting to receive a call from Madeline soon after that and had prepared the response she'd crafted as soon as Madeline had been ordered to bed rest. It wasn't all bullshit, either. Anyone who had half a brain could see how conflicted Madeline was over having this baby in the first place. All Marina had to do was to frame that observation in a psychic context for Madeline. It wouldn't work for Andrew, however, who was absolutely *not* conflicted about having a baby and who was the one who called her, angry, bitter and threatening.

"I knew you were trouble the minute I laid eyes on you," he'd said, his words slurry from alcohol. He was the most unpleasant kind of drunk (and a full-blown alcoholic, she could tell): quiet and mean. She gave him a wide berth, let him carry on as far as his angry line would take him, only occasionally interjecting how sorry she was for both of them and that she hoped Madeline was feeling all right.

Marina knew that she was an easy target for Andrew's anger. His wife had left the house against doctor's orders to see *her*, after all, someone he'd never approved of in the first place. Marina was a handy and obvious choice for blame, but she could have been anyone who'd played the same role for Madeline. At least this was what Marina told herself. What she didn't want to admit was that Andrew's tightly controlled rage was so charged that it frightened her. He finally finished his tirade by telling Marina, "I can tell you one thing: it's over with you. You won't come into my house again. And I won't be giving *her* any money to come see you, either. I know how you people operate—you don't do anything for free, do you? Let's see what a . . . *friend* you are to her without a steady flow of cash." He didn't wait for a response before hanging up.

The call from Madeline herself hadn't come until Christmas. She'd held out longer than Marina had expected.

"Andrew's out," Madeline had said into Marina's voice mail. "We have a tree the size of the Empire State Building in this house. You can't imagine what it's like here. There are all these presents for the baby. He said he didn't know what to do with them, but I think he's just leaving them out to torture me. He blames me for everything. We need to talk, Marina. I know it's Christmas, but . . . I have something for you—a present. And I want to . . .

I'll try you again another time. Maybe we could have coffee. I can meet you somewhere." There was a long pause. Marina could hear the sound of Madeline breathing and the light tinkle of wind chimes in the background. "I could meet you at Darling's," Madeline added finally, "if that's okay. Anyway, I really think we should talk. Merry Christmas, Marina."

When Madeline called a second time, Marina kept the conversation short. Darling's would be fine, she told Madeline, and they settled on a date—today. The conspiratorial tone and abbreviated length of the phone call made Marina feel as if she was planning an adulterous tryst. Perhaps, in a way, that was exactly what it was. Her relationship with Madeline had become very complicated. She felt some sympathy for the woman and that twinge of obligation, but the smart thing to do now was back out. Marina didn't have a strategy in place for how she was going to accomplish this, but planned to take her lead from Madeline. She was glad they were meeting at Darling's instead of the confined and too-private space of her office. But Madeline wasn't the only potentially unbalanced woman she had to deal with today.

Cassie, Eddie Perkins's paramour, was now also on Marina's client roster and was scheduled for an afternoon reading. In Marina's own set of business ethics, it was bad practice to have lovers or spouses as separate clients. Nor did she like to do readings for couples, because they inevitably turned into couples' *counseling*. Were it not for the fact that she'd already bounced Eddie as a client when Cassie came along, she wouldn't have agreed to read for her at all. Not that Cassie was forthcoming about her relationship with Eddie. She'd presented herself as a first-time client, assuming or maybe hoping that Marina wouldn't remember her from Madeline's party. But if there was one thing that defined Marina's powers of observation, it was her ability to remember a face. Cassie's had become more plush and pouty since Marina had first seen it, but it was instantly recognizable. And that added pout had everything to do with Eddie, Marina thought. Eddie—what a nuisance *he* was. Marina couldn't understand Cassie's lovelorn attraction at all. He'd stopped coming around finally, which was a tremendous relief. Gideon had had a hand in that one, too, Marina realized, although again in the most unobtrusive way. He'd just sort of happened to be there the last time Eddie had dropped by unannounced and had just sort of happened to scare Eddie off without saying or doing anything that could be construed as threatening.

"You must get this kind of thing a lot," Gideon had said after Eddie's "visit."

"What kind of thing is that?"

"People coming around, wanting . . ." Gideon had trailed off awkwardly. Marina tried to figure out whether he was talking about needy clients or men who wanted to date her. Either way, there was a parallel to his own motivations.

"Eddie sees himself as a ladies' man," Marina said. "He isn't used to being turned down. I'm not going to date him, so that makes me more interesting. But no, this *kind* of thing doesn't happen to me very often."

"I don't know," he said. "Maybe you just haven't noticed it. I don't like that there are people—men—hanging around here. You're out in the open. A target."

"That's sweet of you," she said. "But I've been taking care of myself for a long time."

"But you have to be careful," Gideon said. "You never know when—"

"We *all* have to be careful," Marina said, and that was the end of the conversation.

Chapter 16

*C*areful. Marina rolled the word around in her head as she turned on her shower and waited for the water to heat up. People told you to *take care* when they were wishing you well. But care was not something Marina was taking when it came to Gideon. She shook out her hair—too long and wild now and badly in need of a cut—and stood directly under the pounding water, feeling the heat soak into her skin as her bathroom filled with steam. Hand at her throat, Marina realized that she'd forgotten to take off her ring and chain as she always did in the shower. Just one more indicator of how distracted she'd become. She closed her eyes and a visual echo of her dream flashed before her—the dark sky and bright stars, running, the rocks under her feet—before dissolving into an image of Gideon's face. Marina let her consciousness stay there, lingering on his features.

If their meal at Lucky couldn't be considered a date, there was no question about the second time they saw each other. He arrived at her office that afternoon carrying a bottle of amarone, an Italian red wine that he said was "made from raisins," and asked if she'd like to drink it on the beach. Spontaneity had never been one of Marina's strong suits, so she surprised herself by telling Gideon that it sounded like a great idea. They drove south down the Coast Highway until they came to a particularly beautiful stretch of beach just past the town of Del Mar, and parked at the edge of the sand.

"I suppose I should have mentioned," Marina said then, "that we're not allowed to have alcohol or glass on the beach. They're pretty particular about that kind of thing around here."

"Well," he said, producing a corkscrew and two plastic cups, "I suppose we'll have to have a toast in the car first, then."

Marina rarely drank and limited the amount when she did. She'd spent an entire childhood with out-of-control addicts and would never allow herself to become one of them. But even she had to admit that sometimes alcohol just made things easier. Alone together in Gideon's truck and out of small talk, they needed the wine until they could relax enough to move on to whatever was going to come next. And there was some push and pull in their conversation. Marina wanted to know more about him, but she'd so thoroughly trained herself to learn through observation that she found it difficult to ask him direct questions about what he did, where he'd come from and why he'd wound up here. Gideon had no such reservations and wasn't afraid to ask her how she'd started working as a psychic, how long she'd been living in California ("Seems like everyone who lives here came from somewhere else," he mused) and what her clients were like. This was where the wine was especially useful for Marina, enabling her to loosen up enough to deflect his questions without seeming like she had anything to hide. "I can't talk about my clients," she told him. "It's the same as if I were a lawyer or a doctor, only my tools are a little different. Tarot cards instead of prescriptions and briefs."

He'd laughed at that, even though she sensed some irritation or impatience beneath the surface, and asked her if she could talk about those tools. So Marina found herself telling him about the symbolism of tarot cards and how they tied into astrology, which went back to the beginning of civilization. She talked about the significance of birth times and the influence of planets. He listened, drank his wine and smiled without condescension.

"You make it sound so legitimate," he said.

Marina bristled but tried not to show it. "You're the one who came to me," she said.

"I did," he answered. "I'm sorry. I didn't mean it to sound that way."

The sun was setting when they got out to stroll on the sand. Marina felt warm and tipsy. It took some time for them to get in step with each other as they walked along the water's edge. Marina was glad for the noise of the rushing ocean and the slight fuzziness she felt from the alcohol. When Gideon stopped and looked out at the glowing horizon, Marina looked up at him and felt a powerful urge to put her lips against his skin and feel the curve of his shoulders under her hands. He turned and didn't smile at her, but after a moment he took her hand in his and held it. It was more intimate than a kiss, Marina thought, and she felt a rush of heat spread through her body. Her cheeks flushed despite the cool salty breeze and perspiration prickled her skin. She felt dizzy and had to look away, down the beach, where she could see a white-haired woman dressed in a long robe sitting behind a small table.

It was a weird enough sight that Marina wondered why she hadn't seen the old woman when they'd first come down to the beach. She squinted through the dying light to try to make out the details. From this distance, the woman looked like one of those old fortune-tellers who sat along arcade boardwalks. Or a caricature of one. But there was something wrong with the whole picture—not least that there was no arcade or boardwalk and the woman was sitting in the middle of the sand. Gideon didn't seem to notice that she was staring, and without letting go of her hand he started walking in the old woman's direction. As they got closer, Marina steeled herself, as if they were about to see something terrifying. The old woman started to look up, and without thinking, Marina tightened her grip on Gideon's hand. He stopped walking and turned to her.

"Marina?"

"Kind of strange, isn't it?"

"What?" he said.

"That woman over there." She tilted her head in the woman's direction. She watched his eyes dart to the side.

"What woman?"

Before she even turned her head, Marina knew that the woman—or what she thought she'd seen—was gone. As she looked out at the beach, empty except for tangles of seaweed and shells, Marina felt her heart sink. The woman *had* been there. It took her longer than she wanted to tell Gideon that it was nothing, she'd mistaken a rock or seaweed for something else.

"It's getting a little cold out here," he said. "Shall we go?"

They rode back to her office in silence and Marina worried—more than she wanted to—that she'd turned him off with her weird behavior on the beach. But then, as she was getting out of his truck, he leaned over and said, "I'd really like to see you again. Maybe a real dinner this time. What do you think?"

For that next date, Gideon took her to dinner at a small Italian restaurant in Cardiff-by-the-Sea where railroad tracks crossed the coast road and the ocean pounded away just beyond that. It was late by the time they finished and Gideon drove her the short distance back to her house. He pulled into her abbreviated driveway with impressive ease considering the size of his pickup and the narrowness of the streets in the Cardiff hills. He turned off the motor but left the key in the ignition. The radio, set to an oldies station, continued to play and they listened as Bob Seger smoked the last day's cigarette and turned the page. They sat without speaking until the song finished and the next one began, and that was the moment when Gideon leaned over without any warning and kissed her for the first time. As his lips touched hers, Marina was besieged by opposing sensations. All at once she had the feeling of déjà vu, as if she knew this kiss and had been here a thousand times before, and the conflicting feeling that this was something entirely new and unfamiliar. Then, suddenly, his hands were in her hair, cradling her head, and her arms encircled him, pulling him in so close that the weight of his chest pressed her ring, tucked inside her bra, deep into the flesh of her breast. A sharp jab of pain shot all the way to her spine and she shivered. Behind her closed eyes, Marina was seeing lightning flashes of light. He let her go then and he lifted his face from hers. His fingers stayed on her face, the tips just grazing her cheekbones as if he were trying to read Braille on her skin.

"Would you like to come inside?" Marina asked. Her voice sounded breathy, low and full of need.

"Yes," Gideon said. "There isn't anything I want more right now." Marina listened carefully to the timbre of his voice, trying to tease out meanings from the tone behind his words, searching for truths he couldn't hide, but hearing nothing except what he chose to tell her. He lifted a curl from her shoulder and rubbed it between his fingers like a rabbit's foot. "But I want to get to know you first," he said. "I mean really get to know you. I have to understand who you are—what goes on here." He touched her forehead. "And here." He pointed in the direction of her heart. "Before I . . . before we . . . It's important to me, Marina. I hope you think so, too."

"You realize that's usually the girl's line," Marina said, instantly regretting how cynical she sounded. She smiled to soften her words, but he didn't follow suit. He just stared at her, boring into her brain with his dark eyes. Something dark and primal—a sharp little fear—twisted in her gut.

"Are you . . . are you attracted to me?" she asked. Marina bit her own lip so hard she tasted blood, but it was too late to take the words back into her mouth.

"Yes," Gideon said, and the deep, thick sound of that one syllable made her feel weak with desire. "I am so attracted to you I can barely see straight when I'm with you." He placed his hand on the side of her neck. Marina's blood went mad, surging wildly through her veins. She could feel her heart beating double time within her chest. "That's why I want to wait," he said. "I need to know that it's not just about sex."

Marina's breath was coming fast. "You surprise me," she said.

"Are you disappointed?"

"Not yet," she said, and this time he smiled with her.

They'd been on a slow build ever since that night, getting progressively closer but never going all the way. It was like some kind of grand experiment, Marina thought. How long can two adults act like clumsy virgins? No, not clumsy. There was something very graceful about the way Gideon was choreographing this dance. And it was working. She wanted him in every way, physically and emotionally. And every time they were together, Marina's world started to spark and expand like some kind of supernova. The strange vision of the fortune-teller on the beach was only the beginning. When Gideon was near her—when he *touched* her—she saw flashes of light and the shadows of people who weren't there. She heard laughter and whispering in her ear. One night, as he kissed her good night on her front step, Marina heard a voice say, "Better watch yourself, girlie," so clearly that she broke away and turned her head in the direction of the sound. But it wasn't the nearness of the voice that disturbed her as much as whom it belonged to: her mother.

She was falling in love and it was making her fall apart. Love, the very thought of which gave her a sick feeling in her stomach, was so messy and uncontrolled and selfish. She was already compromising, cutting back her schedule, and her work was suffering. How long before she started to lose pieces of herself as well? Her clients had noticed the change in her attitude, even though she was more careful than ever to keep her personal life guarded from them. That was the warning in her dream, Marina knew. Stop before it is too late. But she didn't want to stop.

Unwilling to open her eyes, Marina reached blindly for the shampoo and fumbled with the cap. She knew enough basic psychology to understand what her dream was about. In the dream she was moving closer and closer to Gideon, just as she was in life. The warning—the sense of anxiety—was because it was wrong to be getting romantically involved with him. The roses, a symbol of love and romance, were stuffed into her mouth, an even more obvious statement about how conflicted she felt. But . . . Marina grasped at the memory of the dream in her head. She saw herself catching up to him and started to fashion her own imaginary ending.

She ran her soapy hands along her body, moving up from the curve of her hips to her breasts, circling them with her hands, then stroking, then moving downward again over the flat plane of her belly, her fingertips reaching down lower between her thighs. She bent her head and felt hot water cascading off her neck and shoulders. Behind her closed eyes, she saw Gideon on the evening they'd met, when she'd gotten him into the light and looked into his face. She'd felt it right then—the slow magnetic pull of his eyes and the set of his mouth. Her mind's eye traveled down to the warm tan skin of his throat. She could see the steady throb of his pulse just below his jawline. Now she watched him raise his hands, saw his strong square fingers, the roughness of his palms. She turned her own hands into his and she guided them down on her slick wet flesh. Showing him exactly where to go, she caressed, stroked, then pushed hard, harder, all her muscles tensing, until she could hear the sound of herself gasping and felt the shower running cold.

Chapter 17

Madeline was already at Darling's by the time Marina arrived. As she made her way through the busy restaurant to Madeline's table by the window, Marina checked her expression of surprise. She had expected Madeline to be emotional, even angry, but she hadn't anticipated the cold, hard woman she now saw sipping coffee in front of her. Madeline had lost weight; all the softness was gone from her features. Her bright, blond and perfectly coiffed hair covered her head like a helmet. She held herself stiffly, her chin and elbows jutting out at sharp angles, and her shoulders were drawn up and tensed. She was pale and dressed in an expensive white linen suit that looked as if it was brand-new. Marina thought Madeline had never looked more beautiful, but there was something almost frightening about her appearance—it was as if she were encased in a shiny layer of stainless steel.

"You look good, Madeline," Marina said as she sat down. "How are you feeling?"

"Don't you know?" Madeline asked. "Can't you tell?" It was then that Marina could see the shimmer of held-back tears in Madeline's eyes.

"I am so sorry about what happened," Marina responded. "But I'm so glad that you're all right."

Madeline tucked a length of silky hair behind her ear with perfectly manicured fingers. "He's going to divorce me," she said. "He hasn't said so yet, but I know he's going to. He thinks this is all my fault." She picked up a napkin and gently blotted her lips. "Well," she added, "that's not totally true. He also thinks it's *your* fault. He thinks you gave me something in those teas you brought over. Something to make me . . ." She drifted off for a moment, her eyes clouding over. "But of course that's ridiculous. Why would you do something like that? That's what I told him. But he hates me and so he hates you. Convenient, isn't it?" Madeline opened her blue eyes very wide. Frozen in place, her tears did not fall.

"Everyone reacts very differently to stress," Marina said, measuring her words. "This is obviously Andrew's way of coping. I don't believe that he hates you, Madeline."

"Do you believe that he hates *you?*" Madeline said. "I mean, that's really the nutty thing, isn't it? What could possibly be in it for you if I lost the . . . you know? What would you get out of that, right? Right, Marina?"

Willing herself to remain calm and unruffled, Marina spoke in as soothing a tone as she could manage. She'd had plenty of practice with this kind of volatile situation and had learned that it was all about the way you spoke, the image you projected. People who chose to consult psychics were highly suggestible to begin with and responded well to basic hypnotic techniques of quiet repetition.

"You've just been through something tremendously difficult, Madeline," she began. "The intense stress of something like this can manifest in the mind *and* the body. It's important that you allow yourself the space to grieve and to understand what has happened. The important thing is that your body is healthy, and once it has healed, you can work on understanding the lesson in all of this. In our work, we—"

"Oh, yes, our work," Madeline spat. "Our *work*. Our work worked out well, didn't it? Sometimes I wonder. What *was* in those teas you brought me, Marina? You charged me enough for them."

"I'm not the person you are angry with," Marina said softly. "You know I would never do anything to harm you in any way. If anything, the opposite is true. In these last few months, I've felt your pain as if it were my own. I've tried everything I can to guide you in the right direction. I've seen you so much more than I usually see my clients, and perhaps that's been the problem. Perhaps we've both asked too much of the universe." Marina took a breath. "I cannot influence the spirits or the future, Madeline; I can only receive messages and guidance. This is the role I've been given in life. I know you understand that. But this doesn't mean I don't feel for you as a woman. It's not so cut and dried."

Madeline's posture relaxed and her eyes grew softer as Marina spoke. Marina knew she wasn't listening to the words themselves but rather finding comfort in their sound and rhythm. "I know," Madeline said. "You're right. I didn't mean it to come out like that. And maybe this is wrong, but I think of you as a friend, Marina. I mean, don't you?"

Madeline had shifted her body so that she was facing Marina directly, her arms open and hands held out. She was so needy, Marina thought, with such a vast emptiness inside her.

"You know," Marina said carefully, "maybe that's part of the problem. Maybe being friends has made it more difficult to actually do the kind of work we need to do." As soon as the words had left her mouth, Marina knew that she had miscalculated badly. Madeline's face hardened once again and Marina could see her bristling. She hurried to add something that might undo the damage. "Of course I think of you as a friend, Madeline. But what may be happening is that *because* I think of you as a friend I am not as impartial as I should be. My own feelings get in the way and block the messages I need to receive. Does that make sense?"

"I suppose," Madeline said. "And I suppose you can't really *pay* someone to be your friend, can you? I mean, you shouldn't."

Marina sighed, already tired by the encounter, feeling the will to make nice with this woman slipping away from her. All she really wanted to do was to break it off. Madeline had become more of a liability than an asset. Beyond that, though, there was the issue of the time she was spending here. Since Gideon's arrival, Marina had found much more value in her free time. "You aren't paying me to be your friend," she said finally.

"I know," Madeline said. "And I'm not paying you at all right now. Andrew's cut off my Marina allowance. Isn't that pathetic? Daddy says I can't see you anymore." Madeline's eyes filled once more, but she blinked them hard. "So I'm going back to my old business. I used to make these great gift baskets—did I ever tell you that? I stopped doing it after we got married. I don't know why. Yes, I do. I was trying to get pregnant. We were *starting a family.* I have—I mean, I made one for you. I have it—it's in the car. I was thinking I could bring it by your office?" But Madeline didn't give Marina a chance to respond before continuing.

"Andrew can't tell me what I can and can't do. It's ridiculous. I'll make my own money. I've done it before. Maybe by the time he gets ready to divorce me, I'll have enough stashed so that . . . Well, it doesn't matter; I'm still going to sue his ass. Anyway, Marina, the point is—I need a reading. I'm going to pay for it, don't worry. I'm at a crossroads and I need you to look into the future or read my cards or whatever and tell me which way to go." Madeline paused finally, looking down at her coffee cup. "I think you *owe* me that much, Marina," she added softly. "At least that much."

"That's fine, Madeline, but we're going to have to wait a few weeks. I am completely booked at the moment."

They both leaned back in their chairs and Madeline clicked her fingernails on the tabletop. Marina took a long sip of her coffee, debating how best to extricate herself now without further annoying Madeline.

"You know, I've been meaning to ask but I totally forgot, seeing as how I was busy losing my baby the last time I saw you," Madeline said, pursing her lips around the words. "Who was that cute guy you were kissing when I came to your office? How long has *that* been going on? I mean, there's booked and then there's *booked,* right?"

Marina could feel herself redden, but it wasn't from anything as innocent as a blush. "You know, I don't think—"

"Didn't he call the paramedics for me? Since, unfortunately, he now knows a lot about *me,* it's only fair I know something about him. Very good-looking, I have to say. Nice job with that, Marina."

Marina couldn't believe Madeline had noticed—or even remembered. She took a deep breath and prepared herself to respond, but before she could get any words out, the two of them were interrupted by almost the last person Marina wanted to see: Eddie Perkins.

"Marina!" he said, coming over to their table. "What a coincidence. I saw you over here and just had to come say hello." He smiled expansively, creasing his cheeks. His gaze, fixed on Marina for much longer than was comfortable, finally drifted over to Madeline, whom he seemed to quickly assess and approve of in the way a hungry coyote might a kitten. He offered Madeline his hand. "Eddie Perkins," he said. Madeline stared blankly at him for a moment and then asked, "Do I know you?"

"No, ma'am, I don't think so," Eddie answered, his arm still extended like a branch between them. "I'd certainly remember a face as lovely as yours."

Madeline's lips formed a small but definite smile, and Marina wondered not for the first time how Eddie got away with it. He was so full of crap it was practically oozing from him.

"I'm Madeline."

"Like the book?" he asked. "Or like the cookie?"

Madeline's smile grew bigger and she finally reached out and shook his hand. Satisfied with himself, Eddie turned back to Marina and gazed at her with a kind of desperate longing that made her feel sick. "Mind if I join you two?" he asked.

For an absurd moment, the three of them did an updated version of the face-off scene from *The Good, the Bad, and the Ugly:* Marina looked to Madeline, Madeline to Eddie, Eddie to Marina and back around again, each one trying to see the motivations of the others through the thick haze of their own—and each one ready to draw a metaphorical gun. It was Marina who finally broke the silence by standing up abruptly and announcing, "I'm really sorry, but I have to go. I have an appointment and I'm running late." She fished a five-dollar bill from her pocket and placed it on the table. "Madeline, it was great to see you." She nodded at Eddie. "Ed," she said.

"Marina, wait," Madeline said. "We haven't—"

"Take care," Marina said, turning away from them both and walking too fast out of Darling's and onto the street. The jangle of the ridiculous bell on the restaurant's door echoed in her head as she ducked down a side street to take the long way around to her office.

That uneasiness turned into alarm when she finally reached her building. There, tossed against her office door, lay a pile of torn, rotting roses half buried in dark, damp dirt. Small clods of earth were sprinkled along the ground. Fear made a heated knot in Marina's stomach. *Florida,* she thought. *It's Florida all over again.* She looked up and around, as if she could see who had left the mess, even though she knew whoever it was would be long gone. If anything, the street and the parking lot were quieter than usual.

There were many worse things that could have been dumped on her doorstep, but there was something so violent about these dead flowers, clearly torn from their roots and crawling, she could see now, with feasting insects. Marina felt completely powerless and naked. Her eyes stung with sharp tears. But one moment of fear and self-pity was all she would allow herself. By the time Marina had bagged up the rotten dirt and taken it out to the Dumpster behind her office, she had already half convinced herself that there was nothing ominous about a pile of decaying flowers, which had probably been left there by some bored kids with nothing better to do. And as she brushed the last traces of earth away from her front door, just in time for her first client of the day to walk through it, she'd decided that she'd altogether overreacted. Her meeting with Madeline had made her edgy. That was all it was.

Marina had booked her day full to make up for the cuts she'd made in her appointments over the last few weeks to better serve her dating schedule, and she had to work hard to maintain a sense of focus. As the hours wore on, she pushed the morning's anxiety to the farthest corner of her brain and allowed her thoughts to return to Gideon. Whatever feelings of hesitancy she'd had about their relationship in the morning melted away by the afternoon. By the time Cassie arrived for her appointment, the last of the day, Marina's anticipation had turned into fierce longing, and Gideon had become nothing short of a glowing knight waiting to carry her off into the sunset. And all of this only served to make her time with Cassie more annoying.

Marina's hopes for a quick, smooth reading were scuttled almost immediately. The girl was both whiny and demanding, and nothing Marina said was what she wanted to hear. When Marina pulled the Hermit from her tarot deck and explained that it meant Cassie needed to take time alone for reflection, Cassie insisted on pulling another. When Marina said that a transit of Saturn over Cassie's natal Venus showed the need to reevaluate her feelings about relationships, Cassie countered that there must be something else in the stars that had a more positive connotation.

Marina came close to taking the easy way out: telling Cassie that, yes, perhaps there *was* light at the end of her dark romantic tunnel and that her "man" (whom Cassie steadfastly refused to identify) would finally realize that she was the woman he'd been looking for his entire life. But then Cassie, who talked too much and listened very little, offered up a piece of information: She'd lied about being pregnant to buy some time with the object of her affection.

"I know, I know, it's wrong to *lie*," Cassie said, "but it's the only way I can get him to realize how much he loves me."

"And do you think he'll still love you once he finds out you've lied to him?" Marina asked. "Don't you think that might make him angry?"

Cassie shrugged. "He's a liar, too," she said. "How could he get angry with *me?* Besides, I could always *get* pregnant and then it wouldn't be a lie. Let's look at the cards again. Maybe they have something to say about that."

For the first time since she'd met him, Marina felt a stab of sympathy for Eddie. "Cassie—" she began and stopped herself, wondering if it was worth it to make this effort and why she cared to in the first place. "Speaking to you now just woman to woman—not as your psychic—I think this is a very bad idea. People get very hurt and angry when they've been lied to, especially about something like this. You can't build a right on so many wrongs." She shuffled through her tarot deck until she found the Tower. One of the most dramatic cards in the deck, it showed lightning igniting the top of a castle, flames bursting from its dark windows. In the foreground a man and a woman were shown falling, arms outstretched, to the rocks below. Marina placed the card in front of Cassie. "This is what can happen," she said.

But Cassie was neither looking nor listening. She looked at Marina, a dreamy expression on her face. "Have you ever been in love?" she asked. "I mean, really in love?"

Marina remembered the first time she'd met Cassie, at Madeline's party, and how the girl had asked her the same thing then. Gideon's smiling face appeared again in her mind's eye.

No, she thought but didn't say. *Not until now.*

Chapter 18

It was one of those California mornings so sparkling and perfect it begged to be photographed and made into a postcard for the tourism bureau. The air was warm and bright without even the slightest hint of winter, and the ocean mixed a thousand shades of blue as it tossed jewel-studded waves to the shore. Marina stood in the queue outside Rosa's, waiting for her turn to order coffee. Her knees were trembling and her hands were shaking, aftershocks of the earthquake that had torn her apart inside only hours before. But on the outside, nothing had changed and everything looked the same. It was critical she remember that. The most important thing to do—the *only* thing to do—was to pretend that everything was still normal.

In the line ahead of her, beach walkers clad in shorts and spandex halter tops vacillated between cranberry muffins and apple turnovers. There was so little variety in the offerings, but they still agonized over the choice. People always took so much time with the small things, savoring their ability to pick one over the other, rating their decisions later. *I should have had the muffin; this turnover is too greasy. I'm glad I chose the turnover; it's delicious.* The less significant the outcome, the more time spent on the choice. You could control the outcome of breakfast by what you chose to eat and then you could do it all again the next morning. But you only got one shot with the big choices and then everything changed forever. You could never undo a bad choice over a big thing. You couldn't go back the next day and pick the damn muffin instead of the turnover. You could never again decide that it would be worth it to ignore your own rules for the sake of what you thought was love. Once the egg was broken, all the king's men just stood there looking at it. It was a terrible choice she'd made, Marina thought; a huge mistake. And now . . . what? Pretend everything is normal and carry on. It was crisis-mode denial, but it was all she could do.

It was finally her turn and Marina took her place in front of Rosa. The woman gave Marina the abbreviated smile she reserved for regulars and asked, "Coffee today?"

"Yes, please," Marina answered. "Large."

"Muffin?"

"Just coffee, please."

When Rosa turned around to get the coffee, Marina saw the girl who had been standing behind her. Slender and very pale, the girl looked like a much younger version of Rosa. She was barefoot and dressed in what appeared to be a hospital gown. Marina watched as the girl stared at Rosa with an expression of ineffable sadness and then reached out with a thin arm to stroke Rosa's back. If Rosa noticed, she gave no indication; she just carried on hustling hot coffee, Styrofoam cups and plastic lids. The girl looked sick, Marina thought. Why was she working with Rosa, who hardly ever had help anyway? And why was she dressed in a hospital gown? It certainly didn't seem like a fashion statement.

Rosa took Marina's money and made change at the register. The girl reached over again and touched Rosa's face. Once more, Rosa ignored her.

"Thank you," Rosa said, putting the change in Marina's hand. The girl was now standing so close to Rosa that their bodies were touching.

"Is that your daughter?" Marina said, smiling at the girl. "She looks just like you." The girl turned her attention to Marina for the first time, looking mildly surprised, but Rosa's face blanched and her eyes widened, showing both fear and sorrow. Marina was completely confused. Rosa's reaction was so inappropriate it set off loud alarm bells in Marina's head. She could feel the prickle of sudden perspiration along her back.

"What did you say?" Rosa asked. "I don't understand you."

There was something wrong, very wrong, but Marina pressed on. She gestured to the girl. "I just said she must be your daughter. She looks like you. She's . . . lovely. Must be nice to have some help."

Rosa turned to the girl and stared right through her at some unseen point. "My daughter . . ." Rosa started and then choked on a sob, tears making their way down her cheeks. "My daughter is dead. She died last month."

"Oh, I . . . I am so sorry. I didn't . . ." Marina felt heat redden her face. She clutched her cup too tightly and hot coffee spilled on her fingers, burning them. The girl who wasn't there was still staring at her, now mouthing the words *Tell her.* "I'm so sorry," Marina repeated, putting her cup down and slowly backing away.

"Can you see her?" Rosa asked, her voice thick with grief.

Tell her, the girl mouthed.

"Can you *see* her?" Rosa was crying now. "Please tell me."

Tell her tell her tell her tell her.

"I'm sorry, Rosa; I'm sorry. I have to go now." Marina turned and walked as fast as she could toward the beach without breaking into a run. "Hey," she heard behind her, "you left your coffee. Hey!" But Marina didn't turn around or stop until she'd crossed the street, climbed down the rocks and run across the sand to the water's edge.

Marina sat down with her knees up and her head buried between them, making herself as small as possible, trying to figure out what had just happened. There was a fierce pounding behind her forehead and she felt like crying. The sun was warm on her back, but she had started shivering. This was not in the pretend-everything-is-normal plan by half. She'd never be able to go to Rosa's again—not after that performance.

Marina fixed her gaze on a broken piece of shell next to her foot, focusing on the dark wet grains of sand stuck inside its curved edge. She was afraid to look up, afraid of what else she might see that wasn't there. Only the girl *had* been there, Marina was sure of it, and just not in the flesh. Rosa knew. *Tell her,* the girl had demanded. Tell her what?

Marina picked up the shell and gripped it in her hand until the jagged edges bit into her palm; the sharp pain was a welcome reminder of reality. No, she told herself, she hadn't really seen anything at all. In her overstressed paranoid state, she had projected her own fears and discomfort onto the scenery around her. It was a horrible coincidence that Rosa happened to have had a daughter who'd died. And, more than a coincidence, it was just bad luck. Reflexively, Marina reached up to her chest to feel the reassuring weight of the ring around her neck. But it wasn't there—it would never be there again—and she let her hand drop uselessly to her side. Like a fresh burn, a sudden pain pulsed in the spot where the ruby used to rest between her breasts. Her skin had its own memory of what her mind would never be able to forget. But what was worse than the memory was that it obscured those first sweet moments. It would always be the bad that she remembered first, Marina thought, never the slim promise of happily ever after that came before it. If only time could have stopped right there. Yesterday—could it possibly have been just yesterday? She squeezed her eyes shut, trying to lock herself into the amber of that moment.

Gideon had been the good end to a bad day. Her meeting with Madeline, the pile of dead roses and her appointment with Cassie had all swirled into a potent mix of negativity. Marina felt tense and uneasy when she finally said good-bye to Cassie, the sun sinking in time with her mood. Then Gideon called and set everything to right.

"I'm coming to pick you up," he said. "I'll meet you at your house."

"Is there anything special I should wear . . . or do?"

"You're fishing," he told her, "but I'm not biting. It's a surprise. Wear whatever you're most comfortable in. Does that help?"

"Not at all," she said, smiling.

It wasn't until Marina got home that she realized Gideon hadn't told her when he'd be picking her up. She didn't know how much time she had to get ready for whatever it was he had planned for her. She felt gritty and in need of another shower, so she stripped off her clothes and her chain. Halfway to the bathroom, it occurred to her that she wouldn't be able to hear him at the door if she was in the shower. She stood still in the middle of her room for a moment, naked and frozen with indecision. In the end, she opted to stay dry and change clothes. She pulled a pair of old soft jeans from her closet and then, on impulse, she took out an embroidered lace bra that had never before seen the light of day. Marina caught a glimpse of herself in the mirror as she reached around to secure the hooks. The bra was beautiful and alluring and obviously designed to be worn alone. A definite statement of intent, Marina thought, although by the time it was uncovered—*if* it was uncovered—that intent would be obvious. Marina finished her ensemble with a black cotton turtleneck and was about to slip the chain back around her neck when she heard Gideon pulling into her driveway. Tucking the ring and chain into the pocket of her jeans, Marina grabbed her purse and flew to the front door.

Gideon's hand was raised and ready to knock when she opened the door. He took in her appearance and smiled. "In a hurry?" he asked. Marina noticed that he was dressed similarly to her, in faded jeans and a pale chambray shirt. His hair was damp as if it had just been washed and she regretted that she hadn't had time to take a shower. Looking at him spurred a quick memory of how she'd pleasured herself that morning and she blushed.

"Not in a hurry, no," she said. "I just wanted to be ready."

"Do you know where we're going?"

"No," she said. "It's a surprise, right?"

"I thought maybe you . . . considering what you do, it would be difficult to surprise you."

"It isn't like that," Marina said. "Just because—"

"I know," he interrupted. "I'm just kidding." Gideon smiled again, but his eyes were very dark; there was nothing to indicate that he was anything but serious. "Well, since you *are* ready, let's go, shall we?"

Once they were in Gideon's truck and on the road, their conversation dwindled into an expectant but easy silence. Gideon turned on the radio, still set to the oldies rock station, and the sound of Jefferson Starship's "Miracles" filled the space between them.

Gideon drummed his fingers softly on the steering wheel even though the song was heavier on melody than rhythm. For a moment Marina found herself wishing she really was psychic so she could read the thoughts in his head. As he wove through streets heading east along the San Elijo Lagoon, it occurred to her how much she still didn't know about him. It had only been two months, after all, and they hadn't spent that much time together if you added it all up. She knew he was renting a condo in Oceanside, but he'd never taken her there. ("It's ugly," he'd told her. "I'd be embarrassed.") He was a general contractor working on a development near where he lived, but Marina didn't exactly know what he did there. ("Very boring," he'd said.) He claimed to have come from Texas, but he'd offered no details of the place and she didn't know where he'd grown up or gone to school. She did know that he was an only child—they had that in common—but she didn't know if there was an ex-wife or even a child in his past. But maybe that didn't matter; maybe slow discovery was better than knowing all at once. At any point Marina could have pushed for more details, but she never had.

He was driving toward Rancho Santa Fe, the expensive and beautiful neighborhood where Madeline and Andrew lived. Marina knew the way well.

"I guess we're not going to Lucky," she said finally.

"No," he answered. "I think you'll like this better."

"So much cloak-and-dagger," she said, instantly realizing that she sounded ridiculous. She'd spent most of her life perfecting a tone of grave seriousness. Flippancy was a language she didn't know how to speak. But

Gideon didn't seem to care or even notice. He was busy turning left, then right, and then parking on the side of a lushly landscaped hill.

"The mystery is over," he said. "We're here." He took Marina's hand as she got out of the car and he led her through what looked like a miniature community of cottages with little paths between them. It was only when they arrived at a numbered door and he pulled out a plastic key card that she realized they were at a hotel.

"Well," she said softly as he opened the door. "This is . . . something."

The suite was large and airy, a perfect interplay of white down, bleached wood and gray marble. There was a fireplace in one corner of the room and double doors leading to a private patio beyond that. And there was a bed: king-size, four-poster and covered with a canopy. Marina's eyes moved from the bed to the night table beside it, where a giant bouquet of long-stemmed pink roses stretched out of a glass vase. The whole room was full of their scent. Marina flashed on the image of the rotten roses on her doorstep, but then it was gone, replaced by the beautiful scene in front of her. She reached for words that would make him understand how she was feeling, but she couldn't find them. *Surprised* was inadequate, as was *happy* or any of the words she had for joy. She had nothing with which to compare this experience. Nobody had ever done anything like this for her before.

"Do you like it?" he asked. "It's very private."

"It's lovely," Marina said at last.

"You're probably hungry," Gideon said. "I was thinking room service; they have a great restaurant here." He crossed the room and opened the sliding doors to the patio. "Probably not warm enough to eat outside, but we could chance it."

Marina walked over to Gideon and stood as close to him as she could without their bodies touching. She could feel the heat of his skin and smell a trace of lemony cologne on his freshly shaved jaw. She wanted this moment, full as it was of anticipation and longing, to carry on forever. He reached over and cupped her face with his hand, his eyes asking her to take the lead.

"I'm not hungry," she said, her throat so thick she had to clear it. "At least, not yet."

"Okay."

"Okay," she echoed.

"There's also wine," he said, breaking the moment to go stand next to the bed. "I have some amarone here." He pointed to a dark bottle hidden behind the roses and gave her a smiling shrug. "I figured it worked well enough the first time." Marina could only nod. "Should we drink?" he asked.

"No," Marina said, and again she walked over to him. But this time she didn't stop until she was pressed up against him, her arms traveling up the sides of his back and pulling him close. He leaned down, covered her mouth with his and stayed there for a while, just savoring. Still locked in their embrace, he turned her around in a half-twist, guiding her gently backward and down until she was lying flat on the bed and he was on top of her. His heaviness felt both familiar and very strange. She had a sense of *jamais vu*—the feeling that she'd been here before but didn't recognize the place or the man touching her now as if he knew her.

It was happening: the pulling of buttons and zippers, the frantic removal of clothing and the shifting of newly naked limbs. Marina felt her body go hot and cold, her blood rushing. She closed her eyes, but feeling clumsy and blind, opened them again and blinked against the lamplight, which suddenly seemed too bright. He was crushing her now, his full weight pressing into her as she tried to move under him. Her body felt awkward, as if she had lost the ability to operate it, as if she'd forgotten where to put her arms and legs, as if she'd never done this before and didn't know how it worked. Gideon tried to slide her hips beneath his, but she was pulling in the opposite direction. He was working too hard and breathing heavily. The room suddenly felt crowded and airless, and Marina gasped for breath. Gideon stopped, raised himself off of her and then quietly moved to the other side of the bed. Their bodies were still close but no longer touching.

For several moments, neither of them spoke or turned to look at the other. Marina stared up at the ceiling and felt her heartbeat slowly return to a normal rhythm. She wondered what should come next, apologies or laughter. She could almost hear the conversation they would have, each one telling the other something along the lines of "It's not you, it's me," and then the inevitable deconstruction of what had gone wrong and why. Marina didn't want to have that conversation, didn't want to speak at all. But she started forming the words anyway and was about to let them out when Gideon reached over and took her hand, lacing his fingers through hers. Warmth and relief flowed through her. He rolled to his side and put his other hand low on her belly in the hollow made by her hip. It was just enough, that light graze, and she felt desire return, sure and steady. She turned her head and saw his eyes on her, not angry or even confused— just still, patient and waiting.

Marina took his hand and held it against her mouth, first kissing his palm, then moving to his fingers, tasting each one with her tongue. He closed his eyes and smiled. "Well," he said softly. His arm was starting to tremble and once more Marina pulled him close. Now he held her, kissed her, ran his hand still wet from her mouth down the length of her spine. She pushed gently and they turned together so that she was on top of him. Now it was easy, no mistakes, just skin and warmth and pressure. "Better," he said, and then no more words were needed.

Chapter 19

Marina opened her eyes and stared out at the endless ocean. Words were always the problem, she thought. Too much talk, too much conversation. They should have stayed like that—no speaking, no words, just their bodies moving together in an endless loop of lovemaking. It would have been possible, Marina thought, because for hours they didn't speak at all.

They slept, woke, made love again, and then it was near dawn, a cool blue-gray light coming in from the sliding glass doors. Marina was drifting in the place between dreams and consciousness when she noticed Gideon staring at her in a strange way—a look she hadn't seen since the day he'd come to her office. He was assessing her, something cold and hard in his eyes. She was lying on her stomach, her face half buried in her pillow, and it took him a moment to realize that she was watching him watch her.

"You're awake," he said. The hard look receded but didn't disappear. Marina smiled. Gideon placed his finger between her shoulder blades and drew a line straight down her back. "This tattoo," he said. "It must have taken a long time to do. What is it?"

Marina felt her whole body go tense. Her tattoo was out of sight, so most of the time she forgot it was even there. But now it seemed to be burning three-dimensional under Gideon's hand. She pulled herself up into a sitting position and pushed the hair out of her face. "It's—they're the signs of the zodiac. I mean, the symbols for the signs of the zodiac." Gideon's face was uncomprehending. "You know, astrology."

"Astrology," he repeated. "That's some dedication. It must have hurt."

"It did," Marina said. "But it wasn't my idea. I had this done when I was a kid. Actually, my mother had it done. Her boyfriend was a tattoo artist."

"Your *mother* wanted you to have a tattoo?"

"It wasn't . . . She wasn't the best mother, let's put it that way. It's a long story."

"I have time," Gideon said. "I'd like to know."

There was something about the tone of his voice—edged with some kind of longing or need—and the sudden openness in his face—more naked and exposed than his body—that compelled Marina to reveal the story she never shared and hated remembering. It was as if he was offering to take the burden from her and carry it away. So she told him about the traveling, the dirty apartments and the endless succession of men. And once all of that was out, there was no way to avoid talking about the drugs and the constant search for money to pay for them, so she told him about that, too, how her mother had stumbled on the bright idea of pimping her out as a miniature fortune-teller. The tattoo, Marina explained, was just part of the package her mother was selling. It could have been worse, she supposed; she'd never starved, even though there were some hungry days. Marina got caught up in her own narrative, turning her inner eye to the past. She could see a rush of images: overflowing ashtrays and empty liquor bottles. Her mother, passed out wherever she fell. Rafe's dirty, stained fingers on her skin.

"Did you know you were psychic then?" Gideon asked. "Did you even know what that meant?"

But I'm not psychic. There's no such thing; only luck, timing and observation. Marina almost said the words out loud, but she pursed her lips and kept them in. "You don't really question the gift," Marina said finally. "It's just there. I suppose it helped me survive. And not too much worse for the wear. No scars. Permanent ink, yes, but no physical scars." Marina trailed off, remembering suddenly that Gideon was listening.

"Where's your mother now?" he asked. His voice was rough with an emotion Marina couldn't place.

"She's dead. Fifteen years now."

"Overdose?"

"Funny thing about that," Marina said. "She was off drugs—or said she was, anyway. She found a rehab that would take her and she even got a sponsor. She was on the way to a meeting when she crashed her car into a tree." Marina tried to laugh, but it came out sounding more like a shout. "Life likes those kinds of ironies," she said.

After a moment Gideon said, "It sounds like you never really made peace with her. Must be hard for you to imagine what a good mother might be like."

"You have a good mother," Marina said. "Obviously."

"Had," Gideon answered. "My mother died . . . not too long ago. But, yes, she was a very good mother. And she only saw the good in other people."

"That's lucky," Marina said.

"Not for her."

A strange tension vibrated between the two of them for a few moments. Gideon was very still, his head turned in her direction but his eyes focused on some unseen point beyond the room. Marina caught the scent of the roses and was reminded of her dream. It hadn't woken her this morning—the first time she hadn't dreamed it in weeks. And why should it? He was here, next to her. She'd caught up with him. A little clutch of panic gripped her in the stomach. There were only inches of distance between them, but she felt she had to close the gap. She leaned over, a sudden jerky movement, and fell onto him rather than curling into him as she wanted. His arms came up to fold her in and hold her close. He rested his head on hers. Marina's heart was racing. She was struck with an almost uncontrollable urge to blurt out what she was feeling and had to fight it, biting her lip to hold it in.

"Marina," he said, seeming to wait for her to answer. But she couldn't speak, because the words *I love you* would come falling out and she wouldn't be able to pull them back.

"I need to tell you something," he said finally. She lifted her head, looked as deeply into his eyes as she could stand and waited for him to say the words that were in her own mouth. But those words didn't come. What he said was "I think we should get something to eat."

Marina tried to smile, tried to go along with what had to be a joke, but her lips wouldn't make the required movements. "You needed to tell me that we should eat?" she said.

He put his hands in her hair, now affectionate and playful. "Yes," he said. "But that's not all. I just think I have to eat something first. Aren't you hungry? You must be." As soon as he said it, Marina realized that she was famished. She couldn't remember the last time she'd eaten. Yes, it would be good to eat, but still something tugged at her. She didn't want to let him go, even for the time it would take to eat a slice of toast.

"I am," she said. "Very hungry."

Gideon ordered room service and they ate in bed: croissants, berries, melon and muffins, with coffee and mimosas. Why not? Day was night and night was day while they were between these sheets. No need to ever leave this island, Marina thought. Which was why she was disappointed, even unsettled, when Gideon got out of bed and opened the sliding glass doors.

"It's so beautiful," he said. "Shall we sit outside for a bit?"

No, Marina thought. *No, no, no.* But she said, "Sure." Slowly, reluctantly, she climbed out of the bed and walked over to the doors. She leaned into Gideon, wrapping her arms tightly around his bare back, relishing the feel of his skin and muscles under her hands. "Or we could just go back to bed," she said.

He ran his hands across her back and then down her arms, reaching around to tilt her face up to his. "I didn't come to you for a reading, Marina," he said.

"What?" She was confused.

"When we met. I was looking for you. I'd *been* looking for you. It took me a long time to find you." The words themselves were romantic, things a man drunk on love would say. But Gideon's tone—both dark and strangely apologetic—gave them a different meaning. "What I'm trying to say is, you weren't recommended by anyone. I need to tell you how I got here, Marina."

Marina pulled back from their embrace, her heart sinking. "Okay," she said. "Let me—I feel like I should get dressed." She poked around for her clothes, which were haphazardly strewn and mixed with Gideon's on the floor. She picked up her jeans and saw that her ring and chain were about to fall out of the pocket where she'd hurriedly stashed them before running out of the house. She shook her head, not believing that she hadn't thought to put them in a safer place before now, and slipped the chain around her neck. The ring felt strangely hot against the bare skin of her breast. That was when she saw that Gideon was standing very still, staring at her as if . . . *he'd like to kill her.* That was the thought that ran through Marina's head and she felt herself get very, very cold.

"What?" she said. "What is it?" There was panic in her voice—she could hear it. He said nothing, his lips folded into a thin white line, but he finally moved out of his statue pose to come over to her and shadow her like an eclipse. He reached down and for a moment she thought he was going to hit her. His eyes looked murderous. Slowly and stiffly, as if the movement caused him pain, Gideon lifted the ring off her chest and held it between his thumb and forefinger.

Marina felt the force of a huge electric shock take her breath away. The ground under her seemed to be shifting, but she was standing stone still. Her mind was a collision of images she couldn't stop from coming in rapid succession: the red gleam of the ring magnified a thousand times,

Gideon's hateful eyes, her hands on a old woman's soft hands, the ring around that woman's neck, the woman's frightened eyes—Mrs. Golden— they were Mrs. Golden's eyes, her hands, her ring, Gideon's brown eyes, Mrs. Golden's brown eyes, the same eyes. The same eyes. *"He has your eyes."* She heard herself say it and groaned aloud. She was shaking, every- thing in motion as if the floor were buckling underneath the bed. The room went very bright, blinding her, and then completely black before fading in again. She heard laughter, weeping, wails—all in a rush of sound that assaulted her ears. The room was suddenly full of people, climbing over each other, reaching toward her, their faces so familiar but all blending into each other. She shut her eyes and tried to scream but couldn't make a sound. *Stop!* She heard the shout inside her head, and opened her eyes. The room steadied, stopped spinning. The noise and the images were gone.

But he wouldn't let go, wouldn't move away, wouldn't take those eyes—his mother's eyes—off her face. Marina's heart bounced and skipped; the blood drained from her face. She was sure she was going to faint, or that he would kill her with the ferocity of that look.

"How long have you known?" he said. He was so close that she could feel the heat of his breath against her face.

"I . . . I d-didn't kn-know." Marina had started shivering and her teeth were chattering. She struggled to regain some control.

"What kind of person are you?" he asked. "What kind of person does this?" He stood back, but didn't let go of the ring. The chain pulled tight across Marina's neck, jerking her forward.

"You're hurting—"

"Take it off," he said.

Marina could feel the weight of realization crushing her; she'd been wrong about her dream. It wasn't she trying to catch him, but he who had caught her.

"Take it off," he repeated, more menace in his voice now.

"Let go," she said, "and I will."

Gideon let the ring drop and it landed with an audible smack against her skin. There was a thin sharp pain where it fell; a shard of glass piercing her breastbone. She took the chain off, the ring dangling between her fingers for the last time, and handed it to him. He took it, looked down at it and then closed his hand around it, hiding it from her. His shoulders slumped, the anger and menace seeming to drain out of him all at once. She could see his throat working.

"You took *everything* from her," he said. "At the end . . ." Gideon looked at Marina with such misery that she could feel it as an ache in her bones. "She was eating cat food. She didn't have the money to buy real food."

Marina had to look away from him. Feeling more naked now than ever, she pulled on her jeans and the turtleneck she'd finally found on the floor. The light played tricks on her eyes as she went through the motions. Her body looked as if it were covered with thin silvery trails and handprints—*his* handprints. *Cover it,* she thought. Gideon stood where he was, his own nakedness now incongruous and strange. He held out his fist. A bit of gold chain escaped from his grip and dangled from his closed fingers.

"How could you take this?" he asked "How can you be that evil?"

"You've got it wrong," Marina said, suddenly finding her voice. "I didn't take it. She gave it to me."

Gideon's laughter was ugly. "Right," he said. "That's what they all say."

"It's true, Gideon. I didn't want to take it. She asked me to wear it."

"Why would she do that? This ring was so important to her. Why would she take it off and give it to *you?*"

So I could keep you safe, Marina thought, feeling her face flush. There was no way she could explain this to him. She was tried and convicted and the only thing left now was for him to sentence her. "Marina . . ." She felt a pain in her chest at the sound of her name in his mouth. "Is there anything about you that's real? Is there anything that has meaning for you?"

Marina stood up, tried to move in close to him, but there was a barrier between them now as impenetrable as a brick wall.

"I am real," she said finally. "This is real."

"This . . . ," he began, and he stopped for a moment, wrestling with the words. "This was a mistake." He moved away from her, picked up his clothes from the floor and put them on with the grim determination of a soldier suiting up for battle. Marina saw clearly now how much he resembled his mother, whom she could almost see—no, *could* see—standing between the two of them. Marina looked at her hallucination dead on and Mrs. Golden looked back at her, her hand pointing first to her neck and then to Marina's. *Wear it,* Mrs. Golden said. *You promised to wear it.*

"If you knew who I was," Marina asked, turning her eyes to Gideon, "why all of this?"

They were both fully dressed now, only the rumpled bed to indicate that there had been any intimacy between the two of them. Everything about Gideon suggested stony distance, from his face to his rigid posture. He seemed so far away from her, which is why what he said next shocked her into trembling silence.

"I fell in love with you," he said.

When Marina looked back on it later, she couldn't remember any of the specific words that he'd used after that. She'd absorbed his story rather than listening to it—all the pieces hitting her like blows. He hadn't come looking for her until months after his mother had died. It had taken him that long to put it all together. He couldn't figure out where all the money had gone—why she'd been reduced to such a horrible state. She'd never told him anything and by the time he got to her in Florida it was too late. And there was the ring. He knew how much that ring meant to his mother, so far beyond its physical value, and how she wouldn't have parted with it unless . . . well, he didn't know unless what, couldn't even begin to imagine. He'd finally figured out who had taken the money, but somewhere along the line he'd convinced himself that his mother had lost the ring, because by then he'd found Marina and realized that she couldn't have taken it. Whatever else she was capable of, it didn't include stealing the thing most precious to an old woman whose only fault had been to trust her. What was the most difficult thing for him to swallow now was how he had come to believe in Marina as well. That was what he'd wanted to tell her; that he'd come looking for her but that his desire for vengeance had turned into desire for her. He'd convinced himself that his mother hadn't made a mistake after all; that leading him to Marina had been the last and best thing she'd done for him. But self-deception was obviously hereditary. Marina was a liar and a thief—a grifter to the bone. The proof was in his hand.

By the time he was finished, Marina was damp with sweat and breathing hard. Tears she couldn't remember shedding had made her face wet. "Please," she said, "you have to believe me. Your mother asked me to wear this ring. I took . . . On our last session, she gave me three thousand dollars. That's all."

"That's *all?*"

"No, you don't understand! I wasn't the only psychic your mother saw. She had—she had a whole roster of psychics she went to. She knew what she was doing, Gideon. All I took from her was three thousand dollars. She had more than that in her purse that day."

"I don't believe you. You stole her ring."

"No, Gideon, no, no. I didn't steal it. She gave it to me, she asked me to wear it. It's the truth." Marina hesitated, drawing in a breath. She had to tell him why she'd never given it back, although she didn't know herself. Even now, she felt its absence like a hole in her chest.

Gideon's mouth was twisted into a mirthless grin. She needn't worry that he was going to make trouble for her, he told her; she could carry on as she pleased. Sooner or later, she would be called to account for her actions, but it wouldn't be by him. He was leaving, already gone. He picked up the vase of roses and for a moment she thought he was going to walk out with it, but he turned and thrust it at her so hard that the flowers hit her in the face. Several petals came loose, falling like pink confetti at her feet.

"These you can keep," he said. And then, "You'll have to find your own way home." Marina felt the rush of air as he walked past her and heard the door close seconds later. She stood there with the vase in her arms, the scent of roses enveloping her, until her muscles couldn't support the weight any longer and she had to put it down.

Salt water swirled around Marina's feet and receded. The tide was coming in. *Pretend everything is normal.* That warning had sounded in her head the minute Gideon left her alone in that room, and it hadn't stopped since. The only problem, Marina knew, was that nothing would ever be normal again.

A small child ran past Marina and splashed into the water. He was wearing a tiny red bathing suit and had a headful of blond curls. She could hear him laughing as he smacked the wet sand with his little starfish hands. He ventured a little farther out and sat down, the water rising up above his rounded belly. Marina looked behind her and saw a woman in a yellow bikini lying on the sand, her face raised up into the sun as if to catch every tanning ray. Marina knew what was going to happen two seconds before the wave came in and covered the child. She scrambled to her feet and ran into the water, diving down to pull out the little boy. But there was nothing in the surf except sand and seaweed. It couldn't have dragged him out so fast, Marina thought, and turned back to the shore in a panic. The woman was gone now, too. Marina was wet and her eyes stung from the salt. The whole scene had been a hallucination. Marina felt the pressure building behind her forehead, a combination of headache and forming tears. She had to get out of here and go to her office. Today she had to work. Tomorrow she would start thinking about whether it was time to leave California.

She crossed the sand, the wet edges of her skirt clinging to her legs. But she didn't care about being wet; all she wanted at that moment was a cup of hot coffee. It wouldn't be Rosa's. Something else to cross off the list forever. She was almost at the edge of the beach when she saw them coming toward her, the little boy in the red suit and his mother in the yellow bikini. Excited and ruddy-cheeked, he ran ahead of her by several feet.

"Connor!" the mother called. "Slow down!" The boy wasn't listening to her. And soon, Marina thought, she wouldn't be listening to him.

Marina stopped directly in front of the woman. "You need to watch him," she said. "The tide comes in very fast. He could get hurt or . . . You need to watch him. Carefully."

"Who the *hell* are *you?*" the woman said. "What is your *problem?* Connor! Come back here!" This time he came back and stood next to his mother, wrapping one chubby arm around her slim tan leg.

"Just watch him," Marina said, moving forward.

"Watch yourself!" the woman yelled at her. "This is *harassment,* you know. Telling me how to take care of my own kid!"

Marina kept walking. She only looked back once when she got to the main road. The woman had picked up her boy and was holding him tight on one hip as she walked down to the water.

Part II

The Gift

*February–
March 2007*

Chapter 20

The night is so thick and dark that she feels blinded by it. There are no streetlamps, no moon, and the stars give no light. She is walking, walking and her feet are aching. The road feels like a treadmill under her; she can't get there, can't reach him. The smell of roses and smoke clings to her, invades her senses. He is walking several yards ahead, hands in his pockets, looking down at the road. She is running now, sharp rocks piercing her feet, but somehow the running makes her slower. She yells out to him: Stop! But no sound comes out of her throat. She is choking on the smoke and the smell of the roses. He stops walking and turns. She knows this place. Stop! He can't hear her. Now she is right behind him, the distance closed, and he is turning around. She tries to shut her eyes but they are already closed. She hears an echoing cough and watches him turn. There is a flash of light, an explosion, and then everything goes black again.

Marina woke with a start and an unstoppable surge of nausea. She ran, stumbling, to the bathroom, barely making it in time to lean over the toilet and vomit until her stomach was empty and she was racked with painful heaves. It took a long time to stop, and by the end of it she was exhausted and sweating. She leaned her hot head against the cool bathroom tiles and waited for the worst of it to pass. She could not remember ever being so aware of every little flicker and stirring in her body. She could hear the blood moving through her organs; feel the slight twitching of the muscles around her mouth and her neck. And there, deep within the bones of her pelvis, she could feel a growing heaviness, a pulling of tendons, the approaching shadow of future pain. It didn't feel like pre- or postmenstrual cramping. It felt like a rushing together of cells, gathering energy, pulling focus from every other part of her brain and body to that one center point. It felt like an alien invasion.

As soon as she could stand without dizziness forcing her back to the toilet, Marina splashed water on her face, got dressed and headed out the door. A few minutes later, she was standing in the middle of the Rite Aid on Encinitas Boulevard, staring at the vast array of pregnancy test kits. There were early tests, late tests, any time of day tests. Plus sign, you're pregnant; negative, you aren't. Pink stripes, blue stripes. Two for $12.99, store brand for $8.99 plus a $2.00 mail-in rebate, please allow eight to ten weeks for delivery.

Or nine months.

Some careless person who clearly had no right to be a parent had left an infant on the floor in the middle of the aisle, Marina noticed as she moved closer to the rack. The baby couldn't have been more than a few months old, so small and encased in one of those tiny terry-cloth suits. The suit was white (stupid color to put a baby in, Marina thought) with shiny snaps and covered feet. She—Marina could tell it was a girl—lay calmly on the dirty plastic tile of the Rite Aid, looking around with big hazel eyes, kicking up those small covered feet. Marina looked up and over to the pharmacy window, thinking maybe the baby's mother was there waiting for a prescription and would be looking over to make sure the child was all right. But the empty window showed only a listless-looking pharmacy assistant leaning against the jamb.

Marina's eyes flickered back to the baby, but she had vanished. And that was when Marina realized that *it* was happening again. A fresh swell of nausea gathered in the pit of her stomach. Below the nausea, her strange not-quite-pain grew in strength, reminding her why she'd come here. Marina knew what the answer to this test would be, but she had to pick one and buy it anyway. She needed proof.

As she was reaching for the least expensive generic brand (because what did it matter if the test had a brand name?), Marina felt a tug on the hem of her skirt. Looking down, she saw what she immediately knew to be an older version of the disappearing baby from before. This little girl was about five years old, her long dark hair tied in a neat ponytail and her startling green-gold eyes staring into Marina's core. The girl wore a white cotton dress with eyelet detailing on the hem. Her small feet were bare, the small clean toes painted a happy pink. She smelled sweet, like sugary candy. There was a bitter taste in Marina's mouth.

"What do you want?" she whispered to the little girl, who looked so much like Marina at that age. She whispered because she had to speak to this child, hallucination or not, but kept her voice low enough to avoid appearing more like a crazy woman than she already did. She'd seen them plenty of times, those homeless schizophrenics shouting at God and the government, their misspelled cardboard signs begging for help.

The child said nothing. Marina closed her eyes, nausea welling up. For a horrified moment she thought she was going to vomit on the pregnancy test display in front of her. For several seconds Marina just stood there, eyes closed, willing herself back to normalcy. When she could no longer feel the pull on her skirt or detect the sweet smell, Marina opened her eyes and looked around. Nothing—except for an elderly man examining vitamins at the end of the aisle and trying to watch Marina out of the corner of his eye. She needed to leave and get out before she called any further attention to herself.

A teenage girl in white shorts and a T-shirt brushed by Marina too close and bumped her slightly. " 'Scuse me. Sorry."

"It's okay," Marina mumbled, distracted and woozy. The girl breezed by and Marina turned to watch her round the corner, her long dark pony-tail swishing. Before disappearing into the next aisle, she turned and fixed Marina with a smile, hazel eyes sparkling, one dimple, identical to the one in Marina's own face, showing on her left cheek. *What's your name?* Marina wanted to ask her. *Are you happy? Where is your mother?*

The line at the cashier snaked all the way into the shelves of seasonal candy markdowns. Marina didn't know how long she'd be able to stand amidst this crowd, which seemed to be pressing in closer and closer. But then someone must have opened a door, because a breeze suddenly grazed Marina's cheekbones and she felt she could breathe again. The nausea subsided a little and she started to feel almost normal. The people in line next to her looked normal as well—solid and real, not visions. A middle-aged woman in a too-tight suit clutched a chilled bottled coffee drink and a printer cartridge in one hand while her other held a cell phone to her ear.

"I told him we were going to need four of those," the woman was saying. "I know I told him, like, a dozen times at least. I'm not going to be responsible if . . . what? Well, I don't care what *she* says . . ."

The woman was going to get fired from her job, Marina knew suddenly. She was going to be outraged, hire an attorney and attempt to sue for wrongful termination, but then they were going to find out about the petty cash she'd taken for her own use—Marina had a fleeting vision of a very expensive piñata at a child's birthday party with several adults drinking mojitos in the background—and the company was going to end up suing *her.* She was going to go bankrupt and would have to move—Marina could see U-Haul boxes on a scraggly lawn . . .

Marina shook her head, took a deep breath and moved her gaze to the skinny young man with bad acne who was shuffling from foot to foot as he waited in line. He was holding a liter of motor oil, a liter of Coke and a half gallon of generic vodka. Marina had to stop herself from telling him to put the vodka back on the shelf—that if he planned to drink it tonight, and she knew that he did, he was going to get into a car accident. He wasn't going to die, but he *was* going to get arrested and lose his license.

Ahead of her, a young woman—tan, excessively fit, silicone-enhanced breasts protruding from the sides of her small, lime green tank top—was arguing with the cashier about the advertised special on mascara. Marina found herself getting irritated by the sheer ridiculousness of it. *Why bother?* she wanted to ask the young woman. *Mascara isn't going to make a difference. He isn't going to call you tonight, tomorrow or ever again.*

Marina fumbled in her purse for cash. She needed to complete this transaction as quickly as possible and get away from these swirling conversations and mirages.

Finally, the woman gave up her quest for the extra dollar off and left the register with a swish of indignation and it was Marina's turn. She laid her test kit on the counter and looked up. That the cashier was an older version of the three girls she had already seen in the aisles of the store was not a surprise to Marina, but this didn't make it any less disturbing. The cashier smiling at her now, asking if she was paying with cash or credit, looked so much like Marina at twenty years old that she could have been a replica. If not an exact copy, then . . . She could have been Marina's daughter. Yes, that was it, Marina realized now. She was looking at her own daughter—a child whose existence would soon be confirmed by the test Marina held in her shaking hands.

"Ma'am? Cash or credit?"

Marina mumbled something about cash and dug around in her purse. When she looked up again her daughter had disappeared, replaced by a skinny little blond girl who looked to be at the end of her patience.

"I'm sorry," Marina said. "Thank you." She handed the clerk what seemed like the right amount of money and then turned around and left, moving as fast as she could and not looking back.

Marina got into her car and headed to her office, debating how to go about doing what had to be done next. Her pregnancy test had been definitive in a way she was sure nobody else had ever experienced.

Earlier, when she got home from Rite Aid, she was trembling so badly that it had taken several minutes to open the box and then the sealed plastic packet inside. All the while she thought what a pointless endeavor it was; the outcome was obvious. When she finally managed to wrest the test stick out of its packet, she laughed, the way people sometimes did at funerals. The test was of the plus/minus variety: a plus sign for yes and a minus for no. But the answer was already there when Marina opened the factory-sealed, unused test: a pink neon plus sign that seemed to glow in the dim light of her bathroom. She threw the test stick on the floor, hearing it clatter on the tiles, and left her house immediately. She needed the safety and sterility of her office to figure out what to do now that she had her answer.

But Marina didn't know where to start. Did one just open the phone book and start calling doctors and clinics at random? It wasn't as if anyone advertised abortions. Her brain felt thick and stupid. She'd never needed anything like this before, a small miracle in itself really, but still she should know where to go or who to call.

"Like mother like daughter."

At first Marina thought the sound was coming from inside her own head and she blinked hard as if that would shut it off.

"I wanted to do the same thing to you. The sins of the mother . . ."

Marina recognized the voice and it wasn't her own. Nor was it coming from inside her head. Next to her, reclined in the passenger seat, her dead mother sat inspecting her dirty fingernails. Her hair was long and unclean, her clothes were wrinkled and slept in and her bare feet were black with grime. Death, Marina thought, had done nothing to improve her mother's appearance. Marina forced herself to keep her eyes on the road and not engage with the specter, but it was all she could do to keep from pushing her filthy mother out of her car.

"It was a lot harder back then, you know," Marina's mother said. "Abortions were still illegal. Not that going around the law ever meant anything to me, of course. The point is, I didn't care about the law and I didn't want to be a mother. That's right; I didn't want you, Marina. But I didn't have the money and I couldn't find anyone to do it. And then it was too late. Always too late. And now here you are." Marina stole a sidelong glance at her mother, who was smiling, showing a mouthful of gray teeth. Marina looked at her mother's eyes, the same shape and color as her own. She searched her memory for a time when she'd thought her mother was beautiful. There had to be one, but it wouldn't come.

"Why are you talking to me?" Marina asked. Her voice sounded small and stifled.

"Because you need to be told," her mother answered. "I couldn't get rid of you and you won't be able to get rid of that one." She pointed at Marina's belly. "Might as well save yourself the trouble."

"Go away," Marina whispered and turned her eyes back to the road.

"You're going to have to make it right," Marina's mother said. She leaned over, so close Marina could hear the words right inside her ear. "I had to have you and you have to have her. You need to know that."

"No," Marina said. "No, I won't. I don't."

"Your problem," her mother said, "was you always thought you knew everything. You don't listen."

"Why would I listen to you of all people?"

"Because if you don't, I'm going to have to keep coming back," she heard her mother say. "And I'm sure you don't want *that*."

"I don't hear you," Marina said. "You're not really here." She felt a tremor in the air around her and something that sounded like a sigh. Marina glanced to her right. Her mother was gone.

This is how a person went crazy, Marina thought. It happened slowly—excruciating degrees of madness. You saw people who weren't there, heard words that weren't being spoken. And then you started conversing with your own phantoms. So far, she'd been successful about suppressing the urge in public. But how long before she couldn't control it anymore? She was already so close to that edge. For weeks now she'd been holding herself in check even as the constructs of her carefully designed life began crumbling away. Time had taken on a bizarre and unfamiliar shape since the morning Gideon had left her holding that vase full of roses, the moment all this insanity had started. First Mrs. Golden, then Rosa's daughter, and they were only the start. The dead had been mixing freely with the living for Marina, becoming more real as time looped on.

But it wasn't only the dead being conjured for Marina. Taken alone, they would be bearable. But no, at any given moment on any given day, Marina could not be sure if what she was doing or seeing was happening in real time, had already happened or was yet to come. It was like being in a constant state of déjà vu or sleepwalking through a series of layered mirages. This had complicated even the simplest acts, like walking on the beach or ordering a cup of coffee, and made the more complex interactions of her work almost impossible. What had made Marina so successful were her powers of observation and the ability to analyze those observations for her clients. That was all gone now, mutated by the shifting kaleidoscope of visions she saw before her all the time. Marina could only cling to what she thought she was seeing and comment on that. And none of it was what her clients wanted to hear.

Most often, she received the kind of hostile reaction she'd gotten from the woman whose child she'd "seen" drown in the ocean before it actually happened—like the time she met with a first-time client who'd been referred by one of her regulars. The woman introduced herself as Brooke, but as soon as she did, Marina said, "It's nice to meet you, Barbara." The woman bristled immediately and Marina tried to correct herself, but there was nothing to be done—*Barbara* was the only name that would come out of her mouth. "I changed my name a long time ago," the woman huffed, "so I don't know why you want to call me Barbara." But that was only the first thing to go wrong. When Marina commented on the large ornate crucifix Barbara/Brooke was wearing, the woman looked at Marina as if she were certifiable.

"What are you talking about?" she asked. Marina looked again at the woman's neck, which had suddenly become bare.

"I mean," Marina said, struggling, "I *meant* that your faith is very important to you."

"No," the woman said, "I left that behind long ago."

"But that's what's holding you back," Marina said.

"Holding me back from what?"

"There's a woman at the school where you work," Marina said then, completely unable to stop either the images or the words that followed them, "and you are attracted to her. You're in love with her. But you won't go out with her because your faith tells you it's wrong."

The woman stood up so quickly that she almost overturned the table. Her face pinched and white, she said, "I'm not paying you for this. It's . . . it's outrageous." And then she stormed out.

That kind of response was something Marina was starting to get used to, but getting used to it and understanding it were two different things. That Marina was now having visions that could be considered psychic and that those visions were not only unregulated and indecipherable but ruining her *business* as a psychic created a kind of cognitive dissonance within Marina that was impossible to reconcile. Marina wanted to believe that there was a physical explanation for what was happening to her—an alteration in brain function, synaptic messages gone wild—and that it could be fixed or cured. But Marina couldn't be sure of anything except that there was little time to figure it all out. The client base she'd worked so hard to cultivate was disappearing. The new ones seemed either mystified by her behavior or angry with what she said, and the old ones, her core of regulars, seemed to have melted away altogether.

Marina tried to remember the last time she'd seen Madeline and then realized that she'd pushed Madeline away before all of this had happened. But Madeline had never been the type to back off. Nor had Eddie, who suddenly sprang into Marina's mind. She'd wanted him gone, but had always believed he'd stick around, hovering at the fringes of her life. Now she realized she hadn't seen him since that morning at Darling's—the morning of the day that ended with Gideon.

Everything seemed to come back to Gideon. And every night Gideon came back to her in the dream she couldn't stop. Back when the dream was new—it felt so long ago now—Marina had been convinced that Gideon was walking away from her, but now that he really was gone, she was sure that he was walking *to* her, even though she was following him. That she was meant to warn him seemed clear, but everything else about the dream was so confusing. There were the details she couldn't see, blacked out before she could define them, and the sense that she knew the place to which he was heading. She could almost glimpse it. But every night, in every dream, there was an explosion, a flash of light before she could make anything out, and then the sudden horrible knowledge that he was dead. Yes, death was the very clear message of the dream and at the end of it, before it all went dark, Marina had the sense that she hadn't done enough to warn him in time. Before her return to consciousness, Marina felt a physical surge of grief for the loss of him. And as soon as she was awake, the nausea would come—waves upon waves of sickness.

Marina pressed her hands against her belly as if to keep it flat. This pregnancy—she refused to think of it as a *baby*—was the latest and cruelest twist in the story that had begun with Gideon. Her own body had betrayed her, clinging to this piece of him even as her mind knew she had to let him go. He wasn't ever coming back. That was the real message of the dream this time. And she was going to keep having the dream until she terminated the pregnancy, the first step on the path back to normal. In fact, it was probably the hormones that were making her crazy now. She was allergic to pregnancy, Marina thought, and that was just one reason among too many why motherhood was not an option.

Marina had finally reached her office, but had to double back and take the long way around to avoid the construction on the street. She didn't know what they were doing, nor, she suspected, did anyone know why half the street was torn up, but the noise, dust and traffic were choking the neighborhood. By the time she found a parking space, she was exhausted. She decided to just sit in the car for a few minutes and gather herself. At least, for the moment, it was quiet inside this metal shell.

It was not in Marina's nature to wallow or feel sorry for herself. But now she questioned why she'd been singled out for what felt like a tsunami of bad luck. No, not bad luck. It felt much more like punishment. But it was unjust punishment, Marina thought. For a moment the clouds parted and she experienced the kind of clarity she'd once taken for granted but could no longer depend on. It was all about free will, she realized. Every one of her clients, past and present, exercised their free will when they sat down at her table. No arms had ever been twisted. They reached into their pockets to pay her with their own hands. Mrs. Golden had given that ring to Marina because she'd wanted to. Marina's only crime, if it could even be called a crime, was that she hadn't contacted Mrs. Golden soon enough to return the ring before the old lady died.

"You promised to wear it. You promised to keep him safe."

Marina startled at the sound of the words and turned her head to see Mrs. Golden sitting where her mother had been just a few minutes before. This time she didn't try to ignore the vision, although she couldn't tell if it was because she was too tired to resist or if she just preferred Mrs. Golden over her mother.

"I did wear it," Marina said. "I'd be wearing it now if he hadn't taken it back."

"You have to wear the ring," Mrs. Golden insisted. "You have to get it back."

"Well, I don't know how I'm supposed to do that," Marina said. She wondered if anyone was watching her; she surely looked like a lunatic, talking to herself in her car. But then, Marina thought, here in southern California people did the most bizarre things in their cars. Talking to oneself was really the least of it. "He thinks I stole the ring from you," she continued. "I wish you'd tell him what really happened."

"He's not safe!" Mrs. Golden shouted suddenly. "He won't be safe unless you wear the ring!"

"What do you want me to do?" Marina said. She put her head in her hands and pressed her fingers into her eyes until she saw spots. "This is ridiculous," she said to herself. She opened her eyes and turned to her right. The passenger seat was empty once again. "You know," she said to the air, "if you would stick around a little longer, you might be more useful."

Marina got out of the car and walked to her office, laughing at her own craziness. There was nothing funny about it, of course, but she supposed it was better than crying.

Before she even got past her office door, Marina knew that something was wrong. There was a subtle but insistent feeling that the air had been moved—a displacement of molecules. Someone had been inside. There was nothing out of place in the front, but Marina sensed the touch of another person as clearly as if she were looking at glowing fingerprints. She walked slowly to the back, fear and dread taking turns whispering at her ear. She had a flash, not really a memory, of being with Gideon on the day he'd come to see her for the reading he never really wanted. She'd seen what she thought was the shadow of a person exiting through the back door then, although she'd dismissed it as impossible. Nothing was impossible now, Marina thought, and somehow it connected with . . .

Marina looked at what was waiting for her at the table where she did her readings. Her tarot cards were scattered haphazardly on the floor as if they had been thrown up in the air. The tabletop was clear save for two items. In the center, a single dead rose, dried and blackened, lay on top of the one card that wasn't on the floor: Death.

Two thoughts fought each other in Marina's mind as she stared at the tableau in front of her. One was that the person who had broken into her office and staged this scene knew nothing about tarot, witchcraft, voodoo or any other dark arts. Even the greenest practitioners knew that the

Death card didn't signify physical death. Whoever had done this was an amateur. The second thought, rapidly gaining ground, was that it didn't matter. The intent was sinister and Marina was frightened.

She reached over, moved the rose to the side and picked up the card. The room around her seemed to wobble for a moment and then grow darker. Marina's field of vision contracted and when it expanded back she had the sensation that she was no longer in her own body, as if she were looking out through someone else's eyes. She scanned the room, unfamiliar from this perspective, and felt a creeping contempt that wasn't hers, but belonged to the person whose head she was inside of. She smelled rank sweat and something else—some bitter chemical smell. And she could hear thoughts that were not her own as clearly as if she were thinking them.

Goddamn witch. I never should have trusted her. They used to burn them. They never should have stopped doing that. Good idea, burning.

Marina saw the cards fly out and scatter, saw the Death card on the table, saw the dead rose held in a black glove, saw it placed carefully on top.

See how she likes this—something from her own bag of tricks.

Marina felt a wave of hatred, strong and black. But there was something else behind it—something bitter and sad and buried.

Burning—that's what she deserves. Burning like a witch.

Marina felt a sharp jolt, as if she'd been hit in the back of the head, and for a moment the room went completely dark. A second later she was back within herself, her eyes stinging and mouth dry. Her legs suddenly too weak to hold her up, Marina sank into her chair and stared ahead at nothing while her mind tried to make sense of what was happening to her. *Telepathy.* Marina turned the word over in her head, considering its meaning: the connection between one mind and another outside of sensory perception. Before this moment, Marina would have called it a fancy way of saying, "I know what you're thinking." Long-married couples, mothers and children, twins . . . they all shared some telepathic insight, born out of love and familiarity. But what had happened to Marina had nothing to do with love. She'd connected with the mind of someone who hated her enough to want to see her burn alive.

Why is this happening to me? Marina struggled to find the cause. If she could only understand the *why* of it, she thought, everything else—the voices and visions—would all make sense. And if she focused on the why, she wouldn't have to think about *who*. Because there was only one person that angry at her. The name rang loud in her head even as she tried not to hear it. Gideon.

Chapter 21

Madeline sighed, rolled over and kicked the grubby motel blanket off the bed. Her body was shiny with sweat and her lips were throbbing, plumped up and bruised from rough kissing. She could feel other bruises forming, small points all over her hips and thighs where tiny capillaries had been crushed by teeth and fingers. The smell of sex, sharp and earthy, steamed off her like wavy cartoon lines. She was grimy and sticky and she had never felt as satisfied in her entire life.

Those early days with Andrew, when they'd both been in the deepest throes of romantic passion, had come close, but in a different way. Back then they'd both been in love with what the other represented and their emotional wants fueled what their bodies expressed. The heat they generated came from the friction of competing desires as much as it did from their physical lovemaking. That was what made the difference, she supposed. There was love in it, not just sex. But sometimes sex was better without love—or whatever it was that one confused love for. Right now, for example, on this nasty bed that probably held the ragged DNA of a thousand other sinners, Madeline felt something close to physical euphoria. Some secret pleasure center in her brain had come to life, and it didn't matter to her that it had taken this cheap dirty room and the violence of raw need to turn it on.

He wasn't touching her, but she could still feel his hands, his teeth and his tongue all over her body. She shuddered, feeling a tingle at the base of her spine, and realized that she could go again. She wanted more—much more. Wasn't there some kind of animal that had sex until it literally dropped dead? Madeline felt entirely capable of doing just that. Talk about a happy ending.

Her partner in all this sat next to her on the bed, staring straight ahead at the water-stained wallpaper as if he were having a religious vision. And maybe he was, Madeline thought, because she knew it had been at least as good for him. She reached over and ran her hand along the top of his thigh, her fingers questioning his body for response. It wasn't a tender motion. She was salivating, all her senses still on overdrive.

"Damn," he said softly and caught her hand with his. "You got some kind of energy."

"C'mon," she said, and she climbed on top of him, her knees hitting the chipped fake-wood headboard. She grabbed a handful of his hair with each of her hands and pressed herself into him. He stopped her, pulling her hands away from his face before she could get to his mouth.

"I have to take a shower," he said. "And we should probably get out of here."

"Why?"

He lifted her left hand and flicked her wedding ring with his finger. "Because," he said. His mouth curved into a smile but Madeline could see guilt crowding out passion in his blue eyes. And guilt meant that regret wasn't far off, and regret would ruin everything. Right or wrong, what they'd just done had an intensity that rendered it pure and true. Madeline couldn't bear to lose that—not yet.

"No," she said, and she covered his mouth with hers so that he wouldn't be able to answer. It was essential that they not speak now. There was nothing she wanted to know about him other than what she could learn with her hands and hips and tongue. Nor was there anything else he needed to know about her. He mumbled something she couldn't hear and tried to push her away, but she pressed harder, grinding herself into him until she could feel their bones rubbing together. He yielded, becoming passive for only a moment before he clutched at her again, biting her lips and flipping her over as if she weighed no more than the flattened pillows beneath them.

"All right," he said, pushing her knees apart, spreading her legs and squeezing her thighs with his thick fingers. He loomed over her, just long enough for her to see that his whole face was dark with one-pointed need, and then she reached for him and pulled him in.

Afterward, Madeline was completely exhausted and knew if she didn't get up and leave she would have to give in to unconsciousness. The light in the room had changed from noon brightness to the soft glow of afternoon. She had no idea if they'd been there for one hour or three, but it felt as if the clock had stopped and time was up. Her euphoria had given way to something much darker—a heavy front of anger gathering strength and pushing in. He was lying next to her, surrendered and asleep. She nudged his shoulder gently, and when that failed to rouse him she shoved him in the ribs. He startled, reflexively grabbing her wrist so hard that she cried out in pain.

"Hey, sorry," he said, letting go as consciousness flooded back in. "You scared me."

Madeline rubbed her wrist. "We should go," she said.

He lay there for a moment, his brain numbed, and then he sat up and shook his head. "I must have passed out," he said. "Damn. What time is it?"

"I don't know," she said. "No clock in this room. This isn't the kind of place that comes with those amenities. There's probably a Bible in the drawer, though."

That made him laugh even as he was jumping off the bed, awake and all business now. "I have to take a shower," he said. "Wonder what kind of a-men-i-ties are waiting for me in the bathroom."

With great effort, Madeline got off the bed, hating that her bare feet were touching the disgusting carpet. The blood drained from her head as she stood and she staggered a little on the way to her clothes, which she'd at least had the presence of mind to throw on the only chair in the room.

"You all right?" So he'd noticed. Good for him.

"A little weak in the knees," she said. "I'm sure you can understand." She slipped on her shoes first to avoid any further contact with the carpet and then reached for her pants and her bra. Her underwear, a flimsy thong whose price was in inverse proportion to the amount of actual fabric it contained, was destroyed, literally torn to shreds. She'd go without. Madeline looked down at her body as she fastened her bra. She was a mess, bruises on her thighs and red smudges on her breasts. She'd have to check her neck in the bathroom mirror for teeth marks. The rest didn't matter—it wasn't as if Andrew would be seeing it anytime soon. They hadn't had sex since . . . Madeline felt the sharp tinge of bitterness. She couldn't remember the last time her husband had touched her.

"Aren't you going to take a shower?" He seemed stunned or horrified, she couldn't tell which.

"I'll take a shower when I get home. Better amenities there," she said.

He smiled. "Dirty girl," he said. "I like that." He walked over to her and kissed her hard while he slid his hand between her legs, smearing the wetness there. An hour ago those words and that gesture would have sent a thrill through her body, but now it just made her feel sordid. She broke away from him and finished putting on her clothes.

"I'm going to go now," she said. "Okay?"

"Okay."

"I'll—"

"Are we—?"

"Do you—?"

They stopped, words failing them both. "I guess we'll see how it works out," she said finally.

"All right. So good-bye then."

"Right," she said and slung her purse over her shoulder.

A quick shadow passed across his face and his eyes narrowed. "You're not planning to share this with her, are you?" he said.

"*I'm* not going to tell her."

"But you think she's going to know, don't you?"

Madeline shrugged. He waited a beat and then turned and walked into the bathroom without saying anything else. Madeline heard him turn on the water and get into the shower. She took one last look at the ruined bed and headed out, walking fast, making sure to pull the door closed behind her.

Thirty minutes later, Madeline's head was pounding and thick with fury. She hadn't gone home as she should have, but had driven to Encinitas instead, parking on a side street opposite Marina's office. Now she sat slouched and sealed in her car, doors locked and windows rolled up, obsessively twisting the rings on her ring finger until the skin underneath them was red and chafed. Every time it went around, the big four-carat diamond scraped and tore at the delicate webbing between the knuckles. It was showy and heavy—a rich wife's trophy on a rich man's trophy wife—and Madeline wondered if it was sharp and high enough to scratch someone's eyes out.

You're not planning to share this with her, are you?

It was those few little words that had done it, knocked her right off her sexed-up perch and into a swirl of anger. Somehow, everything Madeline did or thought had become about *her*. Even nasty, thrilling sex in a dirty motel room with someone who was so far beneath her standards— even that was somehow about Marina. He'd said it himself—and had known that Madeline was thinking it.

Madeline had tried very hard to make sure there were no tracks leading from her to Marina. She knew about phone records and how easily they could be accessed, so she'd avoided calling Marina from either her house or cell phones. And, this little effort notwithstanding, she'd cut way back on the drive-bys. She'd made a real attempt to scrape Marina out of her mind. But the distance she'd tried to create had ended up working in reverse. Not speaking to Marina only made Madeline more resentful of her. No, resentment wasn't the right word. It was something closer to hatred, but even colder.

It was the rank unfairness of it all that really dug at Madeline. She had poured so much more than money into this woman for psychic insight. Madeline had exposed her deepest, most vulnerable self, had followed every little instruction of Marina's no matter how ridiculous it seemed, had listened slavishly to every word that dropped from her lips. And, of course, there was the money, stacks of it for candles and teas and house calls and readings . . . Madeline ground her teeth. What had it gotten her? She'd ended up with a miscarriage, a ruined marriage and an empty checkbook. But Marina—that bitch had gotten rich spewing her bullshit. But that wasn't the worst of it at all. Marina was fucking *happy*. She had the hot guy and the swell relationship. While Madeline's life circled the drain, Marina's just got better. It was as if Marina had taken everything that should be Madeline's, sucked it right out of her and planted it in her own garden.

So what are you going to do about it?

Madeline heard the sound of her own voice inside her head, harsh and mocking. She twisted her ring, pressing the hard stone into her flesh, feeling the small sharp pain it caused. Yes, she had to do something. She took a long look at Marina's quiet office—nobody coming or going the whole time she'd been sitting there—and started her car. The first step was deciding to act. Everything else would follow.

Chapter 22

Cooper took a sip from his double mocha vanilla latte with extra whipped cream and set it down in the car cup holder, where it fit comfortably despite being an oversize, oversweetened monstrosity of excess. This kind of beverage had become his drink of choice lately, the more fat-filled and sugar-laden the better—part of his own lame attempt at self-destruction. He wondered how long it would take to kill himself with these syrupy coffee drinks and decided that by the time they sent him into a diabetic coma he'd be so fat and disgusting he would have killed himself already. He took another slug from the paper cup and realized that this train of thought didn't even make any sense, but that's how it was these days. Nothing he came up with made any sense. Nothing, that is, except for hating what he'd become. He'd turned into a pale, pill-popping Starbucks addict who spent his days going through old photos and his weepy nights watching old movies and eating raw cookie dough sprinkled with Xanax until he fell asleep. He'd stopped going to the gym, stopped eating anything that couldn't be microwaved in under two minutes and had taken a "leave of absence" from his "job" organizing fund-raisers for his father. Cooper groaned out loud. He was a desperate housewife. That was what he'd been reduced to. Oh, yes, and a stalker, too.

Cooper was parked near enough to Max's office to see when he left the building but not close enough for Max to spot his car. Not that Max would notice, anyway, since Cooper was using a rental car. Yes, that was how insane he'd gotten. Actually, Cooper thought as he used his straw to scoop whipped cream into his mouth, *careful* might be a better word than *insane*. He'd used his own car at first and Max *had* noticed that Cooper was watching his movements—and he was none too happy about it.

"Cooper, I think you might need professional help," Max had said when he'd called. Cooper had been purchasing one of his mondo-grande-cinos when the call came in and he immediately adopted a tone of wounded righteousness.

"Well, that's your specialty, isn't it, Max? Professional help? Physician, heal thy—"

"I'm serious, Cooper. I'm very concerned about you."

"Yeah, I've seen the depth of your concern, Max."

"Look, it's not just the sitting outside my office every day, Cooper, even though you have to stop doing that. Frankly, it's getting a little creepy."

"I don't know what you're talking about."

"Cooper, please. I know you're taking . . . Are you still taking the Xanax?"

"Who is she, Max? Why don't you just tell me who she is? That's all I really want to know."

Cooper heard Max sigh deeply and pictured him rubbing the bridge of his nose as he always did when he was frustrated. There was an ache in Cooper's chest. "I know some really good people, Cooper. I can refer you. It doesn't have to be a permanent thing, but I think you really need to talk to a professional."

It gave Cooper bitter pleasure to deliver his next words. "What makes you think I would ever see a shrink, Max? What makes you think that I'd ever put my trust in another person like *you?*"

"I don't deserve that, Cooper. And you're not helping yourself any."

"Do you care about me at all, Max? Have you ever?"

"You know that I care about you. That's why I want you to get help."

"Fuck you, Max."

"Cooper . . ."

That would have been the time to hang up on him, to make a statement and salvage whatever minuscule portion of his dignity he had left, but Cooper couldn't bring himself to part with whatever piece of Max he had left. And therein lay the problem.

"Please get some help," Max said. "And please don't park outside my office anymore. Or the house. I'm asking you nicely, Cooper." And then *he* hung up. The fucker hadn't even said he was sorry, Cooper thought. That would have been the least—the very least—he could have done.

Cooper had neither sought professional help nor given up keeping a close eye on Max's movements, but it became clear after that conversation that he was going to have to camouflage himself somewhat. Ergo, the Ford Focus that he was sitting in at this very moment.

Cooper understood why Max wouldn't want to identify the woman he was dating. Introducing your girlfriend to your gay ex-lover was obviously not the best way to cement a permanent relationship, although there were probably plenty of women who would take Max as he was as long as he provided a nice house and plenty of spending money. There might even be plenty of women who preferred that kind of double life. They got all the perks—the house, the money, the kids (if they were the types to consider kids a perk) and the shopping—without any of the downsides like sex and . . . sex.

Cooper didn't know if he was being too ungenerous here. He didn't really know if most women found sex with their mates to be a chore or not. He'd never had sex with a woman and he had no idea how their bodies worked on that level. Max had, though. And the information that women would rather do anything than give a blow job (which, of course, was the one thing a man wanted more than anything else) had come from him. But Max was such a fuckup and in such deep denial about everything that he was probably dead wrong about that. Maybe the women

Max had been with just didn't want to suck *his* dick. Anyway, it didn't matter, because he was sure that Max could find a woman willing to be his beard. But Max didn't want a beard—he wanted a real relationship with a woman, sex and kids and all. And that's why Cooper had to know who the mystery woman was. He had to know who Max had found to fool himself with. And maybe, Cooper thought, it was his responsibility to warn her. Yes, that was it—he was performing a public service.

It had, however, occurred to Cooper more than once that Max was simply lying about everything. He'd been watching the man for weeks and had seen him do nothing more provocative than buy a premade fruit tart from Whole Foods. Of course, he hadn't been on Max's trail every minute of every day—and he had drawn his own line at sitting in the car all night—but he had not seen a trace of any kind of woman (or man, for that matter) in Max's life (okay, he *had* gone through the trash, but only that one time). But there had to be someone, because the one thing Cooper was sure of was that deep in Max's confused heart, he loved Cooper. The only reason to end it was if he had someone else.

Whenever Cooper had a clear moment, like now, he told himself that he had to pull it together and start behaving like a grown-up. It wasn't as if Max had ever been anything less than totally honest about what a fucking idiot he was. Relationships ended and life went on and all that other Dr. Phil–flavored crap. But . . . Cooper reached into the pocket of his jeans, pulled out a lint-covered Vicodin he'd put there this morning in case of emergency (and whenever he had a clear moment these days it counted as an emergency) and swallowed it with the last of his sweet drink. Max wasn't just any relationship. That was the difference. And although he could see Max rubbing that crease in his forehead at the very thought of it, Cooper believed that they were *fated* for each other. He didn't know how it was going to happen, but they were going to be together. Without this belief Cooper was lost and homeless, so he had to hold onto it even if it meant acting like a thirteen-year-old girl.

Cooper passed out for a while and when he woke up it was past two and definitely time for another coffee run. The inside of his mouth felt furry and his head felt like it had been hit with a jackhammer. He rubbed his face with his hands and realized it had been days since he'd shaved. He didn't even notice these things anymore. He shifted to get a better look at himself in the rearview mirror and that was when he saw Max leaving the building, walking much faster than his usual saunter, and getting into his car. Cooper wasn't feeling up to a high-speed chase, but really, what was the point of sitting here every day if he wasn't going to do any actual *surveillance?*

Luckily, there was always traffic to help keep a car you were chasing in view. The northbound I-5 was a mess no matter what day or time it was, and it took them half an hour to cover a ten-mile distance. Finally, Max exited on Manchester and turned west onto the coast road. Cooper thought he was finally going to see something interesting from Max, who never ventured this far from the office on a workday unless it was lunchtime and he was meeting someone. He held back a little on the coast road lest Max make him out, so he almost missed seeing Max turn and park in the little lot next to Marina's office, where Cooper himself hadn't been for weeks. What the hell was Max doing here?

Cooper struggled to keep Max in his line of sight without getting into an accident, but it was a losing proposition. He had to park and lost valuable time doubling back to find an available spot on the curb without hitting any bicyclists in their annoying puke-yellow spandex shirts and ridiculous helmets. Always in the fucking way! When he finally managed to maneuver the Focus (definitely not a car on his to-buy list) into a parking space, Cooper got out and hovered just inside the doorway of the café across the street from Marina's office. He flashed on a weird memory of the last time he'd seen Marina. They'd noticed that strange guy hovering at the café and they'd watched him watch her—or the other way around, he couldn't remember. Either way, now he was the strange guy hovering, and he didn't like the feeling.

Max must have gone into Marina's office, because his car was still there but he'd disappeared. Cooper's confused mind was racing, but his reflexes were slow and clumsy. He felt heavy and broad, as if he weighed a thousand pounds.

"Can I help you?"

Cooper turned to the girl, who obviously wanted to seat him. "Can I just . . . ? Um, I'll just be a minute," he said.

"Are you waiting for someone?"

"No. Listen, I'll just be a second."

"Do you want to be seated?"

"Can you just leave me alone for a second?!" Fuck, he'd raised his voice. Now she was going to get her manager. He had about two seconds to decide what to do. Stay, go, hover. But then he saw both Max and Marina exit her office. She locked her door and then they walked to Max's car. He held the door open for her and she got in. Then they drove away. Cooper was stunned. He felt the strangest sensation, as if the floor was falling away beneath him. There was a name for what happened to your brain when you suddenly realized everything you thought you knew to be real was a giant hallucination—as if you'd been the butt of a joke that had taken a lifetime to pull off. What was that term? Max would know . . . he knew all those little psych terms, knew all about pathology. Max, his lover, the man he'd just seen escorting Marina *(Marina!)* to wherever. A hotel? His house?

It was too much. Cooper couldn't think, couldn't breathe. He was suffocating on his own spleen. He was going to pass out right here in the doorway. How could she? What kind of evil did she have within her?

"Sir, if you'd like to be seated I'd be happy to give you a table. But I'm going to have to ask you to—"

"I'm leaving," Cooper said, and he walked out onto the street, the white-hot anger inside his head igniting into a full blaze.

Chapter 23

Eddie was sick of eating chicken. His life had become stuck on the all-chicken-all-the-time channel: skinless, boneless, boiled, baked, roasted. Breasts, wings, thighs. Nothing battered, breaded or fried; no nuggets, buffaloes or burgers (a chicken burger was a travesty to begin with). In short, nothing interesting or flavorful enough to be considered delicious or even tasty. There was only so much you could do with this bird and only so often you could eat it before the entire world started tasting like chicken. God forbid you ate beef anymore with its cholesterol, hormones and mad cow disease; or fish, poisoned with mercury and whatever other toxic sludge filled the ocean. You couldn't even eat spinach anymore because of the *E. coli.* So what was left? Fucking chicken was what.

And it was chicken that would be gracing his dinner table again tonight. Tina was in the kitchen doing her best to torture out another chicken meal while he watched the basketball game in the living room. *Another fowl meal,* he thought, only half enjoying the pun. He couldn't blame Tina, though. She was just doing what she thought was right. In a way that was the story of Tina's life. It was how she mothered their boys and ran their household. This was why their eldest, Jake, took a pill every day for his ADD even though there was nothing wrong with the kid that a little more discipline couldn't fix, and why they had expensive tile in the bathrooms where linoleum would do fine. And this was why they'd been eating chicken since what felt like the dawn of time—because it was part of a healthy diet and a healthy diet was the right thing to have. Eddie went along because all too often he acted not on what he thought was right but on what he knew was wrong.

Eddie turned his head toward the kitchen, a physical response to his guilty thoughts. He couldn't stand to think about his sins now, but it was getting harder to hide from himself inside his own brain, let alone in his living room. That his current X-rated, soap-opera-worthy entanglement was a mess of his own making was too much for Eddie to admit. He preferred to simply consider himself cursed. And hadn't it all gone to shit the minute he'd met that witch? All three of them were witches, come to think of it. They might as well be standing around a bubbling cauldron full of fucking chicken.

He fumbled for the remote and hit the mute button. He could hear Tina singing over the metallic clang of pots and pans. He didn't recognize the song, but that was nothing new. Tina had a tin ear—couldn't hold a note if it was strapped to her—but that never stopped her from warbling on. She sang in the shower, in the kitchen, paying bills at the dining room table. Didn't matter what kind of mood she was in. Singing was the hum of her own inner machinery. He loved that about her— hadn't even realized how much until now. He flipped off the TV and got up from the couch. Hell with the chicken; he was going to take them all out for Mexican. It was Saturday and margaritas had to be on special somewhere. Once, a long, long time ago, he and Tina had loved drinking margaritas together. Tina was a lightweight—one margarita and she was high, two and she was out. Somewhere in between, though, she got very hot, and if they timed it out just right . . . Yes, Eddie thought, margaritas were the thing. And then it finally hit him that Tina was singing Jimmy Buffett. They were on the same page, sharing the same thought. That was a good sign.

"'Margaritaville'!" Eddie exclaimed. "I was thinking the same thing."

Tina kept humming along, oblivious.

"Tina, did you hear me?"

Tina turned around from her preparations at the granite countertop (another pricey upgrade that she'd insisted on), questioning him with her brown eyes made bigger by the dark circles beneath them. She was wearing old jeans and a sweatshirt that one of the boys had grown out of. Her hair was held back with one of those clawlike clips, but a couple of loose strands hung around her face. The sweatshirt was baggy but somehow made her look thinner than she was. Unless, Eddie realized, she'd been getting thinner and he hadn't noticed. Women asked you if they were fat all the time and you always had to find new ways of saying no. After a while you just stopped looking. But he could see now that Tina looked tired and stressed out.

"I was thinking we could go out for Mexican tonight," he said. "Let's celebrate."

"Celebrate what?"

"It's Saturday," Eddie said. "I thought we could have margaritas." He winked and smiled, dimpling his cheeks, a private amorous message that she used to pick up on but was ignoring now. Eddie felt his resolve start to fade along with his connectedness to his unsmiling wife.

"Margaritas are really fattening," Tina said. "Not to mention just plain bad for you. And I'm in the middle of making dinner here, Eddie. You could have said something earlier, you know? I don't want to waste this now."

Eddie studied the bowls and plates she was working on, trying to figure out what she was making, and came up with nothing. "Tina," he said as gently as he could, "I'm really fucking sick of chicken."

Tina didn't miss a beat. "Well, if you can fucking think of something else I can fucking cook that won't fucking kill us, I'll stop making fucking chicken for you. Better yet, why don't *you* cook, Eddie?" She blinked hard. "Right, I thought so."

"Jesus, Tina. I thought you'd be happy."

"Why, because you're home and willing to share yourself with me for five minutes?"

"Okay, what's wrong? Is it Jake, because he—"

"No, Eddie, it's not Jake."

"I don't get it," he said. "You were fine this morning."

"I was fine? Did you even see me this morning? Do you know what I did? Did we eat breakfast together?"

The answer to all three questions was no, Eddie realized, and he felt himself getting sucked into the inevitable vortex of an argument. He did not need this, not now. "Fuck it," he said. "You don't want to go out, fine. Thought you could use the break, that's all."

"And the fucking chicken," she said. "Don't forget that."

"All right, Tina, I'm sorry I said I was sick of chicken. Is that better?" He was getting angry and he couldn't afford to get angry. Better to try to channel it some other way. He walked over to Tina and slid his arms around hers, encasing her from behind. She was tense and stiff, her chicken-slimy hands held out away from her body. He kissed her neck, smelling her light grassy perfume. She always wore scent and always put on makeup, no matter if she was going out or staying in. He'd always loved that about her, too. He reached his hands under her sweatshirt and stroked her breasts, which were covered only by a tank top. It turned him on that she wasn't wearing a bra, and he pressed his groin into the small of her back.

"Eddie, stop."

"Mmm, why? Kids aren't in the house."

"No, really, stop." She didn't move away and for a second Eddie thought she was playing some kind of "no means yes" game, but that had never been Tina's style. There was a tremble in her voice that implied something was very wrong. He froze, then slowly removed his hands and stepped away from his wife. She turned to face him and he could see there were tears shimmering in her eyes.

"I think we should separate," she said.

Eddie felt as if someone had aimed a gun at his temple. "What the fuck are you talking about, Tina?"

She walked over to the sink and washed her hands, then dried them on a dish towel. Because everything suddenly seemed distorted and over-saturated, Eddie noticed the precise pattern of orange and gold starfish on the towel as she wiped her hands. Time seemed to slow down as he watched her hands twist in the cloth, saw her wedding ring go in and out like a game of hide-and-seek. "I thought maybe we should just go to counseling, but it's not me who needs counseling, Eddie, it's you." She gave a horrible choking sob. "I don't have a problem. I haven't done any-thing wrong."

For the first time since he'd met her, Eddie was afraid to touch his wife. "What is it, Tina? What the hell?"

"I know," she said.

"You know what?"

"Are you going to make me say it? You really want me to lay it out?"

No, Eddie thought, the last thing he wanted was a verbal summary of the adulterous images he was having in his head. Ridiculous thoughts flew across his brain. She'd hired a private investigator, she'd followed him her-self, she'd videotaped him. . . . No, no, no. Eddie had kept his lives so well separated. Nobody in his other world even knew where he lived. But maybe that wasn't at all what Tina was talking about. Maybe she just thought he was drinking or smoking or taking drugs. Eddie found him-self having the insane wish that his wife thought he was smoking crack.

"Tina . . ."

"I got a call," she said. "From a woman."

It all came tumbling into his consciousness—who'd called his wife and what she'd said. It was the realization of a pin being pulled from a grenade—no turning back and not enough time to escape. And then Eddie's vision bleached white with sudden, uncontrolled anger, as if some-thing had literally exploded in his brain. His hands clenched, trembling with the desire to hit something, to smash something into powder. In his fury, he picked up the nearest object—a serving platter filled with wine-soaked chicken breasts—and hurled it into the wall. He could see *her* face in his mind—taunting him with that self-satisfied smile—and he wanted to punch it into dust.

"Eddie!" Tina screamed, as shattered porcelain and wine flew back at them both. "Eddie, stop!"

But Eddie, blind and deaf with rage, was only getting started.

Chapter 24

Marina stood at the water's edge with her sandals in her hand and watched the inexorable push and pull of the tide. A gusting offshore wind threw sand at her back; salt water stung her ankles. Even though it had become as hallucinatory and overpopulated as the rest of the places she spent time in, the beach was her last refuge. For a moment she wondered what it would feel like to walk into the waves and just keep going until the water closed over her head. And then, because she couldn't really imagine the act itself, she wondered what it would feel like to have the resolve necessary to do such a thing. Marina certainly didn't have the fortitude. Her instinct for survival was far too strong to allow her the luxury of suicide. There was also the matter of control, something Marina no longer possessed.

It had been two weeks since she'd walked into her office and found the Death card staring up at her, and in that time all she'd managed to accomplish was to get her office locks changed. There was nobody to call, no complaint to file. She pictured a scenario where she tried to explain her situation to the police. *I took his dead mother's ring, then slept with him, and now he's breaking into my office and leaving threatening messages. Oh, yes, and I've also seen into his mind. But I couldn't see into it when I was with him. And I talk to dead people—did I mention that?* No, talking to the cops would be disastrous. And because Marina had managed to insulate herself so well, there were no other *living* people she could confide in.

If nothing else, the last two months had convinced Marina that no hard constructs of reality were safe from demolition. She'd received confirmation of that only hours earlier when she'd tried to end her pregnancy and the doctor had told her there was nothing there to end. If this was the kind of force she was up against, how could a flimsy lock keep anyone out? And in Marina's mind, *anyone* meant Gideon. By his own admission, he'd come looking for her to exact some sort of revenge. Maybe now he'd decided to make good on that intent. Not that this made sense to Marina. The mind could formulate all kinds of untruths, but the body couldn't lie. Their bodies had spoken the truth that night at the hotel and it was love between them, not hate. Not revenge.

But Marina had been wrong about so many things lately. She'd known from the start that getting involved with Gideon was dangerous, but still she'd allowed herself to be swept away. Now the world had cracked open and she was drowning. What had happened at the doctor's office was just the latest unexplainable event. She'd sat in that waiting room for what felt like hours. The office was crowded with women in various stages of pregnancy, and Marina, unable to bury herself in an outdated issue of *Home and Garden,* could hear what every one of them was thinking, their unspoken words creating a cacophony in her head.

Ten more weeks and then I'll be able to—

I know I'm just supposed to want a healthy baby, but I hope it's a girl. I really want—

I have to make sure he schedules the cesarean today because I can't—

I'm not ready for this—

I've already put on twenty pounds and I'm not even in my fifth month—

It's so hot in here. Why can't they—

—go back to work.

—a girl. Is that wrong?

—get my money back for that trip and I don't want to go into labor on a plane.

—I'm just not ready.

—I'm going to look like a damn whale by the time I get to the end.

—turn up the air?

By the time her own name was called, Marina knew every woman's story in excruciating detail. She had no way of regulating the flow of chatter—no way to turn it off or down. It happened when it happened without any indication of why. So when Marina's mother appeared once again after a nurse had taken Marina's blood pressure and a urine sample "just to confirm," Marina had no choice but to look and listen.

"I told you not to bother with this," her mother said. "You're just wasting time."

"You'll have to forgive me if I don't take motherly advice from *you*," Marina whispered.

"Stubborn," her mother said. "As always."

It was a long time before anyone returned to the room, long enough for Marina to realize that something was wrong. When the doctor finally entered, he told Marina that they'd run her pregnancy test twice and it had come up negative both times. Home tests were usually reliable, he said, but every once in a while there was a mistake. Could be any number of things, he said as he snapped on a pair of latex gloves and instructed her to "scoot down" on the table, but most likely she was just late. Sometimes women's cycles changed when they were about her age. Had she heard the term *perimenopause?* There was a nasty stomach bug going around and that could be what was causing her nausea. Had she experienced any fever? Marina gasped as he felt his way around inside her body, prodding and pushing. Yes, her uterus was a normal, nonpregnant size, he said, and everything seemed fine. Looked like it was a false alarm after all, although if she missed another cycle he recommended she see her regular gynecologist for a more thorough examination.

Marina's mother reappeared in the corner of the room. "I told you," she cackled, her voice thick as it had been in life from years of self-abuse. "It's not your decision to make."

And that was when Marina, realizing she'd never had a choice in the matter at all, left the clinic and headed to the first beach she could find. Now, surrounded by competing sounds of crashing surf, seagulls and wind, Marina experienced a rare moment of inner quiet. And, once again, the thought of Gideon came in to fill the empty space. If he'd wanted her to suffer, she thought with sudden bitterness, he had certainly succeeded. She wondered if it would make a difference to him if he knew she was pregnant with his child. For a moment, Marina actually tried to reach him telepathically, to somehow beam her thought—*our baby*—into his mind. Almost immediately, she felt a cruel wave of dizzying nausea crash through her. The wind had picked up again and she was cold. Heavy gray clouds were blowing across the sky, blocking out the sun. Maybe she really *was* crazy, Marina thought. Perhaps the doctor was right and she wasn't even pregnant. Perhaps it was all an illusion created by a sick brain. And maybe what she really needed was a psychiatrist or a neurologist. Or both. Marina thought about Max, the only psychiatrist she knew, and almost laughed at how ridiculous it would be to consult him.

It felt as if it had been years since the day Max had shown up at her office to talk about Cooper, but it couldn't have been more than a couple of weeks. He'd been so intent on convincing her that it wasn't a reading he wanted (because he did not believe in psychics, he was quick to tell her), that he'd taken her to lunch so they could talk about his concern over Cooper's behavior. Although it seemed to physically pain him to say it, Max told Marina that Cooper trusted her more than anyone else in his life and that she was, in effect, functioning as his counselor. As such, she had a certain responsibility to Cooper and he hoped she could see that.

On that day, she remembered now, everything was covered in a haze of color. She'd been distracted by how *red* Max had seemed, as if his blood were literally boiling under the surface of his skin. But when she'd asked him why he was so angry, Max seemed startled and assured her in a slow, calm tone that he wasn't at all angry, only worried about Cooper.

"I'm sure you can't tell me what the two of you have talked about," Max said, his words sounding as bitten off as the half-eaten roast beef sandwich in front of him. "No doubt you have some sort of client confidentiality rule?" Mesmerized by the sparks that seemed to be coming from his head, Marina didn't respond. "But you should know that he's been acting in a very troubling manner. He's been taking . . ." *Pills,* Marina finished silently. It was no wonder Max didn't want to admit to Cooper's drug use. He'd probably prescribed the drugs himself.

"The thing is, he's having a hard time accepting certain . . . circumstances. . . ." Marina experienced a sharp stab of regret that she'd ever encouraged Cooper to stay with this man. It had benefited her to tell him that and it was what Cooper himself had wanted to hear, but it was wrong. "Maybe you could talk to him," Max said, "and guide him in a more positive direction."

"Like lie to him?" Marina asked. "You want to give me a script?"

"I'm not saying—"

"I know what you're saying," Marina cut him off. The air around Max grew darker, she remembered, and she started feeling an unpleasant tingling sensation at the base of her spine. She didn't formulate her next words; they just came tumbling out of her mouth. "You're about to make a very bad decision," she said. "You have to rethink it. It's not too late. Yet."

Max's expression never changed, yet Marina saw both fear and anger rise from him like twin plumes of smoke. "I knew this was a mistake," he said. "I'm sorry to have taken up your time. I know how valuable it is."

He had paid the check and offered to drive her back, but she'd turned him down, not wanting to be confined in a car with him for even the few minutes it would have taken to get back to her office.

M arina turned away from the ocean and started walking toward the main road. If she were going to get any help, it wouldn't come from the likes of Max. She hadn't heard from either him or Cooper since that day. Perhaps

Max had listened to her and made a different decision—not that she even knew what she'd been warning him against. Perhaps he and Cooper had gotten back together and were living happily ever after at this very moment. But even as she formulated the thought, Marina knew it wasn't true.

She felt something sharp under her feet and stepped back just in time to avoid cutting herself on a shard of broken glass in the sand. She wondered why her usually pristine stretch of coast was littered and then realized that she was several miles south of what she'd come to think of as *her* beach. This bit of shoreline looked beaten up and neglected, strewn with wrappers, broken bottles and cigarette butts. Just ahead, she could see a disheveled woman sitting and smoking at the edge of a rickety rundown boardwalk. No doubt this woman's cigarette would soon be joining the other refuse on the beach.

As Marina drew closer to her, the woman began to look familiar and the scene around her took on the softened glow of memory. Marina had the sense that she was looking at a live image from her own past. A few more cautious steps and Marina realized she was looking at her mother, but this time a much-younger, less-ravaged mother than she remembered. This version was attractive, even hinting at beauty. There was still some softness in the lines of her body, some luster left in her skin. And when she looked up, Marina could see that there was light in her eyes. Her mother—or this incarnation of her—regarded Marina without expression, exhaled a cloud of smoke and gestured toward the boardwalk. Marina followed her direction and saw what she was pointing at: an old woman sitting in front of a small table right in the middle of the boardwalk. This, too, had the unmistakable feeling of a long-buried memory, and Marina walked right into it, getting as close as she could.

The old woman was some kind of antique fortune-teller, the sort one didn't see outside of old movies anymore. Marina recognized her as the same woman she'd seen—had *thought* she'd seen—when she was walking on the beach with Gideon. But this time the vision didn't evaporate when Marina drew closer. There was a stack of well-worn tarot cards on the woman's felt-covered table. Next to the deck were four shiny, new, special-edition bicentennial quarters. Marina edged still closer. The fortune-teller sat with her head down so low that her chin was almost resting on her chest. She didn't move as Marina reached over and touched the top of the tarot stack with her fingertip.

"I know this game," Marina whispered in a little girl's voice. "I choose the man with the eight over his head." Her hand trembling, Marina turned over the top card. The Magician stared up at her, the symbol for infinity floating above him. The fortune-teller's head snapped up, making Marina gasp in sudden shock. Her eyes were completely white. Without opening her mouth, she spoke four words that thundered in Marina's ears.

"You have the gift."

The world contracted, the present scene and the memory of it blending into one. Marina watched as if she was looking through a camera's viewfinder. She was five years old, saving those special quarters for ice cream—a rare treat her mother had promised her on this last hot day of summer. *"Just let me do this one thing,"* her mother had said. *"Then you can buy your ice cream, I promise. Just this one thing."* She sat there and smoked her cigarette—angry, Marina knew, at the woman with the cards. Marina loved those cards—all those pretty pictures. But that day it was the same one that kept coming up over and over. Always the man with the eight over his head. Then her mother was yelling and yanking her arm.

"What are you doing?"

"She has the gift."

"Now you know," the fortune-teller said. "Look at your hands."

Marina looked down at her palms. What she saw couldn't possibly be real, and yet these strange, unfamiliar hands were attached to her own wrists. The flesh was smooth. Her life lines were gone.

"I tried to tell you once," the fortune-teller said. "You have the gift."

"What does she mean, Mama?"

"It doesn't mean anything. This crazy freak doesn't know what she's talking about."

Marina looked back to where her mother had been sitting, but the place was empty. She'd been so angry that day, pulling Marina along like a dog on a leash, walking so fast that Marina kept tripping over her own small feet. It was so hot, but her quarters were gone and she never got her ice cream.

What am I supposed to do? Marina asked without speaking the words out loud.

"You must learn how to use the gift you've been given."

What if I don't want it? What if I don't want any of this?

"You do not have a choice."

Why do I have it now?

"The gift is always there. And now yours has been unlocked."

No, I—no . . .

"You cannot choose to have the gift, you can only choose what to do with it."

Help me.

"You must help yourself. You must learn how to use your gift."

I can't do this.

"You will. You must."

Please help me. What should I do?

"Go home," the fortune-teller said. She slid Marina's quarters into her pocket. "Now I go, too," she said. "You will not see me again."

"Wait," Marina said out loud. "Wait!" But the fortune-teller was already gone, vanished into the cold, gritty wind. Marina stood still, her hands curled into fists, staring into the airy space where the fortune-teller had been, trying to will her back into existence. Seconds passed, then a minute, then two. Marina opened her hands and looked again at her palms, expecting to see all the lines restored in the flesh. But her life lines were still missing and now she couldn't be sure if they'd ever been there. All at once, Marina knew that she needed to leave the beach. Suddenly, the space was much too wide and the sky offered no protection.

Chapter 25

Go home, the fortune-teller had instructed, but Marina wasn't heeding that advice. She got into her car and drove with no direction or destination in mind, so intent on escape that she'd gone thirty miles before she realized she had left her sandals somewhere on the beach and was leaning on the gas pedal with a bare foot. She turned on the radio and pumped the volume to the highest level it would go. If she filled her senses with the sight of freeway traffic and the sound of wailing guitars, Marina thought, there would be less chance that anything else—voices, visions, dead people—could get in.

But neither the snarl at the merge of the I-5 and I-805 freeways nor Aerosmith's ear-splitting plea for her to "dream on" could block out the thoughts in Marina's head. First in line—the thought that kept circling like an animal biting its own tail—was that she was more frightened of being suddenly and truly psychic than she was of going insane. But what scared her more than having the gift was that she had no idea what to do with it. The gift had *her,* not the other way around.

A descent into madness almost seemed easy compared to trying to impose rationality onto something that, until now, Marina hadn't even believed existed. She had no choice now but to believe. As contradictory as it seemed, her rational self—the part of her that had guided all her decisions—insisted she accept the unexplainable and unbelievable as true. For Marina, this collision of realities was terrifying. She felt as if she'd been diagnosed with a disease that had no treatment, cure or prognosis.

"*You must learn how to use it,*" the fortune-teller had said. But how? Marina couldn't even figure out what *it* was. But no, that wasn't entirely true. The gift (or curse, as she was coming to think of it) was a mad scramble of unfiltered dreams, visions and premonitions. It was *information,* Marina thought, suddenly hopeful. It was proven science that human beings only used a small fraction of their brains. It was as if— no, *because* the human brain wasn't really designed to tap into that much information, even if it did have the capacity. And maybe this was what had happened to her. Somehow, the circuitry of her brain had come alive, allowing for this flood of supposedly psychic information. The potential had always been there, but some recent trigger had set it all off. Feeling something like relief, Marina clutched at this possibility of an explanation.

Once more, her mind turned back to Gideon. He was the locus—the point where it had all started. The minute he'd walked up to her in the parking lot, her perception of the world around her had begun to change. The closer they'd become, the more distorted her view. And then, finally, when he'd put his hand around the ring—when he'd looked at her with that expression of loathing—and left her alone in that room . . . There was the trigger, Marina thought. Love and fear had literally rewired her brain.

"*You have the gift!*"

The voice was so loud that Marina looked to the side, swerving dangerously, even though the sound was coming from inside her own head. Angry car horns blared through her haze as she righted the steering wheel.

"*Go home, go home, go home, go home.*"

Marina didn't know how long it had been since she'd paid attention to where she was going. She'd been driving blind, not looking. Now she saw

that she was still going north on the interstate, her office and house several exits behind her. The gas gauge was deep into the red zone. She'd been
driving for so long that she'd managed to drain her tank. Gripped with a
sudden sense of urgency, she steered toward the next exit.

"You have the gift—you must learn how to use it."

"Stop it!" Marina shouted. She took the exit too fast and swerved
drunkenly. She needed to turn around, get back on the southbound freeway, but she didn't know if she had enough gas. She spun around and
headed to the Coast Highway. Better to run out of gas there than on the
freeway.

"You have the gift—go home, go home, go home."

The voice had become so loud that it was a siren in Marina's head.
She couldn't concentrate, couldn't focus on where she was going. Where
was the music—what was wrong with the radio? She looked down at the
volume control and punched it hard.

Her eyes came back up to the road and a shock of fear coursed
through her. What she saw could not be happening. Somehow she was
driving north again, heading toward her house from the south, where
she'd already been. She had not turned, had not steered. She had looked
down only for a second. But that wasn't the worst of it. Marina wasn't in
her own car. The hands on the wheel were not her hands. They were . . .

I could just tell her I'm sorry.

. . . Gideon's hands. She was in Gideon's head. She watched as one
hand left the wheel and traveled to his chest. Her ring—his ring—rested
there on the end of its chain. Her fingers—his fingers—felt its small
weight and sharp edges.

Because I love her.

Her eyes—his eyes—shifted again. Her vision was hazy and vibrating.
Marina was back in her car—back inside herself. But she was moving too
fast. The road was a blur of conflated images; she couldn't see where she
was going. She swerved and banked, moved her feet along the pedals,
heard the sound of screeching brakes and felt her body slamming into

something hard and unyielding. The air left her lungs. And then there was nothing.

*H*e walks up to her front door and stands still in front of it. He is holding a bunch of roses wrapped in silver paper. Their scent is thick and strong. He knocks, softly at first, and then louder when nobody answers. Maybe this is a mistake, maybe I shouldn't have come, *he thinks.* But no, I love her. I need to tell her that I'm sorry for leaving her that way. It was cruel, even if . . . But I've thought about it—thought about her. I've done nothing *but* think about her. I need to tell her that. I need to listen to her side of the story. And then maybe we have a chance. *He knocks again and waits for an answer that doesn't come.* She's probably working. It's not that late. I'll go to the office, *he thinks. He turns around, ready to go, but something stops him.*

"*Don't go, don't go, don't go. I am* here, *Marina tries to tell him, but nothing comes out of her mouth, because she is inside him and this is not her mouth. It's too dark and she can't see. Everything is black.*

*S*he swims through layers of darkness, trying to work her way to consciousness. She opens her eyes but it's too dark to make out shapes or colors. This is not her body, not her mind . . . but she hears the thought. It's too dark in here to do what I need to do. *She reaches with arms that are not hers and takes the flashlight from her back pocket. It's small but the beam is bright. She flicks it on and moves it cautiously. She sees pieces of her office illuminated in the moving spotlight. There is her table, her tarot cards, her candles.* Witch. *She feels the thought run cold through the mind she is sharing.* Goddamned witch. Witches deserve to burn. *She smells gas, strong and pungent. She coughs, the sound harsh. She reaches into her waistband to touch the gun she's tucked in there, feels its reassuring weight. She feels a surge of anger.* All of this psychic bullshit—it shouldn't be allowed. There should be laws to protect people from being taken advantage of this way. But nobody ever does anything. Now it's time. *She hears a noise and startles, the flashlight beam bouncing wildly off the wall. And now she wonders if she remembered to lock that door behind her. She clicks off the flashlight and stands still, breath held. It's dark now. Too dark to see.*

*S*he is outside, walking in the dark. There is no moonlight, no streetlights. She is walking as fast as she can, but her feet are bare and she can't get there, can't reach him. She smells smoke and roses, both smells getting stronger as she moves forward. There—there, she can see him. She tries to call out, but no sound comes from her throat. He is walking too far ahead. She tries to run, but rocks cut her feet. He stops walking and turns. She knows this place. Stop! He can't hear her. Now she is right behind him, the distance closed, and he is at a door. He touches the handle. No! Stop! Everything goes black.

*W*ho is that rattling the door? It's not her—damn it, not her. Hand on the gun—just hold onto the gun. What the hell is he doing here? Bad timing—very bad timing. This wasn't in the plan, but there's no other option now. At least here in the dark there is the advantage. Just have to get a little closer. He's moving forward. "Marina?" One long, still second and then, "Marina, it's Gideon. Are you there?"

Time to move.

*S*he wakes up with a start, the smell of smoke and roses clinging to her, suffocating her. She can't see anything, it is so dark. She is in her car and the *smell of gas is burning her throat. How long has she been out? She has to find him. She pushes the car door open and stumbles out into the darkness. Where is the moon? She starts walking, but she doesn't know where she's going. She should have put her shoes on; why didn't she put her shoes on?*

She starts running and the rocks cut her feet, but she doesn't care—she has to find him. She sees him now, too far ahead. He is going to turn. Stop! He can't hear her. The door. He is at her office door. Stop! He starts to turn, but then he stops, leans in. She screams and everything goes black.

*N*o *evidence—can't leave any evidence behind. Must take everything and the rest will burn. Fire cleans, purifies. Burn it down. Must burn it down.*

*S*he *comes to with a start, the smell of gas and smoke choking her. She tries to move, but her limbs are too heavy. Smoke fills her lungs and she can barely breathe. She closes her eyes and sees him walking. He turns the corner. She's too late. There is a flash of light and then everything goes black.*

*S*he *wakes up coughing from the smoke. She is standing on the street in bare feet. She can see everything now. The night is illuminated by flames. Her office is on fire and the whole building is burning. She doesn't move, doesn't call his name.*

He is already dead.

Marina came to, groaning and coughing in the dark. The smell of gas was strong and clinging. Her head was throbbing and her entire body felt bruised. Consciousness was so slow to come that she thought she was still locked inside her dream. She turned her head with effort, eyes adjusting, to the darkness. She was in her car. Reality came through in increments. She had been driving. She swerved, the ground rushed up. She had gone down an embankment. How long had she been here? Her brain, sluggish from concussion, struggled to connect images and meaning. The road, the darkness and the fire gradually linked together to form a patched-together narrative. Gideon was at her office. Someone else was there, waiting. Waiting for *her*. Gideon was in her office. Her office was on fire. That last image was what finally brought Marina to full consciousness.

The driver's-side door was stuck, so she had to crawl across the seat to get out on the other side. She scrambled, tripping in the dirt. It was dark, but she knew where she was going. She could feel his presence—it was so close. She started running. When she reached the Coast Highway, it was as if she'd been thrown back into the thick of her dreams. The feel of the road under her bare feet, the rocks pressing into the soft spots on her heels and the panic that she was going to be too late. Marina kept running.

"Gideon," she screamed. *"Gideon!"*

Her breath was coming short as she turned off the highway to the street that would take her to her office. Her feet were bleeding. And now she could smell the smoke. She was too late, too late. Of course, the dreams were right. The dreams would always be right. It was she who hadn't known how to read them.

And now she was there and the wail of sirens was in her ears. The sky was lit with sparks and leaping flames. She kept walking until someone grabbed her arm, a firefighter who looked at her as if she was insane.

"Ma'am, stay back! You can't go there. Stay back!"

Marina turned to the man and looked up at his face. Was it the reflection of the fire that made his skin seem so red?

"It's too late," she whispered. And then everything went black.

May 2007

Chapter 26

"When are you coming home, Dad?"

Eddie cleared his throat and ran his hand through his unkempt hair. He'd spent the night on his office couch again and he felt like crap. He was way too old for this shit.

"I'm going to see you on Saturday, buddy, remember?" He tried to keep his voice light, hoping he exuded the kind of calm confidence he wasn't even close to feeling. Good thing his son couldn't see him through the phone.

"That's not what I mean," Jake said. "When are you coming *home?*"

Eddie paused, that horrendous Harry Chapin song about the dad who's never home running through his head. He decided just to be straight up with the kid. "Honestly, Jake, I'm not sure."

"Why not, Dad?"

Eddie wanted to say, "Because your mother won't let me," but repressed the urge. This conversation was a minefield and so damn difficult to navigate. Be honest with the kid and risk wounding him now, hedge around the truth and risk wounding him later. And God forbid he trash the mother—that never worked. It didn't matter that Jake was a teenager; he was still miles away from understanding his parents' screwed-up relationship.

"Jake, it's complicated, okay? Your mother and I—"

"Are you and Mom getting a divorce?"

"No. Why, is that what she said?"

"I didn't ask *her*. I'm asking you. I have a right to know how my life is going to be affected by this thing."

Eddie sighed into the phone. "Jake, can you put your brother on the phone? I'll talk to you about this later."

"But Dad—"

"Jake, put Kyle on the phone."

"Whatever."

Eddie heard the phone being dropped on the counter and Jake calling for Kyle. In the distance, he heard Tina shouting at both of them to hurry up.

"Hey, Dad, I gotta go," Kyle breathed into the phone when he finally picked it up. Eddie, tired of feeling so guilty, was almost relieved when the conversation was over in a matter of seconds. It was quiet now, but people were going to start showing up for work within the hour. His office smelled like old coffee and body odor. He needed a shower, breakfast and a change of venue, but he suspected he was only going to manage one of the three this morning.

As Eddie straightened up his office and rummaged around his gym bag for something clean to wear, he realized it had taken him almost fifty years to discover that he was a fundamentally limited person. He didn't have the kind of style or panache that other men used to get through these kinds of things. Plus, he just couldn't shut stuff out of his mind when it started pressing through. That was the worst part.

The day after Tina told him she wanted to separate, he'd gone out and bought her roses—nice, long-stemmed pink ones, because red was such a cliché. He had the florist put them in a big vase with plenty of fern or baby's breath or whatever, and he presented them *without* a card because he didn't want to admit defeat coming in. Begging was not sexy. Women claimed they wanted it, but when a man groveled it turned them right off.

When Tina saw the roses, her mouth flattened into a tight little line and she crossed her arms across her breasts as if to protect them. "You really shouldn't have done that, Eddie," she said. Eddie gave her an it's-the-least-I-could-do shrug and started to smile, but she killed it instantly with "No, I mean you shouldn't have spent the money. These look expensive, and it doesn't change anything."

And that was it—the roses were the extent of Eddie's creativity when it came to apologizing. When that failed, he did what she wanted and just moved out. He'd been crashing around North County ever since, sometimes sleeping in his office, sometimes in a motel, and, on one unfortunate occasion, with an employee who had a week's worth of rotting food in his sink and a vicious Doberman named Ellie May, of all things. He wasn't going to commute from Santee every day, not with gas prices the way they were and not if he couldn't sleep in his own damn bed. Cassie lived up here, of course, and he was sure she would have taken him in in a hot minute, but there was no way—not after what she'd put him through.

"Good news," she'd told him right after all hell had broken loose with Tina. "It was a false alarm; I'm not pregnant." Yeah, no kidding. It was amazing how fast things could turn to shit, Eddie thought. It hadn't been too long ago that he'd found Cassie smoking hot and now the thought of her made him nauseous. It was like *Shampoo,* that movie he'd seen when he was eighteen. Warren Beatty at his prime, playing a Don Juan hairdresser who screwed all his female clients. He had some great lines in that movie, but the one that had stuck with Eddie had to do with how women were just irresistible. They looked good, they smelled good, and there it was. What was a man to do? This reflected Eddie's basic philosophy in a very real way. But look where it all landed.

Eddie's office was as tidied up as it was going to get. He couldn't stand the sight of it any longer and decided that he needed some semipermanent digs until Tina let him move back in, because Tina *had* to let him move back in—he couldn't even begin to imagine his future if she didn't. Although he couldn't have found words to describe it even if he'd been able to admit it, Eddie was lost without his wife. He'd never stopped loving Tina, not for a minute. He'd always been so clear about that, with her, with the other women, with himself above all. None of his affairs had chipped off even a tiny piece of the big love he reserved for her. Tina had always gotten from him everything he was capable of giving her. Now, he wouldn't say, like some men did, that the other women "meant nothing." Sex *meant* something, even if what it meant wasn't always love. But he'd never planned to leave his wife—never. In Eddie's mind, this unchanging emotional commitment should have counterbalanced the consequences of his actions. In fact, Eddie believed what was happening to him now was unfair and unjust. Yes, *of course,* he understood why Tina was so angry and hurt, but the thing of it was, if she'd never been told, she never would have picked up on it—he was *that* good about holding up his end of their marital bargain. He honestly believed that the only thing he'd done wrong where Tina was concerned was to lose control and trash the kitchen. She hadn't deserved that.

The memory of all that broken crockery made Eddie think about Marina, the reason he'd gone ballistic that day, and he bowed his head as the spidery legs of guilt and shame crept up his back. He had no idea why he'd thought it was Marina who'd ratted him out to Tina. Maybe because Marina was the only one he *hadn't* slept with, although he admitted that didn't make much sense. They had *all* seemed like a bunch of goddamned witches. He'd worked so hard his whole life and to see everything he'd gained go up in smoke because of some bitch with a grudge . . . well, he'd snapped—and badly at that. It had actually scared him that he was capable of so much rage. He regretted it later, of course. He hadn't really wanted to hurt Marina—he was *not* that kind of guy. But—and this was where his shame was greatest—he *had* wanted her to suffer. And she had suffered. He had no doubt of that now.

Cassie, on the other hand . . . When he finally calmed down, Eddie figured out that it had to have been Cassie who'd made the phone call to Tina. Not that she'd ever admit it and not that he had any way to prove it—just one reason why he hadn't said anything to Cassie about his wife kicking him out. He hadn't told Madeline, either, come to think of it. Now, *there* was one twisted chick.

Eddie gathered his wallet and keys and headed out, thoughts of Madeline making pinpricks in his conscience. He hadn't for a minute suspected that she'd been the one who called—no reason for it. He and Madeline had some kind of hot, dirty *Last Tango in Paris* thing going on that was totally self-contained, neither one of them needing more or less than what they were getting. All of which made it even stranger that it had gone stone cold so suddenly. Maybe Madeline had gotten scared that her husband would find out. From the little she'd told him, he sensed that the guy was a pretty volatile dude.

Eddie drove mindlessly, pointing his truck toward the Coast Highway. Within a few minutes he was at the little café across the street from Marina's office. He forced his eyes to take it in. It looked terrible still—a blackened-out hole in the middle of the building, like an empty eye socket. The fire had burned hot and fast, down to the metal. The news had made the local papers for a week running, the "psychic couldn't see it coming" angle pretty much irresistible for the press, but then it had died out. He'd watched and listened carefully but hadn't heard or seen anything about the fire for weeks—except, of course, from Madeline.

Madeline's creepy attachment to Marina really unsettled him. At least he had the excuse of being sexually attracted to the psychic. What was Madeline's deal? She'd called him (something she almost never did—they made their arrangements for "next time" in person) after the fire, questioning and probing in a way he found very disturbing. Did he think it was arson or an accident? she'd asked him. Did the cops know who'd set the fire? What did he think? Had he spoken to Marina?

"What's with all the questions?" Eddie had asked her. He got a cold feeling in his gut, like she was trying to get a confession out of him or something. He wondered, not for the first time, how much Madeline knew about his relationship with Marina, if Marina had said anything about his hanging around and showing up without an appointment. He asked her again why she was grilling him, but Madeline got quiet and mumbled something he couldn't quite hear. He waited a moment and then said, "Do you want to—"

"No." She'd cut him off. "Not today. I can't. I'll call you." But she hadn't—not since then. Probably just as well—Eddie had a heap of shit descend on him soon after, so he wouldn't have been able to figure out her behavior anyway.

You could still smell that sick smoke odor from across the street. He felt bad—really bad—for Marina now. Funny how your head could change just like that, he thought. Eddie decided to pay her a visit—just to see if she was okay, nothing more. He polished off a quick muffin and coffee (no more big breakfasts at Darling's for him; he had to watch every cent now), called work to say that he would be in a little late and followed the Coast Highway into Cardiff. It was a short drive, during which Eddie wondered more than once if this was not an incredibly stupid thing to do. What if she wasn't thrilled to see him? Lord knows she never had been before, Eddie thought, ignoring a twist of resentment. And what if she wanted to know how he knew where she lived? It wasn't as if he could just come out and tell her that he'd followed her home, even if he had only done it once or twice. He started formulating some lies and hoped she'd buy one of them if it came to that. On impulse, right before he turned left on Chesterfield to head up into the hills, Eddie stopped at a flower stand and purchased a bunch of fragrant but anemic-looking roses. He hoped she'd take it from where it came. His sympathy (now, anyway) was genuine.

She opened the door before he could even knock, and Eddie was shocked by what he saw. She still had that crazy beauty, but she looked *worked*. The phrase *rode hard and put away wet* danced through Eddie's mind. She'd gained some weight around the middle, but her face looked thin and pale, and there was something haunted about her eyes. Eddie suddenly realized that all of his physical attraction to Marina was gone, replaced by something less visceral but equally powerful—something that pulled him right inside her door.

He stood there way too long, roses in his hand, unable to offer them or even speak while she stared blankly at some unknown point over his right shoulder. His mouth was dry and he was starting to feel very uneasy.

"You broke the fish plate. She loved that plate," Marina said, and Eddie nearly jumped out of his skin. In his rage that afternoon in the kitchen, he'd picked up the huge, unwieldy fish-shaped ceramic plate that he'd always hated and hurled it against the wall, where it smashed into splinters so small that Tina would be sweeping them up for months.

"How do you know that?" Eddie asked.

"You might have been able to talk to her if it hadn't been for that plate," Marina answered. "It really hurt her."

"Did you talk to her? Did you?" But even as Eddie asked the question, the sound of fear creeping into his voice, he knew that Marina was *seeing* him smash that plate. He couldn't explain how he knew this, but there was something about the look on her face, something about the slow, steady way she was speaking—as if she was commenting on a movie she was watching.

"There's a complaint where you work," she said. "And they know you've been sleeping there. They're sending someone down from corporate. You should find somewhere else to stay. You can't afford to lose your job, especially now . . ." Marina stared at him hard, her eyebrows knitting together as if she was trying to work out a complicated math problem. Eddie was thoroughly spooked. He'd never believed that Marina was a real psychic or that such a thing even existed. Now he wasn't so sure.

"You're having a baby," Marina said, a little lilt on the end of her words like she was surprised.

"What are you talking about? You mean I have a kid I don't know about? What are you saying?"

"No, she hasn't been born yet. But her mother . . . her mother doesn't want you to know."

"It can't be," Eddie said. "Tina had her tubes tied after our second kid."

"Your wife is not pregnant, Eddie."

"Fucking Cassie," Eddie swore. "That *bitch*."

Marina looked over his shoulder again, and then back at him. "Cassie can't have children," she said. "She doesn't know it yet and she's going to use that trick again, but it's never going to work."

"So . . . ?"

"So," Marina said, and then it all became clear to Eddie: the sudden cooldown, the weird phone call. He never should have come here, never. He thrust his roses at Marina, the paper covering now damp and tearing from his sweaty hands, and she looked at them as if seeing them for the first time. She looked upset, like she was going to hyperventilate. "Don't go there, Eddie. Please. You're going to get hurt. Please listen to me."

"I don't know what you mean. Go where?"

"Listen, this is important. Does your wife have a friend with . . . with a ruby ring? Do you know?"

That was it. He was rattled way beyond what he could take. "I'm sorry, Marina, I have to go. I'm sorry."

"Eddie, please . . ."

He gave her a last quick look and let himself out. Shit, what a mistake it had been to come over here, Eddie thought. Just one of so many he'd made.

Chapter 27

Cooper was tired in every way. His heavy new body and erratic sleep schedule had drained him physically, and his overworked brain was so exhausted that he could barely calculate change for a dollar. But he was mostly just tired of feeling bad about everything. His own wretchedness had become such a relentless emotional grind that he was almost bored by it. It had been almost impossible for him to drag his ass out of bed this morning and even more difficult to make himself look presentable (since, having left *hot* in the dust a long time ago, presentable was the best he could manage these days), but he'd made the effort because today—well, today could be the beginning of a major turnaround. His eminence, Max, had requested an audience at his office and Cooper was on his way to meet with him.

San Diego was experiencing an unseasonable heat wave and Cooper had to start shedding layers as soon as he walked outside, which was too bad because tight clothing had not been kind to him lately. His T-shirt was already chafing and he worried about showing up with dark sweat circles under his armpits. It had to be at least eighty degrees outside and it wasn't even lunchtime yet. What the hell—this was supposed to be May Gray time, followed by June Gloom. There would probably be a term to describe bad weather in the summer, too, if they could come up with something that rhymed with July—July Surprise? July Good-bye? At any rate, it wasn't supposed to be this hot. He turned on the radio, half expecting to hear news that Earth had spun out of its orbit and was hurtling toward the sun. But instead of a weather report, 102.1 FM was playing "Rehab," that song by Amy Winehouse. They were trying to make her go to rehab, but she wasn't going to go. Cooper appreciated the sentiment.

Of course, nobody was actively trying to get him into rehab, although he figured that was coming soon. His father was incredibly tolerant, but there were limits to the man's patience. Cooper couldn't remember the last time he'd put in a full day's work at his father's office. And between the pills, the Starbucks and the junk food, he'd put on about twenty pounds and his skin had gone to shit. Most of the time, he looked and dressed like he lived on the street. To say he had let himself go didn't even begin to cover it. But the reason he hadn't checked himself into any one of the numerous rehab facilities around here had less to do with a resistance to give up his bad habits and more to do with a desire to punish himself. At first, he admitted, it was about escape, and he'd always been a bit of a partier anyway, but now it was about guilt.

Aside from the little things (leaving his father in the lurch, shutting out his well-meaning friends, not returning his mother's phone calls— crap, it was already May; had he *missed* Mother's Day?), Cooper's deep sources of guilt were gnawing away at him. To begin with, he never should have made those anonymous phone calls to Marina. Besides being just plain nasty, that had been a very dangerous thing to do. His sketchy behavior had already been documented by at least one person at that point, and who knew if Max had gone to the cops (although with Max's pathological desire to remain low-profile, Cooper doubted it). Now, with the fire . . . well, it wouldn't be too much of a stretch for certain people to start questioning whether he had anything to do with it.

Cooper had figured out an excuse—an *alibi*—to cover himself if the shit ever hit the fan (how he hated that expression and its attendant visual): drug-induced psychosis. It was pretty simple, pretty well documented at this point and pretty much true. It was scary to think about, but there had definitely been some nights, even whole days, that Cooper didn't remember with any kind of clarity. And then there were a couple that he just didn't remember at all. One wouldn't think it possible to do too much damage when one was as out of it as Cooper had been, but, unfortunately, it was. Look at what people did on Ambien, for crying out loud. It was supposed to just give you a peaceful night's slumber, but people ended up sleep-eating entire refrigerators full of food. So, yes, if questioned, Cooper could recall most of what he had done and said. But by no means all of it.

Not that concern for himself was what bothered Cooper the most. From the first time he'd met her, Cooper had thought of Marina as his friend. Yes, there was money involved and in a way that meant the relationship was bought and paid for. But the money was also a great leveler; both of them were getting what they needed, unlike most other relationships, where someone was always in emotional arrears. And unlike, say, a *psychiatrist,* Marina was unconcerned about Cooper correcting his character flaws or working on himself, or about transference. She knew him and his secrets and took it all in stride without judging or criticizing. Wasn't that the definition of a friend, with or without the money?

It was stupid—no, it was ridiculous to think that Marina was the woman Max had left him for, and as soon as he'd stopped to give it more than a moment's thought he'd realized how wrongheaded he'd been. Unfortunately, that moment had come after he'd made a series of terrible errors in judgment. No, they were more like *fatal* errors, because he'd effectively destroyed his relationship with Marina. This was a shame because what he needed more than anything right now was a friend. He wondered if he should go see Marina. Or at least call her. That would be okay, wouldn't it? Nobody would question a genuine concern over her well-being, right? Maybe he should take her some flowers. Would that look too guilty? No, what woman didn't love flowers? He knew a place where he could get the most beautiful roses . . .

But first there was Max. Cooper took the Del Mar Heights Road exit off the southbound I-5 and turned left. It would have been quicker to stay on the freeway for one more exit, but Cooper needed the extra time to prepare. He drove slowly through the beige and buff cookie-cutter condo land of Carmel Valley, checking his hair and teeth in the rearview mirror. A shadow of his former self, he was. A very fat shadow. His stomach was doing little flips and his adrenaline was pumping as he got closer. He couldn't believe Max still had this kind of power over him. He thought about swallowing a couple of Xanax for his nerves, but overrode the impulse. Max could always tell when he was high and he didn't want to jeopardize . . . He didn't want to jeopardize the slim (but better than none) possibility that Max had called him here today to tell him that he wanted to give it another chance. Cooper exhaled, feeling dizzy just thinking about it.

Maybe he was foolish to think it was even possible to come back after all the water that had passed under the bridge, but—and here he thought about Marina again—a big part of him still believed that *he* could change Max, that love could conquer all. Marina had always held fast to this motto, which, now that he thought about it, was kind of weird, since Marina didn't seem like the most romantic woman in the world. Anyway, she'd always told Cooper that it was his loving nature that would ultimately bring Max around and, damn it, he *believed* it. Besides, he honestly didn't think Max had a woman at all. Aside from his stupid assumption about Marina, Cooper hadn't caught so much as a glimmer of anything womanlike anywhere near Max. Wouldn't it be the perfect irony, Cooper thought, if all this time he's been out cruising gay bars while I've been crying in my beer at home? But no, Max would rather die.

He'd taken the long way, but Cooper had already arrived at Max's office. It felt weird to be there legitimately after all that time skulking around in that ridiculous Focus. He'd really scraped the bottom of the barrel, hadn't he? Well, that was it; Cooper was this very minute making a pact with God. *Just give me Max back and I'll do it all,* Cooper thought. *I'll get cleaned up, I'll give to charity, I'll go see Marina, I'll make amends. I promise. Just give me Max back.* Cooper wiped his eyes, patted his gel-stiff hair and got out of the car.

The first thing he noticed was the new girl at the reception desk. He remembered the first time he'd come in here, wet from that torrential rainstorm, and how the pretty fat woman with the long hair and nice skin had been so polite but so firm about not letting him go up to see Max. He'd given her that giant vase of sunflowers, he recalled. He wondered what she'd done with them. He'd thought then how great she'd look if she only lost fifty pounds. She could probably say the same about him now. At any rate, she wasn't at the front desk, having been replaced by her polar opposite: an anorexic waif with thin blond hair who looked as if she was about twelve years old.

Cooper gave the waif his name and asked for Max. She pushed a few buttons, breathed into her earpiece and told him to go to the fourth floor. Cooper broke into a full sweat once he was in the elevator. It was kind of stupid to put the shrinks on the top floor, wasn't it? What if they had a jumper? He was starting to get a very uneasy feeling twisting at his gut. Jesus, it was like he was getting ready to go to the prom or something. With the quarterback. He was absolutely *dying* for a few goddamn Xanax.

"I promise," he whispered to himself (and God) as he stepped out of the elevator. "I promise."

Another receptionist guided Cooper into Max's office, where the man himself stood—right next to the woman (it took Cooper only a split second to place her) who used to work in reception downstairs. She looked good, was glowing even, and she'd lost weight. Suddenly, it all felt like a massive setup to Cooper and he wanted to turn around and get the fuck out before the big reveal. But, of course, it was too late; the die was cast.

"How are you, Cooper?"

"Max?"

"Cooper, this is Kiki."

"Kiki?"

"Nice to meet you, Cooper. I've heard a lot about you." Kiki extended her hand to shake. Cooper didn't take it.

"Yeah, well, I *haven't* heard a lot about you. And we've met before." Kiki looked very confused, theatrically knitting her dark, perfectly manicured eyebrows in perplexity.

"Cooper, I wanted you to come here today because I—we—wanted to tell you something and I thought it would be better delivered in person."

"This is a joke, right, Max?"

"Kiki knows about our history," Max said, the words seeming to come out slow and distorted. "She and I do not have any secrets from each other. I want you to know that in case you decide to try to . . . get involved in our lives. It won't work anymore, Cooper."

Cooper looked at Kiki, whose lips were curled in a small carmine-colored smile. "You're okay with this?" Cooper asked her. "Really?"

"I love him," Kiki said flatly. "We are in love with each other."

"Oh, please, you have got to be fucking kidding me," Cooper said, almost laughing—the whole thing was so insane.

"We're getting married," Max said, "and Kiki is expecting a baby. We're having a baby." And that's when Cooper noticed the ring, a huge trillion-cut ruby set in gold, on Kiki's left fourth finger. Of course, Max had found something utterly beautiful and totally unusual. It was so lovely it almost looked familiar to Cooper—as if Max had managed to conjure it up based on a design in Cooper's own head. He thought he might throw up where he stood.

"Oh my *God,* Max!"

"Cooper—"

"No, Max, no. I mean, do you really *think* that getting a fat girl pregnant makes you *not gay?* I mean, do you really?" Kiki's mouth had dropped open at the word *fat* and her eyes were shooting sparks. She didn't give a fuck that her fiancé was gay, Cooper thought, just that he'd called her fat. "I cannot fucking *believe* you."

"I'd really hoped you'd be a little more mature, Cooper. It's totally unnecessary to insult Kiki. She hasn't done anything to you."

"I'm sorry, Kiki. Sorry *for* you," Cooper said.

"I also wanted to tell you that Kiki and I will be going to Andrew and Madeline's party tomorrow night. I don't know if you're invi—if you're planning to attend, but if you are, I want to ask you not to make a scene. Now that you know everything—and you can see that we"—he gestured to Kiki—"are united on this thing—it would only make you look bad, Cooper. It won't serve any purpose."

"I hate you, Max."

"Cooper—"

"No, I really mean it, Max. I fucking hate you."

Cooper turned around and ran out of the office. He couldn't get to his car and his Xanax stash fast enough. Fuck God and fuck promises. He was in hell and there was no God here.

Chapter 28

Madeline speared a slice of mango from the beautifully arranged party platter in her kitchen and shoved it in her mouth. It was delicious, sweet and fresh, so she grabbed another and then one more. Now the symmetry of the platter was ruined and would have to be fixed anyway, so she attacked the strawberries and bananas in the center, shoveling them in, barely chewing as she went. Madeline was starving—truly hungry for the first time in forever—and wanted nothing more than to just eat until she was satisfied. Well, there was plenty of time before the party and there was plenty of food to go around. Besides, the event coordinator organizing this party needed to earn her ridiculously high fee. Fixing a slightly mutilated fruit platter was almost negligible in terms of work. In fact, Madeline thought, turning to the skewers of langostino and lobster, she might just dip into some of the other offerings.

But no. Seafood, Madeline remembered, with all the mercury and whatever else, was dangerous for the baby. No matter how good she felt, she wasn't taking any chances this time. It was so ironic, Madeline thought as she poked around the pineapple plate. All that money, time and anguish spent on fertility treatments had led to sickness, suffering and miscarriage. She hadn't felt well for a single minute after her body had been forced to conceive Andrew's offspring. But now, when she hadn't even been trying, she'd gotten pregnant as easily and efficiently as a rabbit. And instead of feeling ill, she was full of energy. She didn't even feel fat or bloated. Even though it was still very early, Madeline knew that there would be no complications with this pregnancy. There would be no hellish bed rest, bleeding or nausea. Not this time.

Madeline scooped out a spoonful of poi from a brightly colored dish, rolled it around on her tongue and spit it out into a napkin. That wasn't at all what she was looking for. The luau had been her idea, but now Madeline wished she'd picked a party theme with better food. She really wasn't in the mood for Hawaiian. Still, it was going to be a very festive gathering. The event coordinator had set up a miniature beach in the backyard, complete with fire pit, shells, palm trees and hammocks. You wouldn't know you weren't on Maui, Madeline thought. With all the pikake flowers in the house, it even *smelled* like the islands here. It had been so long since Madeline had wanted to let go and have fun. This party was way overdue. "Summer is around the corner," she'd written on the invitations, "so let's have a luau!" She'd had to use the change of season as the official excuse to have a party, because there was the not-so-small matter of figuring out how she was going to convince Andrew she was pregnant with *his* baby before she could tell anyone the real reason she wanted to celebrate.

Madeline wiped her sticky hands on a dish towel and decided it was time to leave the kitchen. She thought about tidying up her mess, but the caterers would be arriving soon and they could deal with it. She poured herself a tall glass of water and walked barefoot through her newly tropical living room and out to the backyard, enjoying the feel of the pristine sand under her toes. Madeline wondered for a moment if it was possible to make fake sand for events such as this one. Surely, these clean, sugary grains under her feet had never seen a real beach or ocean—they had to be synthetic. She took a sip from her water glass and set it down on the edge of the fire pit. She didn't have time to worry about the sand—she had her own fakery to work out.

The essential dilemma was that she and Andrew had not had sex for months, and her husband did not seem remotely interested in changing that situation. It had been so long that Madeline couldn't even remember what his body looked or felt like under his clothes. It was as if sex with Andrew was something she'd read about long ago, but never actually experienced. At first, his excuse for not touching her was that it would be dangerous for her pregnancy. Then it was because she was healing from her traumatic miscarriage. But even weeks later, when she'd been given the all-clear by her doctor, Andrew wouldn't come anywhere near her. He'd started staying up late, drinking and watching TV downstairs, then sleeping in one of the guest bedrooms. The latest excuse was that it was a very busy time at work. Royal Rings was debuting a new engagement ring with a unique design. He was going out on a limb with this thing; people tended to go with traditional rings, even though they claimed to want fresh designs. But if this ring caught on it would be a big deal—very big. He'd said something about Egypt and the power of triangles, but Madeline couldn't remember it. The only thing she heard clearly was that he was busy and stressed and that she shouldn't wait up for him. It wasn't exactly a recipe for intimacy, although, until recently, Madeline hadn't cared about the physical space between them.

He'd been so angry at her after the miscarriage, Madeline knew, all that rage boiling just below the surface, but he wouldn't allow himself to show it outwardly. He couldn't. What kind of man would punish a woman who'd just lost his baby? But Madeline was sure that was when he'd started thinking about divorcing her. Later, she'd found the papers—preliminary proceedings—in his desk drawer. He'd wanted her to make that discovery, she knew. They certainly weren't hidden. So he wanted her to be scared about her future without him. And Madeline didn't need any reminding about their prenuptial agreement. It was funny, Madeline thought, how she hadn't made any fuss about signing that thing. Who could have predicted it would come to something like this?

Someone like Marina, that's who.

Madeline felt a sharp, uncomfortable jab in her brain at the thought of Marina, almost as if the woman were suddenly there inside her head. But this wasn't the first time Madeline had experienced it. A few times since her last encounter with Marina at Darling's, Madeline had gotten the distinct feeling that the psychic was watching her—from within. This was what happened when you imbued a person like Marina with any power. Marina knew too much about Madeline and Madeline was trying to keep too much hidden. Too many balls in the air, Madeline thought. How long before one of them fell? She'd established plenty of distance from Marina before the fire, but she still kept careful tabs on what the papers reported after it happened. It had been a hot story for about five minutes and then disappeared into the swirl of meaningless news blather. People cared more about whether or not their dogs would be allowed on local beaches than an office fire in Encinitas, even if someone had died as a result. That's right—a dead body rated lower than the comfort of someone's pet pooch. It was a homeless man, they said; the investigation was pending. And then, thank goodness, there was nothing more.

Madeline felt a sharp tang of bitterness so strong it made her mouth water. That woman deserved everything she got, and anyone who knew her—*really* knew her the way Madeline did—would have to agree. Madeline wasn't sorry about a damn thing when it came to Marina. She'd run her game too long and on the wrong person. She hoped Marina was every bit as miserable as she had been herself.

Stop it—focus. Madeline unclenched her jaw. She had to concentrate. There was work to do. There was Andrew to think about.

She'd been very careful to avoid pissing him off, especially after she started collecting afternoon delights in a series of sweaty motel rooms. Madeline was almost positive that Andrew would never suspect her of having an affair—or even care if she did—but that tiny seed of doubt was enough to make her extra cautious. But he didn't seem to be angry anymore, and, in a way, that was even more disturbing than his bottled-up fury. He hadn't balked at the cost of this party, for example. Nor had he even questioned her desire to have it. He'd become quiet and strange. His behavior had made her so paranoid that she quickly ditched Eddie (who had obviously served *his* purpose) and attempted to become, once again, the wife that Andrew wanted. Of course, Madeline thought with another wave of vitriol, it was never the *wife* Andrew wanted—it was the children. He wanted an heir, just like Henry the fucking Eighth. Well, Madeline had wants, too. She wanted the baby and she wanted the money. And Andrew could have what he desired if he'd just loosen up.

As soon as she realized she was pregnant, Madeline had tried to get Andrew into bed, a delicate operation considering the emotional distance between them, but he'd been completely unresponsive. She'd been subtle at first, snuggling up to him as he drank his Johnnie Walker Blue neat in front of the flat screen. He'd looked at her, puzzled, as if he'd suddenly acquired some small pet requiring attention, and turned back to the television. She'd gotten a little bolder after that, parading around the house in La Perla lingerie, then sliding up behind him while he was shaving, running her hands up the length of his torso. He'd ignored her until he couldn't any longer, and then he'd just said, "I don't have time for this." Madeline's last attempt had been an appeal to romantic nostalgia. She'd re-created the scene of their greatest passion, where she'd dressed herself up as his personal gift basket and presented herself to him. Andrew stared at the ribbons wound around her breasts, the glitter shining on her perfectly waxed skin, and ran his hand lightly down her arm. "I'm sorry, Maddie," he said. "I just can't."

Madeline finished her water and walked back into the kitchen. She was still hungry—ravenous even. She needed something substantive to eat. Something big. As she rummaged through her Sub-Zero, Madeline realized that everything would be so much easier if Andrew would just disappear. No, Madeline thought, shutting the fridge and reaching for a loaf of coconut banana bread, not disappear—*cease to exist.* If he were to suddenly just die, all her problems would be solved. She thought about the chances of that happening as she sliced a piece of bread and chewed it.

Andrew was having all these health problems lately: high blood pressure and high cholesterol, and he was drinking way too much. But none of those things was likely to kill him anytime soon. The tropical bread was disappointing. She grabbed a skewer of vegetables and soy "chicken" that had been marinating in barbecue sauce and bit into it. Sauce dripped onto her tight white halter top, but she didn't stop to wipe it off. She supposed he could be worked up into some kind of heart attack, but she wouldn't know how to go about doing that. Of course, if he had an accident, like falling down the stairs while drunk, or crashing his car . . .

Madeline stopped herself midchew to allow for the full force of her revelation. The statistics always stated that you were most likely to be killed by someone you knew, someone close to you, but Madeline had never really understood why until this moment. It just made things *so much easier.* When you looked at it like that, murder didn't require a huge mental leap.

But there was still time to make it look like Andrew's baby—barely. She had to force him to have sex with her within the next day or two or else . . . She'd try again tonight, Madeline decided, after the party. She'd make sure he was well lubricated with alcohol, which she'd spike with Viagra. Even though Madeline had convinced herself that Andrew deserved whatever he got, she was willing to give him one more chance. Either way, this baby would end up with Andrew's name and Andrew's money. Nobody else would ever know.

Madeline heard the doorbell and was relieved. Finally, the caterers were here and she could stop shoving food into her face. She rearranged the food on the platter and ran water over her hands. The caterers rang again and then started pounding on the door. What the hell—why were they in such a damn hurry?

"Just a minute!" she shouted. "I'm coming!" As she walked to the entrance, Madeline thought about what she would wear later. Something sheer, she decided—and no bra. She was smiling, thinking about the effect her barely covered breasts would have on a drunk, Viagraed Andrew, when she opened the door. It took less than a second for the grin to fall right off her face when she saw that it was Eddie Perkins, not the caterers, who was standing in front of her. He looked her up and down—her stained top, bare feet, greasy fingers.

"Nice to see you open your own door," he said. "I would have thought you'd have help for that kind of thing."

"What are you doing here?" Her voice sounded raw and shrill.

"Woman," he said, his own voice filled with menace, "you'd better let me in."

Chapter 29

It was going to be another hot day in the middle of a very hot week. Before dawn, Marina had opened all her windows and closed all her blinds in order to keep the air inside cool. Rosa would be arriving soon, and she wondered if it would be more comfortable for them to sit in her tiny living room instead of her larger but west-facing kitchen. She wasn't too worried either way; the heat was intense, but there was no muscle behind it. Even as it swept in, cooking the landscape and upping the danger of wildfires, the heat felt temporary—like a sloppy houseguest who made a mess but didn't stay long enough to create any permanent damage. It was so different from Florida, a place to which Marina's mind returned often lately, where the scorching humidity was a slow torture. The air here was dry and less aggressive—it was as if she were being patiently baked as opposed to viciously roasted. The oven comparison was particularly apt since Marina's body, growing heavier every day, was performing its own version of convection.

For some days, she'd been feeling movement inside, the flickers of tiny fists and heels deep within the bones of her pelvis. In the old days they used to call these flutters the "quickening." Marina was now *quick with child* by those terms—a misnomer, she thought. The activity inside her body seemed to be unfolding in no particular rush. Sometimes, too, the baby talked to her in a language Marina didn't understand, the whispers tickling her inner ear. This communication had started long before the physical movement, but Marina had only just realized what it was. She was trying to make sense of it now, trying to decode and understand it.

Accepting her gift and learning how to use it were now Marina's main concerns. She'd been shown exactly what could and would happen if she refused to work with what she'd been given. She thought about how foolish she'd been the day of the fire; how stubborn, just like her mother had said. That unrelenting urge to explain everything away—to bring the world under her control—had been her undoing. *"Go home,"* she'd been instructed. If she'd listened . . . If only she'd listened.

She was listening now, straining her ears to interpret sounds she'd never heard before, her eyes to gaze upon visions that nobody else could see. Marina's new learning curve wasn't just steep; it was a ninety-degree angle. Her life had become a process of stripping away in earnest—of forgetting everything she'd believed was true and starting over with a completely new set of rules. She was learning to see, to walk, to talk as if for the first time. And she was doing it here—in this little house, in this little beach community, in this slow, pretty county at the bottom of California. Because the first thing Marina had decided after she'd regained consciousness in the back of the emergency vehicle, her incinerated office still smoking, was that she wasn't going to run.

Perhaps it was that her bruised bare feet were bandaged, a clear enough symbol of her inability to flee. Or perhaps it was just that the exhaustion Marina felt went straight through to her core. As the EMT leaned over her, asking questions like "Do you know where you are?" Marina didn't know if she had even enough energy to sit up. But there was more to it than that. Marina knew, finally, that the fire signaled the end of the road she'd been on and the beginning of another. She also knew now that Gideon had come looking for her not for revenge but because he loved her. His fate had been meant for her. She'd been inside that vengeful, bitter mind, but Marina couldn't tell whose body it belonged to. Nor had she been able to get into that mind again at will. Like everything else about her gift, the telepathic connections she'd made happened at random and never by her own design. She searched in the darkness for clues as to who it might be—who had such hatred for her. But there was never enough light to see.

But Marina couldn't have articulated any of this in the ambulance even if she'd wanted to. Nor did she tell the paramedics she was pregnant or that she'd just been in a car accident. And they didn't seem to want to know how she'd come to show up barefoot, bedraggled and half crazed right as the blaze was at its peak.

The cops were a different story. She was questioned as soon as she'd been cleared by the paramedics. She gave up that it was her office right away, but as for the rest of it, there was no explanation she could give that would make them understand why she knew what she shouldn't have known. Anything she said was likely to make her look like the freak who had set fire to the building. As it was, her behavior was outright suspicious. They didn't seem to know yet that there was a body—*some*body, *Gideon*—inside the building, or else they were waiting for her to tell them. Marina was as out of it as she'd ever been at that moment, physically, emotionally and spiritually, but she knew to keep her mouth shut about Gideon. It would all come out soon enough.

Instead, Marina found herself telling the officer—Larson was his name—that the reason she was at the scene (the reason she knew there was a scene to *be* at) was because she was a psychic. *No, really, officer, I* am *psychic.* Marina had uttered those words, or some variation, many times before, but that was the first time she'd truly believed them herself. And there, of course, was the irony.

"You're a psychic," the cop repeated back to her. He had walked her across the street to the café where she'd first seen Gideon and was making notations on a small pad. The light from the fire and all the emergency vehicles flashed blue, red and orange into the shadows. "You see the future? Dead people? That kind of thing?"

"I'm . . . I counsel people . . . intuitively," she said. Old reflexes died hard. Marina realized she no longer had to pretend to be legitimate.

"You counsel people."

So that was his strategy, Marina thought. Just repeat everything until it sounded worse than it was.

"Yes," she said. "I can see certain things. I counsel people based on what I see." At that moment, Marina was indeed seeing something that she knew nobody else could. A pale green glow, flecked with bits of purple and brighter on the left side, encircled Officer Larson. She cast her eyes downward to avoid staring into it and saw a black Labrador retriever sitting with its paws crossed at the officer's feet.

"And so you saw . . ." He flipped back a few pages of his notebook and looked at what he had written. "You saw the fire before it happened? Is that what you're telling me?"

"I had a . . . it was a sort of dream," Marina began.

The dog's tag said "Buddy."

"What is a 'sort of dream'?"

"I was unconscious. I passed out for a while."

"You were passed out. Have you been drinking tonight?"

"No, I haven't had anything to drink."

"So why were you passed out?"

"I had . . . I had a car accident. I must have hit my head."

"Where is your vehicle, ma'am?" Buddy nuzzled Officer Larson's leg and Marina wondered if the dog was real, dead or just a projection of the officer's thoughts. She fought the urge to reach down and pet it.

"It's back . . . I don't know, I just ran. I had this dream. I saw an explosion."

"An explosion? Can you tell me where you were earlier this evening? Is there anyone who can—"

"I went off the road. I had an accident."

"And then you ran here from—?"

"Yes."

"You weren't in the office?"

"No," Marina said. "I told you."

"Excuse me, what are you doing?"

The dog had stood up and padded over to Marina. She could feel its breath on her hand. But when she leaned down to stroke its fur, her hand went right through the animal. Reality was starting to break apart like one of those cheap cardboard puzzles where the pieces never truly fit together. "The dog," she said. "I was just . . ." The glow around Officer Larson deepened and sparked. He tilted his head to the side, nonplussed, assessing her.

"The *dog?*"

Marina closed her eyes, but when she opened them Buddy was still there and sniffing at his master's hand. "I'm sorry," she said.

"Would you mind taking a sobriety test to confirm that you haven't been drinking?" the officer asked her.

"Yes—I mean, no, I don't mind."

It was the first time Marina realized that the police had little use for psychics who were actually psychic, and she knew it wouldn't be the last.

Much later, when Officer Larson had finished with her, Marina saw a tiny black Lab puppy—lost, escaped or abandoned—approach the cluster of cops and firemen gathered on the street.

"Hey, little guy," Marina heard Officer Larson say, "what are you doing here? Where'd you come from, huh, boy? Huh, buddy?"

That was the end of the first night. But it was not the end of the questioning.

There had been several interviews (as the police called their interrogations), most of them in the weeks immediately following the fire. They followed a similar pattern with only minor variations in the questions (and those tossed in only to throw her off balance, Marina assumed):

"Can you tell us where you were the evening of March fifteenth, 2007?"

"I was driving home. I had an accident. I went off the road."

"Do you know who set fire to your office?"

"No."

"Did you set fire to your office?"

"No."

"Do you know who was in your office when the fire started?"

"No."

"Do you know why someone would want to set fire to your office?"

"No."

"Have you been having any trouble with a boyfriend?"

"No."

"The girls from the nail place next door say they've seen a man hanging around your office. Any idea who they might be talking about?"

"It could be anyone. I have—I had a lot of clients. Some of them were men."

"You work as a psychic?"

"Yes."

"And that's how you knew your office was on fire?"

"I had a dream. I saw an explosion."

"But your psychic abilities can't tell you who set fire to your office?"

"No."

"Can you explain that for us?"

"No, I can't."

"Can you tell us where you were the evening of March fifteenth, 2007?"

They never asked her about Gideon and she didn't understand why. It was as if it hadn't really been Gideon who had died in the fire. Sometimes Marina almost believed he hadn't. Dead people with a far weaker connection to her visited her all the time now. Surely, Gideon would have come to her already. And, surely, the police would have identified the body by now—*if* they'd found the body—and made the connection between the two of them? But, of course, this wasn't something Marina could ask them. It had been almost two months since the fire now, and while the investigation was ongoing, her part in it seemed to be getting smaller. This allowed her the thinnest shred of hope that maybe Gideon was still alive in the world and that the body in her office was someone else.

But then, and now, Marina would feel her heart sink—a physical sensation, as if the muscle inside her chest was falling, drowning, and could barely keep beating. She knew what she had seen. Many times since that night, when she was in the deepest part of sleep, she found herself in *that mind* again, in the repeating loop of that single moment. It was the ring she saw, lying against Gideon's chest. *Take it. Take it now.* That was the thought. She woke every time, desperate for more than that glimpse, almost begging whoever it was to come to her. But as yet it hadn't changed. As yet, she was still foundering in the dark. Waiting.

The scent of apple and cinnamon nudged Marina back to the present. Rosa was near. The delicious smell of whatever pastry Rosa was bringing always preceded her arrival by a few minutes. Being able to sense people approaching by scent or sound was just one of the new, if inconsistent, perception skills Marina was trying to get used to. So it was turnovers Rosa was bringing today. Marina would have to act surprised when she opened the fragrant paper bag, but her delight would be genuine. It had taken some practice to wait until people had knocked on her door before she opened it. Marina was learning that disrupting people's expectations of reality made them nervous and unsettled, even if it proved that she *was* psychic. This was another irony that Marina had absorbed but still marveled at. People were much more comfortable with the kind of psychic readings Marina gave before she was actually psychic. Having the gift had effectively ruined her prior business. Once Marina was no longer able to deliver readings based on pure observation and she began telling her clients what she really saw, they became disgruntled at best and angry at worst. In both scenarios they dropped her within a session or two. Marina no longer saw a single one of her old regulars for readings, although they sometimes appeared to her in other ways and forms. This was all, Marina assumed, part of the fortune-teller's message that she'd have to learn how to use her gift.

The knock was tentative, as always with Rosa—as if she felt she was imposing—but it didn't startle Marina, who heard it before it came. In the moments it took to walk to the door, Marina was transported back to her small whitewashed rental in Florida. The heat, the dead snake rotting in the birds-of-paradise, and Mrs. Golden clutching her purse and waiting for whatever calamity Marina would foretell. This was a memory, not a vision, but Marina was visited often enough by Mrs. Golden. The old lady looked in on her with Gideon's eyes; silent now, but expectant.

Where is he? Marina had asked more than once, but the old woman just tapped at her neck where her ring had hung.

Hand on the doorknob, Marina shuddered with faithlessness. Had *they* cursed her with that snake? It wasn't something she'd ever have believed could happen before, but all bets had long been off when it came to the territory of the unknown and the extrasensory. Marina shook her head. It was the first thing those Gypsy frauds said when you came to them looking for answers: *You've been cursed. I need your money to pray on. Only that can free you.* Marina used to think that people who believed and paid for that kind of blatant fakery were fools who didn't deserve to have the money they parted with. Not anymore.

Marina opened the door and smiled at Rosa, who bowed her head quickly and then stepped inside. Rosa's long dark hair was pulled back into an immaculate ponytail. Her clothes were spotless and tidy and would stay that way even after serving food and drink all day in the heat. She held a carafe in one hand and the bag of pastries in the other. There was both hope and trust in the look that they shared.

"It's nice to see you, Rosa."

"*Cómo estás,* Marina? It's so hot outside. Nice in here." Rosa hesitated and then offered the bag of pastries to Marina. "I bring for you," she said.

"We'll put them in the kitchen," Marina said.

Marina could sense Rosa's anticipation edging into impatience as she settled herself at the kitchen table, waiting for Marina to pour two cups of hibiscus tea from the carafe.

"Marina," Rosa began, but she held herself back out of politeness, Marina knew, and respect. Marina took a sip of tea and looked at Rosa, allowing her eyes to soften their focus and her thoughts to still. She waited. After a few moments the girl appeared, as if she had just walked into the room, and stood behind her mother. Her hands rested lightly on Rosa's shoulders.

"*Es Luz?*" Rosa asked. "*Está aquí?*"

"Yes," Marina said. "She's here."

Luz—at least the version of Luz that Marina was seeing—smiled and tilted her head to the side. Rosa came regularly, but the girl didn't always make an appearance. Marina knew that Rosa lived for these moments of communication with Luz and was always disappointed when Marina couldn't see her. It was her unquestioning faith that had driven Rosa to find Marina soon after the fire—showing up at her door, her hands folded, pleading. "You saw my daughter," Rosa said. "I need to talk to her. Please, please, don't send me away."

Marina let her in, never asking how Rosa had managed to find her. In the scheme of things, that detail just didn't seem very important. Nor did Marina question the immediate ease she felt with Rosa or their ability to communicate using few words. Rosa needed no proof of Marina's gift, nor did she try to test it as so many of Marina's previous clients had. Rosa operated on faith and intuition, both of which were deep and strong. She knew, for example, that Marina was pregnant before she began to show. She brought special teas and juices for "*la pequeña,*" along with fruits and pastries. Marina never asked Rosa for money, but sometimes she'd find a ten- or twenty-dollar bill folded into a napkin in her white paper pastry bag. Marina knew that Rosa probably gave her more than she could afford, but out of the same respect Rosa had for her, she never tried to give any of the donations back.

Soon after her first visit to Marina's house, Rosa began referring friends and relatives for readings. That small group had started referring *their* friends and relatives, and Marina was now building a brand-new client base of people who would never have been able to afford her services before. They worked hard and bought lottery tickets on Saturdays. Some of them went to church and all of them prayed. They were superstitious and worried about the weather. They clipped coupons and bought what was on sale. There were no Madelines among them and no Coopers. They were all scraping to get by, and not one of them had time to be bored or disaffected. The biggest difference, though, was that Marina's new clients came to her ready to hear whatever it was she could tell them—not what they wanted her to say.

Sometimes Marina could tell them very little and sometimes she received so much information that she couldn't differentiate between what was important and what was just noise and interference. But this didn't seem to bother any of her new clients, who accepted whatever she could tell them and were thankful for it. Marina knew that their faith and acceptance made them targets for charlatans of all kinds. As with Rosa, Marina took whatever form of payment her new clients were able to give her. Sometimes that came in the form of small bills, but more often she received food, services, even furniture. Thanks to Victor, a mechanic, she wouldn't ever have to worry about paying to have her car serviced. Linda, whose husband was a carpenter, had given her a beautiful, intricately carved rocking chair. Sarah, who sold crafts at street fairs, had given her a large moon-faced clock that glowed softly in the dark.

Marina was grateful for all of it, but it was only going to go so far. She tried not to think about what would happen once her retirement nest egg, which she was now living on, was depleted. And none of her new psychic abilities would tell her what would happen once the baby came. She was going to have to wait until the answer became clearer or try harder to un-cover it—just as she was now doing with Luz, who had stopped smiling and stroking her mother's shoulders and was trying to speak.

"*Dónde está Luz?*" Rosa said. "Can you see her?"

"Yes," Marina said. "I see her."

"What is she doing?" Rosa asked. "What does she say?"

Marina focused all her attention on Luz. She was wearing a white, gauzy dress with red and pink embroidered roses at the neck and hemline, and her long dark hair, so much like her mother's, flowed loose over her shoulder. Luz plucked at the shoulder of her dress and pointed to Marina and then her mother.

"She wants me to tell you about her dress," Marina said. "It's white with roses sewn onto it. I haven't seen her wear this before." Marina didn't tell Rosa that Luz was usually dressed in the hospital gown she'd died in.

Rosa clasped her hands and pressed them against her mouth. Her eyes filled with quick tears. "That is the dress we bury her in," she said.

Luz leaned over her mother, putting her arms around Rosa's shoul-ders. "She's right with you," Marina said. "She doesn't want you to be sad." Luz's presence was so strong that Rosa began to pat her own shoul-der as if she could literally feel the girl's hand there. In a way, Marina sup-posed, she could. Luz raised her head and looked into Marina's eyes. Marina heard the voice inside her head.

Tell her she did everything she could. Tell her she is a wonderful mother. Tell her I love her.

Rosa held her face tight while Marina relayed her daughter's words, but she couldn't stop the small, fierce sobs that escaped from deep within her chest. Luz nodded at Marina and raised her hands, palms up. This time there were no words, but Marina understood exactly what Luz wanted her mother to know.

"Rosa," she said softly, "Luz needs me to tell you . . . She says . . . She's ready to move on. She needs you to let her go."

Marina's voice sounded wrong to her own ears. Her tone was too cold, her words too saccharine and clichéd, like a drugstore greeting card. Luz was communicating without language—as if she were speaking in shapes or colors. It was beautiful, and Marina was frustrated that she lacked the ability to show it to Rosa. She bit her lip and tried again. "It's not a bad thing," she said. "It's better for you—and for her. And you don't have to forget her."

For a moment Rosa didn't respond, and Marina worried that she had caused Rosa to feel the loss of her daughter all over again. Luz stood to the side of her mother now, easing her way out of the room. She wouldn't be coming back again. Marina was about to speak, to reach for words of comfort, when Rosa lifted her head and took Marina's hands in hers.

"I understand," she said. "*Gracias,* Marina. Thank you so much."

Chapter 30

Sudden exhaustion, Marina was learning, was a side effect of her gift. Of all the changes, this was proving to be one of the most difficult to adjust to. There were times when she felt almost literally knocked out and had to sleep in the middle of the day. She might have attributed this to her pregnancy, but it wasn't physical fatigue she felt. After her readings, especially when she was communicating with the dead, Marina found herself drained and light-headed, as if her life force had been drawn out of her body.

Her last session with Rosa had been particularly intense. Marina was so tired afterward that she just passed out sitting in her rocking chair. Sleep was fierce, dreamless and so deep she could barely rouse herself when she heard persistent knocking on her door. Feeling as if she was underwater, Marina made her way to the door on unsteady legs. There was more knocking and then, "Ms. Marks? Ms. Marks, are you there? Police officer. Please open the door."

Marina froze, her senses suddenly alert and buzzing. She opened the door partway and peered through the crack, seeing a bit of blue jacket and tan slacks. Plainclothes, she thought, but her intuition was giving her nothing else.

"Marina Marks?"

"Yes?"

"I'm Detective Franks. I'd like to ask you a few questions. Can I come in, please?"

The "please" was perfunctory and meaningless, and served to make the question sound even more like the command that it was.

"Can I see your badge?" It was something people said often enough in the movies that it had become an accepted response, so Marina threw it out to buy some time. The truth was that she was still woozy enough that she wasn't sure whether or not Detective Franks was a flesh-and-blood presence or a spectral vision. If he showed her his badge, she could touch it and make sure it was real.

The detective sighed, annoyed, but reached into an unseen pocket and pulled out a wallet and badge and thrust it through the doorway. Marina didn't look at it, just ran her fingers quickly across its surface. Solid—and warm. She opened the door.

"Come in."

"Thank you."

Detective Franks was tall and heavyset and had graying blond hair cut in a style that was too boyish for him. Marina felt a wave of embarrassment and her cheeks flushed red. She put her hands to her face, confused, trying to hide . . .

"Something wrong?"

Detective Franks had narrowed his eyes and was looking at her with suspicion. It was *his* embarrassment she was feeling, Marina realized. He'd had very bad acne for years—she could see the scars now—and the pain of it was still real and fresh enough to be a dominant part of his personality. Marina feinted badly, mumbling something about its being hot. She asked him if he wanted a glass of water. He didn't.

"But why not?" Marina asked. "You're thirsty." She dug her fingernails into her palm. She had to learn not to keep stating what was obvious to her and wondered if she would ever be able to stop playing catch-up with her own intuitions. "I mean, you must be thirsty. It's so hot."

"Do you mind if I sit down?" he asked, and he didn't wait for a response, just parked himself on Marina's faded green love seat. He pulled a notebook and pen from his jacket pocket and made a notation. It was for show, Marina knew. He was dysgraphic, unable to write legibly. He'd been covering it for years, developing his own shorthand.

"This is a nice neighborhood," he said. "I haven't spent much time up here. Cute little houses. Probably cost a fortune, though, right? Out of my price range." He gave her a narrow, closed smile. She couldn't tell if his small talk warranted a response.

Marina realized she was still standing. Detective Franks was so much taller that it still seemed he was looking down on her even though he was seated. She sat down in the rocking chair and waited for him to continue.

"How long have you lived here, Ms. Marks?"

"Almost two years. You can call me Marina."

"Marina." He smiled again, a tight curving of his lips. "You live in the right place for a name like that, huh? With the ocean and everything. Were you born on a boat?"

"It's a Russian name. My grandmother was Russian. At least that's what my mother told me."

"Huh. Russian."

Detective Franks made a few scribbles in his pad. He was thinking about the fire, formulating the words he was going to use to ask her what she knew. He had information—she could see it twist like a worm in the corner of his brain—and he was trying to figure out how to use it for maximum impact.

"You said you had some questions for me?"

"I do. As I'm sure you know, we've had an ongoing investigation into the circumstances surrounding the fire on—"

"Yes," Marina said too anxiously. "Have you found out who—how the fire started?"

"As you also know," Detective Franks continued, "this is not just an arson investigation but a homicide investigation. There was a victim."

"Yes," Marina said. "I know."

Detective Franks observed Marina carefully. He was watching her for clues, for tells. He was taking in the way she folded her hands, the direction her eyes moved, whether there was sweat forming on the top of her lip. She watched him watch her, observed the way he tried to look into the core of her being and pull out the truth. It was exactly what she would have done with him had he come for a reading six months ago. For a moment, Marina was jealous. She would never be able to return to that mode of operation and she missed it with an almost physical ache.

"The body was very badly burned," he continued, "which made identification very difficult. Especially when nobody was reported missing. Or was seen in the area around the time of the fire. There was no ID on the body. No vehicle."

Marina said nothing, but continued to watch him. There was a shimmer in the air around him and she had to close her eyes for a moment to refocus. When she opened them, Mrs. Golden was sitting next to Detective Franks on the love seat, her hand pressed against her neck at the empty place where her ring had hung. Marina shifted her gaze to Detective Franks and tried very hard to keep it there.

"You make your living as a psychic, is that right, Marina?"

"I don't . . . That was my office that burned, Detective Franks. I haven't made much of a living at all since then."

"But you *are* a psychic?"

"Yes," Marina said. It sounded like a confession. "I've told the police this before. A few times."

"Must be a tough business."

He didn't know the half of it, Marina thought. "How do you mean?" she said. Out of the corner of her eye, she could see Mrs. Golden tapping at her neck with her index finger and then pointing at the detective.

"Well, I imagine that people come to you wanting things like the winning lottery numbers and that sort of thing. Don't they? Must be difficult if you can't give it to them."

"It doesn't work like that," Marina said. It was a line, the mantra of psychics everywhere, which she'd used even before she knew it to be true. It fell from her lips automatically.

"How *does* it work?"

"It's a gift," Marina said. She could see Mrs. Golden frowning. "Like any gift, you receive what you're given. You don't really get to choose what comes in."

"Still," he said, "I'd guess people might get upset if your *gift* doesn't live up to their expectations. Especially if they're paying for it. Of course, some people will believe anything you tell them. But I think others might feel, I don't know, ripped off. What do you do when that happens? How would you make it right?"

He needs to trust you.

Marina heard the words inside her head. She glanced quickly at Mrs. Golden, who was once again tapping at her neck, and back to Detective Franks, who was now leaning forward, resting his elbows on his knees. Why wouldn't the old woman speak?

"It sounds as if you've had a bad experience with psychics, Detective."

"Well, I suppose you'd know, wouldn't you?" He straightened up and placed his pad and pen on the coffee table. Marina saw his next statement before he spoke it, the words falling like black rain from the top of his head to his mouth and out into the room.

"We've identified the body," he said. "His name is—*was*—Gideon Black. Does that name mean anything to you?"

It wasn't a surprise. Of course, Marina had known all along. But until that moment she hadn't realized how tenaciously she'd been hanging onto the hope that he was alive. Now the physical evidence of Gideon's death came as such a shock to her that it literally took her breath away and she found herself gasping. Her reaction was so intense that it never occurred to Marina to tell anything but the truth.

"Yes," she said, her voice shaky, "I know him. He was my . . . I knew him."

"He was your what?" Detective Franks leaned forward again, his mouth snapping over the question as if he were a hungry fish reaching for food at the top of a tank.

"We were . . . romantically involved. Briefly." Marina felt a fluttery kick from deep inside.

Detective Franks raised his eyebrows, whether in surprise or judgment, Marina couldn't tell. For a few moments he sat very still and just watched her for reaction. It was an old method; say nothing and wait for them to talk. Eventually, they would fill the space just to avoid the silence. But Marina knew enough to avoid this trap and had no fear of silence. He'd have to work for his information.

"He was your boyfriend," Detective Franks said finally. "You were in a relationship with this man."

"Like I said, it was brief."

"How brief?"

"I don't know . . ." Marina struggled for some kind of vision and came up empty. Even Mrs. Golden seemed to be fading into a collection of misty particles on the love seat beside the detective.

"When was the last time you saw Gideon Black?" He was getting impatient. The questions were going to come faster now and they would be more difficult to answer.

"It was . . ." A fleeting spark of her dream lit up behind Marina's eyes. Gideon walking. A flash of light. Fire. The ring. *Take it now.* "I haven't seen him for a long time. I think it was . . . the beginning of the year. January. I think it was January."

"January?"

"Yes."

"Are you sure about that, Ms. Marks?"

"I don't know the exact day in January, if that's what you mean."

"No, that's not what I mean. What I'd like to know is why, if the last time you saw Gideon Black was in January, he came to be in your office on the night of March fifteenth? I'm also a little confused as to why you never informed us that Mr. Black was missing."

"I didn't know!" Marina said sharply. "I don't understand it. He left—he was gone. I hadn't seen him. I don't know why he was there."

"So you were together—a couple—but you hadn't seen him, didn't know why he was in your office. It never occurred to you that the person who died in that fire, in your office, might have been your lover?"

"Our relationship was over," Marina said. Her face was wet, but she hadn't felt the tears fall. "It was over in January."

"The romantic part of it or the professional part?"

"He wasn't . . . There was no professional part."

"When did you meet Mr. Black?"

"I met him . . ." The day she'd first seen Gideon sipping from a bottomless coffee cup across the street belonged to another life. "It was my birthday," she said. "Election Day—November of last year. That's when I met him."

"You seem to have a very clear memory of that day."

Mrs. Golden suddenly appeared close to Marina's ear. *Ask him about the ring!*

"I can't!" Marina gasped out loud and reflexively covered her mouth with her hand.

Detective Franks waited a beat, then two. "I'd like that glass of water now, if you don't mind," he said.

Mrs. Golden followed Marina to the kitchen, chattering as she never had before, stringing together an endless loop of words: *The ringringring you have to ask about the ring the ring is everything you were supposed to protect him you were supposed to help him with the ring the ring is gone you have to ask him about the ring you have to protect him you have to save him—*

"He's dead," Marina whispered. "He's dead! Don't you know—" She dropped the glass she was holding and it shattered, sending shards of broken glass and water in a sparkling starburst on the slate kitchen floor. Marina bent down to pick up the pieces and immediately cut her finger. Now there was blood and water and glass and for a moment Marina could do nothing except watch it all spread. Detective Franks appeared at the entrance to the kitchen, then rushed over to help her to her feet and over to the sink.

"Look," he said as she washed her hand and fumbled in the kitchen drawer for a bandage, "I'm going to be very honest with you, and I hope that for everyone's sake, you'll be honest with me." Marina looked over at him, pleading silently. She was starting to feel dizzy and unmoored. She needed him to leave. She needed to sleep.

"The story you just told me doesn't make a whole lot of sense. Now, I don't know exactly what your relationship was with Mr. Black, but I do know that there's more to it than what you just gave me." He sighed, whether for effect or to release tension Marina didn't know. The ability to interpret gestures was one of the things that were now oddly unavailable to her.

"Some time ago, Mr. Black filed an insurance claim for a very valuable piece of jewelry. Apparently, he'd given it to his mother and it turned up missing from her *estate* after she died." His emphasis on "estate" was sarcastic and bitter. "Mr. Black believed that this piece of jewelry might have wound up with a psychic his mother had been seeing. He believed that his mother had been taken advantage of and that she never would have given up this item willingly. Does any of this sound familiar, Ms. Marks?"

Marina heard his words as if they were coming at her through deep water. Detective Franks, the kitchen, even her own body seemed to fade to shades of gray and white as she watched a rapid series of images go by, as if she was flipping through a magazine. She saw the chain first, half melted and blackened with soot. It was unclasped and empty. Then she saw the ring being polished by a pair of thick, square male hands. Then a different pair of male hands held it; the fingers were long and pale. She saw it being placed carefully into a black velvet box and pushed to the back of a wooden desk drawer. The images speeded up. Still another pair of male hands—small and freckled—holding the ring, turning it around. A handshake. The ring on the left fourth finger of a woman—flesh puffing up around it. A close-up of the ring. A reflection in one of its deep red surfaces. Closer. A face. Gideon lying—

"Marina?"

Detective Franks snapped back into focus, the images gone, just out of reach. "I'm sorry," she said. "I'm sorry."

"I don't know if this is an act or what, but . . . ," he said. He stared at her, as if trying to see inside her head. "But I know you know something about this piece of jewelry. We know you're involved. He knew you before November. The smart thing to do is just come out with it now. Should we start at the beginning? Why don't you tell me what happened in Florida?"

"I don't have the ring," she said.

"But you know the ring I'm talking about?"

"Yes, I do."

"What do you know about it, Marina? Tell me."

Somebody killed him. Somebody took the ring.

"Marina," he said, this time softly, as if he felt sorry for her.

"Please," she said.

"Marina," he repeated. "I'm going to have to ask you to come to the police station with me now. We'll continue our conversation there."

Marina rubbed her eyes with her bandaged hand. Mrs. Golden had vanished. Detective Franks stood tall and solid, but unthreatening. There was nothing clairvoyant about the feeling she had looking at him now— that she could trust him, that he might even be able to help her—just basic instinct, and she had to believe in it.

"Okay," she said. "I'll just need a minute to get ready."

Chapter 31

*S*he is lying on her back beneath the ground, looking up at a bright rectangle of cloudless blue sky. Three birds cut across the space in a fast-
moving triangle of flight and are gone. It is dark down here and close with the
smell of earth. She hears words coming from far above, falling down to her in
fragments. *". . . my shepherd . . . not want . . . walk through . . . shadow . . .
fear no evil . . ."* A woman is sobbing. A trapped insect buzzes in an effort to
escape. The first rose, sweet and white, falls on her face and that is when she
realizes where she is. The white rose is joined by a pink one and then another
white one. The smell is too sweet and holds the odor of rot within it. It fills her
lungs. She can't breathe, can't stay here. She pulls herself up. The thorns press
into her skin. The view shifts upside down. Now she stands above looking in.
Roses pile on the coffin. She can see the sobbing woman, head bent and covered in a black veil, gloved hand to her mouth. Someone whispers, *"That's the
widow."* A heavyset dark-haired woman approaches the widow, her back
turned, and puts a hand on the widow's shoulder. *"I'm so sorry,"* the woman
whispers. *"This must be so hard for you."* She looks at the hand on the widow's
shoulder. The ruby ring catches a ray of sunlight and sparks red laser beams of
light. She turns her head to see—

* * *

Marina woke up gasping for air but was unafraid, wanting desperately to return to the dream, to the funeral she had just attended. She tried to focus on the details before they slipped away into the glare of consciousness, but caught only the quick gleam of the ring—that ring—and the birds flying over the grave. She couldn't even get close enough to the widow's veiled face to determine who it was, although Marina was sure she knew her. She was also sure that the dead husband, in whose grave she'd been lying, was someone she knew as well. But it was the mysterious woman wearing Gideon's ring whom Marina most wanted to see. She closed her eyes, trying to will herself back to sleep, but it was a futile pursuit. Sleep and dreams came to her now when they wanted, not when she decided. She didn't even remember falling asleep in the first place. She'd gone from sitting in her rocking chair reading a reference book about psychic phenomena (conveniently sorted in alphabetical order) to unconsciousness without so much as a blink. Maybe, she thought, she hadn't been asleep at all but in some sort of fugue state, traveling somewhere between past, present and future.

She closed the book now, marking her place between *cartomancy* and *chiromancy* with Detective Franks's business card. *That* encounter had certainly felt real enough. Marina felt a gathering tension between her shoulders as she remembered the interview from the day before. The police did not have enough evidence to arrest Marina either for torching her office or for Gideon's murder—but that didn't mean that they weren't still searching for it.

The questioning she received after she followed Detective Franks to the police station was less kind than what she'd gone through before. They were impatient with her, even though her story never wavered. Most irritating to them, it seemed, was the psychic angle, which stuck in their craws every time they mentioned it.

"If you could see that your office was on fire, why couldn't you see *who* set the fire?" they asked.

"I can't explain it," Marina answered.

"Is that because you set the fire yourself?"

"No," Marina said.

They asked her about Gideon; personal, intimate information that she wouldn't have shared with her closest girlfriend even if she'd had one. But Marina answered because she had to. They had broken up, he had left, she didn't know where he'd gone, and she hadn't seen him in her office on the evening of March 15 or anywhere else that day. And as for the ring, yes, she knew about it. And yes, she'd known Gideon's mother in Florida. The woman visited many psychics and Marina was only one of them. But Gideon had the ring in his possession the last time she'd seen him and she didn't have it now. They were welcome to search her or her house.

It was a long session but in the end it was surprisingly banal, with none of the flash and drama these kinds of scenes had in film or television. Nobody yelled or leaned over her, trying to intimidate her. She didn't demand to see an attorney and never lost control or started crying. The questions they asked were plodding, repetitive and occasionally rhetorical. After a while, they'd let her go home. They'd told her that they'd be in touch again, so if she was planning an out-of-town trip, she might want to rethink it. Detective Franks had given her his card.

Marina startled as if someone had come up from behind her and tapped her on the shoulder. Once again the smell of roses, strong and overly sweet, was thick in her throat. Someone was coming. She jumped up out of her chair and her book fell to the floor, splaying open at the entry for *precognition*. Marina picked up the book, threw it on the rocking chair and walked over to her front door. Her heart was racing. She knew who was on the other side before she opened it and saw Eddie standing there, a large bouquet of already-wilting roses perched awkwardly in his big hand.

Neither one of them spoke. For once, Eddie seemed to have been rendered speechless. For her part, Marina was too distracted by the sound
and vision of breaking plates surrounding Eddie to greet him. She opened
the door wide and he stumbled inside, his eyes sweeping her, confusion
rolling across his face like a dark cloud. Behind him, Marina could see
Eddie's kitchen and his frightened wife half crouching and cringing as
Eddie grabbed a hand-painted, salmon-shaped serving plate and hurled it
against the wall. Marina felt the vibrations of the crash, felt the pain of its
violent destruction.

"You broke the fish plate. She loved that plate," Marina said. She saw
Eddie and his wife walking through the streets of Ensenada, where they'd
gone for their honeymoon, Eddie's wife picking up the plate and laughing
about how it was so ugly that it was beautiful. She heard Eddie saying that
the paint was probably toxic, but he would buy it for her anyway, because
it made her laugh and he loved her, loved her, loved her.

"Hey," Eddie was saying, "how do you know that?"

She could see Eddie's wife crying and understood that Eddie had broken more than just the plate. "You might have been able to talk to her if it
hadn't been for that plate," Marina told Eddie. "That really hurt her."

"Did you talk to her? Did you?"

Now the scene over Eddie's shoulder was changing into that of an office where he was storing his clothes. She saw a toothbrush, fast-food
wrappers and then Eddie arguing with a man in a suit. They were going
to fire him. She could smell desperation on him, acrid and smoky. He
needed money. The images started to come fast, another series of film
clips on fast-forward. Hands holding a pregnancy test strip reading positive. A woman burying the strip in the trash, getting dressed. Her hands
on her belly. Madeline. The woman was Madeline.

"You're having a baby," Marina said in wonderment.

"What are you talking about?"

Marina started laughing, but Eddie wasn't amused. She could see all
the women in Eddie's life circling around him, each one angry with him

in a different way. She supposed she should have known about Madeline, but she'd been so caught up in her own drama with Gideon.

But there was something else. Marina could see Eddie's own anger taking a physical shape inside him, rearing up to strike like a snake. She saw him at the door of Madeline's house. Saw him walking inside.

Eddie handed over his roses and the heavy smell triggered another vision. Once again she was looking up from within a grave. The roses falling on her face. Of course, it was *Eddie's* grave. The widow . . . the woman with the ring . . .

"Don't go there, Eddie. Please. You're going to get hurt. Please listen to me."

"I don't know what you mean. Go where?"

He didn't understand. She had to make him understand. If he went to Madeline's house, he was going to die. And somehow Gideon's ring fit into all of this, but she couldn't see how. It was all just out of reach and floating away. Marina felt the heat of frustrated tears at the backs of her eyes. *Help me,* she wanted to scream, but she didn't know who or what would be listening. Not Eddie, who was staring at her with stubborn incomprehension forming a thick mask on his face. If only she could get through to him.

"Listen, this is important. Does your wife have a friend with . . . with a ruby ring? Do you know?"

"I'm sorry, Marina, I have to go. I'm sorry."

"Eddie, please . . ."

But he was going and then gone. Marina stood staring into the roses until she could no longer stand the smell and went to the kitchen to throw them away.

T he call came as Marina was sitting at her kitchen table riffling through two New Age magazines and the *P* section of the yellow pages.

Her search had started with *Physicians* but had branched out into something else entirely. Minutes after Eddie left, Marina's emotional uneasiness had given way to physical pain. There was strong cramping first and then sharp stabbing pains in her abdomen. It didn't feel like the stretching and pulling of ligaments she'd been experiencing lately, nor did it have anything to do with nausea. Marina felt the first twinge of maternal fear—*What if something is wrong with my baby?*—and realized it was time to find a doctor.

But once she'd pulled out the phone book and settled herself with a cup of Rosa's tea, the pains dissipated and Marina found herself flipping past *Physicians* and into *Psychic Consulting and Healing Services.* Every psychic had a psychic and Marina needed one of her own. She needed help. For psychics, this person was usually a relative or a mentor, but neither option was a possibility for Marina. She'd decided to call all the numbers listed in the phone book and in the magazines and rely on her own intuitive abilities to choose one. She had the phone in her hand, but its sudden ringing stopped her before she had the chance to dial.

"Hello?"

"Hi, is this . . . ? I'm looking for Marina? Is this Marina?"

"Yes, it is."

"Oh good, good. I worried that maybe I had the wrong number or maybe the number was changed because I was given this number a long time ago, and you know people change their numbers so often. I had this number written down on a piece of paper in my desk for forever, so you know . . ."

The silence went on long enough for Marina to ask, "How can I help you?"

"Oh, gosh, I'm sorry! My name is . . . um . . . Claire? I was given your number by my friend a long time ago? She said you do . . . um . . . readings?" The woman's voice got lower and lower until her last word was a whisper.

"Yes," Marina said, waiting for more information.

"Well, I was wondering . . . if I could get a reading?"

"Who is your friend who recommended me?" Marina asked. This was an important piece. If it was one of her old regulars, Claire might be expecting something Marina was no longer able to provide. She thought about what Detective Franks had said about people wanting the winning lottery numbers. Many of her old clients weren't too far off that mark.

"Um . . . she's . . . her name is Frederika? I don't think she's been to see you for a while. Like I said, it was a long time ago. But she thought you were great. She says you really helped her . . ."

The woman kept talking, but Marina had stopped listening. There was a loud static buzzing in Marina's head and an almost physical sensation of being pushed to the edge of her chair. She rarely forgot the names of her clients, even if they came only once, so she was confused by why the name Frederika didn't conjure a visual memory. At the same time, she knew it was important and that Claire, whoever she was, would be able to help her discover why.

". . . so that's why I really need to see you today," Claire was saying. "Is that possible?"

"Today," Marina said, trying to catch up with the conversation.

"It's just that I . . . I've never done this before," Claire said. "You probably hear that a lot. Anyway, I don't know . . . Maybe this isn't a good idea after all."

"No," Marina said, struggling to keep the anxiety out of her voice. Claire was a flopping fish about to dive back into the sea and Marina couldn't afford to lose her. "I mean, it's natural to feel a little hesitation. You've called me and I'm still here. That should tell you something, right?"

"I guess . . ."

Marina closed her eyes, her hand gripped tight around the phone, and focused. She tried to fix on the caller, to pick up any detail. Her mind's eye flashed quickly on the dark-haired woman from her dream. "Claire," she said quickly, "do you have . . . I mean, I'm seeing a ring. Does that mean anything—"

"You *are*? Really? Because that's—"

"I think it would be better if we did this in person," Marina said. "I can see you today, but it will have to be soon. This afternoon is—"

"Where are you?" Claire asked. "I can come right now."

Marina was in trouble. Claire, a dull-haired, birdlike blonde, sat across from Marina at the kitchen table, her sandy eyebrows knotting together in irritated confusion. Not only wasn't she the woman from Marina's dream, but she was also proving to be the most difficult client Marina had ever tried to read.

"You said you saw a ring," she'd said as soon as Marina had shut the door behind her. "It was an engagement ring, right? I shouldn't ask, but what did it look like? No, don't tell me! I want to be surprised."

Marina had had to fight through her frustration and disappointment when she saw Claire, a task made more difficult when it became obvious that nothing she had to offer was going to please this woman. Claire wanted the boyfriend who'd broken up with her to come back, preferably with an engagement ring in his hand. Unfortunately for both Claire and Marina, that wasn't what was in her future. And Marina was literally stopped, as if her tongue was tied, every time she tried to tell Claire something that wasn't true.

"Do you think there's any chance we'll get back together?" Claire had asked.

Marina saw the ex-boyfriend standing on an altar with a bride who wasn't Claire and formed the words, *It might be a good idea to keep your options open.* But what came out of her mouth was "He is going to marry someone else." After a few of these interchanges, Marina stopped trying to do anything except report what she saw before her. Which was how they'd come to this point.

"Well, am I *ever* going to get married?" Claire asked. "Can you tell me *that* at least?"

Marina looked at Claire and saw . . . Claire. She was sitting alone.

There were no relatives around her looking in, no mate waiting in her future and no children. It was the emptiest future Marina had ever seen. Wrestling with the right words to say, she hesitated too long and her silence became Claire's answer.

"Oh, no," Claire gasped. "I don't believe it! Are you kidding me?"

"You know, many people don't—"

"You're the worst psychic ever!" Claire stood up so abruptly that she knocked her chair over behind her.

"Claire, wait—"

"I *knew* this was a mistake. I would have been better off calling one of those 900 numbers. At least *those* people try to give some kind of hope, even if they're all full of crap."

"Claire, I can only tell you what I see."

"You're a liar," Claire spat. "You don't see anything and you're not even a good fake. I have as much right as anyone to get married. You told my friend she'd meet someone and she did. And she's *fat*. Why does she get the happy ending and not me?"

"Your friend?"

"The one I told you about—Frederika. Or Kiki. That's what she calls herself because it sounds *thinner*."

"Kiki . . ." Once again, Marina saw the dark-haired woman from her dream, but now she had a face to match it with: a pretty face with sad eyes and too much bright lipstick. The receptionist who was looking for dates on the Internet. Marina had pulled the Lovers card from her tarot stack and told her she'd be meeting someone soon. She'd smiled, Marina remembered now, and tapped the card with the tip of her polished fingernail. "A doctor?" she'd asked. "Because I do know a lot of them . . ."

"I need to talk to your friend," Marina said. "It's very important."

Claire looked stunned. "You're a piece of work, you know that?"

"I only saw her once," Marina went on, not caring that her words were probably making no sense to Claire, "and I don't have her phone number. There was a fire in my office . . ."

"I'm not paying for this," Claire said and started moving out of the kitchen. "So don't even bother asking for money."

"Do you know a man named Eddie Perkins?" Marina asked. Her head was thick with the sudden memory of her dream and the conviction that Eddie was somehow involved with all of this—and that he was in danger.

"Too late," Claire said, reaching the front door. "You've already told me I'm going to die alone and lonely. Don't try to make something up now to try to get—"

"I never said you were going to die alone and lonely, Claire. I didn't see you getting married. That's not the same thing."

"As good as," Claire said. "And no, I don't know anyone named Eddie."

Chapter 32

Marina had to smile when she saw the house. Small and tidy with almost a gingerbread sweetness, it was nearly identical to her own save for two distinct details. The first was that this house was a bright lemony yellow, where Marina's was a dull white and in need of a fresh coat of paint. The second detail was more telling: a large red neon pentagram surrounded by a circle hanging in the front window. At least the word *psychic* was nowhere in evidence, she thought, a small concession to subtlety.

Marina was on the high north end of Pacific Beach, a neighborhood that straddled the line between expensive and completely ridiculous. The drive had taken less time than she'd anticipated, so she sat in her car for a few minutes, preparing herself for whatever was about to come next.

Marina's need to find a person with even a hint of psychic ability had intensified as soon as Claire had swept off in a cloud of righteous indignation. She'd gone back to her phone book and magazines, making a list and then calling every number regardless of how phony-sounding the names or claims attached to them. The first two calls rang through to voice mail, one with New Age music so loud she could barely hear the outgoing message, and the second asking her to press 1 for "tarot" and 2 for "massage." Marina didn't leave a message on either. The third call was answered by a woman who spoke so little English that Marina couldn't make out more than a few words. In any case, the woman couldn't hear Marina over the din of screaming children in the background. Marina hung up. The fourth number rang seven times, but Marina held on out of sheer curiosity over what kind of person still let a phone just ring. Finally, it was picked up. The voice on the other end seemed to have the dust of centuries within it; the words came slow and cracked. "No, my dear, I don't do that anymore," the voice told Marina. There was a long silence filled with labored breath and then, "But I have the name of someone who can help you." And that was how Marina had ended up here in the bright hills bordering La Jolla.

The psychic's name was Ciel ("Pronounced *seal*, like the ocean animal," she'd told Marina), and she hadn't been the least bit taken aback by Marina's burning need for an immediate reading. "If you can make it over here this afternoon, I can see you," she'd told Marina in a thick, raspy voice. "You need directions?" It didn't matter if Ciel was a total fraud, Marina told herself as she locked her car door and walked up to the house—at least she was trying *something*.

Although by rights she shouldn't have been, Marina was startled when Ciel opened the door before she could knock on it. She was of indeterminate age—maybe forty or maybe sixty—with pin-curled hair the color of orange marmalade. She was solid, but not heavy, and was dressed in a royal blue pullover with matching pants. She looked put together if not quite stylish, and Marina got the distinct sense that she didn't care what anyone thought of her attire.

"Hi, hon," Ciel said. "Don't look so scared. I saw you pull up from the window." She gestured to her left. "Come on in, then."

Inside, the house smelled like sawdust and pungent potpourri, but Marina could see no evidence of either. What she did see was an exhausted-looking sofa and two shabby easy chairs, a beaten-up wooden coffee table and hundreds of paperbacks shoved into two faux pine bookshelves. Most of these books, Marina gathered from her quick glance, had the word *Earl, Duke,* or *Surrender* in their titles.

"Don't look over there, hon," Ciel said. "You're bound to be disappointed by my choice of reading material. Everyone is. But I can't help it; that's my entertainment. We all have to have that, don't we? Come on into the kitchen and I'll get us set up."

"Set up?"

"Well, sure. We'll need a little tea to start."

"Tea?" Marina asked. "Do you practice tasseomancy?"

Ciel raised one well-shaped ginger eyebrow and gave Marina a puzzled smile. "What's that, hon?"

"Are you going to read my tea leaves?"

"Well, I hadn't planned on it, but I suppose I could give it a shot if you want. I was just thinking it would be nice to have something to drink. I have iced tea, but I can make some hot tea if you'd prefer it. It's just that it's so warm outside, you know."

"No, of course, that's fine," Marina said. "I wasn't . . . I mean, iced tea would be fine."

"Well, all right then. Follow me."

Ciel's kitchen was quite a bit larger than her living room but no more modern. The cabinets, state of the art in the 1970s, were in dire need of updating, and the flooring, linoleum that had seen much better days, was faded to a vague shade of greenish blue. A chrome-and-Formica dinette set sat in the middle, laid with two empty glasses and some paper napkins. There were no cards, candles or anything else to suggest Ciel's profession. Marina sat down on one of the three available chairs.

"Hon," Ciel said, reaching into the refrigerator for a pitcher of iced tea, "before we get started, if you wouldn't mind . . ."

Marina stared blankly at Ciel for a moment before her meaning sunk in. "Oh, right," she said, "payment." She reached into her purse for the ninety dollars she'd brought and placed the bills in the middle of the table.

Ciel scooped up the money and replaced it with a small dish of lemon wedges. "Thanks, hon. It's just better that way, you know? Then we can really focus." She poured a glass of tea for Marina, one for herself, and then, from some unseen pocket in the folds her clothing, she produced a worn deck of tarot cards and put them on the table between them. The two women sipped their tea in silence for a minute or two and then Ciel said, "Are you worried about the baby, hon? Because I'm getting a real strong feeling that the baby's going to be just fine."

Marina put her hands on her swollen belly, remembering that she was now big enough for someone who was paying attention to notice that she was pregnant. "Well," she said, "that's good."

"When are you due, hon?"

"I'm not sure," Marina said. "I haven't really figured it out yet."

The look on Ciel's face changed from quizzical to concerned. Lines that Marina hadn't noticed before appeared between her nose and mouth and there were crow's-feet etched into the corners of her faded blue eyes. Maybe she was an older woman after all, Marina thought. "All right," Ciel said. "That's fine." She swallowed some of her tea, picked up the cards and began shuffling them dexterously. "So what happened to your regular person, if you don't mind my asking? Not that I mind getting the business, but one does like to keep up with the competition." When Marina didn't answer, she barked out a quick laugh. "That was a joke, hon. At least the last part of it."

Marina thought about telling Ciel everything, start to finish. She could feel the weight of the confession like a stone on her shoulders and wanted so badly to roll it off and away. But no, that wasn't what she was here for. If Ciel was the real thing, she'd figure it out anyway. And if she wasn't, it wouldn't make any difference to tell her. "I don't have a regular person," she said finally. "To be honest, I haven't had much luck with this kind of thing in the past."

Ciel continued to shuffle, her hands moving faster but never fumbling. "Is that right?" she said. "Well, I guess we're going to have to see what we can do to fix that." Marina watched, mesmerized, as Ciel's fingers moved across the cards with speed and grace. "Want to tell me what's on your mind, hon? Or haven't you figured that out yet, either?" Marina had to smile a little, although she didn't take her eyes off the cards. She liked Ciel's style. She realized something else, too, as the blur of Ciel's hands lulled her into transfixed calm: for the first time in months she felt still. There were no voices, dead people, visions or premonitions—only the here and now and the soft sound of the cards as they slid across each other.

"Cut." The cards hit the table with a smack and Marina startled before automatically reaching over and cutting the deck twice to the left. Ciel placed her right hand on Marina's left for a moment and then reassembled the deck right to left. "You ready?" she asked, and Marina nodded.

"Celtic Cross," Ciel said. She laid out the ten cards, facedown, in the ancient formation of a cross and a staff. The first card she turned over, in the center of the cross, was the Three of Swords. The sight of the pierced heart with the driving rain behind it immediately conjured the memory of Marina choosing this very card for Mrs. Golden and "interpreting" it as a warning that her son was in danger. It was one of the most dramatic cards in the deck and never failed to get a response.

"Oh, hon," Ciel said, "such sorrow for you. You've lost a great love and it was a violent parting." The second card, the Queen of Cups, crossed the first. Ciel sighed and put her hands together, cracking her knuckles one by one. "The greatest obstacle is *you*," she said. There was a hint of surprise in her voice. "You stand in your own way, in the middle of your own path. You must move beyond yourself." Ciel turned over the next card, the Six of Cups. "Ah, but you have an inheritance," she said. "A gift given to you as a child. This is your foundation. You can build on this." Ciel turned another card, the Ten of Swords, a most frightening card showing a man facedown with ten swords buried in his back. "Your immediate past," she said. "Danger, treachery . . ." She frowned and rubbed the bridge of her nose. "This is a card of hatred, enemies. . . . Someone who wants you . . ." She turned the next card quickly, the Five of Swords. "Your immediate future shows theft, deception, manipulation." Ciel was growing agitated, her eyes now focused solely on the cards. Marina knew every one of these cards, had even offered the same words to her clients, and yet she felt as if she were seeing now through a new pair of eyes—Ciel's eyes. "The Nine of Wands," Ciel was saying, "crowns you. You are strong, stubborn and ready to fight. You can win—you have the strength to win. The Eight of Cups here means you are ready to leave behind the life you once lived. The cups are still full. You have much to offer." Ciel turned over the Hanged Man and the Three of Pentacles. "So much loneliness"—she sighed—"and so much sorrow. You are at a crossroads and feel you are getting no guidance. You have lost . . . so much. You must let go. You must trust yourself."

This could apply to anyone, Marina thought, although she realized her heart was beating hard. Ciel's words were a one-size-fits-all garment that could be molded to any body shape. You could stretch it, shrink it, work it until it fit. At least this is what Marina told herself as Ciel continued, turning over the final card in the spread, the one that signified the outcome. It was the eleventh card in the Major Arcana.

Justice.

Ciel touched the card with the tip of her finger, traced the sword and scales held by the red-robed, crowned figure of Justice, and finally raised her eyes to meet Marina's. "You're in trouble, aren't you?" she asked. "All this violence I see . . ." Once more, Ciel reached over and touched Marina's hand lightly with her own. The touch was warm, dry and reassuring. "It will be all right," she said. "It is going to be made right. But it isn't going to be easy."

"What's easy?" Marina said after a while. "Nothing."

Ciel took a deep breath and leaned back in her chair. "What's your story, hon? There's so much going on behind those eyes of yours, I can't even imagine where you've been. There's a lot more to it than what's in these cards, isn't there?"

"I could tell you," Marina said, "but then I'd have to kill you." Ciel just sat there, staring. "That was a joke," Marina added.

"Fair enough," Ciel said, but she wasn't laughing. "But what is it you really came here to find out? I've been doing this long enough to know when there hasn't been enough on my table to satisfy."

Marina was about to protest, but as she was forming the words, she realized exactly what it was she wanted from the woman sitting across from her. "How do you do this?" she asked. "I mean, how do you keep from going crazy?"

"What do you mean, hon?"

"You have to absorb so much energy from everyone else all the time. Everyone's loves and losses and desires coming at you. How can you tell what's what? How do you *sort* it all? How do you keep it straight?"

Ciel looked down at the cards and tapped on the Queen of Cups. "No wonder you wouldn't tell me who your regular person is," she said. "Your regular person is *you*. But why didn't you tell me, hon? I would have given you the professional discount."

"You have a professional discount?"

"Oh, dear. I guess neither of us should be trying to tell jokes, huh? What I mean to say is that you don't need to hide it from me." She tut-tutted softly to herself. "No wonder," she said again. "Always harder to read for readers." She broke apart the spread she'd laid out for Marina and pushed the cards back together. "Come on now, you don't need to look so sad. It's going to work out, hon, trust me. I'm going to pour us some more tea and then we can go on into the living room and make ourselves more comfortable. I don't have anything until my poker game at seven so we have plenty of time to visit." She smiled at Marina, who noticed for the first time that Ciel had a large star-shaped keloid scar at the base of her throat.

"How about you, hon?" Ciel asked. "Anywhere you need to be?"

Chapter 33

The first thing Cooper wanted to do after escaping Max's office (because *escape* was very much what his mad not-waiting-for-the-elevator run down the stairs had felt like) was to shovel a handful of pills down his throat and wash them all down with a bottle of wine. But his instinct for self-preservation (still strong enough despite his emotional devastation) kept him from swallowing his whole stash while he was still in the car. Vanity played a part in his hesitation as well. Something about seeing Max with that woman had drawn Cooper's attention to how far he'd fallen, physically, since this whole fiasco had started. He had a vision of himself crashing his car into a tree under the influence of twenty Xanax and the Jaws of Life having to remove his puffy mangled body from the wreckage. The thought of anyone seeing him like that—especially Max—was too much for Cooper.

As he peeled out of the parking lot, Cooper felt the force of revelation as if it were a punch in the stomach. He'd literally had the wind knocked out of him and it wasn't just from running down four flights of stairs in his weakened condition. If he'd been asked, even right before going into Max's office, whether Max was capable of pulling such a sadistic stunt, Cooper would have denied it was possible. His relationship with Max had devolved into a badly written melodrama full of recrimination, anger and, perhaps worst of all, indifference over the last few months. But even wallowing in the emotional silt that had settled out of what had once been love, Cooper never expected to find cruelty and viciousness. What hit Cooper with the greatest force now was not that he'd lost Max (yet again!), but that there was a very strong possibility he didn't know—had never known—Max at all.

Max thinking he could be happy with a woman—even *be* with a woman once the novelty wore off—was totally insane as far as Cooper was concerned. And that sad, that desperate woman was probably ministering to Max this very second with whatever soothing monosyllables she'd learned from running reception downstairs. How had he even asked her for that first date? Cooper couldn't imagine. Nor could he quite believe she was actually carrying Max's baby. If—ugh—she was, she couldn't be more than five minutes pregnant. When had he found the *time* with his unbelievably important schedule? And then, good Lord, the confession he must have made about Cooper! How had *that* gone over? Cooper tried to picture it, tried to hear the words Max might have used. He knew the tone well enough, anyway—that excruciatingly patient, slow shrink-speak:

It's perfectly normal for a man to experience a time when he is attracted to members of the same sex. The literature shows . . .

No, it wouldn't have been that stupid. Maybe something like *I understand if what I'm about to tell you makes you uncomfortable and I think we should talk about that.* Yes, that was it. He could hear it as if Max were whispering in his ear.

Cooper was so caught up in his mental scenario that he drove past the freeway entrance and started cruising down Del Mar Heights Road. The big hill dipped, then crested, and the ocean, a sparkling blanket of blue diamonds, came into view below. Cooper remembered the first time he'd come into Del Mar with Max on a Sunday date. They'd done the whole touristy thing: walked on Fifteenth Street Beach, then up to the Plaza for lunch. Max had wanted to eat at Pacifica, but Cooper said there were cuter waiters at Epazote across the way. Max had blushed, demurred. They'd each had a three-cheese quesadilla with tomatillo salsa. Neither one of them finished his food. But Max hadn't wanted to split a plate— didn't want to look *gay*, even though they stood out as if they'd been dressed in fucking pink triangles. That was the thing Max never got. He only called more attention to the fact that he was gay by trying so hard not to. It came off him like a rainbow-colored vapor; he just couldn't see it. Cooper had always thought it a mark of vulnerability, since Max was so smart in so many other ways. But maybe it wasn't sweet or vulnerable after all. Maybe it was cold and calculated, just like that horrible setup in his office.

"God*damn* him!" Cooper said out loud, and he banged the steering wheel hard with his hand, causing the horn to blare and the driver in the next lane to flip him the bird. "Fuck you, too!" Cooper shouted, pushing the accelerator hard. The driver sped up in turn, trying to start some sort of macho drag race, but Cooper let him go, already uninterested, his mind still catching and turning in endless repetition. Now that the initial shock was starting to spread and settle, individual elements of the scene in Max's office were starting to press in like nettles under his skin.

What was all that bullshit about Madeline's party, for example? Since when had Max become such a party animal? He'd practically had to *drag* Max to Madeline and Andrew's last party and then he'd spent the whole evening skulking around like some kind of fugitive. Max didn't even *like* Madeline. He'd told Cooper more than once that Andrew had made a mistake by marrying her. Such wisdom coming from him!

But of course, now that he thought about it, it all made sense. Max finally had a legitimate date (oh, he'd been quick to explain that Andrew didn't know anything about Max's *orientation* and wasn't really the kind of guy who could handle something like that, so please, you're just a pal, okay, Cooper?), so why wouldn't he want to parade evidence of his triumphant heterosexuality to the overprivileged denizens of Rancho Santa Fe, half of whom, Cooper thought, were probably banging each other out of boredom anyway? What better place for Max to show off his new bride-to-be, complete with her big, lovely engagement ring?

Cooper swerved and screeched to a halt, just missing a skinny gray cat that was darting across the narrow road. That ring. He *had* seen it before, and not just in his imagination but on a chain resting against smooth skin.

"Hey! *Hey!* What the fuck is wrong with you!"

Marina. The name came to him first, the syllables running through his brain like water, then the image of her face, neck and chest, where the ring lay half buried between her breasts. He'd seen it only once, when he'd reached over a slow-burning candle to hook his finger into the dangling chain and pull it free. But there was no question: It was the same ring that now encircled the fat finger of Max's fiancée.

"Did you hear me? You almost killed my cat!"

Cooper looked up and saw a short, curly-haired woman in a spandex halter top and too-tight shorts running over to him, her little face scrunched up with outrage. Cooper ignored her. *What was Marina's ring doing on that woman's finger?* The question wound itself like a noose around Cooper's brain even as the small, angry woman reached his car and started banging on the driver's-side window. "You can't drive like that here! What's wrong with you? Are you drunk?"

He rolled his window down all the way and gave her his best fake smile. "I'm sorry," he said, "but I didn't hit your cat. I swerved to *avoid* hitting your cat."

"Do you know what the speed limit is here? You're crazy—it could have been a kid!"

"They have *nine lives,* you know," Cooper said, rolling up his window and gunning the engine. "What's one less?" He hit the gas, leaving the woman with her mouth hanging open. As he raced down the twisting road into Del Mar, Cooper felt suddenly invigorated and full of purpose. Those few minutes in Max's office had been some of the worst in his life, and that included the hell he'd gone through in high school and every heartbreak he'd had since. In Cooper's universe, the vision of Max and Kiki (God, that *name* even!) was not possible; it was science fiction and he had been transported to some alien planet. But there, in the middle of it, was Marina, his known quantity. Somehow she held the key that would unlock all of this. As he drove north, he wondered if he'd imagined the ring he'd seen on Kiki's finger. Perhaps his brain—or Marina!—had projected the image there to guide him to her. Either way, fantasy or reality, it didn't matter. He was going to find her, something he probably should have done much sooner. But no, Cooper told himself, everything was happening at exactly the right time, exactly the way it should. He made one stop, at a little flower stand in Del Mar that always had the freshest blooms, for a slim but elegant bouquet of roses. Then he made his way to Cardiff—to her house.

Cooper hadn't expected to be as nervous as he was when he marched up the three little steps to Marina's front door and knocked. Her shades were drawn and the house was very still. He knocked again, a little louder this time, and waited a few beats. The third time he knocked it was out of sheer nerves, a Pavlovian response to standing at a closed door with a bunch of roses in his hand. It was, Cooper thought, one of the most anticlimactic moments he'd ever experienced. He stood there for a few more moments and then turned around and sat down on her front stairs. After a minute or two of that, he realized the neighbors might notice something off and he went over to his car, got in, turned on the radio and waited. Three songs later, he started shifting around, restless and uncomfortable. He turned off the radio and lowered his seat back until he was at a comfortable forty-five-degree angle. He turned his head, the better to keep an eye on Marina's house, and promptly passed out cold with the roses resting on his chest.

He was dreaming of rain, the sound of drops falling on glass, when he woke up to find Marina tapping on his car window. He bolted upright, disoriented but hyper-alert. It was late. The sky was suffused with gold-pink light and the shadows were long. He must have been sleeping for hours. He opened his door and climbed out of his car.

"Cooper? What's happened?"

"Hi, Marina." She looked so different that Cooper thought she'd had some kind of plastic surgery. But it only took a moment to realize that there wasn't any kind of surgery that could effect the kinds of changes he saw in her. She looked both softer and harder than when he'd last seen her. Her body was rounder, plusher, but underneath something had turned to stone. Her eyes seemed to have grown larger and somehow darker. Her face looked not so much thinner as sharply defined—her cheekbones in high relief against her long, wildly curling hair. She was wearing the kind of clothing he'd never seen her in before: stretchy black yoga pants and a baby-doll-style green top that tied in the back. It took another second for Cooper to understand the why of her outfit. She was pregnant. He was stunned and discomfited, as if he were a kindergartner seeing his teacher in the grocery store. It just didn't fit with his image of her. At a loss for the eloquent words he'd planned, he held the roses out and said, "I got these for you," as if he was taking her out on a date or something.

Marina backed up and looked almost frightened when she looked at the flowers. It was the weirdest reaction to a beautiful bouquet he'd ever seen. "Please," she said, "I can't stand to see another rose. Can you put them away, take them home?" Cooper knew he looked totally crestfallen because she added, "Don't take it personally, Cooper, okay?" He tossed the flowers in the passenger seat of his car and turned back to her.

"Marina, I'm sorry."

"You're sorry?"

"For what happened—the fire and everything. I never called you." Cooper bit his lip, remembering the calls he *had* made. "I should have . . . I don't know. I haven't really been myself lately."

Then Marina did the strangest thing. She got up very close to him and lay her hand, palm down, in the middle of his chest as if she were feeling for his heartbeat. He couldn't remember her ever touching him before. She'd always been so weird about anyone getting close to her. "It's okay," she said. "I know."

A dam burst inside Cooper's rib cage. His whole body felt flooded with a tidal wave of emotion—warm, cold, quiet and rushing all at once—and when the water reached his eyes he just started to bawl like a huge baby. Everything he'd felt for the last two years—maybe longer, like since the beginning of his life—came pouring out of him in an unstoppable rush.

"You're going to meet him when you get out of the hospital," Marina said. "He has blue eyes and a buzz cut. He works as a landscaper. There are koi ponds . . ."

"When I get out of the hospital?"

"But aren't you going in today?" Marina asked, genuinely baffled. "For your liver?"

"My liver?"

"I'm sorry," Marina said. "Now I've gotten ahead of myself."

It was starting to get a bit too strange, even for Cooper. Marina had just become so spooky, it was difficult to know how to deal with it. "Um . . ." And then he remembered why he'd come here.

"What is it, Cooper? You came here to ask me a question. What is it?"

Cooper turned his eyes to the collar of her loose top. No chain that he could see. "Do you still have that ring you used to wear around your neck, Marina? The ruby?"

Her hand flew to her neck, clutching at something that wasn't there. "What about the ring?" she demanded. "What do you know about that?"

"I know where it is," Cooper said. "And I know who's wearing it."

Chapter 34

It was never Eddie's intention to show up unannounced at Madeline's house and start growling at her like a wounded bear. For one thing, it was just bad form. Eddie had always prided himself on being *cool* about this kind of thing. It was a woman's job to melt down, lose it and get all emotional. Men were supposed to keep it together, shine it on, walk it off—whatever. Those were the rules as Eddie knew them. But it seemed these days that nobody else was playing by *any* kind of rule book.

Yes, shit happened. Things changed. You got older and your body started to give out. You got high cholesterol and your back started to hurt. The price of gas went up and it got more expensive to live. You argued with your wife. The kids were a pain in the ass. Everything that tasted or felt good wound up being bad for you in some way. Eddie understood these things, even if he wasn't at all okay with them, as basic truths of life. But some things were not supposed to change and some rules were meant to stay unbroken. Yet none of Eddie's usual strategies for keeping his life in order was working.

Start with Tina. It had taken only one phone call for Eddie to bridge the gap between penitent and pissed off. He'd called her a couple of days after he went to see Marina, when he was still turning the scene around and around in his head, trying to get it to make sense. There was just something so *not* normal about the way Marina looked, the things she'd said and the strange tone in her voice. It had thrown Eddie off so badly that he didn't know how to get himself right. What he really wanted to do was talk to his wife and share his feelings; not about Marina necessarily, but about life in general—hell, just to *share,* period—because that was what married people did. He'd called Tina with this in mind, but when he finally got her on the phone, it was not at all the conversation he had been planning.

Two kids and how many years of marriage and suddenly it was fuck you, pack it all in and get divorced? It turned out Jake hadn't pulled the divorce question out of his ass when he'd last spoken to Eddie. Tina had already started discussing divorce with his kids before she'd even brought it up to him. And this he got from Kyle, his younger son, because Jake, "the man of the house," had since shifted all the way over to his mother's side and wouldn't even talk to his father.

"I don't think it's right to tell the boys we're divorcing when we haven't even tried to work this out, Tina," he'd told his wife when Kyle got her to come to the phone.

"I don't believe in keeping secrets from them, Eddie. That's *your* style, not mine."

"What secrets?" he said, ignoring her pointed dig at him. "There's nothing to hide. We aren't getting a divorce."

There was a small tight silence on the other end of the line. "Yes, we are, Eddie," she said. "I've hired a lawyer."

"Jesus, Tina."

"I can't do it anymore, Eddie, I just can't. I still have a chance at some kind of life now, but if I wait much longer it's going to be too late."

"What the fuck are you *talking* about?"

"Are you going to get hostile again, Eddie? Because if you are there's no point in continuing this conversation. I'm going to try very hard to keep . . ."

Eddie stopped listening to her words, hearing only the grating sound of her voice with its long-suffering tone as she laid out the new parameters of their rapidly dissolving relationship. Hurt and angry was one thing, Eddie thought, but this was something else. It occurred to him that maybe she'd been plotting this shit for years, waiting for the right moment. Maybe she'd known about the other women all along and was just letting him dig a hole deep enough to bury himself but good. All the better to make sure she got everything he had once the divorce lawyers started taking a look around. And maybe nobody *had* called her after all. Maybe that was just one big fat fucking lie to get him to admit he'd had an affair. The more she talked, the less he heard and the more furious he became.

And Tina was just the beginning.

With all her talk about broken plates and babies, Eddie had barely listened to what Marina was saying about his job, but it came back to him very quickly when he was called into a meeting with the owner of the store and a suited CEO-type sent down from corporate headquarters. A female employee, and, of course, they wouldn't say who it was, had complained of Eddie's "unwanted advances and lewd behavior." Whoever it was had also asserted that she was "punished" for "rejecting" his "sexual overtures."

In a panic, Eddie ran through every woman who worked at the store and came up completely blank as to who would think up something like this, never mind file a complaint. But maybe no one had, he thought. Maybe this was some sort of frame-up.

"Has this got something to do with my staying in my office?" Eddie blurted. "Because it's only temporary. My wife and I are having a little trouble. . . ."

There was some foot shuffling and throat clearing after that comment, and then they informed him that they really had no other option but to ask him to please remove his belongings from his office and leave as quickly and quietly as possible.

It had been thirty years since Eddie had done his time in prison, but he still looked into the shadows every so often, half expecting the law to jump out and grab him. This vague anxiety spurred him out the door more quickly and quietly than they'd asked, even though he vowed to find himself a lawyer as soon as he was able.

Although he'd known it was a losing proposition, he called Tina to tell her he was finished with her bullshit and that he was coming home to his own goddamn house. Tina told him that if he tried, he'd be entertaining the police before he had a chance to get inside the front door. When he thought about it later, Eddie thought it might have been that threat alone, coming from *his wife*, that pushed him over the edge.

Eddie ran through his short list of options that weren't really options. He couldn't go knocking on the door of his Doberman-owning employee now that he wasn't the guy's boss anymore. He'd sleep in the street before he'd lower himself to go see Cassie, who was probably already fucking someone else in every sense of the word. Sleeping in his truck was just too depressing to think about. So it was time for another motel. Unfortunately for Eddie, North County had hardly any *cheap* fleabag motels. The sleaziest dive in these parts (barring those that charged by the hour) would set you back at least a bill. Feeling much like a cornered rat, Eddie checked into a motel at the northern edge of Encinitas whose bizarre backstory hadn't helped to bring down its rates.

Ten years before, the Heaven's Gate cult had staged a mass suicide in Rancho Santa Fe. Six weeks later, two others who hadn't gotten on that crazy train attempted to take themselves out the same way in that very motel. One succeeded. The other survived but ended up killing himself nine months later in Arizona. Eddie knew about all of this because everyone who lived in San Diego at the time—not to mention the rest of the world—knew every detail, but he was especially familiar with this little bit of the story because he and Madeline had spent more than one scorching afternoon between the sheets at this motel. It was sort of a joke between them: how Madeline lived where the big group had offed themselves, and now here they were at the site of the two pathetic losers who came after.

Eddie lay on the bed in what might have been the very room where those two sad souls had put on their Nike running shoes and prepared to meet the rocket ship that would take them to Jesus, and all he could think about was what a total fucking stuck-up bitch Madeline was. She had the house, the husband, the money and now (oh yes, Eddie *believed*) she had his baby, too. He thought about it all night: how hot she'd been, how she just couldn't get enough. There was nothing he could do that was too freaky or weird. She wanted everything. And then she'd dropped him cold, that ice queen persona taking over as she rode her Mercedes back to Rancho Fucking Santa Fe. He thought about her face, her perfectly done cool blond hair and all her white shirts, skirts and pants. He'd never seen her in any other color. She had that kind of money where you could wear only one color and then spend vast sums to match your whims. He remembered the first time he'd seen her—not when Marina had introduced them at Darling's, but months before in that very same place. He'd been sitting there waiting for his first appointment with Marina and Madeline had run in with some friend of hers, the two of them soaking wet and laughing. She wouldn't give him the time of fucking day then. Too good for him, she was. But Eddie hadn't remembered that little scene until much later, when they were naked and sliding with sweat and she scraped his back with her iceberg-size ring. He remembered the ring then and that she'd been attached to it. He should have known; they were all the fucking same in the end.

Eddie rolled these thoughts around and around in his head until they picked up enough speed and mass to become angry boulders crashing into his brain. What gave someone like Madeline the right to steal from him? And steal is what she'd done. She'd stolen his very essence, his manhood. And now she thought she was going to dump his ass and cut him out of his own kid's life? No. She was going to pay somehow. Eddie was sick to fucking death of being taken advantage of. It was his turn to get a piece of the pie.

It had taken some doing to figure out exactly where Madeline lived. She hadn't been forthcoming about specific names and addresses during their motel sessions. But over the course of their time together she'd slipped enough details for him to put a map together in his head. He didn't know what he was expecting once he got there or what the hell he would say to the husband if he happened to be around. But Eddie was pretty sure he was only going to find the missus at home. How many times had Madeline whined to him about how her husband was never there, didn't love her, etc., etc., etc.? The way he was feeling now, Eddie couldn't blame the guy.

Damn, it was one of the biggest McMansions he'd ever seen, Eddie thought as he approached the front door. He'd had no problem getting in, because the large iron gate at the bottom of the long driveway was wide open, just waiting for him to drive through. He recognized the quality of both the work and the materials on and around the house. Those were imported Chinese tiles he saw on the roof. Must have cost them a fortune. And that was a genuine Italian marble bath that the birds were shitting in. Nice. The landscaping alone, Eddie mused, looking at the rosebushes, bougainvillea trellises and wisteria vines, had to cost a grand a month in upkeep. A grand easy.

He rang the doorbell and heard absolutely nothing from inside the house. Soundproofed, no doubt, as well as wired for armed response lest intruders appear. Eddie leaned on the doorbell again, anger rising up in his craw. He wanted to kill something. When nothing happened after the second ring, he just started pounding the door with his fists. Finally, he heard it: "Just a minute! I'm coming!" Yeah, Eddie thought, he'd heard that before, too. She opened the door and Eddie watched as the quick succession of incomprehension, surprise, shock and finally fear flashed across her face like little bursts of lightning.

"Nice to see you open your own door," he said. "I would have thought you'd have help for that kind of thing."

"*What are you doing here?*" There was real panic in her voice. He was glad.

"Woman," he answered, "you'd better let me in."

"This isn't part of the deal," she hissed back. "You're not supposed to be here." She put her hand on the door frame as if she was going to slam it shut, but Eddie leaned against it with his full weight.

"Well, I am here," he said. "And having my baby wasn't part of the deal, either."

If there had been any doubt in Eddie's mind, it was put to rest as he watched Madeline's reaction. Her surprise and acknowledgment was so instantaneous and genuine that even she knew she'd given herself away.

"What do you want, Eddie?"

"To start, I want you to let me into your house. And then . . ." Eddie paused for effect. "Then *I guess we'll see how it works out.*" That was what she'd said to him the first time they'd been together. He searched her face for evidence that she remembered those words but found none. She was distracted, trying to figure out what to do with him, he guessed. He pushed his way past her and into the house. Inside, even the air felt more expensive; it was heavier somehow and smelled of money. Madeline closed the door and leaned her back against it, her arms crossed reflexively across her chest as if to protect herself.

"This was a stupid thing to do, Eddie. My husband . . ."

Eddie flashed on his meeting with Marina. *"Don't go there. You're going to get hurt."* He felt a quick chill run through his body, a sense of foreboding that made him hesitate, but only for a second. What did it matter? Everything had gone to shit and he had so little left to lose.

"Is he here?" Eddie asked.

"No, but . . ."

"Then don't you worry. I've got some tools in the truck. If he shows up, we'll just tell him I'm the gardener." Madeline's eyebrows drew together in frustration and she bit her lip.

"Fine," he said. "Have it your way. I'm the plumber. Come to fix the sink."

Chapter 35

It was amazing, Madeline thought, how one's situation could go from delicate to desperate in the space of five minutes. It was some kind of insanely bad luck (Madeline refused to think of it as karma) that Eddie Perkins had chosen this moment to track her down and ruin everything.

Madeline had never been much of a plotter, and complicated patterns of cause and effect were not her strong suit. She was the type who needed to follow directions step-by-step in order to do anything, whether that was baking a cake or setting up a DVR. She enjoyed reading suspense novels because, unable to unravel even the simplest plots, she could never figure out who did it ahead of time. For the same reason, Madeline had never been able to play chess worth a damn. Twister was more her game.

But now, watching Eddie stalk around her house like a lost moose, Madeline realized that she was going to have to think not only fast but also strategically. It was a challenge she wasn't sure she was up to. She started with the most obvious approach and prayed it would work.

"What about your wife, Eddie? Aren't you worried about her? I don't think she'd like to hear that you're over here."

"Funny thing about her," Eddie said, running his hand along her stone mantel. "She told me someone called her and told me I was having an affair. You don't know anything about that, do you? Hey, just out of curiosity, how much did this fireplace set you back? Because this is some really fine work here."

"Are you crazy?" Madeline said, starting to think that maybe he was. It wasn't as if she really knew him, after all. "You think I had something to do with that? Why would I call your wife?"

"I don't know," Eddie answered, fingering the inlaid edge of an antique walnut sideboard. "But I'm a guy. I can't figure out how women think anymore. It's a big mystery to me. Oh, this is a nice piece. Where'd you get it?"

"So what does that mean, Eddie? Did you and your wife break up? Is that what this is about?" Eddie didn't seem to be listening to her. He was now picking up silver-framed photographs and studying each one as if he was looking for clues. She wished he would stop touching her things.

"Is this your husband?" he asked, holding a recent photo of Andrew she'd taken with the digital camera he'd given her for some occasion she couldn't remember.

"Yes, that's him," Madeline said. "Why?"

"Not what I expected," Eddie said.

"And what was that?"

"I don't know—fat? Bald? Short?"

"Why?"

"Rich man, pretty woman. You know that story."

"Eddie, can we talk about why you're here? What is it you want?"

"He looks really familiar," Eddie said, still scrutinizing the photo. "I'm sure I know him from somewhere."

"I don't think so," Madeline said. "You two don't really run in the same circles."

Eddie finally turned his head away from the photo to look at Madeline. She saw immediately that she'd made a serious tactical error. His face was full of bruised manhood and wounded pride. And he was angry.

"But that's not totally true, is it, sweetness? There seem to be some circles your husband and I do both run in. I'm looking at one of them right now."

Madeline was starting to feel panicky, and that was very bad, because if she lost it she would make a scene, and if she made a scene, this whole thing was going to blow up. The caterers were going to arrive any second—she couldn't believe they hadn't gotten here already—and Andrew could come home at any time.

"He sees her too, doesn't he?"

"Who? What do you mean?"

"Your husband. I know why he looks so familiar. I've seen him at Marina's place."

"What?"

"I mean at her office, before it burned down. Outside. I'm almost positive."

Several anxious thoughts crisscrossed Madeline's brain at once. One of them was that if Andrew had been hanging around Marina's office he'd been spying on her, in which case he might already know about Eddie. Then it occurred to her that Eddie himself might have been spying on her. But maybe Eddie was making all this up to scare her.

"Eddie, what is it you *want?*"

"Well, for starters, I want to know why you haven't told me about the baby."

Madeline felt her gut twisting, all that rich Hawaiian fruit churning around in her stomach. How could he possibly know that she was pregnant? She hadn't told anyone at all. It had to be a lucky guess, but why guess at that? Men *never* wanted to claim paternity. Unless, of course, they had something to gain by it.

"What baby? I still don't know what you're talking about. There's no baby. Did your wife come up with that, too? Maybe some other woman you've slept with . . ."

"It's true, isn't it?"

"No, it isn't! But even if it were, what difference would it make? You want me to leave my husband and marry you?"

Eddie shook his head as if she just wasn't getting it. "You can't just take, take, take," he said. "At some point you have to start giving something back."

"You want money," she said flatly. "Is that it?"

She saw something change in his face, as if he hadn't thought to ask her, but now that she'd brought it up it seemed like a good idea. Or maybe he was just an idiot and was surprised that she'd guessed. Eddie moved out of the sitting room, where Madeline had led him earlier to keep him out of the way, and into the main living room, where the palm trees and pikake filled the air with the smell of the islands. "Look at this," he said. "You have a whole jungle in here. I've never seen anything like this."

"Actually, it's supposed to be Hawaii," Madeline said before she could stop herself. "It's a luau."

"Is that a *beach* on your back porch?"

"It's not a porch," Madeline said. "It's a patio."

"What does something like this cost?" Eddie asked. "I have to know."

"Stick around," Madeline said, "and you can ask Andrew when he gets home. *He's* the one who pays for this, not me."

The wheels were turning in Madeline's head. She finally had some clarity, and a semblance of a plan was starting to emerge in her calorie-laden brain. Eddie was obviously angling for a share in the life she'd worked so hard to get, but he was a fool, and much stupider than she'd given him credit for, if he thought he was going to get it by intimidating her this way.

"Why a beach?" Eddie asked, still awestruck by the scene in front of him. "What the hell would you need a beach in your living room for? That's the thing with you people, isn't it? You live a few miles from the ocean but that's not good enough."

"I don't think you heard me, Eddie. If Andrew shows up and you're here you're going to fuck everything up." She lowered her voice to a fierce whisper. "If he finds out about you, I'll be done—all this'll be gone. Don't you get it? I have a *prenuptial agreement*. Do you know what that is? I'll get nothing. I'll have to come live with *you*."

"I don't think so," he said. "You think you can take anything you want, but I'm here to tell you that you can't. You're not going to have my kid—"

"You don't give a shit about your *kid,* Eddie, so just shut up about that. I know what you want. But I'm trying to tell you I don't have it to give you."

Eddie fondled the leaves of a fake palm tree. "Well, then, I guess I'll just wait here until you find a way. Things have gotten a little difficult for me lately, Madeline. I'm going to need a little help getting on my feet."

Madeline studied Eddie's face to see if he was bluffing and decided he wasn't. She was also guessing that Eddie wasn't a very complicated man and that what you saw with him was pretty much what you got.

"I'll see what I can do," she said.

"Not good enough."

"I can't write you a check right now, Eddie."

"Can't you?"

"I'll have to get money from Andrew."

"When?"

"I'll call you."

He laughed. "Try again," he said. "I need it now."

Madeline got a quick vision of her possible future. She could put him off now, but he'd be back. He could make a real nuisance of himself and request a paternity test. He wouldn't stop, Madeline thought, once he got a taste. And she'd spend the rest of her life dodging bullets. She chewed her lip in frustration, that desperate feeling coming back like a tightening vise around her head, but then, in a stroke of inspiration, the answer came to her.

"I have to get ready for this party, Eddie. It's all planned; I can't change it. You have to go now. Just give me a few hours. Come back tonight, after the party's over. I'll meet you . . . I'll show you where, and I'll give you some *help.* Okay, Eddie? Okay?"

The sound of the doorbell made Madeline jump, an exaggerated reaction that betrayed how nervous she'd become. "Shit, that's the caterers," she said. "Eddie, you have to go."

He hesitated, but finally started making some movement toward the door. "Okay," he said, "but I'm coming back, Madeline. I'm coming back tonight."

"Not that way," she said quickly. "I'll show you another way out where I'll meet you later. Come back at . . . at midnight would be good. Everyone should be gone by then and Andrew should be passed out." As she spoke, she guided him out through the patio doors and around to the side entrance near the garage and their many rosebushes. The doorbell rang again. "Just a minute!" Madeline called. "Okay, Eddie, go. Midnight, okay?"

"I hope you're not yanking my chain," he said, "because that would suck for you."

"I have to go," she said and turned, leaving him staring into her American Beauties.

Chapter 36

As small as Marina's orbit was, in order to get anywhere she still had to contend with the traffic that was slowly driving the populace into a state of collective insanity. Rush hour never started; it was constantly in progress. And there were no back roads to take to avoid the crush of cars whose drivers all had to get there *now*. Those shortcuts, the byways that locals always found to avoid the freeway-bound hoi polloi, had become as congested as the interstates. Everyone was now a local.

The sun had gone down on a Saturday evening and the roads were still as packed as a Monday morning. As Marina inched toward Rancho Santa Fe, she had plenty of time to think about what she was doing and all the rational arguments for why she shouldn't be doing it. She was a pregnant woman, alone, about to go to a place where, at the very best, she would be unwelcome. Several people at this party had reason to avoid her, to fear what she knew. She knew about their lies and infidelities, the small and large cruelties they'd inflicted on the people they claimed to love. But Marina wasn't crashing this party to release skeletons from closets. She was looking for Gideon's ring. What happened once she found it was for fate to decide. This, Marina realized, could not really be called a reasonable plan.

The *reasonable* thing would be to call Detective Franks, whose card she'd stuffed into her purse as some sort of talisman, and tell him what she was doing. He'd called and left a message for her yesterday, telling her "we have a few more questions we'd like to ask you, so if you could give us a call back . . ." Marina's initial surge of alarm over that message had given way to dull anxiety when she realized that if he'd wanted to—if he had enough evidence—Detective Franks could have just shown up at her door as he had before and taken her to the police station. That he'd chosen to leave a cordial voice-mail message meant that her cooperation was still voluntary. But it wouldn't be for long, Marina sensed. They were closing in on her.

But how could she call the detective now and tell him that she knew Gideon's ring was on Kiki's finger? That Kiki had been a client of hers? That Max, who had given it to her, couldn't possibly have been the person who had ripped it from Gideon's neck because Max was gay and hiding so much already that he'd never flaunt the evidence of a crime in plain sight—that it just wasn't his way? That someone *had* killed Gideon and had taken the ring and if she could just touch it she'd know who it was? That she'd promised Gideon's mother she'd wear it until the danger was past? No, Marina thought, none of that would seem reasonable and all of it would make her seem guiltier than she already did.

But it was all moot anyway, because reason no longer guided Marina's decisions. If the police were going to arrest her, reasoning out a plan would do nothing to stop it. She could only keep moving ahead in the direction she was being pushed and hope that she wasn't halted before she could get there. Fate had become Marina's primary driving force, perhaps the most powerful change in the series of cataclysmic upheavals that had begun the night she met Gideon.

Of the myriad categories that people could be broken into, Marina thought the most basic was the one that separated the believers in probability from the fatalists, a difference more elemental than gender. The only thing that allowed the two types to coexist was that they both accounted for a measure of free will. Those who figured they could beat the odds lined up to buy lottery tickets right next to those who were reaching for their destinies. Marina had always been so far on the side of odds that she couldn't even see the view from where the fatalists were standing. But now she believed the very concept of randomness was something created to stave off the crush of inevitability. Marina's old sense of reason was like a phantom limb. She could try to use it, but it was no longer there, and she found herself being pushed forward by a different hand. This was exactly how she'd come to be on this road, headed to Madeline's house, a crawling sense of danger growing with each mile.

It troubled Marina that Cooper's observation and not her own vision had provided the first place to search. That he'd gotten a good enough look at her ring to recognize it on another woman's hand made her wonder how much else she'd missed. Marina had always been so intent on studying others that she hadn't realized how carefully they were looking at her. Poor Cooper didn't have any idea how twisted a story he was part of, but he knew that there was something very wrong about where that ring had ended up. "You can see for yourself," he'd told Marina as she led him inside her house. "They're having a 'coming out'—ha!—at a party in Rancho tomorrow night. It's at—well, you know Madeline, don't you? Of course you do, that's where I met you." Then he'd started babbling, so relieved that she wasn't angry at him, he'd said, because he'd done some things, some things that weren't at all what he was about, but if she only knew how hard it had been and . . . And then he'd passed out; he'd literally listed to the side and then down into the soft folds of her couch. By the time the paramedics had arrived he was conscious enough to smile at her and attempt a weak joke about the extremes some people would go to to get attention.

"You're going to the hospital," she told him, "but you're going to be fine, Cooper."

"You said," he mumbled. "A gardener, right?" By the time she'd made sure Cooper was settled and resting royally in the hospital, which had a wing named after his father, Marina had already decided to crash Madeline's party.

Memories descended thick and fast as she got closer to Madeline's house. Passing the San Elijo Lagoon, she remembered her ride with Gideon, how quiet and full of mystery he'd been on the way to the hotel. She searched for his face in her mind's eye, but it remained frustratingly out of view. So she tried to focus on the details she could see: the big white bed full of promise, the way the dawn light had muted and softened the colors in the room, and the roses. The roses. Marina could smell their sweetness again mixed with the tang of smoke.

"Gideon, where are you?" she said out loud. *I'm sorry,* she added silently. *I should have gone home. I should have listened. I should have been there.* And then there was more, the slow leak of useless regret. She'd promised the old woman that she'd wear the ring and keep him safe. If she'd kept it hidden, if she'd never let him see it—take it . . .

The line of traffic finally thinned as Marina left the main road and started maneuvering through the dark plush interior of Rancho Santa Fe. She knew the way by heart from here, the muscle memory of all those visits to Madeline coming back to her. Madeline in repose on the red chaise longue, her pale hands resting on the swell of her belly. Madeline twisting her wedding ring around and around on her finger. Andrew, dark and glowering, hovering at the edges of doorways, watching and disapproving. His hand clutching a cut-crystal glass.

Marina's heart started beating fast, pushing adrenaline through her veins. She smelled it first, strong and harsh, and then she tasted the bitter burn of scotch whiskey on her tongue. Her stomach turned in revolt. More came down, filling her nose and mouth as if she were swallowing great gulps of liquor. Marina coughed, her throat closing up, and felt as if she was going to vomit. Her head swimming, she pulled over on a soft shoulder and opened her window to let in some air.

Not drunk enough. Not even close.

It was *that head* again, and this time it had invaded hers. Her vision wavered and she gagged. She opened the car door and leaned out, spitting the vile taste in her mouth onto the road.

Where are you going?

I'll be back in a minute.

Marina closed her eyes and leaned back in her seat, trying to slow her breathing. Behind her closed lids she saw a swirl of color come slowly into focus. Palm trees and a blue-and-white-striped hammock. A man in a Hawaiian shirt drinking out of a coconut and talking to a woman wearing a grass skirt. The vision swung a hard right onto a dark patio where several people were sitting around a fire pit, their bare feet buried in a pile of sand. Another dizzying spin and she was looking into the maw of a huge punch bowl filled with something red. There were bursts of loud noise: laughter, the crash of a glass breaking, several people talking at once. It became a deafening, blinding din and Marina opened her eyes.

Shut up—just shut the fuck up.

Then there was nothing except for the nauseating taste of scotch and the smell of roses. Marina opened her eyes. Five minutes of slow, steady breathing later, she was still shaking from the violence of the *attack*—the only word she could think to describe what had just happened to her. She started her car and pulled back onto the road. As she drove unsteadily toward Madeline's house, her vision seemed to tunnel and shrink as if she were looking through the wrong end of a telescope. For the first time since she'd left her house, she felt the baby kick, bringing her back into her own body. If this were a movie, Marina thought, the violins would be screeching to a foreshadowing crescendo right about now, and the audience would be thinking, *Don't go there; turn around!* But, of course, the character would keep going, oblivious, even though any idiot could see the danger she was heading into. And this was exactly what Marina did.

Marina found a fleet of Jaguars, Mercedes, BMWs and Hummers clogging not only Madeline's driveway but a good portion of the street in front of her house. She was forced to park much farther away from the house than she wanted, and as she wove her way between the cars in the dark, she remembered the crowd at Madeline's last party: the people thronging around their human sushi platter and her own carnival tent at the other end of the room. Madeline had hired a valet service for that one—an "LA thing," Marina remembered someone telling her. Only at the really chichi LA events, the valets gave you roses when they brought around your car.

Marina caught her heel on a loose piece of gravel and stumbled. She felt a thump and couldn't tell if it was coming from inside her or if the ground beneath her was shaking. The smell and taste of scotch was burning her throat again. She could hear ukulele island music coming from the house now, the sound of a party in full sway, and she realized that what she'd seen in the car a few minutes before was what was going on inside the house now. Once again, she felt the frustration of always being simultaneously one step ahead and two steps behind herself. It made trying to figure out what was going on in the present an almost impossible task. But there was something else she was hearing now.

Marina? Marina, it's Gideon. Are you there?

She was there again, in the heart of that night, hiding in the back of her office as she saw Gideon approaching. He'd come to tell her he loved her, to apologize for leaving her, to try to work things out. He wanted to listen to her story, to understand. And she would never be able to tell him, because she raised the arm that wasn't hers and brought the gun down hard across his skull, hearing the crack of it, watching him fall.

Must get rid of the evidence. Can't leave anything behind. Take his wallet and his keys. What's that around his neck? What kind of pansy wears a ring like this on a chain? A piece like this is worth . . . take it. Must take it. Have to burn this place down. Fire burns everything clean.

Marina's lungs were thick with smoke. She coughed and gasped for breath. It was hot: burning, agonizing heat. *No, no!* Marina's tears scalded her cheeks. He was still alive when her office went up in flames. The blow to his head had knocked him out, but the fire had killed him. If she'd gotten there just minutes earlier . . . Just minutes would have made the difference between his life and his horrible death.

Marina kept walking as the remnants of her vision fell away from her.

She could feel the presence now—that cruel mind she'd shared—and she could tell it was very close. The sound of her racing blood sang in her ears and her face was wet with tears. She was almost there. Finally, at the top of the long driveway, Marina veered off to the side of the house and the entrance she'd always used when she'd come here before. It didn't occur to her until she was past the garage that she probably shouldn't be using what she'd always thought of as the service entrance. No matter; if the door here was open it would be easier to slide in undetected.

But Marina didn't even get as far as the door. Just as she reached Madeline's blooming rosebushes, a man smelling strongly of alcohol stepped in front of her and blocked her path. Andrew.

"Witch," he said, "what the hell are you doing here?"

Marina's senses sharpened to a razor's edge. She saw the anger inside Andrew as a roiling mass, barely contained and pushing to get out. Her own head pounded. Panic thickened her throat and she couldn't speak.

"I mean, you must have some kind of balls to show up at *my house.*" He was drunk, but steady on his feet, and there was no slur in his words, just cold dark hatred. "Either that or you're even stupider than my stupid bitch wife."

Marina saw it then—the scene unfolding like a film clip in her mind. Gideon approaching her office and peering into the darkness, where he'd seen the flashlight flicker. There in the back, Andrew waiting with his hand on his gun. He'd left the door unlocked and Gideon had just walked in. Andrew, consumed with hatred and bitterness over a life that hadn't produced what he wanted from it. And all of that dark loathing spilling out of him. There at her desk, over her tarot cards and candles, Andrew's hate met Gideon's love and the two exploded in flames. It was she who should have been in the center of that vortex, not Gideon.

"It was you," Marina said.

"You're like a bad penny," Andrew said, moving closer to her. "Like a black cat. And you won't go away. I knew you were fucking trouble the minute I saw you." He was practically on top of her now. She could feel his liquored breath on her face. "You should have quit while you were ahead," he hissed.

Marina tried to back away, but he grabbed hold of her arm and pulled her still closer. His face was so contorted with anger that it was starting to look like a Halloween mask. Her vision telescoped again, Andrew's face seeming to tunnel backward, and now she saw him through Gideon's eyes. He was leaning over, his hands pulling, grabbing, taking wallet, keys and now the ring—yanking it, snapping the chain.

"No!" she shouted. Everything went black; she couldn't see. She struggled to move, to open her eyes, but she was dead weight. Smoke filled her lungs. She couldn't breathe; she was burning, choking—

—Andrew's hands were on her throat, her mouth, shaking her. "Shut up, shut up!" The words came through his gritted teeth.

"You killed him," she gasped. Her voice was dying in her throat and he was squeezing harder, his fingers locked around her windpipe. She grabbed at his hands, her fingernails piercing his flesh but unable to loosen his grip. He was too strong and she was choking. He was going to kill her. She was going to die. Bright spots danced in front of her eyes and time slowed. It was not her life flashing in pieces through her mind now but the last seconds of Gideon's. She saw herself, soft and smiling, a version she'd never seen with her own eyes. She felt his love and hope as he reached for her. She heard his heart calling out her name. *I'm sorry, Marina. I understand now.* He didn't want to let go, wasn't ready to leave. There was so much unfinished.

There was no more breath. The light went out. Her body went limp. Marina fell.

There was a rush of blood to her head, the sharp scrape of thorns and the sweet smell of roses. With a crash of broken branches, a body fell and landed heavily next to her. Soft petals rained down on her face. She coughed and sucked in air, turned her head and saw Andrew's dead eyes staring into hers. She felt the scream, but no sound came from her damaged throat.

"*Marina!* Are you all right?"

She turned to the voice and saw Eddie leaning over her, reaching out with his hands to lift her. "Can you speak? Are you all right?"

Marina clung to him, trying to get to her feet. "What happened?" The words scraped out raspy and wounded.

"Goddamn insane bastard. He would have killed you." Eddie put his arms around her, supporting her full weight with his body, and carry-dragged her away from the rosebushes. "He would have killed you," he repeated, his voice wavering. "I had to . . ." He turned his head and Marina followed his anxious eyes to where Andrew lay half buried in the roses, his legs splayed and twisted. Something that looked like a length of pipe was resting on the ground next to him. "I didn't hit him that hard," Eddie said. "Fuck, we need an ambulance. You need to go to a hospital." Marina felt his muscles tensing. He wanted to run. She tried to let go of him, but her weak knees wouldn't hold her up. "It's okay, it's okay," he said. "I won't leave you."

"Eddie . . . it's all right. You saved my life."

As soon as she got the words out, everything around them exploded into a mad whirl of color and sound. A door opened, spilling light and music, and Madeline walked out, a small group of partiers trailing her.

"I don't know where he's gotten to. Andrew! Andrew, we have *guests* here!"

"Yeah, you don't want to miss the limbo, Andrew!" someone added. Marimbas blared from inside.

"—hope he didn't run away from home, Maddie."

"—went to get some ice for—"

"—seen their rosebushes? They're ama—"

"—that was *Don* Ho, stupid—"

"Andrew! Where are you? What—"

It was Madeline who reached them first, her face blanching the shade of her diaphanous white gown as she registered first Eddie, then Marina.

"Oh my God, oh my God!"

"What is—"

A woman shrieked, the sound of it knifing through the air.

"Somebody call nine-one-one!"

Madeline turned and saw her husband's body. It took no more than a second, but Marina saw it. Madeline flicked her eyes back to Eddie, her face registering not shock or grief, but indecision. She was trying to come up with the best, most genuine reaction so that her witnesses could attest to it later. Instantly, the look was gone. Madeline opened her mouth wide and screamed.

"It's all right," Marina whispered to Eddie. "It's going to be all right."

August 2007

Chapter 37

Cooper ran his fingers through his freshly cut hair and surveyed the effect in the long salon mirror in front of him.

"You want to see the back?" Cassie said. "It looks awesome." She handed him a round hand mirror and swiveled his chair so that he could get a look at the back of his head. She wasn't wrong, he thought, checking her work. The short, ultra-professional style suited him perfectly. Of course, it would have looked like crap a few months ago when his face was fat and sallow. The triumph of this haircut owed as much to the rest of Cooper's new look as it did to Cassie's talent as a stylist. Nevertheless, he had to give credit where credit was due.

"Love it," he said. "It's a new me."

"Definitely," Cassie said. She spun him back around so that they were both staring into the big mirror and put her hands on his shoulders. "You know, if you want, I can get rid of those grays, too," she said, lowering her voice. "A lot of guys do it. More than you think. It would look really hot." She brushed off his shoulders with her hands even though all the stray hairs were already gone, her fingers lingering on the bare skin of his neck.

"Something to think about," Cooper said, giving her a small smile. He knew he must be back in prime form if women were starting to come on to him. On the other hand, he felt bad that this one was so clueless—

or desperate. It reminded him of Max's "bride" and, despite his new philosophical approach to that whole thing, the memory still stung.

"Well, you can come in anytime," Cassie said. "I've just started here, so I'm working a lot of hours to build up my client base. Why don't I give you my number for when you decide about the color? Here, I'll write down my cell so you can make sure you get *me* and not someone else."

Part of Cooper's new philosophy (borrowed from several twelve-step programs) was to avoid trying to change things he had no control over. The old Cooper would have said something like "Thanks, and I'll send my boyfriend in, too," but the new Cooper knew better than to get even that deeply involved. He thanked her, tipped her well and left the salon after giving himself one last go-over in the mirror.

Cooper picked up a fresh carrot juice with a wheatgrass shooter at the Jamba Juice next door to the salon and headed over to the hospital. The backseat of his car was packed full with boxes of dolls and games, and he planned to distribute them to the sick kids in the children's ward. Another part of Cooper's new approach to life was to try to be less selfish and to give back to society in the form of charitable works. At least that was the way he'd explained it when he'd asked his father for funds to implement this charity. It was his brush with death that had really done it, Cooper explained. How many people got a second chance? It was actually his responsibility to make the most of his new lease on life.

Of course, Cooper hadn't actually walked through the tunnel toward the light, but he *had* been sick and he *might* have died if, instead of collapsing at Marina's house and being taken away by paramedics, he'd passed out at home alone (or, worse, on the road). What he had was an inflamed and fatty liver along with some related "insult" to his pancreas and kidneys. Cooper's attempt at sexy self-destruction, it seemed, had resulted in an extremely *un*sexy, if curable, illness. After the initial drama of the emergency room and admittance to the hospital, Cooper had the self-awareness to be embarrassed by the nature of his medical problems. Despite that, though, he still believed that Marina had saved his life. More important, he believed his was a life worth saving.

It was also Marina who had pointed him toward love—real love this time—with her prediction about the landscaper he was going to meet. It hadn't just happened, of course. After he'd recovered and gotten back into shape, Cooper had called every landscaper in the phone book to come over and assess the state of his cactus garden, each one of them decidedly hetero and totally confused as to why he sent them away so fast. He finally met Michael, "a landscape artist" who'd been putting in a koi pond at a neighbor's house. He'd been watching the parade of his competitors with much amusement and finally came over to see what Cooper was up to.

"I'm just curious," Michael had asked Cooper. "Are you waiting to find the one who can feel the pea under all the mattresses?"

It was as close to love at first sight as one could get, Cooper thought, and he had Marina to thank for it. And he had been thanking her in as many ways as he could since the day she'd sent him off in the ambulance. He still felt guilty that he'd been too sick to go with her to that party and felt somehow responsible for her nearly getting killed, although who could ever have guessed that Andrew was such an insane psychopath? So his first order of business was to make sure that she had expert medical care right through her delivery. ("Yes, Marina," he'd told her, "I *did* notice that you were pregnant.")

The next thing he did was go with her to Andrew's funeral. Or, more accurately, *he'd* gone to Andrew's funeral while Marina waited nearby with a cop she knew. Just as she'd told him, Max's fiancée, Kiki, was there at the graveside, the ruby ring sparkling in the sunlight. Max, curiously, was not in attendance. Avoiding as usual, Cooper thought at the time. Although it didn't jibe with Cooper's newfound charity, he had to admit he got a catty satisfaction out of telling Kiki that a police officer was waiting to talk to her about her engagement ring. He was only sorry he couldn't be there when she asked Max why he'd given her a ring (subsequently taken into evidence) that had been stolen from a murdered man.

But he did find out what eventually happened when Max called him a few weeks later.

He'd started with a long, insincere bit about how he'd heard Cooper was sick and was calling to see how he was faring and blah blah blah until Cooper cut him off by asking how his pregnant fiancée was doing and about the wedding plans. Max gave one of his famous pauses and then informed Cooper that it wasn't going to work out with Kiki after all. Sadly, she'd suffered a miscarriage (read: never pregnant in the first place, Cooper thought), so there wasn't going to be a wedding. Cooper kept quiet, refusing to say he was sorry because he absolutely wasn't. And then Max said he wanted to make sure Cooper knew he had nothing to do with that man's death or any of the trouble Marina had been through. "I just bought the ring from him," Max said pathetically. "Andrew was Royal Rings, for fuck's sake. How could I have known?" Although he realized Max must have been really rattled if he used the *f* word, Cooper still said nothing and let him carry on, using Max's own shrink trick on him. Max said it was important to him what Cooper thought of him. He said he was taking a sabbatical from work to "think through some things." And then he paused for so long that Cooper was sure he was going to finally say it: *I miss you, I love you, I made a mistake, let's get back together.* But for one last time, Max pulled the chair out from under Cooper. "So you believe me, don't you, Cooper?" he said. "If someone asked . . ." And for one last time, Cooper hung up on Max. Marina, Cooper thought now, had always been right about Max, too.

The funny thing was, now that he was ready, open and *enlightened* (about certain things, anyway), Marina didn't want to read for him anymore. She told him that he could come by as often as he wanted, but it was no longer "right" for her to read for him. Whatever that meant. Marina may have gotten shaken and stirred over the last few months, but she still had that mysteriousness about her.

No matter, though. In a show of real good nature, Marina had given him the name of another very competent psychic who lived above La Jolla. Ciel would only let him see her once every three months—*no exceptions*—but he was okay with that, too. After all, too much looking into the future made you less inclined to actually live it.

That, at least, was one thing Cooper was sure of.

* * *

MADDIE—

LET'S TOAST TO THE SALE OF YOUR HOUSE!!!
POINT FIVE OVER THE ASKING PRICE!!!
CONGRATS!!!
—JOY

Madeline crumpled the note, filled a champagne flute with the Dom Pérignon her Realtor had left to celebrate the sale of her house—and her own hefty commission—and sucked it down in one gulp. She'd begged off a get-together with Joy, who was a talented Realtor but an irritating person, by telling her that she was having trouble dealing with everything—all the arrangements, the money, the lawyers and, because she was selling Royal Rings, the business advisers as well. Joy had dropped off the champagne anyway, perhaps hoping that Madeline would share it with her at a later date. Not likely, Madeline thought.

She took the bottle and glass into her nearly empty living room and sat down on the floor. She could barely hear the movers packing and crating in the kitchen. The odd sound of clinking silverware and china was the only indicator that they were there. Madeline felt the warm glow of the Dom spread golden through her solar plexus. It felt so good, she poured herself another glass. She'd forgotten how much she enjoyed the taste and buzz of good champagne. It was time to take up this particular habit again. Madeline had spent so long chained to the demands of a breeding body that she had to remind herself that there was no longer anything that was forbidden. For the first time in she couldn't remember how long, Madeline wasn't trying to get or stay pregnant. One of the very first things she'd done after *that* night was to have an abortion. She went way out of town to a ratty clinic where there was no chance of her being recognized by anyone, handed over four hundred dollars in cash and was on her way home less than an hour later.

She'd expected to feel some sadness, maybe even regret. But Madeline hadn't shed a single tear either before or after her visit to the clinic. The only thing she felt was an overwhelming sense of relief that she'd gotten her own body back and a determination never to let anyone else control it ever again. Not that she'd ever have to. Madeline's need to produce an heir died the same moment Andrew did.

Madeline had and continued to put on a show of grief worthy of an Oscar, but the deep inner truth was that she was glad Andrew was dead. If it had happened at any moment before that night, Madeline would have felt something more. If not an agonizing sense of loss, at least sorrow of a kind. She *had* loved him, after all. But the side of Andrew she'd seen that evening before the party—so deeply ugly and frightening it made her uncomfortable to think about it even now—had effectively extinguished any affection she still had for him.

Eddie's unexpected visit had put a real crimp in Madeline's post-party seduction plan for Andrew, and she'd had to revise—to try to get him into bed *before* the festivities. This ended up as one of the most spectacular failures Madeline had ever experienced. Andrew was already drunk and surlier than usual when he arrived home less than two hours before the party was supposed to start. He took one look at her Diana, Goddess of the Hunt outfit and asked her what the hell she thought she was wearing. She'd stayed cool, plied him with Johnnie Walker Blue, ran her hands up and down his back and moved down between his legs. Then he'd grabbed both her hands and barked at her to stop it. She acted wounded, desperate, and slipped off her dress and put the full naked breasts he'd bought and paid for in his drunken face. Then he slapped her hard in hers.

"You should try not to be so obvious about being a whore," he said.

Hand to her stinging cheek, Madeline was too shocked to cry or speak. But whatever slim hope she'd held out for their marriage vanished with his next statement. "This isn't going to work, Madeline. We'll have to come to some kind of agreement, but this"—he gestured around the room and then at her—"is over."

Madeline remembered what Eddie had said about seeing Andrew hanging around Marina's office, and suddenly she figured it out. His animosity toward Marina, the way he'd cut Madeline off from seeing her, his long disappearances after the fire when Madeline finally dropped her. He was having an affair with *Marina*. In a weird, nothing-left-to-lose kind of panic, Madeline turned to him, still naked and flushed with shame and fear, and demanded to know how long he'd been sleeping with her psychic. His reaction—she shuddered in the memory—was terrifying. He'd grabbed her by the back of her head and yanked her hair until tears of pain formed in her eyes. He got so close to her face that she could feel the alcoholic moisture of his breath on her lips. "Don't. Ever. Mention. That. Name. Again." He pulled her hair a little harder. "That witch is the cause of all this grief. Do you hear me? And I blame *you*. You spoiled brat. You brought that devil woman into this house and everything went to hell."

"Andrew . . ." She was whimpering. "Please . . ."

"You're lucky I didn't kill—" He stopped himself, but not before Madeline saw the most intense look of hatred she'd ever seen shooting from his eyes.

"Andrew, you're hurting me."

He let her go and pushed her away. "You'd better go get ready," he said. "We're having a goddamned luau."

M adeline poured another glass and drank. It was pretty amazing how quickly you could kill a bottle of bubbly, she thought. But still she felt nothing more than the soft glow. Well, it was enough for now, anyway. The sound of methodical packing and stacking continued to come from the kitchen. She longed for peace—real quiet—but she was still afraid to be alone. She'd kept the house full of people—lawyers, movers, friends and Realtors—for months. At night, when there was nobody left, Madeline went to the Inn at Rancho Santa Fe and checked into a room. That lonely trek would soon be over, though. The house was sold and she'd soon be moving into another—one that would be hers only. She hadn't been completely honest with Joy. She knew much more about the money than she let on. The lawyers *were* handling it, but Madeline was well in charge of the lawyers. It wouldn't be long now—not long at all and she'd have everything she'd wanted.

Well, almost everything. There was no man in Madeline's life, and she expected it would be a long time before there was again—if ever. Her gratitude to Eddie was genuine but it wasn't love. Whatever his motivations for being there that night, he hadn't just saved Marina's life, he'd saved hers, too. She'd rewarded him—quietly, carefully, but making sure he knew—but she didn't want to hear from him or see him again. It was time she started over, fresh. On her own terms.

Chapter 38

Eddie sat in Darling's, not-reading the *North County Times* and waiting for the latest in a string of increasingly surly waitresses to come and take his breakfast order. The name of this place was a pretty good joke if you thought about it, he mused. Never in the dozens of times he'd been into this place had he ever been served by anything resembling a "darling" of any kind. Lots of skinny, black-haired, pale-faced, nose-ringed girls, but no darlings, sweeties or even honeys. Not that Eddie would ever again refer to a woman by any of those endearments, anyway. Just one more thing to add to his I-will-never-understand-women list.

He stared out the window onto the Coast Highway and watched the sun glinting off the cars as they whipped by. It was before nine, but there was already a heat shimmer coming off the road. It was going to be a scorcher today; the beaches were going to be packed. Eddie was glad he'd be working in an air-conditioned house, doing nothing more taxing than installing a faucet. The house was close, too, just down the road in Solana Beach. He'd be done by post time. If he hustled home to shower and change, he could be over there by the third race. He couldn't believe that he'd lived in San Diego for more than half his life and this summer was the first time he'd gone to the races at the Del Mar Fairgrounds. About time, is what it was. He planned to take his boys this weekend when they came to stay with him. Tina hadn't liked the idea at first, thinking it was all cigars and dirty old men at the OTB, but he'd set her straight.

"Hey, sorry to make you wait; we've been totally swamped this morning."

Eddie turned his head and saw the cutest little thing ever to wear an apron in this place. She was white-blond for one thing, and curvy instead of bony like the rest of them. Her white Darling's T-shirt was about two sizes too small (on purpose, he guessed) and hugged her plump breasts as if it were in love. His gaze made it up to hers just a shade too late and he saw her big round blue eyes narrow in annoyance that he was staring at her tits. *Why wear a T-shirt like that,* he wanted to ask her, *if you don't want me to look? Just why?* But he was going to die without knowing the answer to that one question.

"Yeah, okay, hi," he said.

"Any questions about the menu?" she asked. "Or are you ready to order?"

"Oh, I know what I want," Eddie said. "I'm a regular here. You must be new. I haven't seen you here before. What's your name?"

The eye roll she gave him was so dramatic that her irises almost disappeared. "Listen, would you mind just, like, ordering if you're ready? I'm super busy."

"Coffee," Eddie said. "Scrambled eggs, wheat toast, small oatmeal."

"Great," she said, and she swept the menu off his table. "Be right back with your coffee."

Hell with her, Eddie thought, training his eyes back on the road. Hell with all of them. But no. He didn't really mean that. Because, not to put too fine a point on it, this was the first time in thirty years that Eddie was without a wife, lover, mistress or any combination of the three. It was weird. But it was probably good for him. Like oatmeal. He'd always known that women were his weakness, his Achilles' heel. But that hadn't stopped him. Who knows how long he would have carried on if they, the women themselves, hadn't put an end to it? As it was, he'd ended up killing a man . . .

Eddie felt his waitress splash the coffee down next to him, but he didn't turn around to look at her again. Of course, he hadn't *murdered* Andrew, not like Andrew had murdered that guy—who, in a weird twist, turned out to be Marina's tough-guy boyfriend. It was just lucky that he'd been suspicious of Madeline's motives for having him wait out there in the dark. He'd gone to his truck and picked up that piece of pipe just in case. He hadn't planned anything, though, and what Eddie had done was totally justified. You could actually see the black-and-blue marks on Marina's neck. Andrew would have choked the damn life out of her if Eddie had gotten there two seconds later. How did you get there? Eddie wondered for the thousandth time. How did you get to the point where you put your hands around a woman's neck and strangled her? Here was a guy who had everything—he was Mr. Royal Rings, for God's sake. He was beyond loaded, he had a hot wife, a *mansion*. . . . How bent did the man have to be to try to murder a woman at his own house while a thousand of his closest friends partied inside? It was an insane form of evil that Eddie couldn't begin to comprehend.

But Eddie hated being responsible for the loss of any life. The coroner's statement said it was possible that the blow Eddie had landed on Andrew's head might not have killed him. When he opened the bastard up, the coroner found evidence of a massive stroke that must have happened around the same time Eddie swung his bit of pipe. There were charts and diagrams of angles and skulls that all seemed pretty impressive, but Eddie still wasn't sure—would never be sure. But just as Marina had promised when she whispered to him through her bruised larynx, it *was* all right. Madeline, of all the people in the world, had made sure he had one of the best defense attorneys in the county, even though she'd done it on the down low. There was never much chance he was going to jail or even to trial for what he'd done, but Madeline's lawyer had made certain that possibility went down to zero.

Eddie felt a pang thinking about Madeline. Despite the bitter feelings he'd had toward her and despite the sketchy things she'd done, he might have been a little in love with her after all. The last time they'd met—in secret on the beach like something out of an old French film—when she'd handed him the money and asked him not to contact her again, he'd seen something soft and vulnerable underneath that snowy exterior that he hadn't been able to find before. It made him want to protect her. He was genuinely and unexpectedly saddened when he'd asked her about the baby and she'd just told him, "No, Eddie, there's no baby."

He shook his head as if to clear it of the memory. It wasn't as if he didn't have enough on his plate with the two kids he did have. Tina was intent on going through with the divorce even though he'd finally just broken down and begged her to take him back. But having just seen how much trouble domestic anger could cause, he gave up being mad at her and was working on patience and understanding. You never knew— maybe if he lost a few pounds, got a new haircut, ate a whole lot more oat- meal . . . You just couldn't tell with women. At least he was working now and had a place for the boys to stay. Madeline's money had enabled him to start his own handyman business and rent a small but comfortable place in Solana Beach. He'd become very fond of beach life and didn't know if he could ever go back inland.

"Small oatmeal?"

Eddie looked over and saw one of the usual Darling's skinnymalinks. Had his blond beauty passed him off to another waitress? "Yeah, that's mine," he said. "But I also ordered—"

"Yep," Skinny said, "coming up in a sec."

Eddie was starting to get really annoyed. What was it with these little chicks? He deserved better, if only because—and how he hated to admit this—he was old enough to be their father. A little respect, please. Eddie thought about that for a moment and realized that here was another one for the strange-but-true file: the one woman in Eddie's life who actually *was* giving him respect, or at least offering warmth and friendship, was

Marina. Well, he *had* saved her life. If that couldn't get you a few props, you might as well throw in the towel.

A few months ago, he would have given his right arm to spend any time with Marina, but now, and this was the strange part, it just made him uneasy to be around her. It wasn't that he disliked her or found her any less attractive, even as big and pregnant as she was now. Eddie had never believed in all that psychic shit. But it was an entirely different story now. Those green eyes of Marina's could see things he didn't want to know and reach into places he didn't want to go to. When it came down to it, Eddie didn't want to be told what was in store. It was hard enough being here now.

"All right, scrambled eggs and a side of wheat toast."

Blondie was back, leaning over and sliding the plate between his elbows. He gave it one more shot, smiled at her as she straightened up, and she almost returned it, the corners of her mouth quivering in a maybe. "Can I get you anything else?" she said.

"Sure," he said. "I'll take some more coffee. And your name."

The barely there smile was gone, replaced by a look of disgust and a turned back as she flounced off to get the coffeepot. *Hey,* Eddie wanted to yell after her, *you could do worse. I saved a woman's life, you know.*

I saved a woman's life.

Epilogue

September 2007

The days were hot but getting shorter. Every day the sun set a minute or two earlier, the only indication of a change in season. Outside, the air was dry, sharp with the smell of wildfire smoke. Light breezes came and went, blowing dust through the screens of open windows.

Marina's time was getting close. She was heavy and still. She'd moved her rocking chair next to her living-room window and spent most afternoons there, staring out onto her street, her bare feet against the warm wood floor, pushing her back and forth. She watched cats darting through her neighbor's azaleas and black crows flying over a palm in a graceful, ominous circle. People moved along the street, getting in and out of cars, walking their dogs, running with their headphones turned up loud. Marina saw bits and pieces of their lives as they passed and heard fragments of their thoughts. She was learning to focus this way, figuring out what to shut out and what to let in. It was a lot like tuning a radio to find the right frequency.

Usually, Marina fell into something like sleep during these sessions, the scenery outside her window bleaching out to white behind her closed lids. She rested her hands on her belly and felt the baby's feet moving under her palm. The baby was getting quiet now, too. Her movements were slower and less frequent and she had dropped down low in preparation for descent.

She was waiting and suspended in that nowhere/everywhere space between death and life.

Marina drifted, her eyes following the erratic flicker of a late-season butterfly as it searched for a bloom. A worry, small but insistent, wormed its way to the surface. What would happen when she looked into her daughter's eyes? Marina couldn't stand the thought of knowing every hurt and danger before it happened. If there was one thing she had learned in the last nine months, it was that destiny was unalterable and that knowing one's part in it only emphasized how little control one had over it. It might be something close to torture to see into her child's future. The last time they'd spoken, Ciel told Marina that things were going to change as soon as the baby was born. "Babies give, but they also take something away," she said. "The energy gets shifted. You'll see." Marina felt a pulling of muscles, an almost-pain between her hips, as if her body were signaling agreement. She shifted in her chair, leaned her head back and closed her eyes. The sun had moved and was shining hot on Marina's face. Her hands relaxed against the taut skin of her belly. A slight rumble came from inside, the gathering tension before an earthquake, and Marina breathed in deeply.

She felt the disturbance in the space around her first—the displacement of air to make room for something solid. Then she felt his hands on hers, the fingers so warm and solid. Marina opened her eyes and saw Gideon leaning over her. His face, so clear in every detail now, was very close to hers. He was smiling. He had forgiven her, and he had come back. Marina was flooded with trembling relief. She lifted her hand and stroked the curve of his cheek, so comforting and real beneath her hand.

"You're here," she said. "You're not dead." Water filled her eyes, blurring her vision, then splashed onto his hands. He didn't answer, but she felt him sigh, saw his eyes cloud with something sweet and sad. "I'm sorry, Gideon," Marina said. "I'm so sorry. I didn't get to tell you . . ."

"It's all right," he said. "I already know." She felt the vibration of his voice deep inside her body. He opened his hands wide so that they covered the baby beneath her skin, holding her. "You'll know what to do," he said. "She'll help you. And I will always be here."

"I thought you were dead," Marina said again. "I couldn't see you. I thought you were angry . . ."

"I have something for you," he said. She saw it then, the love and reluctance in his eyes, and she knew he was going to leave her again. His lips brushed her forehead and he pressed something small and heavy into her hand. "This is yours," he said. "You'll know what to do."

Marina opened her hand. Gideon's ring lay sparkling on her palm between the lines of heart and fate. She stared at it, mesmerized by its deep red gleam.

"Please don't leave me again," she said, but when she looked up he was already gone. Bright motes of dust swirled in his place, a vast twinkling emptiness, and Marina felt her throat constrict.

"Gideon, come back." Marina blinked, her tears dropping big and heavy until her face was wet and hot with them. Then there was physical pain, crashing through her in waves. It was too hard, she thought, trying to catch her breath. It was too hard to lose him again, even if it was only a cruel dream that had produced him. Marina opened her hand. The ring was gone. She pressed her empty palm flat against the tight skin of her belly.

This is yours. You'll know what to do.

She was fully awake now and no longer resting easily on her chair. She needed to get up, to move. Another intense pain, sudden and brutal, made Marina gasp and clench her fists. She was in labor. The pain crested and ebbed, but Marina knew that another would soon be following. She pulled herself up and took a deep steadying breath. It was early, but she was ready. She looked at the moon-faced clock on the wall above the phone and noted the time.

She stroked her baby one last time from the outside. "Ruby," she said, "it's time to be born."

Acknowledgments

While writing is a solitary endeavor, a finished book represents the efforts of many people and I owe a huge debt of gratitude to those who helped me with this one. Were it not for the encouragement of my agent, Linda Loewenthal, *The Grift* would have remained just an idea. Her intelligence, intuition and support have made this entire process so much easier. Many thanks to my editor, Sally Kim, and the entire team at Shaye Areheart Books, whose professionalism and dedication are second to none. My deepest appreciation and thanks to all the wonderful, devoted booksellers who have supported me and my books throughout the years, and the readers who have followed me and written to me along the way. Thanks and love, as always, to my family for all their help in ways large and small. Finally, I would not have been able to finish this book without Maya and Gabe, who read and listened on demand, offering feedback that was sublime, ridiculous and invaluable.

About the Author

Debra Ginsberg is the author of the memoirs *Waiting, Raising Blaze,* and *About My Sisters* and the novel *Blind Submission.* She lives in southern California. Visit her at www.debraginsberg.com.